ALSO BY P. DJÈLÍ CLARK

The Black God's Drums
The Haunting of Tram Car 015
Ring Shout

A MAST

OF DJIN

A MASTER OF DJINN

P. DJÈLÍ CLARK

TOR
DOT
COM

A TOM DOHERTY ASSOCIATES BOOK · NEW YORK

A MASTER OF DJINN

Copyright © 2021 by P. Djèlí Clark

Edited by Diana M. Pho

A Tordotcom Book
Published by Tom Doherty Associates
120 Broadway
New York, NY 10271

www.tor.com

Tor® is a registered trademark of Macmillan Publishing Group, LLC.

The Library of Congress Cataloging-in-Publication Data
is available upon request.

ISBN 978-1-250-26768-9 (hardcover)
ISBN 978-1-250-26767-2 (ebook)

Our books may be purchased in bulk for promotional,
educational, or business use. Please contact your local bookseller
or the Macmillan Corporate and Premium Sales Department
at 1-800-221-7945, extension 5442, or by email at
MacmillanSpecialMarkets@macmillan.com.

First Edition: May 2021

Printed in the United States of America

0 9 8 7 6 5 4 3 2

For Claudette,
who many others called Liz, and I just called Mom.
Thanks for all those library visits.

A MASTER
OF DJINN

CHAPTER
ONE

Archibald James Portendorf disliked stairs. With their ludicrous lengths, ever leading up, as if in some jest. There were times, he thought, he could even hear them snickering. If these stairs had eyes to see, they would do more than snicker—watching as he huffed through curling auburn whiskers, his short legs wobbling under his rotundity. It was criminal in this modern age that stairs should be allowed to yet exist—when lifts could carry passengers in comfort.

He stopped to rest against a giant replica of a copper teapot with a curving spout like a beak, setting down the burden he'd been carrying. It was shameful that someone of his years, having reached sixty and one in this year 1912, should suffer such indignities. He should be settling down for the night with a stiff drink, not trotting up a set of ruddy stairs!

"All for king, country, and company," he muttered.

Mopping sweat from his forehead, he wished he could reach the dampness lining his back and other unmentionable regions that his dark suit, by fortune, hid away. It was warm for November, and in this overheated land it seemed his body no longer knew how *not* to sweat. With a sigh, he turned weary eyes to an arched window. At this hour he could still make out the sloping outline of the pyramids, the stone shining beneath a full moon that hung luminous in the black sky.

Egypt. The mysterious jewel of the Orient, land of pharaohs, fabled Mamlukes, and countless marvels. For ten long years now,

Archibald had spent three, four, even six months in the country at a time. And one thing was certain: he'd had his fill.

He was tired of this miserably hot, dry place. Thirty years past they had been ripe for becoming another conquest in His Majesty's Empire. Now Egypt was one of the great powers, and Cairo was fast outstripping London, even Paris. Their people swaggered through the streets—mocking England as "that dreary little isle." Their foods troubled his stomach. Their praying came at all times of day and night. And they delighted in pretending not to understand English *when he knew they very well could*!

Then there were the djinn. Unnatural creatures!

Archibald sighed again, running a thumb across a lavender G stitched into his kerchief. Georgiana had gifted it to him before they'd married. She liked these sojourns no more than he, being left in London, with nothing but servants to order about.

"Just a few more weeks, my dear." A few more weeks and he would be on an airship heading home. How he would welcome seeing his "dreary little isle," where it was a sensibly cold and rainy November. He'd walk its narrow streets and savor every foul scent. For Christmas, he would get smashingly drunk—on good, hard English whisky!

The thoughts lifted his spirits. Hefting his bundle, he started up again, marching to the hum of "Rule, Britannia!" But a spot of patriotism was no match for these vexatious stairs. By the time he reached the top, the vigor was leached from him. He stumbled to a stop before a set of tall doors made of dark, almost black wood, fitted into a stone archway, and bent hands to knees, huffing noisily.

As he stood, he cocked his head at a faint ringing. He'd heard the odd sound off and on now for weeks—a distant echo of metal on metal. He'd inquired of the servants, but most never caught it. Those who did claimed it was probably unseen djinn living in the walls, and suggested he recite some scripture. Still, the sound had to be coming from—

"Portendorf!"

The call sent Archibald straight. Adjusting, he turned to find two men striding toward him. The sight of the first almost made him grimace, but he willed his face to composure.

Wesley Dalton reminded Archibald of some caricature of the aristocratic Edwardian: golden hair neatly parted, moustache waxed to fine points, and a self-assurance brimming from eyebrows to dimpled chin. Altogether, it was nauseating. Walking up, the younger man delivered a hearty clap to Archibald's back that almost tipped him over.

"So I'm not the only one late to the company's soirée! Thought I might have to give my apologies to the old man. But walking in with the little kaiser should save me from a striping!"

Archibald smiled tightly. *Portendorf* had been an English name for centuries. And it was Austrian, not German. But it was poor form to get riled by a jest. He offered greetings and a handshake.

"Just flew in from Faiyum," Dalton related. That explained the man's dress—a tan pilot's suit with pants stuffed into black boots. He'd probably flown one of those two-man gliding contraptions so popular here. "I was relayed information of a mummy worth exploring. Turned out to be a hoax. Natives constructed it out of straw and plaster, if you can believe it!"

Archibald could quite believe it. Dalton was obsessed with mummies—part of proving his theory that Egypt's ancient rulers were truly flaxen-haired relatives to Anglo-Saxons, who held sway over the darker hordes of their realm. Archibald was as much a racialist as the next man, but even he found such claims rubbish and tommyrot.

"Sometimes, Moustafa," Dalton went on, stripping off a pair of gloves, "I think you delight in sending me on these fool's chases."

Archibald had near forgotten about the second man, who stood silent as furniture—Dalton's manservant, Moustafa, though it was increasingly difficult to find natives for that sort of work. Mummies were hard to come by, as Egypt's parliament had restricted the trade. Moustafa, however, always seemed able to find Dalton some new lead—each one fruitless and, Archibald suspected, conducted at great expense.

"I only seek to serve, Mr. Dalton." Moustafa spoke in clipped English, taking the gloves and folding them within his blue robes.

Dalton grunted. "Every hand out for a little bit of baksheesh. As bad as any London street urchin and will rob you blind if you let them." Moustafa's eyes shifted to Archibald, the barest smile on his full lips.

"I say!" Dalton exclaimed. "Is that . . . the item?"

Archibald snatched up the bundle from where it rested. He'd gone through quite a bit of dickering in acquiring the thing. He wouldn't have the man's fumbling hands all over it.

"You'll see it when everyone else does," he stated.

Dalton's face showed disappointment and some indignation. But he merely shrugged. "Of course. Allow me, then?" The heavy doors rasped across stone as he pulled them open.

The room on the other side was enclosed by a round wall patterned in shades of gold, fawn, green, and umber against a royal blue. The smooth surface shimmered beneath the glare of a hanging brass chandelier cut with small stars in the Arab fashion. Along the sides stood rows of columns, their curving arches bearing stripes of ochre. Quite a show of Oriental decadence that was only fitting for the Hermetic Brotherhood of Al-Jahiz.

A pair of boilerplate eunuchs stepped up, their blank inhuman faces unreadable sheets of brass. Between tactile metal fingers, each automaton held white gloves, black robes, and a matching black tarboosh with a gold tassel. Archibald took his own, slipping the long garments over his clothing and fitting the hat atop his head—making sure the embroidered gold scimitar and down-turned crescent was forward facing.

There were twenty-two men in the hall, adding Dalton and himself. Moustafa had respectfully stayed outside. All were adorned in the Brotherhood's regalia, some with colorful aprons or sashes to indicate rank. They stood conversing in knots of twos or threes, waited upon by boilerplate eunuchs serving refreshments.

Archibald knew every man here, all of standing in the company—there were no other means of joining the Brotherhood. They called greetings as he passed, and he was honor-bound to stop and give the proper handshake and cheek-to-cheek embrace—a ritual they'd picked up from the locals. Each eyed the bundle, which he assiduously kept from reaching hands. It was tedious business, and he was happy to make free of them, leaving Dalton in their company. Clearing the assemblage, he caught sight of the man he'd come to see.

Lord Alistair Worthington, Grand Master of the Hermetic Brotherhood of Al-Jahiz, struck an imposing figure in resplendent purple robes trimmed in silver. He sat at a black half-moon table, in a high-backed chair resembling a throne. Behind him, a long white banner hung from a rear wall, bearing the Brotherhood's insignia.

Archibald could sparse remember a time when Lord Worthington had not been "the old man." With snowy hair and bold patrician features, the head of the Worthington Company seemed to fit his role as elder priest of their esoteric fraternity. He had founded the Brotherhood back in 1898, tasked with uncovering the wisdom of al-Jahiz—the disappeared Soudanese mystic who had forever changed the world.

The fruits of their labor lined the walls: a bloodstained tunic, an alchemical equation reputedly written by his hand, a Qu'ran from which he taught. Archibald had helped to procure most, much as the bundle he now carried. Yet in all their searching, they'd not stumbled across divine wisdom or secret laws governing the heavens. The Brotherhood had instead become home to romantics, or crackpots like Dalton. Archibald's faith had dwindled with the years, like the wick of a candle burned too long. But he held his tongue. He was a company man after all.

When he reached Lord Worthington, the old man wasn't alone. Edward Pennington was there, one of the most senior men in the company and a true believer, though half-senile. He sat between two others, nodding his wizened head as both spoke into his ears.

"The Germans are making dreadful trouble for Europe," a woman commented, the only one in the room: a dusky-skinned beauty with black kohl beneath her large liquid eyes and braided hair that hung past her shoulders. A wide collar of rows of green and turquoise stone beads circled her neck, striking upon a white dress. "Now the kaiser and tsar trade daily insults like children," she continued in heavily accented English.

Before Pennington could reply, a man on his other side spoke. He wore, of all things, the pelt of a spotted beast over his heavy shoulders. "Do not forget the French. They have unfinished business with the Ottomans over Algeria's territories."

The woman clicked her tongue. "The Ottomans are too stretched. They expect to regain the Maghreb when they're up to their ears in the Balkans?"

Archibald listened as the two went on, poor Pennington barely getting a word in edgewise. This pair was a reminder of how far astray the Brotherhood had wandered.

"I only hope Egypt isn't drawn into your conflicts," the woman sighed. "The last thing we need is war."

"There will be no war," Lord Worthington spoke. His voice rang with a quiet crispness that silenced the table. "We live in an age of industry. We manufacture vessels to traverse the seas and airships to roam the skies. With our manipulation of noxious vapors, and your country's recovered skills of alchemy and the mystic arts? What new hideous weapons could this age create?" He shook his head, as if clearing away nightmarish conjurations. "No, this world cannot afford war. That is why I have aided your king on the coming summit of nations. The only way forward is peace, or we shall surely perish."

There was a pause before the woman lifted her cup. "Egyptians are as fond of toasts as you Englishmen. We often say, '*Fi sehetak'*—to health. Perhaps now, we should toast, to peace."

Lord Worthington inclined his head, holding up a goblet. "To peace." The others followed, even senile old Pennington. Somewhere between, the old man sighted Archibald.

"Archie! I feared we might not see you! Come on, man. Why, you don't even have a cup!"

Archibald mumbled apologies, lifting a cup from a boilerplate eunuch. Making the usual formal introductions, he sat beside the woman, who exuded a heady sweet perfume.

"Archie was instrumental in putting together our Brotherhood," Lord Worthington related. "Oversaw the acquisition of this very house—a hunting lodge built for the old basha. Back then, Giza was still off the beaten track. Archie holds the title of my Vizier, much as . . ." The old man trailed off, blue eyes twinkling at the bundle leaned against a chair. "Is that . . . ?"

"It is indeed, sir," Archibald finished, placing the bundle atop the table. Every eye took in the dark cloth, their conversation dwindling. Even senile Pennington gawked.

Lord Worthington reached out an eager hand, then stopped. "No. We will present this gift to the Brotherhood." As if on cue, a loud bell tolled, announcing the hour. "Ah! Impeccable timing. If you will give the call to order, Archie?"

Archibald rose to his feet, waiting for the bell to stop before shouting: "Order! Order! The Grand Master calls the Brotherhood to order!" The din died away as men turned forward. At this, Lord Worthington rose bringing the table to their feet as well.

"Hail! Hail! The Grand Master!" Archibald called.

"Hail! Hail! The Grand Master!" the room responded.

"Thank you, my Vizier," Lord Worthington said. "And welcome, brothers, to this momentous gathering. Ten years we have carried out our quest to walk in the footsteps of al-Jahiz, to uncover the mysteries he laid upon the world." His left arm gestured to the banner bearing the order's insignia, and the words *Quærite veritatem* written in golden script. "Seek the Truth. Our Brotherhood is not bound by robes, or secret words, or handshakes, but by a higher and more noble purpose. It is important we remember this, and do not lose our way between bombast, and ritual!

"The world sits at a precipice. Our ability to create has exceeded our ability to understand. We play with forces that could destroy us. This is the task the Brotherhood must take up. To recover the most sacred wisdom of the ancients, to create a greater tomorrow. This is what we must stand for. This must be our greater truth." The old man's fingers moved to the bundle. "What better emblem of that purpose than what we have procured today." Pulling back the cloth, he lifted out its treasure. "Behold, the sword of al-Jahiz!"

Gasps went up. Archibald could hear the woman murmur what might have been a prayer. He could not fault her, as he looked upon the finely wrought hilt that held a long slightly curving blade—all a shade of black so dark it seemed to drink in light.

"With this holy totem," Lord Worthington declared, "I rededicate the purpose of our Brotherhood. *Quærite veritatem!*"

The gathering was set to return the rallying cry—when there came a sudden knock.

Archibald's eyes went to the doors with everyone else's. The knock came again. Three times in all. The doors shook with each blow, like a great hand pounded upon them. A bout of silence followed—before they were forcefully thrown open, one nearly coming off its hinges as the bar that bolted them snapped like a twig. Cries of alarm followed the sound of shuffling feet as men backed away from the destruction.

Archibald squinted to find a figure stepping through the archway. A man, garbed all in black—with long billowy black breeches tucked into boots, and a shirt draped tight across his torso. His face was hidden behind a black mask, with only his eyes revealed through oval slits. He stopped at the broken doors to survey the room, then lifted a gloved hand to snap his fingers.

And there were two of them.

Archibald glared. The man had just . . . doubled himself! The twin figures regarded each other, before the first snapped his fingers again. Now there were three. Snap! Snap! Snap! Now six of the strange men! All identical and seemingly pulled from air! As one, they turned masked faces upon the stunned gathering, and crept forward like shadows.

New distress gripped the room. Men stumbled back at the strangers' silent approach. Archibald's mind raced, grasping for sense. This was a trick. Like he'd seen performed on the city's streets. These were locals—thieves perhaps? Thinking to rob some wealthy Englishmen? When the six reached near the center of the room they stopped, still as statues. The odd standoff was broken by Lord Worthington's outraged voice.

"Who dares trespass this house!" No answer came from six sets of unblinking eyes. Lord Worthington rapped the table in anger. "This is the sacred place of the Brotherhood of Al-Jahiz! Be on your way, or I shall have the authorities lay hands upon you at once!"

"If this is the house of al-Jahiz," a new voice came, "then I am here, by right."

A figure strode between the broken doors—a man, tall and draped in black robes that flowed as he walked. His clasped hands were concealed behind gloves of dark chain mail while a black cowl covered his head, hiding his face from view. Even still, his presence filled the chamber, and it felt to Archibald as if a weight had been borne down atop them.

"Who are you to claim such a right?" Lord Worthington demanded.

The strange figure took his place at the head of his companions, and gave answer by pulling back his cowl. Archibald's breath caught. The man's face was concealed by a mask as well—carved in the guise of a man and adorned in strange script that appeared to move upon its golden surface. The eyes behind those oval slits were black pits that burned cold.

"I am the Father of Mysteries." He spoke in deeply accented

English. "The Walker of the Path of Wisdom. The Traveler of Worlds. Named mystic and madman. Spoken in reverence and curse. I am the one you seek. I am al-Jahiz. And I have returned."

A stillness descended like a heavy shroud. Even Lord Worthington seemed at a loss. Archibald gaped, too stunned to do more than stare. It was a bark of laughter that jolted him.

"Nonsense!" someone shouted. Archibald groaned silently. Dalton.

The man shouldered his way forward, pushing past others to stand before the black-clad figures, staring down their leader with all the impertinence of aristocracy and youth. "I know for a fact you are no al-Jahiz! Brothers! Look over this specimen. Tall, with long arms and legs, a build typical to the tropical climes of Soudanese Negroes. But I contend al-Jahiz was no Negro, but in fact, a Caucasian!"

Archibald willed Dalton to stop. For the love of God. But the fool carried on, gesturing dramatically at the stranger. "The true al-Jahiz descends from the rulers of old Egypt. That is the secret to his genius! Were you to place him on Baker Street or among the teeming crowds of Wentworth, I daresay he would be indistinguishable from any other Londoner! I state with conviction that beneath this mask is not the fair complexion shared by our own Anglo-Saxon lineage but instead the sooty, low-browed countenance—"

Dalton cut off as the stranger, who had stood quiet, lifted a chain-mailed hand. The sword in Lord Worthington's grip suddenly began to hum and vibrate. The noise grew to a whine, so that the old man shook with its movement. With a sharp pull, it tore itself free, sailing through the air until it was caught by the stranger's outstretched fingers. His hand closed around the hilt, and stepping forward, he lowered the blade at Dalton.

"Speak another word," the masked man warned, "and it will be your last."

Dalton's eyes went momentarily wide, crossing to look down at the sword's pointed edge. Once again, Archibald willed the man—for all that was holy—to for once *keep his mouth shut*! But alas, it was not to be. The natives here often joked of Englishmen too stubborn to heed cautions of keeping out of the punishing midday sun, until they toppled over from heat exhaustion. Young Dalton appeared determined to follow in that trope. Fixing the stranger with a look that carried all the haughtiness of British pride and imperial hubris, he opened his mouth to begin upon another half-baked tirade.

The masked man didn't move. But one of his companions did. It was swift, like watching stone come to life. Gloved hands reached for Dalton and blurred—sending up an odd wrenching— before the figure flowed back into his statue-like pose. Archibald blinked. It took him a moment to make sense of what he was seeing. Dalton still stood in the same place. But his head had been turned fully around. Or perhaps his body had. Either way, his chin now rested impossibly on the back of his robes—while his arms extended out behind him. He made a full tottering cir-cle, looking almost comical, as if trying to sort himself out. Then stopping, he gave them one last befuddled look before falling flat onto his wrong-way face—the tips of his black boots pointed up into the air.

Around the room men cried out. Some retched. Archibald tried not to join them.

"There's no need," Lord Worthington pleaded, face ashen. "No need for violence."

The stranger turned black pupils to the old man. "Yet there is need for retribution. Upon men who claim my name. Masr has become a place of decadence. Polluted by foreign designs. But I have returned, to see my great work completed."

"I am sure we can help," Lord Worthington said urgently. "If indeed you are who you claim to be. If you could show us some sign that you are truly al-Jahiz, then you will have me at your dis-posal. My wealth. My influence. I would give you all I hold dear if you prove yourself worthy of the name you claim!"

Archibald turned in shock. The old man's face bore the look

of someone who desperately wanted to believe. Who *needed* to believe. It was the most disheartening thing he'd ever seen.

The black-robed figure stared appraisingly at Lord Worthington, eyes growing darker still. "Give all that you hold dear," he spoke bitterly. "You would at that, wouldn't you? I have no more need for anything you can offer, old man. But if it is a sign you require, I will give one."

The stranger raised the sword, pointing the blade at them. The room went dim, the light filtering through shadows. That unmistakable presence emanating from the man grew stronger, building until it felt to Archibald he would fall to his knees. He turned to Lord Worthington—to find the old man burning. Bright red flames crept across his hands, shriveling and blistering the skin. But Lord Worthington didn't seem to notice. His eyes stared out at the chamber, where every member of the Brotherhood was also burning—bodies alight in smokeless fire the color of blood. The strange flames left their clothes untouched, but singed away skin and hair as their screams filled the room.

Not just their screams, Archibald realized. Because he was screaming too.

He looked down at the fire wreathing his arms, devouring the flesh beneath his unmarred robes. Beside him, the woman shrieked, her death cries mingling into the terrible cacophony. Somewhere past the pain, past the horror, before the last bits of him were given to the flames, Archibald grieved for his London, for Christmas, for dear Georgiana and dreams that would not be.

CHAPTER
TWO

Fatma leaned forward, puffing on her hookah. The maassel was a blend of pungent tobacco, soaked in honey and molasses, with hints of herbs, nuts, and fruit. But there was another taste: sweet to the point of sickly that tickled the tongue. Magic. It made the fine hairs along the nape of her neck tingle.

The small crowd that had gathered watched her expectantly. A big-nosed man in a white turban leaned so close over her shoulder she could smell the soot that covered him—an ironworker by the stink of it. He shushed a companion, which only made others grumble. From the corner of her eye, she caught Khalid giving both men a withering glare—his broad face drawing tight. Never a good idea to upset the bookie.

Like most, they'd probably wagered on her opponent, who sat across the octagonal table. All of seventeen, she guessed, with a face even more boyish than her own. But he had already bested men twice his age. More important, he was a he, which still held weight even in Cairo's flaunted modernity—which explained the smile on his dark lips.

Some more traditional ahwa still didn't cater to women, especially where hookahs were smoked, which was most. But this seedy den, tucked into a disreputable back alley, didn't care who it served. Still, Fatma could count the women on one hand. Most left gambling to the men. Three sitting at a far-off table in the dim room were unmistakably Forty Leopards, in garish bright red kaftans and hijabs, with blue Turkish trousers. From their disdainful looks, you'd think them wealthy socialites—not the most notorious thieving gang in the city.

Fatma filtered everyone out—gambling men, smug boys, and haughty lady thieves alike—fixing on the water bubbling in the hookah's bulbous vase. She imagined it a flowing river, real enough to wet her fingertips as she inhaled its scent. Taking a long pull from the wooden pipe, she let the enchanted maassel work through her, before exhaling a thick column.

It didn't look like regular smoke—more silver than gray. Didn't move like smoke either, knitting together instead of dissipating. It took some seconds to coalesce, but when it did, Fatma couldn't help feeling a bit of triumph. A vaporous river snaked across the air as a felucca sailed its surface, the triangular lateen sail stretched taut, and leaving ripples its wake.

Every eye in the coffee shop followed the ethereal vessel. Even the Forty Leopards looked on in wonder. Across the table, her challenger's smile gave way to open-mouthed astonishment. When the magic was spent and the smoke cleared, he shook his head, setting down the tube of his water pipe in defeat. The crowd roared.

Fatma sat back to praises as Khalid stood to collect up his money. Enchanted maassel was a banned substance: a slapdash of sorcery and alchemical compounds that mimicked a drug. The addicted traded away their lives chasing the next great conjuration. Luckily, a milder form had been popular back at the women's college at Luxor. And as a student, she'd taken part in a duel or two. Or three. Maybe more.

"Ya salam!" the kid called. "Shadia, you're as good as the Usta claimed."

Al-Usta was Khalid's nickname. The old Turkish title was addressed to drivers, laborers, mechanics, or craftsmen—anyone really who was very good at what they did. She was sure Khalid had never done an honest day's work in his life. But when it came to handling bets, there was none better.

"One of the best, I tell you," the bookie added, sitting to count through a wad of bills.

Khalid had come up with that name, Shadia. The big man was her guide into this seedier side of Cairo, where Fatma el-Sha'arawi, special investigator with the Egyptian Ministry of Alchemy, Enchantments, and Supernatural Entities, would draw unwanted attention.

"Wallahi!" the kid exclaimed. "Never seen a conjuring so real. What's your secret, eh?"

The "secret" was what any first year picked up in lessons on mental elemental manipulation—choose real experiences over imagined ones. Hers had been an uncle's boat she'd sailed dozens of times.

"As Khalid—the Usta—said, I'm one of the best."

The kid snorted. "Wouldn't have figured it." He tilted a chin at her suit—an all-white number with a matching vest that looked sublime on her russet-brown skin. Fatma ran fingers down the length of a gold tie, certain to show off the glittering cuff links on her dark blue shirt.

"Jealous?"

The kid snorted again, folding arms across a tanned kaftan. Definitely jealous.

"How about you give me what I came for, and I'll send you to my tailor."

"Gamal," Khalid said. "Let's get on with business. Shadia's been patient enough."

More than patient. That trait wasn't her strong suit. But undercover work demanded it. Thieves were inherently distrustful, and only some penchant for their vices ever put them at ease. She checked a golden pocket watch fashioned like an antique asturlab. Half past ten.

"Night's not getting any younger."

The kid cocked his head. "What do you say, Saeed? Shadia look like a business partner?"

Gamal's companion, who sat beside him, stopped chewing his nails long enough to mutter, "Let's be done with it, okay?" The lanky youth looked even younger than Gamal, with jutting ears and a halo of coiled hair. His eyes never met Fatma's, and she hoped it was because of the persona she worked to project: a young socialite willing to pay heavily for pilfered goods.

"Then let's go somewhere private," Khalid offered. He gestured to a back room and rose to go. Fatma smoothed back her mop of cropped black curls before putting on a black bowler, preparing to stand. She stopped halfway, noticing neither young man had moved.

"No," Gamal said. Saeed looked as perplexed as they did.

"No?" The way the big man stretched out the word should have cowed anyone. But not the kid.

"Wander off to secret places and you give people ideas. Maybe come up on one of us on our way out and try to find what that secret is. We can conduct our business right here. What's the big deal? Wallahi, no one's even paying us any mind."

Fatma was certain everyone was paying them every bit of mind. In a place like this, you grew eyes in the back of your head, the sides, and the top. Still, kid had a point. She met Khalid's questioning gaze. He looked ready to snatch the kid bodily out of his chair. But as entertaining as that might be, probably best to not create a scene. She lowered back into her seat. Khalid sighed, doing the same.

"So let's see it, then," Fatma demanded.

Saeed unslung a brown satchel from his shoulder and set it on the table. As he reached inside, Fatma found her hand gripping the lion-headed pommel of her cane. Patience.

"Wait." Gamal put out a restraining arm. "Let's see the money."

Fatma gripped tighter. This kid was becoming annoying.

"That isn't how we conduct business," Khalid chided.

"It's how I conduct it, Uncle." His eyes fixed on Fatma. "You have it?"

She didn't answer right away. Instead she met his gaze—until some of his bravado wilted. Only then did she reach into her jacket to pull out a roll of banknotes. The blue-green paper affixed with the royal seal glittered in the kid's eyes, and he licked his lips before nodding. Saeed looked relieved and drew out an object from the satchel. Fatma's breath caught.

It looked like a bottle made of metal instead of glass, with a pear-shaped bottom inlaid with flowering gold designs that ran up a long neck. Its surface was tarnished a dull bronze, but she guessed it was brass.

"It's old," Saeed noted, fingers tracing the engravings. "I'm thinking maybe from the Abbasids. That's at least a thousand years."

Good eye. So under that nervous gaze was a scholar.

"We found it fishing. I was thinking it was meant to hold perfume or used by early alchemists. But this . . ." His hand went to a stopper at the bottle's top, running along a jade ceramic seal engraved with a dragon. "Never seen its like before. Chinese maybe? Tang? Don't recognize the writing either. And the wax is fresh, like it was just put on yesterday—"

"You haven't removed any of it, have you?" Fatma cut in.

The sharpness in her tone sent his eyes wide.

"Usta Khalid told us not to. That the seal intact was part of the sale."

"Glad you listened. Or you might have wasted all our time."

"Aywa," Gamal sighed. "What I want to know is what's so special about it? Saeed and I find lots of junk. Every day, wallahi. Everything people throw into the Nile comes up again. We sell them to rich people like you. But no one's ever offered so much, wallahi. I've heard other things—"

"Gamal," Saeed cut in. "It's not the time to start that again."

"I think it's a fine time," Gamal replied, eyes fixed on Fatma. "My old setty used to tell me stories of djinn imprisoned in bottles being thrown into the sea—long before al-Jahiz brought them back into the world. She said fishermen would sometimes find them, and when they freed the djinn, it would grant their greatest desires. Wallahi! Three wishes, that could make you a king or the richest man in the world!"

"Do I look like your setty?" Fatma asked. But this time, the kid's bravado didn't waver.

"No deal," he said suddenly. Grabbing the bottle, he pushed it back into the satchel. In her mind, Fatma howled.

Saeed looked flummoxed. "Ya Allah! What are you doing? We need that money!"

Gamal made a chiding sound. "Ah! Wallahi, you're only smart with books! Think! If this is what I believe it is—what *she* believes it is—we could use it ourselves! Ask for money to rain from the skies! Or turn a whole pyramid to gold!"

"The two of you are making a mistake," Khalid warned. His dark face was like a storm, and the white hair that surrounded it bristling clouds. "Take this deal and go your own way. By the Merciful, it isn't wise—"

"Isn't wise?" Gamal mocked. "Are you a shaykh now? Going to start reciting hadith? You don't frighten us, old man. So eager to take the bottle off us when we came to you. Then when we refused, you were even more eager to set up this deal. The two of you in this together? Thinking to cheat us? Best be careful. Might use one of our wishes on you, wallahi!"

Fatma had heard enough. Should have known the kid wouldn't be an honest broker, not with all the wallahis he threw around. Anybody who swore to God that habitually couldn't be trusted. So much for doing this the easy way. Reaching back into her jacket, she drew out a bit of silver and placed it flat onto the table. The old Ministry identification had been a set of bulky papers with an affixed daguerreotype. They'd switched to this badge in the past year—with an alchemical photograph melded to the metal. Blowing her cover hadn't been her first plan. But watching the brashness drain from Gamal's face was worth it.

"You're with the Ministry?" Saeed croaked.

"Pretty hard to get one of these otherwise," she replied.

"It's a trick," Gamal stammered. "There aren't women in the Ministry."

Khalid sighed. "You two should read the papers more."

Gamal shook his head. "I don't believe it. You're not—"

"Khallas!" Fatma hissed, leaning forward. "It's over! Here's what you need to know. There are four other agents in this room. See the man at the door?" She didn't bother to turn as the two peered over her shoulder. "There's another talking everyone's ear off at a table to your right. And a third, enjoying his hookah and watching a game of tawla on your left. The fourth, I won't even tell you where he is."

Their heads swiveled about like meerkats. Saeed visibly trembled.

"So here's what happens now. You hand over that bottle. I give you half of what we agreed on—for making this difficult. And I won't haul you in for questioning. We have a deal?"

Saeed nodded so quickly, his ears flapped. Gamal was another matter: shaken, but not broken. His eyes darted from her to the badge to the satchel and back. When his jaws tightened, she cursed inwardly. Not a good sign.

In an explosion of movement the kid flipped the table over. Khalid went sprawling, his chair tipped out from under him. Fatma caught herself before falling, stumbling back. Gamal stood with the bottle in one hand and a small knife in the other. So much for not making a scene.

"Now I make the deals! Let us out of here! Or I break this seal and see what happens!"

"Gamal!" Saeed protested. "We can just go! We don't have—"

"Don't be stupid! She's not going to let us go! They'll take us in and our families will never hear from us again! Experiment on us! Or feed us to ghuls!"

Fatma frowned. People had very strange ideas about what went on at the Ministry. "You don't know what you're doing. And you're not leaving here. Not with that. Now hand it over. Last time I'm going to ask."

Something on Gamal's face snapped. Snarling through clenched teeth, he drew the blade across the wax seal, which broke and fell away.

There was a moment of stillness. The entire ahwa had turned

to stare at the commotion. But their eyes were no longer on the small woman in a white Westerner suit, the big man they knew to be a local bookie picking himself up off the floor, or the two young men standing behind an overturned table.

Instead, they stared open-mouthed at what one of the young men held—an old antique bottle pouring out bright green smoke. Like enchanted maassel, but in greater amounts. It formed something that looked more solid than any illusion. When the vapor vanished, a living, breathing giant was left in its wake: with skin covered in emerald scales and a head crowned by smooth ivory horns that curved up to brush the ceiling. He wore nothing but billowy white trousers held up by a broad gold belt. His massive chest swelled and retracted as he took deep breaths, before opening his three eyes—each burning like small, bright stars.

Even in the world left behind by al-Jahiz, it wasn't every day you saw a Marid djinn simply . . . appear. The exact scenario Fatma had tried so hard to prevent was now playing out right before her. She allowed a momentary wave of panic, before finding her resolve again.

"Don't move. Let me talk—"

"No!" Gamal shouted. "He's ours! You can't have him!"

"He doesn't belong to—!"

But the kid was already brandishing the emptied bottle at the djinn. "You! Look at me! I'm the one who freed you!" The Marid, who had been silently gazing across the room, turned his fiery gaze. That should have been enough to make anyone cower. But the kid—quite stupidly—stood his ground. "That's right! We freed you! Saeed and me! You owe us now! Three wishes!"

The Marid stared at the two, then uttered one word that rumbled and echoed: "Free." He formed the word again between lips surrounded by a curling white beard. "Free. Free. Free." Then he laughed, a low bellowing that set Fatma's teeth on edge.

"It has been ages since I have needed to utter this mortal tongue. But I remember what 'Free' means. To be unbound. To be not fastened or confined." His face contorted into something terrible. "But I was not bound, or fastened, or confined. No one imprisoned me. I slumbered, at my own choosing. And you woke me, unbidden, unasked, undesired—so that I would grant you wishes. Very well. I will grant you only one wish. You must choose. Choose how you will die."

That was enough. People jumped up from chairs and tables and made hasty runs to the exit. Even the serving staff joined the stampede. The ahwa's owner disappeared into a closet, locking the door behind him. In moments the place had emptied, leaving behind Fatma, Khalid, two young men, and one very ill-tempered Marid.

Gamal looked staggered—Saeed ready to faint. Fatma shook her head. This was precisely why you didn't go around opening up mystical bottles. Why was that so hard for people to understand? Well, time to earn her pay.

"O Great One!" she called out. "I would petition for these two who have wronged you!"

The Marid turned his horned head, that fiery gaze scrutinizing. "You have been in the company of other djinn." His sharp nose inhaled and wrinkled in distaste. "Among other creatures. Are you a mortal enchantress?"

"Not an enchantress. Dealing with magic is just in my line of work."

The Marid seemed to accept that answer. Or he didn't care. "You seek parley on behalf of these two"—a clawed hand waved at Gamal and Saeed—"fools?"

Fatma bit back a smile. "Yes, Old One. The two *fools*." She spared a direct glance at Gamal. "Surely you are magnanimous enough to look past any slight two *stupid* children could offer one so powerful and wise."

The Marid ground his sharp teeth. "The dissembling flattery of mortals. That, I also remember. Do you know why I bound myself to slumber, not-enchantress? Because I grew tired of your kind. Greedy. Selfish. Ever seeking to satisfy your wants. I could no longer stomach the sight of you. The stink of you. Your ugly little faces. I slept to escape you all. In the hopes that when I next awakened, you would be gone. Struck down by a blessed illness. Or slaughtered in one of your endless wars. Then I wouldn't have to hear your monkey-like chatter. Or need speak your inarticulate tongues ever again. But here I am. And you are still here."

Fatma blinked at the tirade. Of all the djinn these two had to go and wake up, it had to be a bigot. "Right. You can go back to sleep, Old One. You can sleep for as long as you like. I'll even see that your vessel is sent somewhere far away. Where you'll be undisturbed." Maybe the heart of a volcano, she thought idly.

The Marid inspected her the way a butcher might a goat bleating out a proposal to stay the knife. "And why, not-enchantress, should I deign to make bargains? When I could simply pluck your head from your neck? Stain these walls with your entrails? Or fill your belly with ravenous scorpions?"

Fatma didn't doubt those threats. Of the classes of djinn, Marid were some of the most powerful and ancient—possessing preternatural strength and formidable magic. But if this half-awake tyrant thought she'd wilt under his intimidation, he had another think coming. Tipping back her bowler at an imperious angle, she moved closer to the towering Marid, craning her neck to meet those three burning eyes.

"You've been in self-exile in that bottle for at least a thousand years. So let me catch you up. There are more of us chattering mortals than you might guess. Lots more. More of your kind, too, crossed over to this world. Djinn live among us now. Work with us. Follow our laws. You want to smear me to a pulp?" She shrugged. "Go ahead. But you'll pay for it. And the people I work for, they know how to make even slumbering for eternity in a bottle extremely unpleasant. Try extending that third eye of yours. See what's become of the world while you slept."

The Marid didn't react right away. Finally, he closed both his eyes, at the same time widening the third on his forehead until it flared with brilliance. When he reopened his remaining eyes they looked startled.

"You speak truth. Your kind has truly multiplied. Like locusts!

So many more djinn in this world. Working alongside mortals. Living among them. Mating with—"

"Yes, all of that," Fatma cut in.

"Disgusting."

"Reality. So that brings us back to our bargaining. I'm sure you'd rather get back to sleep. Wait and see how things pan out. My offer still stands. You have my word."

The Marid snorted. "The word of a mortal? Empty and weak as water. There is no worth in that. Present me with something to bind. Something that makes your offer true."

"My honor, then."

"What is mortal honor to me? You try my patience, not-enchantress. Make your offer worthy, or offer it not at all."

Fatma gritted her teeth. Damn djinn and their bargaining. There was one other thing she could give. Though she loathed it. But her options seemed slim.

"To make my offer true," she said, "I offer you my name."

That made the Marid's eyebrows rise. Djinn were big on names. They never gave their true names, instead calling themselves by geographic locations—cities, rivers, mountain ranges. Either that or majestic titles like the Queen of Magic or the Lord of Thursday. That lot were insufferable. By the look on his face, however, it seemed even mortal names held some worth.

"Your *true* name," he demanded.

She bristled at this, but nodded acceptance.

"The offer is accepted. But there is still the matter of granting the fools their wish."

Fatma started. "What do you mean? We just settled on that!"

The Marid's dark green lips pursed into a smirk. "Our arrangement, not-enchantress, was your offer that I return to my vessel and you assure me uninterrupted slumber. Not that I spare the lives of these two. The wish is still binding."

"That was implied!" But even as she said the words, she knew the fault was hers. You had to be careful when bartering with djinn. They took every word literally. Why so many of them in this age made good lawyers. She cursed her mistake and tried to think straight.

"So the wish still stands?" she asked.

"What was requested will be given."

"But you already set the parameters."

The Marid shrugged and cast a baleful glare to Gamal and Saeed, who shook visibly. "The asker should have taken more care to specify their wants."

"So all they can get from this wish is death?"

"What comes to all mortals in the end."

Hardly fair. But fair usually accounted for little in dealings with immortals. Her mind worked to find a solution. This Marid had lived countless lifetimes and was very good at this. But she was a Ministry agent. That meant protecting people from the world of the supernatural and the magical—even when they ran stupidly headlong into it.

"I have a proposal," she said at last, taking care with her words. "For their wish, I ask that you grant these two fools death—as old men, in their beds, at the end of their natural lives."

It was a beautiful thing to see the arrogance evaporate from the Marid's face. She expected him to protest, find some little crack in her logic. But instead, he merely nodded—appraising her anew—then smiled a terrible smile.

"Well played, not-enchantress," he pronounced. "And done."

◆　◆　◆

A half hour later, Fatma stood, wiping off her badge. Between the table flipping over and the stampeding patrons, it had ended up halfway across the room. Khalid had found it sitting in a pile of spilled charcoal ash.

"There weren't any other agents, were there?" the big man asked, holding a cup of tea. He'd managed to coax the coffee shop's owner from the closet and convinced him to brew a pot.

Fatma rotated her shoulder, feeling the slightest twinge. She'd injured it on a case this past summer. And though it had healed remarkably fast, it still flared up now and then. "Good thing they didn't know that."

Khalid chuckled, glancing to Gamal and Saeed, who sat dazed as black-uniformed Ministry agents questioned them.

"Good thinking on saving those two. For a while there, I thought that Marid had you."

"For a minute, so did I."

Khalid grinned before his face turned serious. "You do know what you've done? What you've granted them?"

Fatma had known the moment she spoke the words. Gamal and Saeed were all but guaranteed to live to old age. They'd never need worry about being killed by an automobile. Or falling off the ledge of a building. Not even a bullet. The Marid's power would protect them for the remainder of their mortal lifetimes.

"I don't think they realize it yet," Khalid mused. "But they'll figure it out in time. Saeed, I believe, will put it to good use. The boy really wanted the money for a trade school. Though I think he'd probably be better at a university. But Gamal . . . that one could steal the eyeliner from your eye, and still not be content."

"It's worse than that," she said. "Their wish grants them long life. But it doesn't say how. They could live out their whole lives with a terrible disease, unable to die. Same thing if an accident leaves them in unbearable pain. Their 'gift' could easily become a prison."

Khalid slowly lowered his teacup and murmured a prayer. That was the thing a lot of people didn't understand. Magic abhorred imbalance. And always exacted a price.

"I'll keep an eye on them, then," he said soberly before adding: "Thanks ya Jahiz."

Fatma nodded at the familiar Cairene slang—evoked with praise, sarcasm, or anger, at the long-disappeared Soudanese mystic. The very one who some forty years past bored a hole into the Kaf, the other-realm of the djinn. She was young enough to have been born into the world left in al-Jahiz's wake. It was still at times a dizzying affair.

"The kid was right, you know," she said, eyeing him. "You didn't have to tip me off. You could have kept that bottle for yourself. Tried to get your own wishes."

Khalid scoffed. "And risk Muhammad Ali's curse? God forgive me for such a thing!"

Another bit of Cairene slang. Muhammad Ali Basha, the Great, was rumored to have consolidated his power with the help of a djinn advisor—who abandoned him in his greatest time of need, answering the old Khedive's pleas with laughter that echoed unceasing in his head. When the aging ruler was forced to abdicate, many blamed the djinn's curse for weakening his mind.

"Unlike the young," Khalid continued, "I know the difference between what I want, what I need, and what might just kill me. Besides, I thought all that business about djinn locked away in lamps was some bad Frenchman's writing." He looked to where Supernatural Forensics was gingerly placing the Marid's vessel into a wooden crate for transport. They'd get a proper seal back on and find someplace to store the thing—allowing its ornery occupant to wait out humanity's demise.

"Lamps are overdone," Fatma said. "Bottles, on the other hand . . ."

She didn't get to finish as she spotted a man walking toward them. In that red kaftan, not with Supernatural Forensics. At second glance, not a man either—a boilerplate eunuch. By its lithe frame and sleek gait, one of the newer messenger models.

"Good evening and pardon my intrusion," it stopped and spoke. "I bear a message for the recipient: Agent Fatma el-Sha'arawi. The sender is: Ministry of Alchemy, Enchantments, and Supernatural Entities."

"That's me," Fatma indicated. A message at this hour?

"The message is confidential," the machine-man stated. "Identification required."

Fatma held up her badge to the sensors beneath the boilerplate eunuch's featureless face.

"Identification confirmed." Its mechanical fingers produced a thin cylinder and handed it to Fatma. She opened the casing and unfurled the note, quickly scanning it.

"More work?" Khalid asked.

"Aywa. Looks like a trip into Giza."

"Giza? The way you're going, won't get much sleep tonight."

Fatma stuffed the note away. "Sleep is for the dead. And I plan on doing lots of living."

The big man chuckled. "Go in peace, investigator," he called as she walked away.

"God protect you, Khalid," she replied before stepping from the ahwa into the night.

CHAPTER THREE

T he ride into Giza by automated wheeled carriage was about forty-five minutes this time of night. But Fatma would be happier when the aerial tram extension got up and running. The Transportation Ministry claimed it would make the trip in a quarter of the time.

As she rode, her mind cataloged the night's events. It had taken days to follow up on Khalid's tip. Identifying the bottle. Arranging the meetup and creating her undercover persona. She'd even gotten a new suit—to perfect the look of the eccentric socialite. Things hadn't exactly gone as planned. Then again, did they ever? Who thought that kid had it in him to summon up a Marid djinn and then demand wishes?

"A fool's heart is forever at the tip of his tongue," she muttered. One of her mother's sayings, for every reason or occasion. Of course, this was Egypt. You could hear such adages everywhere, uttered from a hundred lips, and often unsolicited. Only her mother seemed to use them every other sentence. That had to be some kind of record. Not just Egyptian either. She seemed to pull them from who knows where. Her father joked she must have begun spouting them at birth, chastising the midwife, and keeping it up right through her subu'.

Thoughts of her mother, as usual, reminded her of home. She hadn't been home in months. Not even for Eid. Too busy with work, she'd told her family. It wasn't that she didn't miss them. But whenever she visited her village, it all felt so small. She remembered when Luxor had been the biggest city in the world to her eyes. But compared to Cairo, it seemed like a big town full of old ruins.

The glare of lights made her sit up to peer out the window, meeting the ghost of her reflection—dark oval eyes, a fleshy nose, and full bold lips. She was in Giza. The city was growing, filling with newcomers escaping the cramped neighborhoods of Cairo. Paved lanes and newly constructed buildings stretched across the plateau—illuminated by electric lamps like lotus columns in Neo-Pharaonic style. The girders of an unfinished mooring mast jutted over rooftops, where cargo airships would soon be making dock, turning this place into a hub of commerce. Still, whatever Giza was becoming its past remained prominent—the skyline dominated by towering pyramids, ancient sentinels to this modern age.

The carriage passed through downtown, moving along shop-lined streets onto a road surrounded by flat desert. After what seemed an eternity, the unvaried landscape was broken by a large well-lit structure—the pyramids in its background looming up like mountains.

The Worthington estate was a thing of squares and rectangles, as if several buildings had been lined up unevenly against each other—so that it stretched out lengthways. The architecture was a traditional style, with towers, minarets, and colonnades of beige stone, accented with dark wooden balustrades and porticos. It sat in an even larger garden: an oasis of palm trees and leafy bushes that presented the image of a floating island.

The carriage stopped at the estate's entrance to let Fatma out. Several other vehicles were parked, bearing the blue and gold of Cairo's police. Making her way up a set of stairs she rapped the door with her cane. It was opened by a tall older man in a white gallabiyah.

"Good night, young master—" he began in English, then paused, his gaunt face curious. When he spoke again, it was in Arabic. "Good evening, daughter. I am Hamza, night steward of the house. How may I assist you?"

Fatma took both mistake and correction in stride. The suit and boyish face threw most people off at first glance. His eyebrows jumped further at her badge. But she was used to that too. Opening the door wide, he bowed slightly and ushered her through.

They stood in a spacious rectangular room that looked to be a parlor. Vintage inlaid silver lamps hung from a high ceiling of dark wood, their light shimmering off the floor—an expanse of white tiles shaped like stars. The walls were decorated with an assortment of antiques: from a vibrant Safavid painting of polo players to a pair of swords in red-brown leather scabbards. They were broken up by four bulbous equidistant archways, and the night steward escorted her through one, down a corridor no less opulent. Colorful carpets lined the walls like tapestries—a Tabriz of red florals, some burgundy Anatolians, a green Bokhara with yellow prints, all alongside delicate lattice mashrabiyas. As she eyed them a faint sound came to her ears. Like the clanging of metal. Then it was gone.

"I regret welcoming you to this house in such a time," the steward said. "It blemishes the beauty put into its making."

"How long have you been with the estate, steward Hamza?"

"Since the beginning. Well over ten years now. And I've watched Lord Worthington's house grow into its present magnificence!"

Fatma wasn't certain she'd call this fairy-tale palace magnificent. But to each their own.

"Were you close to Lord Worthington?"

"A master can only be so close to a servant. But Lord Worthington always treated me with respect. That can be a rare thing." They stopped at a set of stairs. "The others are gathered above." He paused, face grave. "Whatever you find in there, it is only a vessel and not the man. We all belong to God. And to Him we must return."

He departed, leaving Fatma to climb what might have been the longest stairs in the world. By the time she reached the top she wasn't winded exactly. But close. From somewhere to her left came voices. Wrinkling her nose at a terrible smell, she followed both to their source.

The room she found was missing its doors. One hung by a hinge. The other lay fractured on the floor. She stepped past them, noting the splintered wooden bar, before surveying the rest. The round space was filled with people. Policemen. Identifiable in their khaki jackets and trousers. They bustled beneath an immense brass chandelier, which shone on the grisly scene.

The missive Fatma received had been short and to the point—casualties reported at the Worthington estate; check for supernatural activity. That hardly did it justice. Bodies covered in white sheets were strewn about the marble floor. A quick count gave her almost twenty. More were at a table in the back. That terrible smell was almost overwhelming now. Burning. But worse. Coppery and almost metallic. Like the most unappetizing cooked meat.

She was still taking it all in when a policeman walked up. He looked her age—twenty-four, maybe twenty-five. But he stormed over, chest out and scowling, as if readying to pull his younger sister from a hashish den.

"You! You can't just walk in here! This is a crime scene!"

"That would explain the dead bodies, then," she replied.

He blinked dumbly, and she sighed. Wasting good sarcasm was annoying. She flashed her badge, and he squinted from it to her and back again before his eyes rounded.

"It's you!"

Fatma had come to learn "It's you" could mean a lot of things. It's you, the sun-dark Sa'idi from some backwater village. It's you, the woman who was all but a girl in their eyes that the Ministry had made a special investigator—and assigned to Cairo no less. It's you, the strange agent who wore Western suits. A few others tended to get less polite. Egypt boasted its modernity. Women attended schools and filled its booming factories. They were teachers and barristers. A few months back, women had even been granted suffrage. There was talk of entering political office. But the presence of women in public life still unnerved many. Someone like her boggled the senses completely.

"Constable! Are you bothering the agent?"

Fatma looked up to a familiar face—a middle-aged man who wore a fancier police jacket with gold epaulets. It fit his tall and thick frame a bit tightly so that his belly preceded him. The young policeman jumped, turning and coming face-to-face with Inspector Aasim Sharif.

Aasim was a member of Cairo's police force and a liaison with the Ministry. Not a bad sort—a bit vulgar, but amiable enough when not brooding at the inconveniences of the modern world. He'd even gotten comfortable around her. As comfortable as she could expect. He glared at the young policeman from behind a set of thick long graying whiskers. Big overwrought moustaches had fallen out of favor in modern Cairo's ever-shifting fashion trends, though they still held sway further south, as her uncles could well attest—and among older conservative Cairenes like Aasim. Prideful badges of nostalgia, she supposed. His whiskers always reminded her of some antiquated Janissary, and they twitched in annoyance.

"I asked you a question! Are you bothering the agent?"

"No, inspector! I mean I didn't know who she was, inspector. I mean—"

He gulped as Aasim scowled deeper.

"Why don't you make yourself useful. Run to the kitchens and fetch me some coffee."

The younger man started. "Coffee?"

"Coffee," Aasim repeated. "Do you not know what that is? Do I need to explain coffee to you? Should I begin reciting a history of coffee? No? Then why are you still here? Yalla!"

With some stammering, the young policeman scurried off.

"You enjoyed that entirely too much," Fatma accused.

Aasim's lips set into a smirk. "You know what's funny? I don't even like coffee. Tastes like dishwater to me. I do, however, love breaking in new recruits." He turned to Fatma. "Good evening, agent. You're looking very"—his eyes took in her suit—"English."

"This one's American. From New York."

"I don't believe such a place exists."

She made a face at him. "You have some case here."

Aasim scratched a shaved chin. "You haven't seen the worst of it." He invited her to walk beside him. "Hope we didn't wake you. But I thought it prudent to call the Ministry."

"You asked for me personally, of course?"

"Of course. I know how much you enjoy a challenge."

"I do have a personal life, you know."

He shook his head. "I don't believe that for one instant either."

"Well, at least catch me up."

"We got a call sometime before ten," he began. "From the estate's night steward."

"Hamza. Met him," Fatma noted.

"Man was a wreck. Came in and found the bodies. Called every station he could screaming about murders. Most here are Giza policemen. But they reached out to Cairo for help. We got here and found all this."

They stopped before a mass of white sheets that smelled of burning. Or was that the policemen all standing about, puffing on their Nefertari cigarettes? At seeing the inspector they hurriedly put out the thin brown sticks. Aasim detested smoking at his crime scene.

"Twenty-four dead," he informed her, pulling his glare from the officers.

Twenty-four. Merciful God.

"All burned to death," he added. "Hoped covering them up would mask the smell."

"You called the Ministry over a fire?" But even as the words left Fatma's lips she noticed the obvious. No scorch marks. In fact, no burn marks anywhere.

Aasim handed over a kerchief. "You'll need this. Stinks like burned hair under there."

Fatma followed him to one knee as he pulled back the sheet. Even with the kerchief pressed to her nose, the stench was strong. The scorched corpse looked like charred wood, the blackened head with emptied sockets that poured out wisps of smoke. Whoever he'd been, he'd died screaming, his gaping mouth showing soot-stained teeth and bits of gold replacements. What stood out, however, was his dress: long black robes over a dark gray suit, with white gloves and a black tarboosh still attached—and unscathed.

"Only the flesh is burned," she murmured.

"Very unusual for fire, don't you think?" Aasim asked.

Fatma only paid him half attention, her mind running through various controlled conflagrations, of the magical and alchemical varieties: fires that could melt steel, stick to surfaces like oil, or even be shaped into the likenesses of beasts. Fires that consumed flesh but left clothing untouched? That was new. Pulling out a pair of Ministry-issued spectral goggles, she fitted on the copper-plated spectacles and peered through the round green lenses. Magic was everywhere. Not on the clothing. But it clung to the corpse in a faint luminous residue.

"They all like this?" she asked, removing the goggles.

"Every last one. Well, except our friend here." Aasim gestured to a corpse set apart from the rest. Pulling back the sheet revealed a burned body dressed in the same unblemished clothing. But something was wrong. It took a moment to actually see it.

"His head's on backward," she remarked, unable to keep the shock from her voice.

"Don't see that every day, do you? We were confused too until we turned him over."

Fatma leaned down to inspect the bizarre corpse.

"His face. There's no screaming. He didn't die by fire. This happened before."

"You have any idea the strength needed to do *that* to a human body?"

"Can't say I've given it much thought. But I'm guessing *inhuman* strength?"

Aasim sighed. "Back when my grandfather was a policeman, the most he had to worry about were pocket pickers. Cheaters trying to beat up the market inspector. On an exciting day, maybe a counterfeiter. What do I get? Magically burned bodies and inhuman strength."

"Not your grandfather's Cairo," Fatma retorted.

Aasim grunted his acknowledgment. "Thank ya Jahiz."

Fatma stood, looking past the shrouded bodies to take in the room itself. For the first time she noticed the ceiling, with its concave underside like a honeycomb. Muqarnas. A Persian style that had flowed to Egypt along trade routes centuries past. The blue walls with gold and green repeating flowers were Persian too—but with hints of Andalusian, and some Arabic calligraphy. The columns running along the sides were Moroccan and inscribed with verses from the Qu'ran. It wasn't uncommon to see all of these styles in Cairo, given the city's long history as a crossroads of culture. But like the rest of this house, something about the room's construction made it appear more a mishmash than anything approaching aesthetic coherence: an outsiders's valiant but overwrought attempt at authenticity.

There were items on the walls too, under glass boxes. She spied a book, bits of clothing, and more. To the back a white banner hung. Two interlocking pyramids on its front formed a hexagram, displaying an all-seeing eye in its center surrounded by seven small stars. In each corner of the hexagram were signs of the zodiac, with a sun disc placed at its left and a full moon on its right. The odd assemblage was encircled entirely by a fiery serpent devouring its tail. Beneath sat a gold scimitar above a down-turned crescent that ended in fine points. Her eyes flickered to the black tarboosh still worn by the dead man with his head turned backward, bearing the same gold sword and crescent.

"What is this place?" she asked. "Who are these people?"

Aasim shrugged. "Some kind of cult maybe? You know how Occidentals like playing dress-up and pretending they're ancient mystics. Order of the this . . . Brotherhood of the that . . ." He led her to the half-moon table in the back with more bodies. Some slumped where they sat. Others lay on the floor. Aasim stopped at the table's center, pulling back the sheet to reveal a seated figure in a deep purple robe.

"The one thing we know for certain," he said, "is that this is Lord Alistair Worthington." He lifted the dead man's hand. Fitted onto the smallest blackened finger was a large silver signet ring. The engraving on its flat front was a crest: a shield with a rearing griffin, capped by a knight's head and an armored arm wielding a sword. Beneath was a singular scripted W.

"This is *the* Alistair Worthington?"

"The English Basha himself," Aasim replied.

Fatma was familiar with the moniker, as she was the Worthington name. The Englishman who helped broker the Anglo-Egyptian Treaty, and granted special rights by Egypt's new government. His money and influence had maintained peace, secured trade, and built up Giza.

"The English Basha, found murdered," she corrected.

Aasim grimaced. "I was hoping you'd tell me this was just a spell gone wrong."

Fatma shook her head. "I saw those doors. Someone forced their way in here." She studied the bodies. "Sent everyone running to the back. The one with the broken neck—maybe he got brave. Tried to fight. The rest, all burned alive."

Aasim nodded. He'd likely come to same conclusion but was hoping for an easy out.

"Murder. You have any idea how much paperwork this is going to be?"

"Did the English Basha have any enemies?" Fatma asked, ignoring the question.

"Rich people always have enemies. Usually, that's how they became rich."

"Wasn't he supposed to be helping in the king's peace summit?"

"You mean the one to stop Europeans from launching a fresh crusade against each other? You're thinking this might be related?"

"I don't know," she answered. Why commit a massacre on this scale just to murder one man? No, whoever did this, the time and place was intentional. This scene was meant for everyone to see—like a gory painting. She looked back to the hanging banner. At the very bottom was stitched *Quærite veritatem.* Seek Truth, if she was translating the Latin right.

"One more thing," Aasim said. He bent to pull a sheet from a crumpled body on the floor. Burned like the rest, but one thing was different—this victim wore a close-fitting white dress that reached to the ankles. "The only woman in the room," the inspector remarked.

More than that. A broad collar of colorful stones circled her neck hanging down to her chest. A wesekh—jewelry fallen out of fashion some two thousand years past. She knelt to eye gold earrings peeking beneath a wig of black braids: carvings of a woman with outstretched wings.

"Any more like this?" Fatma asked. "I mean, in . . . costume?"

Aasim pulled the sheet from another body. This one a man, with the spotted hide of a cheetah slung over his shoulders. And she'd thought this night couldn't get more bizarre.

"Must have been some party," Aasim mused.

A very odd one. Her gaze flickered to another body, where a hand protruded from the white covering—as if trying to reach back into the world. She peered closer. A kerchief with a lavender G stitched in cursive was clutched between his charred fingers.

"You think this might be necromancers?" Aasim asked. His moustache gave a nervous twitch. "Maybe an attempt at making ghuls gone wrong?" The man blamed necromancers for everything. Let him tell it, masters of the undead lurked behind every crime. And he hated ghuls. Then again, who didn't?

"Unlikely," she answered. "Making ghuls doesn't include turning corpses combustible." The very thought of fiery ghuls sent Aasim's moustache into spasms. "Besides, I didn't see any takwin under the spectral lens." Necromancers used a corruption of the alchemical substance to make ghuls. The sorcery she'd seen was something else. "Any witnesses? The night steward?"

Aasim shook his head. "It seems when Lord Worthington has these gatherings he dismisses his *human* staff. The night steward arrived after the festivities. That left only them." He motioned to a row of boilerplate eunuchs that stood unmoving, even as people worked around them. Reports claimed some machine-men had achieved sentience—a phenomenon that baffled the Ministry. Didn't seem to be the case here.

"There is someone, however," Aasim continued. "Lord Worthington's daughter."

Fatma turned to him sharply. "Daughter? Why didn't you mention her before?"

The inspector held up his hands. "She's been recovering. I'll take you to her." They walked from the room and descended the lengthy stairs. "Abigail Delenor Worthington. Seems she arrived home after all this. The night steward found her in the parlor, unconscious. Says she had a run-in with a mysterious character. Maybe a survivor. Or the perpetrator. But it's better if she explained it. Just, whatever you do, don't let her speak to you in Arabic."

"She speaks Arabic?" Fatma asked.

"Not at all. Only she doesn't seem to know that. We've had the night steward translating. But you might do better."

At the bottom of the stairs they turned down a corridor that ended where two policemen stood guarding a set of doors. At seeing Aasim they pulled them open to allow passage. The room was the clash of architecture that defined the rest of the house. But instead of fine rugs or swords, there were books. Endless books, fitted onto wooden shelves. A library. The books were broken by framed paintings in vivid Orientalist style, many displaying crumbling edifices with noble fellahin or sultans in garish dress. Others were salacious, where barely clothed alabaster women lounged about, waited upon by dark-skinned servants.

There were five people gathered—not counting a boilerplate eunuch with a tray of crystal bottles. Four stood around a modish moss-green Turkish divan with long curving silver legs. It looked made for lounging, but now held a woman who sat propped against a pile of cerulean pillows with mustard tassels. Dressed in a cream gown, she looked in her mid-twenties, slender and long-necked, with dark red tresses that fell about the lace stitching and ribbons at her shoulders. Her tanned features were pronouncedly English—a short pointed nose and an almost heart-shaped face. Abigail Worthington, Fatma presumed. At the moment, a thin and short dark-haired man in a formal evening jacket and gray striped pants knelt bandaging her hand.

"About time you got back!" someone snapped.

Fatma looked to the other man in the room, whose broad frame filled up a black waistcoat and white shirt partly unbuttoned—tie loosened. His head was topped by a halo of golden curls that formed generous sideburns.

"You just leave us locked up and guarded by your gendarmes?" he spouted in refined English. His waving arms sloshed about the contents in a drinking glass.

"Lay off, Victor," his companion sounded nasally. "Everyone's on edge already." The bigger man seemed set to the retort, but Abigail Worthington spoke up.

"Percy's right." Her melodic voice came hoarsely. "It won't do any good to yell at these people. They can't change what's happened." She lifted her head to set puffy red eyes on them, confusion passing across her face as she took in Fatma's suit. That was better than the other women. The two stood gawping, trading whispers behind their hands. When Abigail spoke again, it was in Arabic. "Sorry. Brandy. Victor. He drink. Much. Make stupid."

Fatma winced. Aasim hadn't exaggerated. The woman's Arabic was an assault on her ears. Deciding to save them all, she replied in English. "It's fine, Miss Worthington. You've had a trying night. May I offer my condolences."

Abigail's blue-green eyes widened at Fatma anew. So did her companions'. The two whisperers stopped talking altogether. "You speak English! And with the most delightful accent! Though I can't quite place it. How splendid!" She wiped tears from her cheek. "Thank you. And please, just Abbie."

"Abbie, then," Fatma agreed. "I'm Agent Fatma, with the Egyptian Ministry of Alchemy, Enchantments, and Supernatural Entities."

"An agent," Abigail mouthed in awe. "First your country grants women the vote, now I learn they let you be police officers!"

"The Ministry aren't police. I work with Inspector Aasim on matters dealing with the . . . unordinary. I'm afraid your father's death falls under that heading."

Abigail's face turned grim, and she pressed her lips tight. "They haven't let me in to see . . ." She swallowed. "I understand, there was a fire?"

"Yes, but more than that." Fatma delicately explained the state of the bodies.

"My God!" Victor cried out. He downed his brandy. "Murder! Sorcery, then?"

"What else could it be?" Abigail whispered. "Poor Father. I hope he didn't suffer." She looked on the verge of weeping again, but pressed a hand against an orange sash at her waist and spoke levelly. "How can I help, agent?"

"Inspector Aasim says you came across someone?"

Abigail shivered visibly. "Yes. I'd just come home. The house was strangely quiet when I entered. I hadn't made it out of the parlor before *he* arrived. A man, in black robes."

Fatma jotted down the information on a notepad. "Not one of your servants?"

Abigail shook her head.

"Could you describe him?"

The woman's expression turned awkward. "Not exactly. He wore a mask of some kind." She touched her own face, as if imag-

ining it there. "Gold. With markings. I remember he was tall. So
very tall! And his eyes. I've never seen such intense eyes!"

"Did he do that?" Fatma indicated her bandaged hand.

Abigail's cheeks colored. "No. I . . . well, you see, I fainted.
Dead away at seeing that horrid man. Silly goose that I am, I
landed on my own hand. Percy's been a dear to wrap it up."

"I've done what I can," the thin man said, standing.

"Can you tell us anything else about this man in a gold mask?"
Fatma pressed.

Abigail shook her head regretfully. "I was passed out until
Hamza found me."

"Wish I'd been here," Victor said hotly. "I'd have shown the
masked devil a thing or two!" He downed another glass and
turned to Fatma. "I want to know what you and this inspector are
doing to apprehend this criminal. Shouldn't you be out hunting
him?"

Fatma regarded him flatly. There was always one like this. "I
didn't get your full name?"

He stuck out a square chin. "Victor Fitzroy." As if it should mean
something.

"Forgive my manners," Abigail interceded. "These are my
friends. The hotheaded one is Victor. My play physician is Percival Montgomery." The dark-haired man smirked behind a
small but thick moustache. "And this is Bethany and Darlene
Edginton, my erstwhile partners in mischief." The two women
nodded, though the haughtiness in their hazel eyes remained.
Sisters. Fatma could see it now—the same upturned noses, sand-
brown hair, and pinched, drawn faces.

"We all made our way back after Abbie rang us," Percival said.
"Poor old man Worthington. May his soul rest in peace."

Abigail sobbed, dabbing her eyes.

"Just a few more questions. Did your father have any enemies?"

"Enemies? Who would possibly want to harm my father?"

"Maybe someone in his employ? A business rival?"

Abigail shook her head. "I suppose such a dreadful thing is possible. Though I don't know much about my father's business. Alexander is the one with a head for such things."

"Alexander?"

"My brother. He manages our family's business affairs. He's overseas."

Fatma wrote hurriedly. "One last thing. Do you know anything about what your father was doing tonight? Who all the people were with him?"

"A secret brotherhood," she replied. "One of my father's eccentricities."

"Any reason to think this brotherhood might have enemies?"

"I can't imagine why. It's fuddy old men wearing silly hats over drinks and cigars. Who could take them seriously enough to want to kill them?"

Fatma wanted to point out that someone may have done just that. But she folded away her pad. "Thank you. May the remainder of your father be lived in your life."

"Please do all you can to bring this murderer to justice, agent," Abigail said, her glistening eyes pleading. "My father deserved more."

Fatma nodded, and she and Aasim took their leave. Outside, he gave her an impressed look. "Your English is as sharp as your suit. I only caught half of all that. Learn anything?"

"Other than some masked man? Not much."

"Well, we'll have to go with what we have. We've sent word to this Alexander. Assume he'll be arriving in the next few days. By then, this will be all over the dailies." He shook his head. "The paperwork will be unbearable."

"Paperwork is part of the modern world. I'll start looking in the morning. Have your people send me the forensics report. I'll check back when—"

She stopped abruptly as someone rounded a corner, almost running into them. The young policeman. He held a cup, trying and failing to not spill its contents. His face registered surprise at seeing her, then relief at finding Aasim.

"Inspector! Your coffee?" He offered up a cup that looked half-full. Aasim accepted with a flat look.

"Agent Fatma," the policeman greeted, more polite than before. "Looking for you as well. There's someone to see you." He turned. "She was following right behind. I hope I didn't—ah, there she is now!"

Fatma looked to find another figure darting around the corner. A young woman, wearing a black coat and long dark skirts that swished as she moved. At seeing them, her face lit up from within a sky-blue hijab.

"Good evening," she greeted, catching her breath. She took in Aasim before turning to Fatma. "Agent Fatma, I managed to catch you. Praise God!"

Fatma looked her over uncertainly. "I'm not sure we've met . . . ?"

"Ah! Where's my head?" The woman began fishing about in a tan leather bag slung over a shoulder. After an awkward while, she retrieved something quite unexpected. A silver badge bearing her likeness and the words EGYPTIAN MINISTRY OF ALCHEMY, ENCHANTMENTS, AND SUPERNATURAL ENTITIES.

"I'm Agent Hadia," she said. "Your new partner."

Fatma thought she could almost hear Aasim's moustache twitch at the words.

CHAPTER FOUR

T he boilerplate eunuch at the Abyssinian coffee shop set down two white porcelain cups before leaving in a whir of spinning gears. Fatma took her own, a strong floral Ethiopian blend, which was fast edging out the more traditional Turkish varieties in the city. She took a sip. Just right—one spoon of coffee, one of sugar, with just enough foam. The shop was more a café than a traditional ahwa, boasting modern amenities and a modern clientele. It also stayed open all night, and she came here often at the end of a shift to unwind.

At least, that was the usual routine.

Fatma rested her cup to sift through the papers in the folder in front of her. She'd shared an awkward and silent ride from Giza looking them over—at least three times. Either that, or be forced to actually have a conversation. Now, she spoke aloud as she read. "Hadia Abdel Hafez. Twenty-four years old. Born into a middle-class family in Alexandria. Studied comparative theological alchemy at university there. Graduated top of your class." She paused, looking up. "Spent two years teaching at the Egyptian College for Girls in America?"

Hadia, who sat with hands wrapped around her cup of black mint tea, perked up beneath her coat—looking relieved to finally be talking. Fatma had almost forgotten what the Ministry's uniforms for women looked like, since she'd long opted out of wearing one. There was also that sky-blue headscarf that so blatantly stood out. Patterned or colored hijabs were still frowned upon by more traditional or rural Egyptians, even here in Cairo. She obviously wanted it known she was a thoroughly modern woman. "I thought the queen's mission might let me put my degree to good use," she answered.

Fatma arched an eyebrow. "They're not too fond of alchemy in America."

"The mission is in New York—Harlem. Worked with immigrants in Brooklyn too—Roma, Sicilians, Jews. All people suspected of bringing in 'foreign customs.'" She wrinkled a bold nose in distaste.

No need to explain. America's anti-magic edicts were infamous. "Returned to Egypt and accepted into the Ministry Academy on your first attempt. Graduated in the 1912 class and was assigned to the Alexandria office. But now you're here. In Cairo. As my . . . partner." Fatma closed the folder, sliding it back across the table. "Not every day a new partner arrives, at a crime scene, carrying her résumé."

Spots of color bloomed on Hadia's beige cheeks, and her fingers fidgeted around the folder's edges. "Director Amir intended we meet tomorrow. But I was already up late at the Ministry when I got word of the case. So I took a carriage over and decided to introduce myself. And maybe now, thinking about it, that wasn't the best idea . . ."

Fatma let her trail into silence. The Ministry had been pushing for agents to take on partners. She'd managed to wriggle her way out of it. Everyone knew she worked alone. Amir certainly did. Likely he'd planned to spring this on her tomorrow, once everything was official.

"Agent Hadia." The woman perked up, her dark brown eyes at attention. "I think there's been some mistake. I didn't request a partner. Nothing personal, I just work alone. I'm sure they can pair you with someone else. There's an investigator in the Alexandria office—Agent Samia. One of the first women in the Ministry. I'll put in a letter if you like." There. She even managed a sympathetic face. No need to be cruel.

Hadia stared, mulling something before setting her tea down.

"I was told you might not take to having a partner right away. I was given an assignment with Agent Samia on graduation. Turned it down. Told her I wanted to work with you."

Fatma stopped mid-sip. "You turned down working with Agent Samia? To her face?" Agent Samia was one of the most imposing women she'd ever met. You just didn't say no to her.

"She wished me God's good fortune. And here I am."

"But why work with me? I don't have anywhere near Samia's experience."

Hadia looked incredulous. "Why work with the youngest agent to graduate from the academy—at twenty? Who was assigned to the Cairo office? Who made it to special investigator in just two years? Whose cases are now required reading at the academy?"

Fatma grunted. This was what notoriety got you.

"I thought you'd like to know that I didn't waste my trip to the Worthington estate tonight." Hadia pulled out another folder, opening and setting it on the table. Fatma's eyes rounded. Sketches of the crime scene!

"How did you—?"

"I have a cousin on the force." She grinned, showing off a slight overbite.

Fatma leaned forward, flipping through the sheets. Aasim would have sent her information on all this by tomorrow. But he was particularly stingy about his sketches.

"Never seen burns like these," Hadia remarked. "Some kind of alchemical agent?"

"Too controlled," Fatma muttered. "There's magic at work."

"I thought this was interesting." Hadia lifted one sketch out. It was of the woman. Her fingers traced the broad collar and earrings. "This was an idolater, wasn't it?"

Fatma looked up, eyes narrowing. Good catch. The arrival of djinn and magic pouring back into the world had impacted people's faiths in strange ways. It was inevitable a few would go seeking Egypt's oldest religions, whose memory was etched into the very landscape.

"What do you know about them?" Fatma asked.

"More than the police. I don't think they've caught on yet."

Not yet. Aasim and his people believed the adherents of the old religions a small group of heretics. They wouldn't be looking for them at the mansion of a British lord.

"From the banner," Hadia went on, "Lord Worthington looks to have been in some kind of cult. Maybe the idolater was their priestess. There was a man with his head turned backward. Some kind of sacrifice? I've heard—"

Fatma closed the folder, cutting her off. "First thing they should have taught you at the academy is not to take rumors you hear on the streets as fact. I haven't had any cases of 'idolaters' twisting people's heads about. So maybe we wait until we have some evidence before starting up about human sacrifices."

Hadia's face colored. "I'm sorry. I was just thinking aloud."

Fatma reached into her jacket for her pocket watch. Already past two. She stood up. "It's late, Agent Hadia. Not a proper time to think clearly. Let's get some sleep and pick up on this in the morning." *And, hopefully, get you reassigned.*

"Of course." She gathered up her things and stood in turn. "I'm honored to be working with you, Agent Fatma." And the two parted ways.

◆   ◆   ◆

Fatma could have taken a carriage. But the walk home from the coffee shop wasn't far. Besides, she needed to clear her head. She wasn't certain why Hadia's words had been so irksome. She'd heard similar things a thousand times. It was why she didn't mention it to Aasim. Maybe she was smarting at being assigned a partner without a say in the matter.

Or maybe you're taking out your weariness on some starry-eyed recruit. Bully. She could hear her mother's chiding: "Well, look at the big investigator. Her face is to the ground."

Fatma turned the corner to her building: a twelve-story high-rise of tan stone, with Neo-Pharaonic columns along the sides and rounded like a turret in the front. Outside broad black doors worked with gold stood an older man with receding graying hair. At seeing him, she smoothed the annoyance from her face. Every apartment in downtown Cairo had its own bewab—porters, doormen, and general watchers of all things. This one had no problem offering unsolicited advice, and could read faces with uncanny accuracy.

"Uncle Mahmoud," she greeted, walking up with taps of her cane.

The man fixed her with a look that could have come from the sphinx. His sharp eyes seemed to weigh and judge her on a scale, before his red-brown face broke into a smile.

"Captain," he replied, using the nickname he'd given her—on account of the suits. His Sa'idi accent didn't hold a hint of Cairene. With that long gallabiyah and sandals he could have stepped right out of her village. "Wallahi, the Ministry is keeping you out later and later these past nights."

"It comes with the job, Uncle."

The bewab shook his head. "And you don't even come home to sleep in the afternoon like a civilized person, always going like one of those trams." He gestured at the network of cables that crossed the city's skyline. "Wallahi, that's no good for the circulation!"

She wanted to ask when it was he slept—given he seemed to be out here at all times. But that was rude. Instead, she tapped her chest and bowed in thanks. "I'll take the advice."

That appeared to satisfy him, and he opened the doors. "See? You listen to an old man like me. Some arrive here and forget all decency, wallahi. But you are a good Sa'idi, with proper manners. In our head and heart, we must always remember we are Sa'idi. Wake up healthy." She returned the same and walked into the lobby, ignoring her letter box and stepping into a lift.

"Ninth floor," she commanded a waiting boilerplate eunuch. Leaning back, she felt the day's toll take hold as they rose. By the time she got out, she was trudging along and thinking fondly of her bed.

Opening her apartment door, she found the inside dark. By memory, she hung her bowler on a wall hook by a leafy plant. Fumbling, she searched for the lever to the gas lamp. The building owner had been promising to move to alchemical lighting, or even electricity. But so far, she hadn't seen any work started, despite the small fortune she paid for the place. A few quick pumps lit up the dim space—enough to at least see.

"Ramses?" She thrust her cane into a rack. Where was that cat? Mahmoud came in to feed him and would have said if he'd gone missing. She unbuttoned her jacket. "Ramses? I know it's late, but don't be angry."

"Oh?" a voice purred. "And what does Ramses get when you find him?"

Fatma tensed, spinning on her heels and reaching instinctively for the janbiya at her waist—only to find the blade wasn't there. Damn. Her other hand clutched at her service pistol, still nestled in the holster. She got it halfway out before stopping dead at the sight before her.

Lounging casually in a high-backed Moroccan chair of dark wood and cream-colored cushions—*her* chair—was a woman. Dressed in a loose-fitting one-piece black fabric, she sat with her legs crossed. Sharp dark eyes stared out from an almost perfectly oval face, the hair atop her head cut close to the scalp except for a curly tuft in the front. Each finger on the woman's gloved hands was capped by curled points of sharp silver, which casually stroked the fur of the cat in her lap.

Before Fatma could speak, the woman gently deposited Ramses on a cushion. The cat mewed in discontent, but only blinked his yellow eyes once before curling into a silver ball. Rising, the black-clad woman walked forward—her padded feet soundless on the wood floor. Her gait was sauntering, almost intentionally lazy. Yet she seemed to move remarkably fast, reaching to tower over Fatma in quick strides. Her gaze dropped down to the half-drawn pistol.

"Plan on shooting me, agent?" she purred. "Where's that knife you always carry around?"

Fatma eased her grip and released a held breath. "Didn't wear it tonight. Had an undercover case. Would have stood out."

The woman gave a throaty laugh from her slender neck, running a silver claw under Fatma's chin and down the length of her tie. "As if you don't stand out in these little suits." She took firm hold of the tie, wrapping it about her fingers and pulling until the two touched—and Fatma couldn't tell which of their hearts she felt pounding. "And I do so love these little suits."

Then in that quick way she leaned down and gave Fatma a kiss.

It wasn't a hard kiss, but it was a hungry one. The kind that spoke of need and want, of things long denied and yearned for. Fatma at first held back, her senses momentarily overwhelmed, her own lips and tongue awkward and out of step. But that hunger was in her too. It fast stirred awake, full of craving, playfully seeking the right tempo until it fell into rhythm.

When their lips parted, Fatma's head was swimming. The air felt electric, and she drew in breaths to refill her lungs. "Siti." She spoke between heavy breaths. "What are you doing here?"

Siti smiled a lioness's smile, blinking a set of curving eyelashes, and Fatma felt her insides flutter. "I think that's rather obvious." She loosened Fatma's tie and somehow began unbuttoning her shirt with those curled claws.

"Mahmoud didn't say I had any visitors."

Siti's dark face wrinkled as she worked Fatma out of her jacket. "That bewab is nice—but too nosy. You wouldn't want him telling the neighbors about your late-night visits from some infidel woman, would you?"

"Then how—?" Fatma broke off the question to discard her jacket as Siti started up on the waistcoat. Her eyes caught the cotton curtains of her balcony, flapping in the night breeze. "Do you ever use a door?"

"Not if I can help it."

A playful push pinned Fatma against a wall. It always amazed her how strong Siti was. Not that she was doing much resisting. A set of claws ran across the nape of her neck, setting off shivers. She let them travel up, drawing softly through her black curls.

"Your hair needs washing."

"And you cut yours. When did you get back? I haven't seen you in months."

"Miss me?" Siti pouted.

Fatma wrapped her arms about Siti's waist, relishing the familiar feel—and pulled her close.

Siti grinned, dark eyes flashing. "I'll take that as a yes!"

"You know, I planned to come home and go to sleep. I was very tired."

"Oh? Still tired?"

Fatma answered with a kiss, and decided she wasn't so tired after all.

◆   ◆   ◆

Sometime later, Fatma found herself seated on her bed among red-gold cushions and matching damask sheets. Dressed in a plain white gallabiyah, she leaned back against Siti, who combed through her still-damp hair.

"If you don't keep your scalp oiled, it's going to get dry in this heat."

"I have a barber," Fatma replied.

Siti tsked, pouring oil onto her curls and then massaging it in with nimble fingers. Fatma sighed, content, breathing in the faint nutty sweetness. This might have been one of the things she missed the most.

"What is that?" she murmured.

"An oil my mother and aunts taught me. Helps keep the hair healthy."

"What's in it?"

"A little of this and that—old Nubian secret. We don't share it with outsiders."

Fatma twisted her head around to Siti, who was in one of her gallabiyahs. The crimson garment was entirely too small and fit her more like a shirt. But she wore it like it had been tailored for her. "I think I'm entitled to know. My father says we might have a Nubian ancestor, some great-great-great-grandmother or something."

Siti rolled her eyes, turning Fatma's head back around. "You're just a Sa'idi with pretty lips. Get back to me when you're sure. Aay!"

Fatma turned to find Ramses had hopped onto Siti's shoulder, gripping with his claws.

"That hurts!" She shooed him off, and he jumped down to the bed. "You're certain he isn't a djinn? Half the cats in Cairo are probably djinn, you know . . ."

Fatma laughed, tracing a hand along the underside of Siti's bent right leg while eyeing the left. They were long, like all her limbs—as if she'd been stretched out. Well-toned too, so that Fatma could feel the muscle beneath. She considered herself reasonably fit. But next to Siti, she felt like she could spend more time in the gymnasium.

"It's good to see you, Siti." Then more softly. "But what are you doing back?"

"Hmm? In Cairo? Or your bed?"

Both actually. Fatma had met her the past summer, on a case. What started as a few dinners fast blossomed into . . . whatever this was. It had been giddy and new and wonderful. Then it ended with the summer, and Siti went off to do . . . whatever it was she did. A few letters came, postmarked from Luxor, Qena, Kom Ombo. Fatma fell back into the frenzied life of a Ministry agent, telling herself it had just been a fling. Now, Siti was back. And all the giddiness with her.

She sat up, turning around. Might as well be direct. "Guessing this isn't just a social visit. Or you'd have worn something a little more casual." She gestured to where the black outfit lay discarded, silver claws piled atop.

Siti stared back, impassive, eyes hard as black stone. Something gave, and she sighed. "I got back to Cairo by airship today. And yes, I was sent to deliver a message. From the temple."

The temple. That was the other thing about Siti. She was an adherent of the old religion. Pledged to Hathor, the goddess of love and beauty once worshipped in a long-gone Egypt. An infidel, without question. Hadia's "idolater" wormed into her head, and she shook it off.

"What's the message, then?" she asked, cooler than intended. It didn't matter if she had come here partly on business—did it?

Siti frowned at the tone. "It's about what happened tonight in Giza."

That was unexpected. "How do you even know about that? It's barely been a few hours." Her eyes narrowed as understanding dawned. "You have a policeman who belongs to one of your . . . temples."

"Why do you think it's just one?" Siti asked. "Anyway, two of the victims were followers. I didn't know them well. They were from other temples. But word is out about the way they died. We might have information. Figured you're the best person to approach."

Naturally. Fatma was one of the few authorities in contact with them. "What kind of information? Are you involved in this?"

"Me? No! I just got here. I don't know much of anything, except that this Worthington—the one they call the English Basha—had dealings with the temples. You'll have to ask Merira more. She wants to meet, tomorrow."

Merira. A priestess of the local Temple of Hathor who seemed to know the oddest things. "We'll meet, then, tomorrow. Anything else?"

"Yes."

Siti leaned forward and kissed her, gentle but filled with warmth enough to keep back the coldness swirling in Fatma's thoughts. She fell into it even as the woman pulled away.

"I missed you these past months," Siti said, seeming to read what lay behind Fatma's eyes. "I *did* plan on coming here, message or no. It's all I could think about. It's all I've thought about for so long." Lying down, she put her head onto Fatma's lap and curled in close. "For the rest of the night, promise me we'll stop talking about murders, and investigations, and whatever's happening out there. Just for tonight, let's forget about the world. And just *be* here."

Fatma ran a hand along the thin covering of hair on Siti's scalp, playing with the tuft in front between her fingers. She could do that. The world, after all, would be waiting.

It was the sound of the muezzin calling Fajr that stirred her awake.

Fatma blinked to adjust to the dark room. A nearby clock read just past 5:00 a.m. Shifting, she reached out to find empty space. She lifted up and looked about but found herself alone. Her gaze drifted to the balcony, where a breeze blew in from the predawn morning.

Siti had opted for her usual exit, it appeared.

Like old times. There was even a folded note on the pillow. Guiltily—knowing she would not be getting up in time for prayer—Fatma lay back down and closed her eyes. Ramses purred in her lap, and she curled around him, trying to ignore the emptiness beside her.

CHAPTER
FIVE

orning, Uncle."

"A morning of roses, Captain," Mahmoud returned. "Is that a new one?"

She glanced down at her ensemble: a dark forest-green suit with thin magenta stripes and matching waistcoat. She'd paired it with a fuchsia tie showing hints of purple, over a soft white shirt. "Been hiding in the dresser. Felt like being a bit . . . bold."

The bewab raised bushy eyebrows, holding open the door. "You seem lighter this morning, Captain. God is great to send you good dreams and sleep."

"You could say that." Stepping outside she flicked the brim of her bowler and bid him farewell. The truth was she felt remarkably rested—though she'd only slept a few hours. She hadn't felt like this since the summer, after spending time with . . . Siti.

A smile touched her lips, and when she stopped to get her shoes shined, the little man in a white gallabiyah and turban eyed her, curious. She hid her flustered face behind a newspaper as a hand drifted to her jacket pocket—patting Siti's note, an invitation to breakfast.

Hopping a street trolley she found it packed with commuters— factory women in telltale light blue dresses and hijabs; business-men in suits of Turkish fit and red tarbooshes; government clerks wearing kaftans over crisp white buttoned-up gallabiyahs, com-plete with shirt collars in the ministerial fashion. A goat-headed djinn in a tweed jacket and pants sat reading a newspaper, the long hair on his chin moving as he chewed absently. Catching the headline, Fatma hastily checked her own.

Shocking Death of the English Basha was the lead story, with condolences from the business community, a statement by the government vowing the peace summit would go on, and the ensuing investigation. Nothing about flames that burned only flesh, a corpse with its head on backward, or a mysterious man in a gold mask. The rest of the front page included speculation on the growing closeness between the German kaiser and the Ottoman sultan, the usual worries of war, and a write-up on another daring heist by the Forty Leopards. Maybe Aasim had managed to keep the press in the dark after all.

She tucked the paper away and hopped off the trolley at a backed-up intersection. Cairo's infamous traffic had struck again: an accident involving a sleek silver automobile and a donkey-drawn wagon overturned with melons. The two drivers stood yelling, pointing and wagging forefingers in the air. The donkey ignored both, trying to pick up a melon with its teeth.

Fatma headed off the main street, winding through back roads to her destination. Makka was a sleepy-looking Nubian eatery to the unsuspecting but had grown a loyal crowd. Every table was full, and chairs barely left space to weave between. The décor mimicked a traditional Nubian house, with yellow window frames on blue walls and floors of green-and-brown tiles.

She was barely inside before a white-haired man gave her a boisterous welcome. Uncle Tawfik, the owner's son. He peppered her with questions. Why hadn't he seen her in so long? How was her family? Didn't she want to see his mother? She was herded to the kitchens—where scents of cumin and garlic wafted through the air. Tawfik's sisters were no less effusive and querying. She endured them, until she was placed before the proprietor of Makka, Madame Aziza—a sibling of Siti's grandmother. The stately matron sat in a chair like some Meroitic queen surveying her realm. She returned Fatma's greetings and looked out from beneath a more traditional black hijab.

"A nice cane," she rasped, tapping the floor with a wooden staff. "But I like mine better. Come to see my niece?"

"Siti—I mean Abla—asked me to meet her here." Fatma was so accustomed to the nickname, she sometimes forgot to use Siti's given name.

"Abla. That one can't stay in one place. Like a wind blowing this way and that. Too much of her father in her."

Fatma didn't reply. Siti rarely spoke of her father—whom she hadn't known. It had been some kind of scandal, from what little Fatma understood.

"There was a story in my village," Madame Aziza went on, "of a woman who was as light as a feather. She was like that wind— and her husband couldn't keep her in one place. So he recited poetry, and she would settle down long enough to listen. Can you recite poetry?"

Fatma opened her mouth, trying to think of an answer—and was rescued by Siti's arrival down a set of steps. She'd exchanged the outfit of her nighttime jaunts to something more her usual style—a Nubian dress of gold and green prints tied up near her knees, over a pair of snug white breeches tucked into tall brown boots. She started up a whirlwind of chatter while tying on a red hijab, before taking Fatma's arm.

"Yalla! If we don't get out now, they'll have me waiting tables all morning!"

Fatma managed some farewells as she was all but pulled from the kitchen. "Your aunt, what does she know . . . about us, I mean?"

"Auntie Aziza? She's ninety. I doubt her senses are all there."

Fatma peeked back over her shoulder, meeting that watchful gaze. They weren't giving the old woman enough credit.

"I thought we were having breakfast?"

Siti shook her head. "No time. Merira wants to meet now."

Now? Fatma had hoped to sit and talk. Eyeing a bowl of ful reminded her she was also hungry. "I need to eat something."

Siti answered by taking two bundles from Uncle Tawfik, handing one to Fatma. Fresh-baked kabed, stuffed with what looked like mish. Siti was already biting into the bread and cheese, eating heartily. Fatma grumbled slightly; she would have preferred the bean stew. They walked to the main road where the accident was clearing up, and Siti waved down a wheeled carriage. Fatma fell into a cushioned seat just as they lurched off.

"I already signed up for the late day shift," Siti complained. She usually stayed at her aunt's restaurant when in Cairo, working tables. "My lazy cousin thinks I will take her shift too?" She sighed, then looked apologetic. "Malesh. I haven't even told you good morning properly." Her fingers ran down Fatma's tie. "Or complimented this gorgeous suit!"

"It's fine," Fatma answered, finishing her meal. "Whenever I go home my aunts put me straight to work. Last time, I was swept into my cousin's wedding."

Siti made a face. "Try a Nubian wedding. They can last about a week. And the henna . . ."

"Not too much different. I have an aunt who does all the henna. But I've been her *helper* for as long as I can remember. Think she always thought I'd been an apprentice. Anyway, we spent half a night working on the bride."

Siti reached to wipe a bit of mish from Fatma's lips. "You'll have to practice on me." She winked, turning to look out the carriage. "Has this city grown since I was gone?"

Fatma followed her gaze to where the morning sun beat down on Cairo—a mix of towering modern buildings and factories. Newer ones went up by the day, their steel girders like bones awaiting skin, amid streets crammed with carriages, trolleys, steam cars, and more. The skyline was no less busy, traveled by speeding tram cars that left crackling electric bolts in their wake. Even higher, a blue airship hovered like a skyborne whale—six propellers pushing it toward the horizon.

"Thanks ya Jahiz," they both said on cue. And meant it.

The carriage made its way into Old Cairo. Here, the roads were narrower and covered in paving stones. On either side loomed masjid and architecture spanning Cairo's ages—from the Fatimids to the Ottomans.

Siti signaled for the carriage to stop, insisting on paying the fare. They stepped out along a busy thoroughfare at Al-Hussein square and followed the crowds toward a stone gate showing spandrels adorned with geometric designs. On the other side was the market of Khan-el-Khalili.

The open-air souk had been built over the centuries with no rhyme or reason to its layout. Storefronts with colorful doors lined narrow streets, outnumbered only by stalls that took up every space: coffeehouses and machinist kiosks, bookshops and alchemical fragrance peddlers, boutiques of silk and shelves stacked with boilerplate parts. Vendors shouted into the morning, while others enticed passersby with whispered promises. Amid the haggling, a hundred scents—perfumes, spices, and sizzling meats—dizzied the senses.

"Now this I missed," Siti said, strutting the souk with confidence. She led Fatma around giant cylinders for aeronautic motors and past young men shouldering high-pressure steam urns who poured tea into fine porcelain cups. "You can get just about anything in this place. Do you know, there's supposedly an angel somewhere down here? They say she grants miracles."

Fatma ducked under hanging brass lanterns before turning down another passageway. An angel? In the Khan? Angels had appeared sometime after the djinn. Or rather, beings calling themselves angels. The Coptic Church ruled they couldn't be angels, insisting all such divinities resided in heaven with God. The ulama was equally skeptical, insisting true angels had no free will. The enigmatic creatures were not elucidating on matters either way. That one of them would take up residence in the souk was bizarre. Then again, what about them wasn't?

"Seen enough angels," Fatma replied. Siti grunted her agreement. The case where they'd met this past summer had involved an angel named Maker, who went very, very wrong. They both tried not to talk about that too much.

Siti stopped near the end of a small alley, facing a shop with two doors. One was labeled in black calligraphy as an apothecary, bushels of dried leaves and pungent herbs decorating its front. The worn wood of the other was painted with a great eye of celestial blue surrounded by gold stars and red candles. At its top was etched in white: HOUSE OF THE LADY OF STARS.

Opening the door set off ringing chimes as they walked into a faded blue room. A lone old woman sat at a table, pushing pieces across a game board, an empty chair her opponent. At hearing them enter, she looked up to mouth silent greetings—waving a hand up and down for quiet.

Half the rectangular space was cordoned off by a curtain of red and black beads, behind which sat three figures at a table. One was Merira, in a black sebleh decorated with stars, and a long headscarf draped in coins and red pom-poms. The persons opposite her wore green dresses cut in a mix of Parisian and Cairene styles—so common these days—their faces hidden by veils. Upper-class women, come seeking a fortune-teller in a back alley of the Khan. The three spoke in hushed tones: something about an ailing father, a dirigible shipping magnate, and an inheritance.

Whatever Merira revealed didn't appear to go over well, and the pair took to loud bickering. After several failed attempts at intervention, Merira let out a frustrated shout. A gust of wind rattled the curtain and swayed the gilded gas lamps on their chains. Fatma clutched her bowler in the gale. Siti yawned, examining her fingernails. The old woman's clothing whipped about, but she never looked up from her game.

The wind died away, but it had the intended effect. The two rich women stopped their quarreling, eyes fixed on Merira, who silenced one of their protests with a quick "Tut!" When both finally took their leave, they left an obscene amount of money along with their gratitude.

Merira emerged looking wearied, but at seeing Siti and Fatma put on a bright smile, greeting them with kisses. The priestess affected a matronly air, accentuated by age, a set of doting eyes, and plump cheeks. That was all a role, however, like acting the fortune-teller. Fatma knew better. Behind those ever-smiling lips was a shrewd mind that knew all the workings of this city—both in the light and the shadows.

"Your clientele has gone up a notch," Fatma noted.

Merira rolled her eyes. "Even the wealthy want to know their fortunes. And the bills must be paid." She laid down the generous stack of notes on the table beside the old woman. "And thank you, Minya, your timely display stopped me from throttling those two!"

The space above the empty chair rippled, and an inhumanly tall woman appeared, with marbled aquamarine skin and bright jade eyes. Her ephemeral body was as transparent as her sheer dress, which billowed as if caught in a breeze. A Jann. One of the elemental djinn. That explained things. The Jann moved a piece on the board, causing the old woman to exclaim and bite her hand.

"Peace be upon you, Agent Fatma," the djinn greeted, voice echoing. "It is pleasant to see you again, despite the circumstances."

"And upon you peace, Minya," Fatma replied. The Jann was a devotee to Hathor. Djinn, after all, could be of any religion, or none at all. She turned to Merira, who had removed the headdress and was now applying black kohl on the honey-hued skin beneath her eyes. "I'm guessing the 'circumstances' have to do with last night? You have information?"

"Not just me. Come." The priestess led them past another curtain of beads, these gold and blue, to a narrow hallway and then a door. A quick set of patterned knocks gained them entrance, and the three stepped into the Temple of Hathor.

Lit by bright lanterns, it was furnished with mahogany tables and cushioned chairs. Colorful wall murals depicted gods with the heads of animals, or wearing divine crowns. At the temple's center stood a black granite statue of a seated woman, curving horns adorning her head with a disc in their center. Hathor. The

Lady of Stars. The venerated goddess of old Egypt, reduced to a small group of faithful in the backstreets of Khan-el-Khalili.

Those who opted to follow these forgotten gods did so in secret. Though the Ministry wasn't sure of their numbers, it was guessed to be in the thousands—and growing. There was only one occupant of the temple today: a young woman in diaphanous white robes. She bowed to Merira, who pulled off the sebleh to reveal a gold pleated dress. The young woman took the garment, helping the priestess into her layered wig. Siti had gone her own way, stopping to pray at a second granite statue—this one a woman with a lioness's head. Hathor, made over as the Mistress of Vengeance and Lady of War—the goddess Sekhmet.

Fatma observed from a distance. She wasn't intolerant. But she believed in God, and that the Prophet—peace be upon him—was His messenger. Even after all she'd seen in this line of work, this was still strange. When Siti finished praying, she walked over, and Fatma shifted beneath those knowing eyes. They tried their best not to talk religion.

"Merira went this way," was all she said, leading them to another part of the room. The priestess of Hathor was already seated in a broad burgundy divan with legs ending in animal paws. A black cat lay near her side, earrings of gold piercing its nose and ears alongside a collar of lapis lazuli. And there was someone else.

Seated at a long coffee-colored table across from Merira was a man. Fatma had never seen a man in the temple. She'd thought the followers of Hathor all women. But as she caught sight of his face, she wondered if he were a man at all. His complexion was completely gray, with bland undertones of olive, as if his actual color had been faded in the sun. He had no hair at all. None on his rounded scalp, even his brow. Despite that, his strange skin didn't look smooth. Instead it held a leathery quality, and she imagined it feeling rough under her fingers.

"Agent Fatma," Merira introduced, "this is—"

"You may call me Lord Sobek," the man spoke. His voice was

almost guttural. And his teeth! Were they sharpened to points? "Master of the Waters," he went on. "The Rager. Lord of Faiyum. Defender of the Land. General of the Royal Armies."

There was a stretch of silence. Merira kept a stoic face. The young attendant fixated her gaze elsewhere. Siti sighed, pulling up a chair and inviting Fatma to sit. "This is, um, Ahmad."

The man scowled but nodded sharply.

"Ahmad is the high priest of the Cult of Sobek," Merira explained.

The name clicked on in Fatma's head. Sobek. The crocodile-headed god of the old Egyptian pantheon. She looked over the man, who wore dark brown robes that frayed at the ends. Not exactly high priest attire, but there *was* something decidedly crocodilian to him. Now that she looked closer, she could see what she'd mistaken for black eyes were actually a deep penetrating green. Like a Nile crocodile.

"Two of our own were lost in last night's tragedy," Merira said.

Fatma turned to her. "A man and a woman. You knew them?"

Merira nodded, arranging a set of black tarot cards upon the table. Fatma didn't understand why a priestess of Hathor needed such things. Tarot cards for divination were likely a European invention with some Mamluk influences, not a practice of the pharaohs. But here she was in an Englishman's suit. So perhaps, not one to quibble.

"The man was a high priest of the Cult of Anubis." Merira overturned a card, depicting a black jackal holding a reaper's scythe. "The woman was a high priestess of Nephthys." She flipped another card—a seated woman holding a staff.

Nephthys. A funerary goddess as Fatma recalled.

"Nephthys," Ahmad spoke, "was my divine consort. The wife of Sobek."

Fatma frowned. "I thought Nephthys was Set's sister-wife." Siti shook her head quietly. Too late. Ahmad's generous nostrils flared as he gritted his sharp teeth.

"Why is everyone so slavish to texts written thousands of years ago?" he snapped. "Gods can change. Grow apart. Try new things. Besides, Set was a jerk. He never knew how to treat her properly. How to worship her."

Fatma looked on dubiously. Were they talking about gods or people?

The anger drained from Ahmad's eyes, and he reached into his robes, drawing out a photo—an image of a woman. "Nephthys. My love. My divine one."

The woman in the picture was young, quite pretty—with a joyous smile that extended to her eyes. Quite a contrast to the charred remains she'd seen last night.

"May God give you patience," she told him. "May I ask her given name?"

"Ester," he spoke softly, withdrawing the photo. "Ester Sedarous."

A Coptic name. She was a Christian. Or had been, once.

"What was she doing there last night?" Fatma asked, directing her question to Merira. "Did Lord Worthington join one of your temples?"

"Quite the other way around." Merira turned over another card. This one depicted an old bearded man in purple robes holding a glowing lantern. "The Hermit seeks truth." She flipped another card, and Fatma's eyebrows rose. It was a replica of the banner at Lord Worthington's estate: two interlocking pyramids making up a hexagram encircled by a fiery serpent devouring its tail, all above a scimitar and down-turned crescent.

Fatma had no idea how the woman did that, and didn't much care. "Enough, Merira. I want to know everything you know. No more parlor tricks. Just talk to me."

The high priestess sat back, disappointed. She did love her dramatics. "The Hermetic Brotherhood of Al-Jahiz." Her fingers tapped the card depicting the banner. "The hexagram, a symbol of alchemy representing the great elements." She touched the four zodiac signs and the all-seeing eye respectively as she spoke. "Air, fire, earth, water, and spirit. The sun and moon for the many unknowable worlds that may be. Beneath, the sword: honor in defense of rightness, of purity, the balance of life and death. Under that, the down-turned crescent—the light of wisdom in the face of darkness." Her forefinger traced the fiery serpent. "The unending and eternal quest. *Quærite veritatem.* Seek Truth."

Fatma was puzzled. Since the return of the djinn, esoterics and spiritualists had flocked to Egypt—an array of men in odd hats. But one dedicated to al-Jahiz? "I've never heard of any such thing."

"Neither had I," Merira replied, "until we were approached to join. The Hermitic Brotherhood of Al-Jahiz was founded by Lord Alistair Worthington. Sometime in the late 1890s."

"A decade or so after the routing of the British at Tell El Kebir," Fatma noted. "Lord Worthington was instrumental in brokering the peace and independence."

"For which he was granted special privileges," Merira continued, "the so-called English Basha. It seems he put them to use, founding his secret brotherhood. They've spent years hunting every trace of al-Jahiz. They reportedly have a vault of relics."

Fatma recalled the ritual room at the estate—built, it seemed, as a dedication to al-Jahiz.

"It does seem a bit contrived, doesn't it?" Merira asked. "I was certain there was some nefarious plan, when he called on the heads of the temples." Her hand tapped the Hermit card. "Yet all I saw was an earnest man seeking a higher purpose. He truly believed himself on a holy quest. That the secrets of al-Jahiz would bring peace to the world."

"Our great and noble English savior," Siti remarked wryly.

"Yes, well. That too."

"I still don't understand how you're involved in this," Fatma said. "If I were creating a group dedicated to al-Jahiz, you people wouldn't be the first on my list. No offense."

"We weren't," Merira replied. "The Brotherhood were mostly Englishmen—from Worthington's company. But he became convinced that the key to recovering al-Jahiz's secrets was to get, how did he put it, 'the more pure-blood Nilotic type in our ranks, whose minds might work as his.'"

Fatma winced. Merira shrugged.

"He attempted to bring in other Egyptians, wealthy associates. But what few he floated the idea with—Muslims and Copts alike—balked. He even went after some Soudanese."

Fatma tried to imagine recruiting someone from the Mahdist Revolutionary People's Republic of Soudan to your occultist brotherhood. Probably have to endure a three-hour rebuttal featuring Sufi writings and two more in Marxist rhetoric.

"Those closest to Lord Worthington warned he would be seen as an outcast if he persisted," Merira said. "Us on the other hand? We're long past that."

"You're the only ones who would take up his offer."

"Even a rich man must sometimes eat with beggars," Ahmad remarked.

That sounded like something her mother would say. The strange man pulled out a packet of Nefertaris, slipped one between his lips, and was prepared to flick a silver scarab beetle lighter before Merira cleared her throat loudly. Taking the hint, he sighed and replaced the cigarette. The high priestess of Hathor narrowed her gaze on Fatma.

"I can see that look on your face, investigator. You think we were being used. Some wealthy Englishman comes along with his nonsense cult mocking our culture, and we don't even have the dignity to tell him no—like some old-time guide offered to carry bags for a little baksheesh."

"Not quite that. But you were being used."

"And we used him back," Merira retorted. "We demanded a high price for our presence. Our cults can't keep going like this. Hiding in back rooms. Meeting in secret. Worthington money would help us build and locate an actual temple. A place to worship out in the open, where we won't be harassed or hounded. Why do you think Siti's been traveling?"

Fatma's head swerved to Siti, who didn't meet her eyes. She looked back to Merira. "I'm not here to lecture you on how to run your temple. But we're talking about murder. Your people's involvement is going to get out sooner or later. That'll bring exposure—and not the kind you want. I don't need to tell you how quick fingers could get pointed your way."

Ahmad growled something about senseless bigotry, and Merira's face tightened.

"Which is why I'm being as open as possible. I will aid you as best as I can. My word, by the goddess."

"Good," Fatma said. "So tell me, did this brotherhood have any enemies?"

"I can't say. We only dealt with them recently."

"How about the other temples? I've heard you have rivalries."

Merira's eyes rounded. "Rivalries yes, but for members. Or over interpretations of theology. But murdering two of our own? The high priests and priestesses meet every month for coffee. We hold inter-temple potlucks. Why, Sobek and Set are roommates."

Fatma looked to Ahmad, who shrugged. "It's how I met Nephthys. Besides, you know how hard it is to find an affordable one bedroom in central Cairo?" Actually, Fatma did. So she let the issue drop.

"We know about the bodies," Merira said. "The odd burns. Minya? Your thoughts?"

A strong breeze picked up at mention of the Jann's name, and she materialized.

Fatma started. Had the djinn been there all this time? "You know something about those burns?"

The Jann's face creased in thought. It wasn't exactly a human face—and not just because of the near-transparent marbled skin. Her eyes—equally marbled—were overly large, her mouth too broad and jawline too defined. This was an immortal face that spoke of eternity.

"I did not view the dead myself," the Jann answered, echoing. "But I have heard it described: a fire that consumes flesh but leaves all else unmarred." She rippled, as if discomfited. "I cannot be certain, but I sense the touch of my cousins at work."

The djinn waved long slender fingers over the table. One of the tarot cards slowly turned over to show a sword wreathed in flames.

"They, truly formed, of smokeless fire," Minya intoned. "The Ifrit."

Fatma's breath caught. An Ifrit! One of the other elementals. Beings of flame. They were considered quite volatile and didn't live among mortals or even other djinn. In fact, no one had actually *seen* an Ifrit in the forty years since al-Jahiz's opening of the Kaf. "But why would an Ifrit want to murder Lord Worthington?" she asked.

The Jann whooshed, like wind moving through the branches of a tree. "Perhaps these mortals sought to bargain with an Ifrit. Such attempts have rarely ended . . . without consequence."

"Who would be fool enough to try to bargain with an Ifrit?" Siti muttered.

Someone playing at forces he didn't understand, Fatma thought. One of the greatest problems in their age. And it rarely ended . . . without consequence.

"One more question. Do you know anything about a masked man in black?"

"What man?" Ahmad asked. A low growl sounded in his throat.

"Lord Worthington's daughter ran into a man dressed in black last night," Fatma explained, unnerved at his reaction. "Wearing a gold mask." Ahmad's teeth ground together, but he said nothing. Fatma filed that away for later.

Merira shook her head. "I'm sorry I can't offer you more, investigator."

"You've provided a lot. I'll do what I can to see you're not too caught up in all this."

"You will do all you can to find who has committed this atrocity," Ahmad said.

Fatma frowned. Was that a request or a demand? "I always solve my cases."

The man's dark green eyes stared, as if they could discern truth. "Nephthys didn't deserve her end," he said, voice almost cracking. "Bring her murderer to justice. Man, or djinn, let them stand before the gods and have their soul weighed and judged for this crime!"

♦   ♦   ♦

Fatma stepped from the House of the Lady of Stars into the backstreet of Khan-el-Khalili. Siti came out a moment later.

"Is he for real?"

Siti frowned. "Who? You mean Ahmad?"

"Lord Sobek," Fatma replied dryly. "He really thinks he's some crocodile god?"

"Well, not *the* Sobek. More like Sobek's chosen here in the mortal world. Someone in direct communion with the entombed god, a part of whom now resides within him."

Entombed gods. That much Fatma understood of the old religionists. The faith claimed the gods had never truly gone away, but instead lay interred deep beneath the earth of Egypt—not dead but entombed within colossal sarcophagi like the pharaohs of old. Adherents believed the more people turned back to their worship, the more the old gods stirred in deathless slumber, reaching out to touch the mortal realm—bestowing followers with bits of their power. One day, they claimed, when enough chanted their names and once more made offering in their sacred temples, the gods would break their eternal fast, taking their rightful place as the true lords of this land. The thought, Fatma admitted privately, at times made her shiver.

"You alright?" Siti asked.

Fatma pushed away visions of hoary desiccated gods wrapped in mummified shrouds and adorned in shimmering crowns with the heads of beasts rising from Egypt's depths—and answered with a question. "You're looking for a place for this grand temple? That's where you've been these past months? And you never told me?"

Siti propped back against a wall. "I told you I was out doing work. You never asked much more. Or seemed to want to know. We don't really talk about that kind of thing."

True enough, Fatma conceded. Still. "This attempt at opening up some public temple. That doesn't sound like a good idea."

"I thought you said you weren't here to lecture."

"I'm not lecturing. Just being honest."

Siti folded her arms. "What's your 'honest' not-lecture, then?"

"The country is still getting used to djinn and magic. Now you want to tell them there are ancient gods entombed beneath their feet—that you're trying to wake up? People aren't ready."

Siti's voice tightened. "How long should we wait until they're ready? A year? Ten?"

"As long as it takes." Fatma could hear her own tone heating. "Until people accept you."

Siti cocked her head. "Like you accept me? Don't you think we hide enough as it is?"

The two said nothing else for a moment, only glaring. Slowly, their faces untensed.

"Did we just have a fight?" Siti asked, a smile forming. "I think we just had a fight!"

"We had a fight," Fatma agreed. Her irritation all but vanished at the realization. It was a wonder it'd taken this long.

"How about tonight you make it up to me—" Siti began.

Fatma's eyes rounded. "Make it up to *you*?"

"Make it up to *me*, by taking me to the Spot. It's still there, isn't it?"

"The Spot is always there."

"Then looks like you've got a date, investigator. Dress sharp."

Fatma gave a slight snort as Siti turned to walk inside. She always dressed sharp.

CHAPTER
SIX

The Ministry of Alchemy, Enchantments, and Supernatural Entities sat in the center of downtown Cairo. When it was founded in 1885, its headquarters had been relegated to a warehouse up in Bulaq. It moved to its current locale in 1900—one among the wave of new constructions by djinn architects.

Fatma traced the building's outline as she approached: a long rectangular structure capped by a glass dome. A row of bell-shaped windows lined the front of its five floors, each fitted with mechanized screens of black and gold ten-pointed stars and kites, which constantly shifted into new geometric patterns. Walking through a set of glass doors, she gave a quick greeting to a guard—a young man whose uniform was always too big for his gangly frame. One of these days, she'd introduce him to a tailor. Not breaking her stride, she bounded across the marble floor—where the Ministry's insignia, a medieval symbol for alchemy superimposed upon a twelve-pointed star, had been formed from a mosaic of red, blue, and gold stone.

She spared an upward glance, where giant iron gears and orbs spun beneath the glass dome, like some clockwork orrery. It was, in fact, the building's brain: mechanical ingenuity forged by djinn. Smaller replicas allowed aerial trams to self-pilot without the need of a driver. This one helped to run the entire Ministry. The building was alive. She tipped her bowler in good morning to it as well.

Her cane stopped the closing doors of a crowded lift, allowing her to slip inside. With apologies to the other occupants, she named her floor and checked her pocket watch. Still some morning left, but not much. In her head, her mother's voice came on cue: *Time is made of gold.* The lift stopped at the fourth floor, and she stepped out, passing agents on the way to her office—men in black with red tarbooshes. She pulled down her bowler, avoiding their glances.

"Agent Fatma!" someone called.

She gritted her teeth. No such luck. Turning, she met a tall, broad-shouldered man in a well-pressed Ministry uniform, silver buttons gleaming. A smile lined his square jaw, and she relaxed a bit. "Good morning, Agent Hamed."

The man frowned at a clock on the wall. "Wait, is it still morning?"

"I didn't know you were funny now."

He smirked beneath a short dark moustache, sipping from a cup of tea.

She and Hamed had graduated from the academy together, back in '08. Not that they were great friends back then. He'd been older, bigger, and always bragged of coming from a family of policemen—the kind of person she usually avoided. But, by chance, they'd reconnected just this past summer. Turned out, he wasn't all that bad. A bit stiff and conservative—like his starched white collarless shirt—but alright, once you got to know him.

"Keeping late hours," he remarked. Then in a lowered voice. "Heard you were out in Giza, working the English Basha case. The papers say it was a fire. But if you're involved . . . ?"

"You know better than to trust the papers, Hamed," Fatma chided.

He looked disappointed at seeing no more was forthcoming. "Fine. But this office is terrible at keeping secrets. The longer you hold out, the more inventive the story's going to get."

Fatma frowned. Men were so gossipy. "Please tell me there's not another pool?"

"Oh, there's a pool. But not on that. The bet's on how long before you chase off your new partner."

Fatma inhaled sharply. Hadia! Between Siti's return and this morning's meeting, she'd completely forgotten! Her eyes scanned the office. "Where is she? Did they already get her a desk?"

Hamed bit his lip, failing to hold back a smile. Lifting his teacup, he motioned straight to her office door. "Onsi's in there with her now. He's bringing her up to—"

Fatma spun on her heels, no longer listening. She found her office door wide open, and walked inside. She'd been granted this space upon making special investigator. It was big, with windows that looked out on the Nile and space enough to hold a desk and furniture, including a wardrobe chest—where she kept her backup suits. You could never be too careful. Now, it held a second desk. Hadia sat behind it. At seeing Fatma she stood straight up.

"Good morning, Agent Fatma," a voice greeted.

Fatma glanced to the squat man across the room. Agent Onsi. Hamed's partner. His brown face beamed, as usual.

"I was just talking to Agent Hadia. Did you know we were in the academy together? Why I—" He stopped, frowning through wire-rimmed silver spectacles. "Agent Fatma, are you well?"

"The desk was already here when I came in," Hadia blurted.

Fatma turned about and left, not saying a word. She was vaguely aware of people watching as she strode to Director Amir's office. She gave a quick knock before being called in.

At first glance, Amir didn't fit expectations of a director. His graying hair, sleepy eyes, and drawn face affected the air of an overworked bureaucrat. His uniform had a dull, rumpled cast, and his desk was a clutter—covered in folders and paperwork. But he'd run the largest of the Ministry's offices for over ten years. Most in his position barely lasted half that long. Currently, he stood engrossed with riffling through a large book, as if searching for something.

"Thought I'd be seeing you," he said. "Surprised it took so long. Have a seat."

Fatma sat in a narrow, uncomfortable chair. Her eyes fell on a photo of a young Amir framed on the desk, wearing an outdated Ministry uniform and smiling. It was hard to believe he'd ever been young—or that he smiled.

"I suppose you've met Agent Hadia."

"We met last night," Fatma replied.

"She showed up at the Worthington estate? Impressive."

That was one word for it. "I don't think this partnership is going to work out."

"Oh?" Amir mused distractedly. He was taking more books off shelves, opening and shaking them. Fatma steeled herself. The man was notorious for throwing you off your intent.

"I've done fine as a special investigator without a partner. I believe my record speaks for itself. Therefore, I can't see why I would need one now. I know the Ministry has been pushing for agents to be paired up. That works for some people, but not everyone. I think Agent Hadia deserves a proper mentor, which I'm uncertain I will be." There. Succinct and to the point.

Amir said nothing for a moment, shaking out one last book. With a frustrated grunt, he returned to his desk, settling into a worn chair. He was a lanky man, and when he set his half-closed eyes on her it felt like she was being hovered over by a vulture.

"Ask me how many people, right here in Cairo, have blood sugar sickness," he said.

Fatma blinked. "I don't—"

"No, go ahead. Ask me."

"How many people in Cairo have blood sugar sickness?"

"Ya Allah! I have no idea! I'm terrible with numbers!"

"You just *told* me to ask you."

He kept on talking. "You know who's good with numbers? My wife. A statistician at the Health Ministry. Put together a report on blood sugar sickness and how it's an epidemic in Cairo. Her probability model says that I could have blood sugar sickness and not know it."

He leaned forward.

"So, do you know what she's done? She's thrown out every

sweet we have in our house. It got so that I took to hiding sugary things in secret places. Last Moulid, I bought several little candy horses and kept them here. I reasoned she'd have an eye out for sesame candy or malban—not confectionaries made for children. But now it appears she's found even those so that I can't grab one sweet thing to nibble on."

Fatma stared. He'd done it. He'd completely thrown her off.

"Is it frustrating? Of course. A grown man should be able to eat a sweet when he wants!" He sighed, and his face relaxed. "But my wife is doing this for my own good. So how can I dislike that? Do you see now what I mean?"

Fatma shook her head. How could anyone see what he meant?

"You're getting a partner for your own good, agent," Amir snapped. "Whether you believe you need one or not. You've done commendable work. But it also gets dangerous. Ghuls. Djinn. That sordid business with the angel. It's not safe for a lone investigator. The Ministry wants its agents paired, to watch each other's backs."

"But, director," Fatma protested, "I often work in liaison with the Cairo police. They—"

Amir shook his head. "Not good enough. You don't work with police all the time. And they're not Ministry. Look, it's not often that I put my foot down." He motioned at her suit. "Do I ever say anything about your flagrant flouting of proper Ministry uniforms?"

"You bring it up at least once a month!"

He frowned. "Really? Well, you don't appear to pay attention to me, but you'll have to do so this time. This comes directly from the top. The Ministry commissioners want Agent Hadia here, in Cairo. And they want her with you."

Commissioners? Fatma thought, bewildered. Ministry brass were involved?

"Why? What's so important about this?"

Amir leaned closer. "How many women agents are there? I can count them off on one hand. Agent Samia in Alexandria. Agent Nawal in Luxor. Then you. And you're far younger than them. Agent Hadia is the first woman recruit we've had since.

A few months ago, women were granted the vote. We might see women soon in parliament. There's rumors of women joining the police force. The Ministry can't be seen lagging! Not with those Egyptian Feminist Sisterhood types monitoring everyone, then writing up reports for the papers!"

So that was it. Fatma had proposed new ways to recruit women *years* ago, and was mostly ignored. Now the Ministry was playing catch-up. And she and Hadia were to be some kind of public relations campaign.

"Honestly, I'm surprised. I'd think you'd welcome more women in our ranks. You know I've always supported you. Do you know, I was an early subscriber to *La Modernite?*"

Fatma groaned silently. *La Modernite* had been an Egyptian magazine featuring prominent thinkers, among them women who became early feminists. Amir liked reminding her of his more liberal past—frequently.

"If the Ministry wants more women recruits," Fatma said, "then it should work on recruiting more women. The more the better. But that doesn't mean I want a partner."

Amir shrugged, settling back in his chair. "And I would give anything for a sweet right now. We don't get everything we want, do we?"

By the time Fatma returned to her office, Onsi was gone. Hadia remained standing, nervously fidgeting with a deep blue hijab, her brown eyes expectant. Fatma closed the door, hanging her bowler on a wall hook before falling into the chair behind her desk.

"You can sit down, Agent Hadia."

"It wasn't my idea to put a desk in here," she said, sitting.

"I know. I think Amir was trying to make a point."

"Some of the other agents said you might throw me out."

Throw her out? Gossipy men! They'd like nothing more than to see the bureau's two only woman agents in a tumult. Then again, she'd tried to get her reassigned. But that wasn't the same. Was it? She gave Hadia a hard look, remembering her own arrival in the office. How might she have felt, to be rebuffed by the only woman agent here? Her face flushed, and for the second time she heard her mother's chiding of the embarrassed girl whose face fell to the floor.

She cleared her throat. "Agent Hadia. I may have misspoken last night. I've never had a partner." The word still sounded strange. "So this is going to be new for both of us. But I think we can manage to figure it out."

Hadia gasped. "Thank you! I mean, that's wonderful! I mean, I'm overjoyed to—"

Fatma held up a hand. "It's going to take a while. So let's maybe go slow for now?"

Hadia cut off her exclamations, giving a solemn nod. "Slow. I can do slow."

Well, that was at least a start. Her eyes fell on Hadia's desk, to the typewriter amid a stack of folders. Following her gaze, the woman grabbed a paper and walked over.

"I started typing up the case report. I thought you'd want to get on it right away. Plus, I like doing paperwork. I hope I didn't overstep?"

Fatma took the sheet. She *liked* paperwork? Was that a joke? Everyone had their thing, she supposed. Maybe this partner business had its advantages. She thought of Aasim sending new recruits to fetch coffee. No, that would be too much. She read over the paper.

"Not overstepping at all. Where did you get all this?"

"The police. Had to ring three times to get the file sent by boilerplate courier."

Fatma smirked. Three times? Oh, Aasim was going to like her.

"I've been going through them," Hadia continued. "The police identified most of the victims from a list Lord Worthington kept of his guests. Last names anyway."

Fatma read them over . . . Dalton, Templeton, Portendorf, Burnley. All English.

"Two bodies were unaccounted for."

"The woman and one other man," Fatma guessed.

Hadia nodded. "From their dress, I'm betting they weren't English."

"Good bet. Pull up a chair, Agent Hadia. I'll fill you in on what kept me this morning."

For the next twenty minutes Fatma related what she'd found out: the identities of the unnamed man and woman; the Brotherhood of Al-Jahiz; and what the Jann revealed about the mysterious fire. When it was done Hadia gaped.

"An Ifrit," she breathed. "And God created Jinn from fire free of smoke."

Fatma was familiar with the ayah, one of many mentioning the djinn.

"You learned all this in one morning? From some informants among the idol—" Hadia halted, cheeks coloring. "I mean, adherents of the old religion?"

Fatma hadn't given names. Not Merira's. Certainly not Siti's. But she'd made her sources plain. "I've dealt with them before. A strange bunch, but trustworthy. They certainly don't go around burning people." Hadia flushed further.

"None of this solves our case, though," Fatma continued. "Why would this brotherhood bargain with an Ifrit? Fire didn't kill our friend with his head twisted around, so who, or what, did? And then there's this man in a gold mask."

Hadia scribbled in a notepad. "Feels like we have more questions."

"It'll feel that way until the end. At least now, we have clues." Her eyes went to the stack of folders. "Let's take a look at what else Aasim sent over." Hadia stood, turning to retrieve them. "And, agent," Fatma called, rolling up her sleeves. "Welcome to the Ministry."

The woman positively beamed.

CHAPTER
SEVEN

It was half past ten when Fatma arrived at Muhammad Ali Street. Snatches of music filled Cairo's liveliest hub, as patrons dipped into establishments with glaring signage. The Electric Oud blinked in green alchemical bulbs, while a red silhouette of a cabaret dancer flashed above another. A welcome reprieve, after today.

They'd spent hours searching through files on Lord Worthington: his business, personnel, financial transactions. The Worthington Company had built itself through trade and construction contracts—because even in a world of magic and djinn, you needed mundane things like investors and capital. And when rich people were killed, it almost invariably led back to their wealth. But they'd come up empty. By evening, she called it a day and sent Hadia home. Not much to do but wait and see what Aasim's people turned up Monday. The whole thing left her frustrated, and even more eager for tonight.

She turned off the main boulevard, onto one of the area's backstreets. Not as numerous as the Khan but easy enough to get lost in. At a barely lit square, she walked beneath an archway and down some steps to an almost hidden door. Using her cane, she rapped a pattern: three quick, two slow, three quick. Up top a slot opened, showing two eyes with shifting purple irises.

"You lost?"

"Looking for some jasmine tea," she answered.

"How much sugar?"

"Just a touch."

The slot slammed shut, and the door was opened by a heavily muscled djinn wearing a black tailcoat. He flourished an arm, those purple irises glinting. "Welcome to the Jasmine." Fatma walked inside, a cacophony of music and carousing washing over her like a small storm.

The Jasmine wasn't listed in the directory. Outside, no one ever said its name. They just called it the Spot.

Patrons sat at tables talking or laughing as boilerplate eunuchs in tuxedos and red tarbooshes swapped out empty glasses. At the Spot, the drinks flowed freely. Mostly beer, Egypt's favored intoxicant. But there was wine too and a trendy bubbly champagne with enchanted elixirs that, quite literally, left you light on your feet.

But no one came here just for the alcohol. You could get that readily enough anywhere in Cairo, even the foreign stuff. It was the clientele that placed the Jasmine off the beaten path. At one table, two women in Parisian dresses smoked from slender tortoiseshell cigarette holders—socialites come to do some slumming. They flanked a tall milk-white djinn with an unnaturally handsome face, as he pulled from a hookah and blew out spinning silver orbs. Beyond the tables, young men with the swagger of street toughs moved as gracefully as cabaret dancers—partnered with upperclass women who'd never be seen with them elsewhere, day or night. Some of those young men danced with each other. Everything hummed to the mesmeric music belted from a raised stage.

Navigating the crowd, Fatma sauntered over to the bar. A short djinn bartender with six arms doled out drinks. She caught hers as it slid past and lifted it to take a contented sip.

"You act like you drinking something," someone commented in English, "when all you got in there is sarsaparilla!" She turned to find an older man in a tanned suit some seats down.

"Sarsaparilla with mint leaves and tea," she corrected. "You should try some."

The man huffed. "I like my drinks as *drinks*!" His brown face broke into a grin. "How you doing, Fatma?"

She smiled back. "Alright, Benny. Been a while."

"Been a minute!" He moved beside her, setting down a silver cornet.

Benny was from America, like most musicians at the Jasmine—a place called New Orleans. Cairo brought in people from all over. Some looking for work or drawn by stories of mechanical wonders and djinn. Benny and the others had come fleeing a thing called Jim Crow. They brought with them their hopes, their dreams, and their fantastic music.

"You playing tonight?" Fatma asked.

"Every night."

Their attention was drawn to a blaring trumpet onstage. The man leaned back as he played, fingers moving in a blur that made his instrument squawk in a mix of ragged whines and shouts, like lovers in in the late of night or a quarrel in the morning. Behind him, a band joined his tirade with the multitudinous harmony of clarinets and trombones.

Benny didn't have a name for what they did. Said it was just the New Orleans sound. But he claimed it was going to be the biggest thing in the world one day. Fatma could believe that. She'd been riveted the first time she heard this hypnotic, beautiful music. The syncopated rhythm and melodies crept up your spine, willing you to move, live, and be free.

"That Bunky can blow!"

Fatma turned to find others arriving to sit around them. One with a jowly face in a blue suit was Alfred, nicknamed Frog—a trombone player. A small tight-lipped man wearing a red tarboosh and hugging a clarinet case was Bigs. The one who'd spoken, a skinny younger man in an all-gold suit and matching hat, was a piano player. She wasn't sure of his real name, because he only answered to Mansa Musa.

"Yeah, you right." Benny nodded. "Seen better, though."

Mansa Musa squawked. "Name someone better!"

"I can name you three. But only need to say one."

"Then say it."

"Buddy Bolden."

Mansa Musa groaned. "Why every time we talk music, you bring up Buddy Bolden?"

"If you'd ever seen him," Alfred croaked, "wouldn't need to ask."

Nods came all around.

"I remember this one time I saw Buddy play," Benny related. "Fatma, I'm telling you it was something. He played so loud, his horn blew back the whole row of people seated in the front. No, I'm telling you true! Them people pitched right over! This one woman, she went rolling right up on out the place. Kept rolling all Saturday night, and no one could find her until she rolled up into church Sunday morning!"

The group erupted with laughter as Mansa Musa threw up his hands. Fatma smiled.

"Well, Buddy's gone now," Alfred put in. "Left him, Jim Crow, and old New Orleans behind." He lifted a glass. "To King Bolden. They never gon' take away your magic."

The rest raised their glasses, chanting the same. When al-Jahiz sent magic back in the world, it hadn't just happened in Egypt. It had happened everywhere. The whole world over. In America, the return of magic had been met with persecution. Benny and the others still whispered wide-eyed about a sorcerer named Robert Charles who'd nearly brought New Orleans to its knees. They claimed this Buddy Bolden worked another kind of magic with his music, and had suffered dearly for his gift.

Alfred sighed. "I do miss home sometimes. No ways I miss Jim Crow, though."

"Amen!" Benny added. "Ain't no Jim Crow in Cai-ro!"

A chorus of "Yeah, you right!" came from all around.

"Don't know about all that," Mansa Musa cut in, swirling his drink. "I get treated fine enough, because I ain't from here. Other folk dark as us, though, not so lucky. Seen them get put out places plenty. Even spit on. Slapped in the streets. And who you find in the slums? Boo-coo faces look like ours. Same as back home."

Fatma couldn't deny those accounts. Egypt had its own problems. Al-Jahiz being Soudanese had made things somewhat better. There were even calls to ban discrimination by law. But ingrained beliefs were hard to break.

"Don't make sense," Benny grumbled. "Back home, Fatma here be riding the Jim Crow car. Half here couldn't pass a paper bag test."

"Lots can't even pass for octoroon," Alfred said. "Hell, not even quadroon."

Mansa Musa grunted. "They don't know that, though."

"Some octoroons and quadroons don't know neither," Benny quipped.

New laughter came as Fatma listened in fascination. She'd picked up a lot of her English from them. Even learned their cadence and inflections. But some of the vernacular still escaped her. What in the world was an octoroon?

"That's why I stay draped down wherever I go," Mansa Musa related. "People treat you right when you got this suit on. Where y'at, Fats? That's a nice one you got on tonight!"

Fatma gave her usual flick of the bowler. She'd gone for bright burgundy, with a brocaded waistcoat. Her dark olive tie was fastened with a silver ball tie pin, over a rose-blush pin-striped shirt and a club collar. He was right. People did treat you different in the suit.

"You all know I taught Fatma how to dress, right?" Mansa Musa asked.

Fatma gave him a flat look. "But all your suits are gold."

Benny barked a laugh while Alfred bellowed till his jowls shook, slapping the counter.

Mansa Musa huffed. "You all need to watch how you talk to the king!" He'd taken up the sobriquet after hearing about the medieval Mali emperor, who'd passed through Egypt on hajj, dispensing enough gold to ruin local markets—or so the stories claimed. He ended his sets with a shower of fake gold coins, which people snatched up like treasure.

"Uh-oh!" Benny exclaimed, looking past them. "Here comes trouble now!"

Fatma followed his gaze, to a tall figure standing near the entrance. Siti. And Benny was right. She looked absolutely like trouble—in a long red evening gown of lace and chiffon that fell draping to her feet. Under the sheer gossamer top a fitted bodice sewn with bead netting glistened in the dim light, while a matching sash cinched her waist.

Siti's eyes caught Fatma, and she set out in a slow sashay toward them, drawing more than a few eyes. A chorus of chatter met her arrival. Benny and the others treated Fatma like one of them, but Siti was another matter—a woman to shower compliments and who could poke jabs just as quick. After the hubbub died down, she slid in front of Fatma, reaching to tug her tie.

"Funny running into you here."

Fatma glanced to a golden diadem nestled into a short braided wig Siti now wore—the front engraved with a lioness. "You look . . ."

"Like the fiery wrath of the goddess made flesh on Earth?"

"I was going to say 'beautiful.'"

"I'll take that." She caught a drink from the bartender, downing it in one go. Her eyes went to Fatma's glass. "Sarsaparilla? With mint leaves?"

"And some tea."

Siti tsked. "We're in here to be bad. Break the rules."

"This *is* me breaking the rules."

"Don't take this wrong, but those bright brown eyes of yours look tired. Long day at Spooky Boys Central?"

Spooky Boys? "You know how tedious it is reviewing financial reports of a transnational business with dozens of subsidiaries?"

"No. And I don't want to know. Ever."

"Even with Hadia there, took hours."

"Hadia?"

"My new . . . partner." The word didn't sound any less strange.

Siti's eyes lit up. "Partner? Another lady Spooky Boy? Pretty like you? With a thing for suits and infidels? Should bring her by."

Fatma tried to imagine Hadia at the Spot, and failed. "I think she breaks fewer rules than me. All bright and eager. Had to chase her out of the office. Likes typing up reports, though."

"Agent Fatma and an eager lady partner. Can't wait to meet her."

Fatma stopped mid-sip. Meet? Siti laughed, covering her mouth.

"Relax. But you're going to have to figure out how to explain why she keeps running into you in my company. I'm pretty memorable."

"That mean you plan on staying around awhile?"

Siti answered by downing another drink, which wasn't an answer at all.

The sudden roll of a snare sizzled the air, joined by the faster pace of palms hitting darbukas. It hadn't taken long for that New Orleans music to blend with local styles—as if the two were reunited kin. It created a vibrant mash-up that beat with the soul of modern Cairo, drifting from these underground lairs and onto the streets. The sounds stirred anticipation through the crowd who rushed the dance floor.

Mansa Musa slid over, offering a hand to Siti. "Let the king escort you out in style."

She answered by wrapping an arm into Fatma's. "Afraid this dance is taken. Yalla!"

Fatma rose, sparing a shrug and bowler flick for Mansa Musa. He laughed it off, flicking his gold hat in return. They reached the dance floor just as the blare of a horn started. Siti spun as Fatma stepped forward, catching her waist and drawing her close, finding each other's rhythm. The two shared knowing smiles, letting their movements do the talking. As far as Fatma was concerned, if this wasn't magic, nothing was.

◆ ◆ ◆

Hours later, they walked the backstreets near Muhammad Ali Street. Fatma kept pace with her cane, Siti on her arm, dancing lightly, as if trumpets and drums lingered in her head. That, or the drinks.

"Where to now?" she slurred.

Fatma looked her over. "I'm thinking you might be a bit much for your family."

"I sleep in Auntie Aziza's room. She doesn't notice much."

"Not so sure of that. Just come back to my place."

Siti winked. "As if that's not where I was going all along."

"You'll have to settle for the front door. I don't do windows."

"Going to explain me to that nosy bewab? He's *always* there."

The man *was* always there. "He can think whatever he wants. I'm the one paying rent."

Siti snickered. "We don't have to go yet. I still have my dress on under this." She gestured beneath her dark kaftan.

Fatma looked dubious. She'd barely survived all-nighters with Siti before. "How about we go home, I make tea, and we catch up. It's Friday. We can even sleep in."

Siti nuzzled her ear. "Such a romantic. Going to start wooing me with poetry next?"

Fatma raised an eyebrow. "You like poetry?"

"Only the old stuff. I can recite the poetry of Majnun by heart."

"Impressive. You have a thing for Persian romances?"

"Nothing quite like tragic and unrequited love. Know some Antar too."

"That explains your aunt. She thought I should recite you poetry."

"Auntie Aziza told you that?"

"Aywa. Said it might win over your heart."

"Crafty old woman," Siti muttered.

"She said you had too much of your father in you. And that's why you like to wander." The ensuing silence made Fatma want to take the words back immediately.

"Well." Siti said after a while, her arm loosening. "Auntie does like to talk."

"Sorry," Fatma said, cursing her runaway mouth. "I shouldn't have—"

Siti gestured as if to dismiss the comment—or maybe her absent father. "I think some tea and talk sounds fine." She tapped beneath one eye. "But is he coming with us?"

"What?" Fatma turned to look, but Siti clicked her tongue. "Not right at him!"

She settled for glancing out of the corner of her eye, catching a dark shape. They were being followed.

"How long has he been there?" she hissed.

"Not sure. Probably followed us from the Spot."

Fatma gazed about. Lots of shadows for skulking in these backstreets.

"Isn't this how we met?" Siti asked.

"You pocket-picked me to get my attention. Because you're strange. He's likely a thief."

"Or a homicidal maniac! Who preys on young women out about town!"

"Too bad for him."

Siti's rejoinder was almost a growl. "Too bad."

The two turned a corner, passing under a pointed archway and down stairs leading to shadows. There they parted, taking positions at opposite ends. Fatma gripped her cane's pommel, easing the sword out a few inches. People always wanted to learn the hard way the thing wasn't just for show. Siti was on the balls of her feet, teeth bared and eager.

Their pursuer's approach sounded in the quiet. He hesitated before descending the stairs and entering the shadows. A figure in a dark cloak and hood, walking right between them.

Amateur, Fatma thought. She waited until he passed before drawing her sword, letting the sound of sliding steel reverberate. He spun just in time to catch the flat of the blade on both knees. A howl of pain came as his legs folded. It was cut off as Siti pounced, bearing him down with a hard *smack*! She pinned his chest with a knee as he fought to catch his breath.

"Picked the wrong women to go hunting! Are you a maniac or what? Talk!"

The man struggled, flailing in his robes and gurgling.

"I don't think he can talk with you on him like that," Fatma noted.

"His problem. Not mine." She pressed her knee harder, and the man yelped.

Fatma bent down, pulling back his hood. "Listen, friend, you'd better—" She stopped at seeing his face. Bald, with skin a pale shade of gray. And no eyebrows.

"Ahmad?" Siti asked, lifting her knee.

He gasped before rumbling weakly. "You may call me Lord Sobek. The Rager. Def—"

"Ahmad!"

He winced, running a pink tongue over sharp teeth. "Yes?"

Siti jumped up, giving Fatma a confused gesture. "What are you doing here, Ahmad?"

The strange man climbed to his feet. His dark green eyes flickered to Fatma. "I came looking for you. Saw you enter that place. Then Siti. Figured you'd leave sometime."

Fatma frowned. "You followed me? How long?"

"Since your apartment." He backed off as she stepped forward. "I had good reason!"

"For stalking me?"

"I wanted to see how you were handling the case!" Fatma paused, and he took the moment to speak. "I expected the Ministry to be working day and night to catch Ester's murderer. Instead, I find you cavorting as if nothing matters!"

Fatma was taken aback. "I don't need you to tell me how to do my job. I get to have a life."

"Have a life?" Skin rose where eyebrows should have. "I went to the police today, to identify Ester. So that her family could know." His face twisted. "The body was so burned I couldn't make out her face. I couldn't . . ."

Fatma's anger eased. He didn't have the right to follow her. But she understood grief.

"Ahmad," Siti spoke gently. "I'm sorry for what you must be going through. But prowling in the dark after us isn't helping. Why didn't you just come up and talk?"

He shrugged. "I was waiting for a good time. Didn't want to seem . . . creepy."

Siti blew out a breath. "That ship's sailed, Ahmad."

"The Ministry's doing the best we can," Fatma told him. "We're hunting every lead."

Ahmad's dark eyes glittered. "I think I've found one of those. A lead." He met their puzzled looks. "I'll take you there. It's something you have to see for yourselves."

◆   ◆   ◆

Fatma snuck glances at Ahmad opposite her in the automated carriage. The man had pulled out his silver scarab beetle lighter to start a third Nefertari, blowing cigarette smoke out the window. There was a more crocodilian look to him: as if his face had elongated.

"Didn't he have more of a nose this morning?" she whispered.

Beside her, Siti spared a look. Her voice had lost its slur, and she seemed sober and alert. "He's been like this for a while. Whatever's happening seems to have sped up."

"What kind of magic is that?" Fatma asked.

"No idea. Not my temple."

"Looks like some kind of transmogrification. You're not into anything like that, are you?"

"Don't worry. Hathor isn't turning me into a golden cow, if that's what you mean."

"And Sekhmet?"

Siti flashed a lioness's grin. "Can't tell you all my secrets. But the Lady is always near."

Fatma tried to imagine the fierce goddess inside the woman, peering out from behind her eyes. On second thought, she decided that wasn't an image she wanted to conjure up. She returned instead to trying to judge their location. Somewhere outside the city proper. They'd been riding for almost a half hour, and their guide was tight-lipped on where they were going.

"You really think this is a good idea?"

"Figure we can at least see what this is," Siti answered.

"What if he's what you first said? A homicidal maniac? He thinks he's a crocodile god."

Siti mocked seriousness. "You think he's taking us to be eaten by his crocodile minions?"

"I hope you can still tell jokes when we're being fed alive."

"Sobek holds no taste for mortal flesh," Ahmad broke in. "But has excellent hearing."

Siti laughed while Fatma, a bit abashed, returned to the window. The carriage turned off a main road into one of the old factory districts, where dilapidated buildings rose up about them.

"We get out here," Ahmad said, flicking away a cigarette butt.

Fatma winced as they stepped onto the dirt roadway, dust settling on her cognac brogues. This had been an early factory district in Cairo after the coming of the djinn. People streamed in from villages, eager for better pay in the bustling city. The factories eventually closed up—moving out to new manufacturing hubs like Helwan and Heliopolis. But many people remained: packed into slums arrayed around the decaying remains of industry.

"This way." Ahmad walked out ahead. They followed, picking across uneven ground. What passed for houses here were barely shacks: hovels of brick, mortar, even mud. In some, small fires burned, and at times the occasional lamp of luminous alchemical gas.

"Easy to forget places like this exist," Siti murmured, eyeing old women bearing buckets.

"Modernity has its drawbacks," Fatma added as several young men ran by excitedly.

"What are all these people doing out so late?"

Fatma was wondering the same. Places like this always had

activity, even their own after-hours entertainment. But these people milled about like it was midday. She looked harder. Not milling. Most were headed in the same direction as they were, to a towering old factory building near the slums' center.

She caught up with Ahmad. "Where are you taking us?"

In answer, he stopped someone: a boy of no more than twelve in an ill-fitting gallabiyah. He scrunched up his snub nose and opened his mouth to protest but froze at Ahmad's face.

"A bit of your time," the man hissed. "And something for your trouble."

The boy's eyes grew, and his fingers quickly snatched up the coin in Ahmad's hand.

"God reward you, basha. I mean, djinn."

Fatma smirked. Honest mistake.

"Tell the lady where you're going," Ahmad said.

"To see the man in black!" the boy blurted excitedly. "The man with the gold mask!"

Fatma stared at Ahmad, then back to the boy. "What man in a gold mask?"

The boy recoiled. "They say it's ill luck to speak his name! But he performs wonders! Wallahi, I have seen them with my own eyes!"

Fatma wanted to press further, but Ahmad released the boy, who promptly ran off. "What's going on?" she demanded.

He walked faster. "When you told me of a mysterious man at the Worthington estate, I recalled rumors I've heard. Whispers, of a man in black, visiting places like this."

"And you didn't think to tell me?"

"I wanted to be certain. Until today, I'd thought it a street tale."

"I haven't heard about any of this," Siti said, looking dubious.

"You've been away. And while the Temple of Hathor cultivates more upscale worshippers, the acolytes of Sobek walk among the less fortunate."

"We don't have an upscale—" Siti began defensively, but Fatma cut her off. This wasn't the time. Besides, they'd reached the old factory. It turned out not to be much of a building at all but the crumbling frame of one: missing a roof and two sides. In the space, a crowd had gathered in the dozens. She followed their rapt gazes to the top of a wall, where a figure stood speaking.

Fatma gaped.

He was exactly as Abigail Worthington had described—tall and draped in black robes. He wasn't alone. To his right stood a figure in black shirt and breeches. He remained still, as the tall man's words echoed in the night.

". . . I have come to find my people lost," he rumbled. "Cairo has become a place of decadence, where wealth is hoarded, while many are left in destitution. Where is the rich man who gives alms? Where is the physician to heal? Where is the promise modernity offered?"

Cries of approval came from the crowd, amid calls to continue. Fatma pushed past Ahmad, striving to get a better look.

"When I first came, I walked among those like you," the man continued. "Those society had discarded. I have returned now, not among the mighty but the low. To fill ears that will listen! To teach who would learn! To set right what was turned wrong!"

More cries now of consent. Fatma reached the front of the crowd, craning her neck to see. She leaned in close to an old man beside her.

"Uncle, who is this?"

"It is him!" he answered, never lowering his gaze. "The one who has returned!"

"Who?" she demanded. "Who has returned?"

He looked at her this time, his white bearded face incredulous. "They say we should not speak his name, but it is the Great Teacher, the Inventor, the Master of Djinn." He whispered in wonder. "Al-Jahiz!"

Fatma stared back, stunned. She looked to Siti, who seemed equally dazed.

Ahmad gave a solemn nod. "On the streets of Cairo, in the places we have forgotten, people say al-Jahiz has returned. A mysterious man wearing a gold mask. Just as the one fleeing the murder of a brotherhood dedicated to al-Jahiz. What do you suppose are the chances of that?"

Not answering, Fatma instead peered back to the man on the wall. He stood, arms behind his back, drinking in the crowd's praise. He surveyed them and then looked directly to where she stood. For a moment their gazes locked, and she shuddered. His face was concealed behind a gold mask. Yet even from this distance she could see his eyes—the intensity of them. For a moment the two only stared at each other. Then he held up a hand and pointed down. The silent figure beside him jerked his head as if coming alive—before hurtling from the wall toward the ground below.

She gasped. He should have died from that height—at least four stories. Or broken half the bones in his body. But they landed in a crouch, boots sending up billowing dust.

Fatma blinked. Wait, *they*? One man jumped from that wall. She was certain. But now there were two! Identical! Wearing the same masks: black and carved in the faces of men. They glanced at one another before stalking forward, lanky bodies moving like jackals.

"Fatma!"

Siti's warning came just as one of the figures rushed them. Fatma barely had time to bring up her cane, blocking a fist and dancing back as he came at her again. There was a growl, and Siti surged past, aiming for the man. But his companion joined the fray, legs darting kicks she was forced to slap away.

Fatma stumbled as the crowd pulled back from the combatants. The man was fast—unnaturally so. There was no hope in getting her sword out; he never gave her a chance. She was forced to use her cane to block as he pressed the attack. She needed to do something soon or—

In a blur he was in her guard, and a fist connected with her side. There was a flaring lance of pain that would have doubled her over. But she didn't even have time before he slapped her chest with a flat palm. It felt like being hit by stone. Her feet lifted off the ground, and she landed hard on her back. God! That hurt! Everywhere! Stunned, she looked up to see him slinking forward like a cat after prey. Fumbling for her sword, she got it free just as he descended on her, a fist drawn.

"Keep back! Or—"

Before she could finish, he threw himself on the blade. It slipped through shirt and flesh, burying into his chest. He stopped, inspecting the weapon that had probably punctured a lung. He'd be spitting up blood in that mask soon. Damn! She hadn't wanted that! He lifted his head up to stare at her with unblinking eyes—black on black with not a hint of white. Then he pushed forward, driving the sword through him. Fatma glared in disbelief. No blood appeared on the silver blade. Instead she thought she saw a fine mist of black, like particles of sand. He pushed closer, until their faces almost touched—staring, with those inhuman eyes.

There was a sharp call, and the man pulled back, black mist forming where a wound should have been. Fatma watched as he moved to his twin, whom Siti had been fighting. The two touched—and in a blink were one. With a terrific leap he flew into the air, landing back atop the wall beside the man in the gold mask. Fatma scrambled to her feet, ignoring her stinging chest to clutch her side and stare up at them. What in all the worlds was going on?

Siti, however, was having none of it.

With a lioness's roar, she snatched off her wig and flung it up at them. Then she hurled herself at the wall—hanging on by something sharp and metallic. Fatma recognized the gloves with silver claws. Did she take those things everywhere? Growling, she began to climb, still wearing her gown but barefoot now.

Ahmad wasn't the only one gifted with odd magic. Siti carried her own peculiar sorcery: magic that made her faster, stronger. She scaled a third of the bricks in moments, carried up by anger and sheer bullheadedness. Watching her ascent, Fatma wondered if a goddess didn't reside within the woman. Then the wall erupted into flames.

Fatma reared back as the fire's glare lit the night, red as blood, its heat on her skin. Siti let go. She should have landed in a broken heap, but managed to drop on all fours—as graceful as a cat. Before either could say a word, the flames vanished. Atop the wall, both figures had vanished as well.

"Cowards!" Siti shouted. "I almost had him!"

"You okay?" Fatma staggered toward her.

Siti flexed a set of smoking claws. "Didn't even touch me." Her angry eyes rounded in alarm. "You're hurt!"

Fatma grunted in pain as the taller woman reached over to support her. "Took a hit to the side. Think he might have—" She let out a breath. It hurt to talk. "Cracked a rib."

Siti wrapped an arm about her, taking her weight. "They were stronger than they looked."

Fatma nodded. She recalled the corpse with its head turned around. *Inhumanly* strong.

"I don't think they meant to injure you," Ahmad said. He'd backed off with the crowd during the fight and now returned. He looked over Fatma, reassessing. "Not gravely at least."

Siti rounded on him. "A lot of good you were! Some help would have been nice!"

The man gave a crocodilian wince. "I thought you were handling things. Besides, I think their intent was to send you a message, nothing more."

"What message was that?" Siti asked testily.

Ahmad gestured to the wall. The brick was scorched, but in some places the stone remained untouched, leaving script written from top to bottom.

"Okay," Siti admitted. "That's a message."

As Fatma read the words, she felt her teeth clench along with her stomach:

BEHOLD, I AM AL-JAHIZ.
AND I HAVE RETURNED.

CHAPTER
EIGHT

nlike most government offices, the Ministry didn't close on Fridays. It was manned by a skeleton crew, and a custodial staff of boilerplate eunuchs maintained by the sentient building. As Fatma walked with Hadia, she barely paid attention to the emptiness or the odd quiet. Her mind was still on last night.

"I usually spend Friday with my cousins," Hadia was saying. "But I'm glad you rang."

Fatma realized she hadn't asked Hadia to come in—just sort of demanded it. That was rude. But it spoke to how rattled she was. She'd made up her mind to come in this morning. She'd even opted for a sensible suit—blue with a maroon tie and sturdy brown shoes. Playing the dandy would have to wait. Well, except for the gold tie pin and matching cuff links. Not to mention the bowler and cane. Did the violet pin-striped shirt count as dandy?

Anyway, she was going to be serious. It was hard to admit, but Ahmad was right. She should have followed up on this masked man. Instead, she'd pushed the case into the background, waiting on Aasim. Part of that was Siti—whose return affected her in more ways than she cared to admit. But just because she took time off, didn't mean this city did.

"Stay prepared," she said as they reached the elevator. "Best advice I can give you as an agent." Hadia wore her Ministry coat, with the long dark skirts, a bag slung over a shoulder. Her hijab however was a dark forest green. Was she trying to match Fatma's past suit? "But thanks for coming in. There's been a development in our case."

"Of course. Although I'm curious to know what kind of development happened between last night and this morning?" The doors to the elevator parted, and they stepped inside.

"More than you'd guess," Fatma answered. "Basement."

The elevator began to descend, and she turned to find Hadia waiting expectantly. Choosing her words, she recounted the previous night—leaving out Siti, of course, and referring to Ahmad as an "informant." As she spoke she let a hand fall at her side. Siti had carried her home, bandaged the wound, then curled around her in bed, humming a song that brought on a deep sleep. When she awoke, the woman was gone, of course. So was the pain. Nothing now but a dull sting. Odd. Maybe she hadn't cracked a rib as feared—just taken a glancing blow. When she finally finished, Hadia breathed out, as if she'd been the one talking.

"Your night was definitely more exciting than mine. Al-Jahiz! Returned!"

"Stop elevator," Fatma commanded, and they halted with a lurch. She fixed her eyes on Hadia, voice stern. "This figure in black. Whoever he is, he may be involved in a mass murder. He may be a criminal. But he's *not* al-Jahiz. A lot of our work deals with peeling back illusion. Don't get caught up in it."

Hadia accomplished a wincing nod. "You're right. Of course."

Fatma ordered the elevator to resume.

"But you're thinking there's a connection," Hadia reasoned. "A man about the city claiming to be al-Jahiz leaving fiery calling cards. Members of a brotherhood dedicated to him found burned alive."

"And someone fitting his description identified at the scene of the crime," Fatma added.

"But why did this . . . imposter . . . attack you?"

Fatma had pondered that, and still didn't have a good answer. "Maybe I stood out."

"What about the Ifrit? Did you see one?"

"Not exactly. Saw fire that moved oddly, but that's all."

Hadia looked confused. "Then why are we going to the basement?"

"Because that's where the library is located."

"Right. And we're going to the library because . . . ?"

Fatma fixed her best blank look. "Because it has all the books." The elevator doors parted, and she stepped out, leaving Hadia with a baffled expression that soon turned to awe.

The Ministry housed one of the largest libraries in the city. It took up much of the lower parts of the building—two whole floors of books and manuscripts that spanned centuries, from all over the world. As she understood, a few weren't from this world at all. They sat in wall shelves, extending almost to the high ceiling—reached by ladders that slid along railings. Other shelves were stacked neatly on either end. A second level in the center held rarer works. At the back of the room, an enormous pendulum swung back and forth, made up of an iron cable ending in a giant gold sun disc inscribed with geometric patterns. At the top of the antique clock was a half-moon dial that gave time with signs of the zodiac.

"Ayou!" Hadia gawped.

"You haven't even seen the vault." Fatma smirked, walking off.

Hadia hurried to follow. "Wait? There's a vault? What's in the vault?"

Fatma didn't answer. Some things a new recruit just had to learn for themselves. She took them to a space in the center of the floor, where long tables with runners were arranged for reading. Standing before one was the library's only occupant.

Zagros was the Ministry's librarian: a Marid the size of a rhinoceros, if it stood up on two legs. And you dressed it in longsleeved indigo blue robes embroidered with lilacs: what she thought was a khalat. Unlike a rhinoceros, the djinn had skin of pale lavender, and four golden twisting ram horns striped in amethyst. But his disposition was similar to a rhinoceros. He guarded the library zealously and was infamous for banishing agents for the slightest infraction. Most complained he was fussy, unlikable, and easily irritated. Fatma knew better. The truth was, the djinn was just an incredible snob.

Affirming her assessment, it took three calls of his name before he deigned to look down at them. His half-lidded gaze behind a pair of silver spectacles held a mix of boredom and annoyance. "Library's closed," he bellowed lazily. "Come back during regular hours." He lifted a manicured clawed hand adorned in rings, waving them away like children.

"The library isn't closed on Fridays," Fatma replied.

The djinn's pointed ears twitched as he muttered in Farsi before returning to Arabic. "Well, look at you knowing things. Good for you! I'm busy, however, so all the same." He gestured to the table, where fragments of yellowed papyri lay pressed between sheets of spectral glass. There were gaps in the parchment, and bits more sat in a small nearby box.

"Is that Meroitic?" she asked, eyeing the script. "Second-century?"

Zagros turned, pursing a set of violet lips before drawling: "Third. But Meroitic, yes."

Fatma leaned in, appearing to take an interest. When he was in a mood, it helped to impress his innate bibliophilia. Getting the century wrong was a special touch. Because his type lived to correct people. "I thought Meroitic was indecipherable. The lost Nubian language."

"It has remained stubbornly unknowable," Zagros admitted. He pointed to the bits of parchment between the infused glass, which glowed a slight jade. Where his claws touched, the script shifted and reformed into Arabic. "This we know means 'door.' This one 'bird.' But what does that mean when put together?"

Fatma almost suggested "door-bird," but the librarian wasn't known for his sense of humor.

"Deciphering words hasn't helped us understand the *language*," he bemoaned. "Two different matters, you see. I'm working on a theory that the syntax may be magically locked, purposefully obscuring itself. Quite crafty."

Fatma glanced to Hadia, nudging in the djinn's direction. She caught on quick. "Where is this book . . . from?" she asked.

"The mortuary tomb of Amanishakheto!" Zagros answered, his golden eyes excited. "One of the famed Kandake! This could be a funeral dirge: a lament to their gods or philosophy on the afterlife. We have it on loan from Soudan. It's been sitting in their collections, while those Sufis spend all their time searching for radical numerology in sacred geometry. You let some people read Marx . . ." Catching himself, he looked to them as if seeing wholly new people. "It is refreshing to hear an appreciation of alphasyllabic script. How may I help you today, agents?"

"We're looking for works on al-Jahiz," Fatma said.

The djinn arched an eyebrow. "More than a few of those."

"The better biographies and contemporary accounts."

Zagros tapped contemplatively on a pair of ivory tusks that curved up from his mouth. The tips were capped in silver and stringed with tiny bells that tinkled at his touch. "The more popular historical biographies are by Ghitani. Then there are the literary accounts by Mahfouz and Hussein. Religious interpretations by Soudanese fakirs . . ." He turned, muttering and walking out into the library.

Fatma and Hadia followed close. The djinn was faster than his size suggested, and they kept up by catching glimpses of his fluttering robes around corners—and the chiming of tiny bells.

"That was a quick turnaround," Hadia whispered. She yelped, just managing to catch a thick tome tossed by Zagros.

"Djinn are a lot like the rest of us," Fatma said. She plucked a book out of the air that came flying, without stopping her stride. "They just want to know the odd things they're interested in are appreciated."

"Like my cousin who collects automata birds," Hadia noted. "But why are we doing this again?" She caught a second book atop the first and smiled in satisfaction.

"You said it earlier," Fatma answered, casually catching two more. "Someone is running around the city claiming to be al-Jahiz. Someone who was at the scene of a murder of a brother-hood dedicated to his memory. Al-Jahiz is the one thread that ties the two."

"You're thinking whoever is masquerading as al-Jahiz proba-bly created his persona based from books like these. And Lord Worthington's brotherhood did the same. We're not building a profile of al-Jahiz; we're building one on how people remember him."

The woman was good, Fatma had to admit. There was a yelp as another large tome soared at them, causing Hadia to drop her stack. But she was going to have to get better at catching books.

Some hours later they sat amid stacks arranged along the length of a table—the only sound the constant whoosh of the swinging pendulum. The librarian had provided them with more material than they could get through. They'd tackled the popular ones first before moving to the obscure titles. Hadia took notes with pen and paper as they went, unable to convince Zagros to let her bring down a typewriter—what he called a vexatious and cacoph-onous machine. Still, she'd written up several pages. Reaching the end of a sheet, she stopped to flex her hand.

"I think it's cramped." She winced.

Fatma rested her own book, and her exhausted eyes. "Read back what we have."

Hadia rummaged through her sheets, before lifting one out.

"Al-Jahiz. Well, the first thing is, no one really knows his name."

That was something all the books and accounts agreed upon. Al-Jahiz wasn't actually a name, more like a sobriquet. The most famous man in modern memory couldn't even be assigned something as simple as a name.

"It's uncertain whether he adopted the title or if it was given," Hadia continued. "Either way, most writers agree it's the source of the arguments over his origin and the schools of thought that have popped up. The Temporalist school claims he's a time traveler, and one and the same with the ninth-century al-Jahiz of Basra."

"Abū 'Uthman 'Amr Baḥr al-Kinānī al-Baṣrī," Fatma recited.

"Nicknamed al-Jahiz." Hadia nodded. "The boggle-eyed. Not very flattering. Most today think he suffered from a malformation of the cornea. Not much is known of his early life, but he's credited with writing over two hundred books—if the stories are to be believed—on everything from zoology to philosophy. The Temporalists claim the two al-Jahizes are one. However, there's nothing about the medieval al-Jahiz that says he was an inventor. They've probably mixed him up with the thirteenth-century al-Jazari. The mistake's been pointed out, but they're pretty insistent, some even claiming al-Jahiz came back first as al-Jazari. They don't even have his background right! The first al-Jahiz was likely Abyssinian. Everyone agrees the modern al-Jahiz is from Soudan. And no one mentions him being boggle-eyed. So the reason for the title remains a mystery."

"People find all sorts of ways to make their logic work," Fatma replied. Temporalism had become popular among mechanics and the more science-minded. Every few months, the Ministry got a case of one of them attempting to build a time machine using unlicensed magic and unstable alchemy. The last one tried inside his apartment building. Didn't time travel, but managed to transport half his floor ten blocks away—into afternoon traffic.

"Then there are the Transmigrationists," Hadia read. "The school arose among some Sufis, who use the concept of tanasukh to argue for metempsychosis. They claim the modern al-Jahiz is a reincarnation of the first. But it's considered heretical, denounced by the ulama and even the majority of Sufis. Most of its followers today are Buddhist or Hindu. There's a festival for it in Bengal."

Heretical or not, ideas of al-Jahiz reborn were widespread, and not just among unorthodox Sufis. Despite it being dismissed as some rural custom, you could easily find Cairenes who said the same.

"There are about a dozen more schools about his origins." Hadia lifted up several sheets. "The Sufis in Soudan think he's a herald of the Mahdi. Some Copts see him as a harbinger of Armageddon. None make any more sense than the other."

"They don't have to. Al-Jahiz's ambiguity lends itself to interpretation."

"People define him how they want." Hadia caught on. "So, an imposter . . ."

". . . never has to get specific," Fatma finished. "That crowd last night. They saw al-Jahiz in that man in the gold mask. Never mind if they all had different ideas of who he was. Al-Jahiz is so wrapped up in myth and rumor, he can be whoever they want him to be."

"That's dangerous."

"Why the Ministry takes men claiming to be al-Jahiz seriously. He's not the first. But they're always trouble, because of what they stir up in people. People willing and wanting to believe. Even when they're half-mad."

"Did this one look that way? Half-mad, I mean?"

Fatma shook her head, remembering those eyes. Intense, yes. But nothing about them looked mad. "So we know what we don't know about al-Jahiz. How about what we do know?"

Hadia shuffled her notes again, lifting out another page. "The first mention of al-Jahiz is usually given to al-Hajj Umar Tal, the later conqueror and founder of the Tukulor Empire. In 1832 he was a wandering mystic. On his way back from hajj, he meets Ibrahim Basha, then a military commander on campaign in Syria. Umar Tal healed the future basha's son of an affliction before famously prophesying the coming of a man he claimed would shake up the world. He called him by the title 'the Master of Djinn.'"

Fatma recalled what the old man in the crowd had said. The Master of Djinn—one of al-Jahiz's famous honorifics.

"It's thought that around this time the man who would become al-Jahiz was part of the basha's Soudanese regiment, made up of slave soldiers. Some even claim he was sent with a battalion to Mexico to put down a rebellion against Napoleon III in the 1860s. But that sounds like another rumor. Because by then he's no longer in the Egyptian army. He appears for the first time with the title 'al-Jahiz' in 1837 in Soudan, preaching against slavery in the company of a tall mysterious figure—that most people now think was a djinn."

"Eighteen thirty-seven," Fatma echoed. She picked up a book, flipping to what she wanted. "The same year of the Egyptian-Abyssinian border skirmish, after tax collectors kidnapped an Ethiopian Coptic priest in Soudan. The Abyssinians handily defeated the local Egyptian garrison, freeing the priest. The survivors claimed the Abyssinians used 'sorcerous weaponry.'"

"Al-Jahiz vanishes from all accounts for thirty-two years," Hadia picked up. "Then, in 1869, inexplicably arrives in Cairo. Starts teaching alchemy and what he calls the 'lost arts,' performing some of the first 'great wonders.' His secret street schools start gaining followers."

"Then in 1872, Isma'il Basha annexes Abyssinian territory, starting a war," Fatma read.

"Which we lose, again," Hadia added. "In just two days! This time people pay attention to soldiers talking about magic. Those years al-Jahiz was missing, it's now thought he was in Abyssinia, following in the steps of the Prophet—peace be upon him. Likely the source of their weaponry."

"Which the Abyssinians won't confirm one way or the other," Fatma groused. It was confounding why the monarchy was so secretive. There was a treaty between them now, and no hostilities in decades. Then again, Abyssinian rulers also kept live lions wandering about their palaces—which reportedly had the ability to speak. So maybe that wasn't the oddest thing.

Hadia flipped through her notes before tapping an area with a pen. "After the 1872 war, Isma'il Basha learns about al-Jahiz and has him arrested as a traitor. But al-Jahiz wins him over with his teachings. The Khedive sets him up in Abdeen Palace to work his experiments. That's where he makes most of his machines and transcribes his many books. It's also where 'it' happens."

Fatma didn't need a primer. Every first year in the Ministry knew the story. Of how al-Jahiz built some grand machine of alchemy and magic. Of the day the entire palace was engulfed in light, that made the stone seem to warp and shimmer. Back then people had called it the work of the Khedive's Soudanese sorcerer. Today, it was remembered as the boring into the Kaf, the weakening of the barriers between the many realms that forever changed the world.

"No one knows why he did it," Hadia read. "Curiosity, mischief, malice. But the science has never been replicated."

Fatma held her tongue, eyes wandering to the vault behind the swinging pendulum. That wasn't precisely true. Al-Jahiz's grand formula—the Theory of Overlapping Spheres—had been replicated exactly once, through a machine built by the angel Maker. He called it the Clock of Worlds. Maker had sought to use his invention to bring about the end of their world, until she and Siti destroyed it. The files on that case remained sealed to most. And what remained of the clock now sat only feet away in the vault, where the Ministry housed its most precious secrets.

"Over the next few months," Hadia continued, "djinn begin appearing in small numbers throughout Cairo. Other places too. They keep mostly hidden, but the Khedive senses something grand is happening and makes a move for greater independence with the Ottoman Porte. Asks al-Jahiz to construct him weapons of magic. But he refuses. Angered over this, Isma'il Basha sends soldiers to confiscate his inventions. By the time they arrive, al-Jahiz is gone." She looked up wryly. "Only about a dozen different versions of how *that* happened."

That was understating things. Al-Jahiz had made the Khedive's soldiers blind, before walking through their midst while they groped about. He had turned them into wisps of smoke. No, he'd turned them into winged rams that bore him away. Or had he flown off on the back of a djinn? No, it was a mechanical djinn. A chariot pulled by djinn. Or golden-winged rukhs.

And so it went.

The only thing anyone knew for sure was that in 1873, al-Jahiz disappeared, taking most of his machines and writings with him.

"I have a cousin who fancies himself an augur," Hadia related. "He swears al-Jahiz left piloting a great contraption that spun with endless wheels. And that even now he travels between the many worlds, bringing magic with him. But I guess none of that really matters. Because what impacts us today mostly happened after he was gone."

"Aywa," Fatma agreed. The ten years after al-Jahiz's disappearance saw the rise of a nationalist movement as Isma'il Basha fell into debt and ceded greater control to European powers. The djinn mostly hid behind the scenes, but they were there too. It wasn't until Tell El Kebir in '82 that they made themselves fully known—where djinn magic joined nationalist fervor to drive the British from Egypt and into the sea. That event was now commemorated as the Emerging. Whatever became of al-Jahiz, it was them who created this new world.

"I just did the math," Hadia said, scrunching up her face. "Al-Jahiz was maybe in his twenties in the 1830s. So by the time he disappeared he was in his sixties. Anyone claiming to be him today would have to be what—a hundred years old?"

"The man I saw last night definitely didn't look a hundred," Fatma confirmed.

"You'd think people would take that into consideration. Wish we had some of his earliest followers around to speak against this imposter."

"No chance of that," Fatma said. Al-Jahiz's core followers had disappeared shortly after he did, supposedly to take his most secret writings into hiding. The youngest of them would likely be in their seventies now, if still alive. The Ministry had been searching for them for decades, but had come up with nothing.

"What about these others last night?" Hadia asked. "The man who was really two? That part kind of confused me."

"Still confusing to me," Fatma replied. She rubbed at her side again. "I don't know what that man was. Or how he did what he did. Had to be sorcery involved."

Hadia nodded thoughtfully. "So what's the connection to Lord Worthington?"

Fatma strummed fingers along the top of a book. She'd been considering this as they put together their profile. "Lord Worthington was a man so infatuated with al-Jahiz he created a brotherhood dedicated to him. From what I saw, they were hunting down even scraps of clothing, personal possessions—anything. Like holy relics. Men obsessed with al-Jahiz to the point of wanting to own him, to be a part of him, to maybe be him."

Hadia's eyes rounded. "You think the imposter belongs to Worthington's brotherhood?"

"It's the best I can come up with. Someone immersed in al-Jahiz. Someone in the know about Lord Worthington's brotherhood. Even the night it meets up. And where. Someone who could get into his mansion unseen and undetected. Too many pieces there to not fit."

"But why?"

Fatma closed the book. "Maybe a resentful employee. Someone who wanted the English Basha out of the way. Or a member of the Brotherhood who took this al-Jahiz thing too far."

"Sounds plausible. But it doesn't explain the possible Ifrit."

"No," Fatma admitted, recalling the strange fire. "But one mystery at a time."

They were interrupted by Zagros, coming to tower over them.

"The both of you do realize," he drawled, "that it's polite to be quiet for other patrons."

Fatma looked around the empty reading room. "We're the only patrons."

"Then you should be quiet for your own sakes."

The two women exchanged glances. It appeared their good graces had worn off.

"It seems, however, today I'm not only a librarian but a messenger." The djinn extended a small rolled tube, disdainfully held between clawed thumb and forefinger. "This arrived for you by boilerplate courier. They weren't able to come further than the lobby, so I was forced to walk up an entire flight of stairs— since these lifts can't accommodate my healthy weight—and back down again. Only to find, the missive wasn't even for me. Isn't that a delightful story?"

Fatma accepted the message with thanks, though the librarian had already taken his leave.

Hadia watched after him. "Is he always like that?"

"No. Sometimes he's actually in a bad mood." She read over the note. "I think we might have a reason to go out into the field today. Ever been to Cité-Jardin?"

Hadia shook her head. "No one I know has that kind of money."

"Then consider this a chance to visit. Just got a tip. Someone there we might talk to, who knows something about this Brotherhood of Al-Jahiz. Let's grab lunch first. Hungry?"

"Starving!" Hadia all but whimpered. "But, umm." She gestured toward the dial of zodiac characters above the swinging pendulum. "Do you think we can make time for al-salah? It's Friday. There's a masjid that opens to women. It's on the way, I think. And the sermon's quick."

Fatma turned to eye the clock, a bit guilty at her impatience.

"Or we could just pray here," Hadia offered. "Just staying steadfast on deen."

"No," Fatma said. New partner, new concessions. "It's fine. I actually wouldn't mind." Just the thing to clear her head. "Only, I don't have a hijab. Just more bowlers."

Hadia reached into her bag, pulling out a blue headscarf. "Stay prepared!"

CHAPTER
NINE

E ntering Cité-Jardin was always jarring. One moment you
were in the bustle of downtown Cairo—with shops and
restaurants still open on a Friday for locals and the trolleys
full of tourists. But walk over a few streets, and you crossed into
a place with no honking horns or crackling aerial trams, no pe-
destrians chattering politics or shouting street vendors. Just the
humming of birds and wind rustling the branches of leafy trees.

Cité-Jardin had been built by a djinn architect. He'd lived
in this world before the coming of al-Jahiz and had sailed off
with Napoleon's armies to see Paris. He returned to Egypt after the Emerging and convinced the new government to let him
design a development—one he claimed would speak to Cairo's
place as an international city. The result was modernity accented
with inspiration drawn from the natural world. The buildings—
mostly embassies—were carved with leaves or repeating vines.
The houses were mansions: multistory villas with archways and
columns in the likeness of bundled reeds, all encircled by a forest
of trees and bushes. Incandescent electric lamps lined the roads,
like saplings crowned with orbs of colored glass.

Fatma took in the organic opulence and serenity. Prayer had
been a good idea. She remembered as a girl staying home on
Fridays while her father and male relatives all went to the masjid.
Being able to share that today with other women was . . . refreshing. And it always helped clear her head—*Probably you should
make a habit of doing it more.* She silenced her mother's admoni-
tions, listening instead to Hadia.

". . . so I tell him just because Friday prayer isn't an obligation for women doesn't mean I can't attend. What children am I caring for?" She had been sharing thoughts on women and faith since leaving the masjid, hardly stopping as they ate lunch on the go—skewered beef kofta and baladi bread. "I've heard in China there are masjid just for women. Can you imagine? Maybe we could try that here. Should bring it up at an EFS meeting."

"You're in the Egyptian Feminist Sisterhood?" Fatma asked. They watched an automobile roll past—a six-wheeled black luxury vehicle with ivory running boards.

"Spent my summer in Alexandria marching for the vote." She made the victory sign of the suffrage movement. "I have a cousin in the Cairo chapter. Supposed to attend next week."

"You have a lot of cousins." Fatma had lost track of how many.

"We're a very big family. Would you like to come? To an EFS meeting? Always looking to bring in women from the professions—to show we aren't all just factory workers." Then added hastily, "Not that there's anything wrong with factory work."

Fatma could think of many things wrong with factory work—low wages, unsafe machines, harassing male bosses who often acted like jailers. But she got the point.

"I'll think on it," she replied, noncommittal. She donated to the EFS and generally supported their causes. But who even had time for politics? Hadia was set to say more—perhaps a recruitment pitch—when someone slipped alongside them.

"Nice day for a walk," Siti said by way of a greeting.

Fatma started at the woman's unexpected appearance. She wore a tied-off sun-yellow kaftan that looked amazing against her skin, paired with blue breeches and tall laced tan boots.

"Rang your office three times before I sent the messenger eunuch," Siti continued idly, matching their pace.

"Wasn't by a phone," Fatma said. "Didn't think you'd have anything for me so quick. Didn't expect to run into you either." She hoped her face fully conveyed the what-in-damnation-are-you-doing-here she was trying to affect.

On the trek home last night they'd come up with a hasty course of action. Things seemed to be coalescing around Lord Worthington's mysterious secret society. Siti was to talk to Merira about the Brotherhood's members. Fatma would head into the office, and get a refresher on al-Jahiz. This, however, was not part of the plan.

"Never underestimate me." Siti winked. She turned to Hadia. "You must be the partner. A new lady Spooky Boy! The Ministry's going to get a glowing write-up from the EFS."

Hadia, who had watched their exchange, looked understandably confused.

"This is Siti," Fatma said. "She's . . ." Words, for some reason, sent her tongue into a knot.

"One of Agent Fatma's informants," Siti stepped in smoothly.

"Oh! Yes, of course. I'm Agent Hadia."

"Good to meet you, Agent Hadia," Siti returned, accepting an offered handshake.

"How do you know Agent Fatma?"

Siti grinned roguishly. "We've worked closely." She leaned in, whispering, "You see, I'm an idolater!"

Hadia's eyes grew to look like dark plums, and she froze, still holding Siti's hand. Fatma wanted to pull her bowler over her face. Why was the woman like this? When Hadia found her voice again, she only said: "I thought 'idolater' was offensive."

"Only when *you* use it." Siti released her hand. "But we call each other that all the time." She shrugged at Hadia's bafflement. "It's an idolater thing. You wouldn't understand."

"What we don't understand," Fatma quipped, "is why you're here. Not what we agreed."

Siti appeared unfazed. "We never agreed on anything. I told you I'd speak to my people and get you a name—which I did. There was no discussion on where I should or shouldn't be. I think I have a right to be here. Two of this killer's victims were from my community. We watch out for our own."

Fatma knew it was pointless to protest. Siti's mind was stubbornly unchangeable once made up. She could declare this Ministry business—order her to leave. But the woman didn't respond well to authority.

They settled into an awkward silence. Hadia, who strode between, glanced at both several times before working up the courage to speak. "Might I ask, what, ah, *temple* you belong to?"

"Hathor," Siti answered. "But I'm more partial to Sekhmet."

"Sekhmet. In theological alchemy we studied ancient and Hellenistic Egypt. If I recall, she's a goddess of battle?"

"The Eye of Ra. When humankind sought to overthrow Ra, his daughter Hathor didn't take too kindly. In her anger, she became Sekhmet—the fiery lioness. Then broke some things."

Hadia frowned. "Didn't she almost wipe out the world?"

"The goddess *really* gets into her work. Lucky for humankind, Thoth tricked her with beer she thought was blood. Put her right to sleep. Woke up in a better mood."

Fatma could almost hear the ayah Hadia was likely reciting in her head. To her credit, she held her composure. "So what is it you do at the temple?"

"I look after things. Fix things. Put things together." Siti flashed a sharp smile. "Sometimes, if I'm lucky, I get to break things too."

"We're here," Fatma said, eager to end the conversation. They stood before a white house that boasted some three stories. It was capped with triangular red roofs in Western fashion, but with a stone façade cut to mimic mashrabiyas. If windows were anything to go by, it held at least a dozen rooms—or more.

"That's fancy," Siti remarked.

Fatma confirmed the address on the message. "How'd you find this"—she looked again at the name—"Nabila al-Mansur? Wait, is she related to the al-Mansur steel industrialists?"

"Same family," Siti confirmed. "Though they have their hands in a bit of everything now. Merira put the word out among the temples. My head priestess," she explained for Hadia's benefit.

"Anyway, there was one curious tip. From someone who works at *Al-Masri*."

"The newspaper?" Hadia asked. "A reporter?"

"Better. A secretary. To the editor. Belongs to the Cult of Isis. Haughty types, but we get along alright. Anyway, notice how lacking news stories are about Lord Worthington's death?"

Fatma had checked the paper again today. "They make it sound like the fire was at best an accident. Nothing about a secret brotherhood. Strange."

"Purposeful," Siti replied. "The secretary says the morning after Lord Worthington's death, she arrived at work to find the printers in a snit. They had to dump an entire batch of morning dailies and reprint the headlines—on orders that came in at 4:00 a.m. That day, she took a call for the editor. She listens in every now and then, to keep the temples up on things. This caller thanked her editor for keeping talk from the paper that might embarrass the English Basha. Pressed him hard to keep it up."

Fatma had thought that Aasim's work. This was even more interesting. "Let me guess. The caller was one Nabila al-Mansur."

Siti winked. "You're catching on. The secretary also passed on that the al-Mansur family is a major financial benefactor to the city's papers. Betting she made that call more than once."

"So much for a free press," Hadia muttered.

"Talk that might embarrass the English Basha," Fatma repeated. "Like dying at a meeting of his own secret occult society."

"I'd put that high on the list," Siti agreed. "Merira said that before he approached the temples for his little club, he tried to entice a more high-class crowd. The al-Mansurs fit the bill."

Fatma suspected the same. They walked a tree-lined path to the front door—its black surface carved with interlocking stars. It took two heavy poundings of the brass knocker to bring someone. The servant, a young woman in white, took in the trio blankly until Fatma flashed a badge, and she scurried off to fetch her mistress.

When Nabila al-Mansur came to the door, the idea Fatma had

formed of the woman didn't do her justice. She wasn't tall but of surprising girth—not plump but sturdy, wearing a modern silk gallabiyah with gold fringes, contrasting with a hastily wrapped traditional black hijab. Well past her middling years, her face bore its share of wrinkles, but her eyes were two sharp points. She stared down at them over a hawkish nose, with a measuring glare only a patrician could master.

"Well?" she asked with an impatient click of the tongue.

"Peace be upon you, Madame Nabila. I'm Agent Fatma, and this is Agent Hadia. We're with the Ministry of Alchemy, Enchantments, and Supernatural Entities."

Madame Nabila scanned their badges, one hazel eye glaring like an owl. "What does the Ministry need of me?"

"We wanted to ask you about Lord Worthington."

"He's dead. Has that changed?"

So she was going to be difficult. "His death took place in the company of a certain brotherhood that we have reason to believe you know about."

That got her attention. Her lips pursed tight as her eyes drew sharper. After a while, she settled back to adjust her headscarf. "Very well, come in." Her gaze flickered to land on Siti. "But your abda is going to have to wait outside."

Fatma stiffened, and beside her Hadia gave an audible intake. The slur was common enough—hurled against Nubians and anyone with dark skin. A none-too-subtle reminder of a recent past. But Cairo was the boasted modern city. And it was now frowned upon to use such language. At least in public.

"She's not my . . . servant," Fatma said, unable to properly explain Siti's presence.

"Whoever she is, she waits here. I won't allow abeed in my home."

Fatma opened her mouth in a flare of anger, but Siti cut in.

"Fine by me." Her tone was nonchalant. "Don't think I want to go in there anyway." She paused, thoughtful. "You know what's funny? My family's been living along the Nile for thousands of years. Certainly, much longer than the descendants of some Mamluks—so jumped-up and full of themselves they forget they came here only recently. As *slaves*." She said the last word with emphasis, before turning in a carefree stroll.

Madame Nabila scowled at her back. "How rude. Abeed. God put no light in their complexion." Shaking her head, she led them inside.

Fatma spared a glance at Siti before following, letting a servant shut the door behind.

"I used to have abeed work for me," Madame Nabila went on. "Terrible thieves. Wallahi, you had to watch the women make your bread in the morning, or they would pilfer sacks of flour. I dismissed them outright when I discovered it and will not have their kind back."

Fatma studied the house—with walls in gilded flowering, marble floors covered in lavish rugs, a grand brass chandelier composed of perhaps a hundred spheres of glowing alchemical gas, and ornate furniture fitted with velvet cushions. Was this obscenely wealthy woman complaining about the theft of some flour?

"We aren't here for your political views," Fatma said, cutting off the harangue.

Madame Nabila stopped, eyes inspecting. "You disapprove of the way I talk. No wonder. You carry a bit of the abeed around the nose and lips. In the skin too. I thought el-Sha'arawi were a wealthy and respectable family in the south."

"We're not them," Fatma replied. "Your mistake."

The older woman's appraising gaze swung to Hadia. "At least you look to have some untainted blood."

Hadia regarded her coolly. "And among His wonders is the creation of the heavens and the earth, and the diversity of your tongues and colors. For in this, behold, there are messages indeed for all who are possessed of innate knowledge." Finishing the ayah, she smiled. "Before God, our *blood* means nothing. Virtue is in deeds, not the skin."

Madame Nabila's face drew to a fine point, obviously unused to reprimands from someone half her age. She turned, muttering about "liberal philosophies," beckoning them along. They were led through a room of vivid panoramas, including one of airships hovering over the Saladin Citadel.

"You've interrupted my hydrotherapy," Madame Nabila grumbled. She lifted the hem of her gallabiyah to climb a winding staircase, with railings that twisted like vines. "So you'll just have to talk while I steam."

At the top she led them to a room with a large bath whose floor and walls were covered in green tiles overlaid with yellow octagonal stars. Several attendants stood—more women in white—beside a large silver box.

As Fatma and Hadia sat on a bench, two attendants helped the woman disrobe. Two more worked dials on the silver box, which parted at a seam that ran down its middle. Inside revealed a small seat, where Madame Nabila stepped in and sat. It was closed again, leaving only her head visible, which craned out from a hole at the top. The box began to hum and hiss, as steam curled up from the hole about Madame Nabila's head that gave off a sweet, dusky, floral scent. Fatma sniffed. Was that cardamom? Was she steaming herself . . . in tea?

"Rich people are strange," Hadia whispered.

That was ever the truth.

"Now," Madame Nabila said. "What do the two of you want?"

"Information about Lord Worthington," Fatma said. "You two were acquaintances?"

"Alistair and I?" She frowned. "Yes, we were acquainted. Nothing improper. He was a friend of my husband, who passed years ago. We were more business associates. Though for some reason he believed he could confide in me, the way he confided in my husband. Occidentals are always needing someone to confide in, I find."

"Did he confide in you about the Brotherhood of Al-Jahiz?"

Madame Nabila made a face. "Alistair's great project. He was always going on to my husband about al-Jahiz. Pestering and questioning, as if we know anything about that madman. After my husband's passing, he attempted to recruit me. I said no, of course! Warned him he'd be a pariah if it got out. But he was stubborn."

"What do you know about the Brotherhood?" Fatma asked.

"Not a great deal," Madame Nabila answered as an attendant flicked sweat from her brow. "That they went about hunting al-Jahiz's secrets and held odd rituals. Alistair believed those secrets could bring a new age to the world—as if we don't have enough on our hands."

"*Quærite veritatem*," Fatma quoted.

Madame Nabila huffed. "You've seen that outrageous emblem? I think he truly believed it all. Doubt you could say the same for half his brotherhood."

"If they didn't share his vision, then why join?"

"Standing and advancement. The Brotherhood became a way for ambitious men at the company to get close to Alistair. The only way, when he picked up from England and moved to Giza permanently. They could even procure funds for projects. Quite the game many played. Though most were wasting their time."

"Why do you say that?"

"Alistair barely ran the company anymore. Too invested in his brotherhood."

"Then who was running it?" Hadia asked.

"I assume his son, Alexander."

"Why did you contact the newspapers to cover for Lord Worthington?" Fatma asked.

Madame Nabila's eyes widened. "How did you . . . ?" She sighed. "Well, I only have the same answer. Alexander Worthington."

"You're saying Lord Worthington's son asked you to hide details of his father's death?"

Madame Nabila clicked her tongue. "He was panicked. Begged me to talk to them."

"And you obliged?"

"I don't expect you to understand the burden of societal standing. Lord Worthington was a respected member of Egyptian society. The English Basha. As heir to the Worthington fortune, Alexander knew his father's death in such a . . . compromising situation could embarrass more than just his family. It could hurt the Worthington stock and trade. Hurt markets on two continents. Not to mention the peace summit to which the Worthington name is vital. It was in everyone's interest to keep the matter quiet."

"You can't keep something like this quiet," Hadia put in. "Not forever."

Madame Nabila chuckled. "Girl, you don't need to keep something quiet forever. You just let it come out in drips, to give everyone a chance to prepare for it. Then when the larger story is released, the impact is diminished and it's soon forgotten."

Fatma could see the reasoning behind that. There was so much going on in Cairo at any given moment, you could bury even a story like this if you let enough time pass.

"Is it true?" Madame Nabila asked. "About the way Alistair died?"

"We're not calling it an accident," was all Fatma answered.

The woman whispered a prayer. "I warned him about who he was getting close to. In the end, he consorted with all sorts of low types. Not just commoners but idolaters! Can you imagine? If there is a jackal's hand behind this, look to them. You can be sure of it!"

"Did he have enemies?"

"Business rivalries. No one capable of such depravity."

"How about among his brotherhood?"

"Unlikely. Never more than twenty or so. And all of them perished with him."

All of them, Fatma thought. So much for her theory.

"Terrible business," Madame Nabila complained. "No wonder Alexander looked so distraught. Thought he might get down on his knees for my help. Quite undignified."

Fatma frowned. "*Looked* distraught? Alexander Worthington

asked you this in person? On the morning his father died? He's in Cairo?"

Madame Nabila blinked. "Yes, he'd just come into the country, to such dreadful news."

Fatma shared a look with Hadia. That was new information. "One last question. Was Alexander part of the Brotherhood?"

The woman shrugged. "God knows best. But given his father's convictions, I find it hard to believe it could be any other way."

Fatma considered this. So maybe there was one surviving member of the Brotherhood of Al-Jahiz after all.

Madame Nabila didn't bother to end her hydrotherapy to see them out.

"She was pleasant," Hadia grumbled.

"As my mother says, it's always the wicked who have lots of money. Good work earlier. With the verse. Think your pushback made her more pliable."

"Wasn't even thinking all of that," Hadia muttered. "Just couldn't stand her bigotry."

"Lots of that to go around," Fatma assured.

Hadia made a face. "When I was in America, everything was about color. Where you could eat. Where you had to ride. Where you could live or sleep. When I got back to Egypt, I couldn't believe I'd not noticed it before. With my friends, my family. In the Alexandria EFS, none of the officers were darker than me. At our protests, Nubian and Soudanese women marched in the back. Quoting scripture came in handy to fight against it." She sighed. "Maybe we aren't so different than America after all."

Fatma hadn't needed to travel to know that. She'd suffered her fair share of slights. Nothing near what Siti endured, but not absent either. Magic and djinn hadn't changed everything.

They reached the front door, which the servant opened to let them through. Siti stood waiting on the street. She met them, sniffing. "Why do you two smell like tea?"

"Let's catch a carriage," Fatma said. "I'll tell you on the way back."

They had to leave Cité-Jardin to actually find a carriage—so Fatma talked on the way. By the time they caught one, the three were already tossing around ideas.

"Alexander Worthington here in Cairo," Siti murmured. "And his sister claimed otherwise?"

"Told me he was away," Fatma said.

"Why lie about that?" Hadia asked.

"That's what I'd like to know," Fatma muttered.

"You're thinking he has something to do with all this?" Siti asked. "Maybe hired this man in the gold mask to do in his own father? Treacherous. Even for an Englishman."

"Or maybe he's the imposter," Fatma said.

Hadia inhaled. "That's . . . elaborate!"

Siti looked dubious. "Our friend last night didn't sound English. Their Arabic is usually terrible. Worthington's heir running around Cairo as al-Jahiz is *very* elaborate."

Fatma knew as much. Plus, none of this explained a possible Ifrit. Or the man they'd had fought last night—or whatever he was. She was grasping.

"You're right," she admitted. Probably best not to make wild speculations.

They reached the Ministry in short order. As they stepped out, Fatma pulled Siti to the side. "About what happened before . . . with Madame Nabila."

Siti made a gesture commonly used to dismiss unruly children. "You think that's the first time anyone's called me abda? Insulted my family as a 'pack of stinking abeed'? Or made some comment on my skin? My lips and nose? Maybe men asking me to be their little gariyah? I assure you, it's not uncommon."

Fatma wasn't naive. "Still, doesn't make it right."

Siti smiled. "Protector of my honor. I might swoon." Her eyes flickered over Fatma's shoulder. "Though that might have to wait."

Fatma turned to find a familiar figure in a khaki uniform exiting the Ministry.

"Inspector," she greeted. "Another unexpected visit."

"Agent," Aasim replied. Then to Hadia, "I mean, agents." He glanced to Siti, but she turned as if ignoring them. "Rang your office. When I didn't get you, decided to stop by. Only one who had seen you was a djinn in your library. I think he insulted me five times just to tell me you weren't there."

"I'm sorry that happened to you," Fatma mocked.

Aasim grunted, wrinkling his moustache. "Do the two of you know you smell like tea? Anyway, I followed up on what you told me about last night. Your encounter with al-Jahiz." He said the name sarcastically. She had called him first thing in the morning. The police had more people than the Ministry to search the streets.

"And?"

"We found him! At least, we found out about him. Seems you were right. This imposter's been running around Cairo for at least a week now. Maybe longer. Don't know how we missed it. But once we put an ear out, the streets were buzzing."

"Anything on who he might be?"

Aasim shook his head. "No, but we found out where he's going to appear next. Sunday night. Thinking of attending, with a few of my friends." His moustache twitched. "Want to come?"

ver the next two days, they planned.

Aasim secured an arrest warrant, listing every complaint and criminal code he could get away with—and some he probably couldn't. Fatma coordinated on how things were to go. The police had the numbers. But if the Ministry were to be involved, she would have some say.

That meant keeping Aasim's people under control. Cairo police had a reputation. She wanted to expose this imposter, not start a riot. So no guns. This gathering was likely to be full of poor people, the old, even children. Last thing they needed was bullets. Amir had let her build a special team of agents. Hamed was her first pick. He helped find four more—men who could keep their heads, and whose size made people think twice.

The hardest part was convincing Hadia to stay behind. An operation like this was no place for a recruit. If things went bad, no guaranteeing her safety. Nothing the woman wanted to hear. Fatma had to quote Ministry rules and explain she'd serve better running logistics from the police station. Onsi would be with her. Everybody was suited for what they were suited for.

The one snag was getting a chance to interview Alexander Worthington. Frustratingly, she had no cause for a warrant. Despite Madame Nabila's claim he'd been in the city on the night of his father's murder, passport documents showed him arriving by airship a day later. There'd been sightings of this supposed al-Jahiz at least a week prior. Documents could be forged, of course. He could have even hired someone to play the part of this imposter. Fatma had suggested that they bring him in for questioning to clear things up. But Aasim had already been warned to back off by superiors—who were getting an earful from politicians and businesspeople. Worthington's heir was grieving, they claimed, and preparing for the burial of his father, in some English custom. He wasn't a suspect. And could be interviewed later.

"Rattle the gates of people like that and they send out their hounds," the inspector said. "Let's nab this imposter. If Worthington's involved, the person he has pretending to be al-Jahiz is likely some small-time con artist. Or worse, a theater actor. I know how to crack both. They'll give up whoever put them up to this."

It made sense, she supposed. But by Sunday night, she was on tenterhooks.

She sat in the back of a police wagon, one in a procession that rumbled through Cairo's streets. Hamed sat directly opposite, in a pressed Ministry uniform—silver buttons gleaming and pants sporting a perfect crease. He looked like a picture right out of a guidebook—down to the red tarboosh. The only thing out of place were his shoes: black military issue, with thick ridges. The three other men sharing the van—all broad-shouldered and thick-necked—wore the same.

Fatma had thought of putting on a uniform. For about ten seconds. Suits were so much more comfortable. This one was a coal gray: sober and minus her usual flair. Well, except for the ivory buttons on the jacket and waistcoat. And perhaps the cobalt-blue tie with slashes of mandarin was a bit showy. However, her shoes were a perfectly ordinary black—though on the glossy side. They were made for running and jumping. She'd come prepared too. Just more fashionably.

"You're expecting a crowd out there tonight?" Hamed asked. His hands idly gripped a black truncheon sitting across his lap.

"If what I saw Friday night is anything to go by."

"Do they really think it's him?" another agent asked. "Al-Jahiz, I mean?"

"Some do. I think others are just curious." There were no posters advertising tonight. Not a word in the papers. But you could find evidence of it everywhere—scribbled on walls in back alleys or whispered in underground dens. Cairo was at times a two-sided coin with completely different faces.

"I've heard things," a third agent ventured. "That he performs wonders." His look said he was waiting for her to confirm or refute it.

"I didn't see any wonders."

"But there was an Ifrit?" the fourth quipped. He sounded hopeful, which was crazy. No one should *want* to come across an Ifrit.

"All I saw were some tricks with fire," Fatma answered.

An uneasy quiet settled before Hamed spoke up. "Doesn't matter who he says he is or what magic tricks he performs. We're Ministry agents. Nothing we can't handle."

"What about this other man?" The skeptic again. "Who you say can become more than one person?"

Fatma grimaced at the memory. "Hoping the four of you can handle him. Or them."

"That's what these are for." Hamed held up the truncheon—a rod almost long as his arm, with a bulbous head. A flip of a lever at its base set off a humming whine, and the head crackled with blue bolts. The others cheered, lifting their own truncheons. One even thumped his chest with a fist. Men, Fatma decided for perhaps the hundredth time, were so strange.

When the police wagon stopped, Fatma was the first out, landing on the uneven ground in a small puff of dust. She nudged up her bowler with her cane and looked about. Under the light of a full moon that hung in the black canvas of the sky, the City of the Dead sprawled in every direction.

El-Arafa, the Cemetery, as most called the old necropolis, lay nestled at the foot of low hills. They had once been an ancient quarry for limestone, and their tops still carried a broken and sawed-off look. The Cemetery sat in the valley between: a dense grid of tombs and mausoleums built up over 1,200 years. The families of Egypt's rulers had been buried here—military commanders, Mamluk sultans, even some Ottoman bashas. Their tombs were miniature palaces and had been the site of spectacles, even Sufi schools. El-Arafa became a hub for seekers of wisdom and custodians overseeing its care.

But that was long ago.

The late years of Ottoman rule had seen most of the Cemetery's well-to-do inhabitants leave for more alluring parts of Cairo. Rapid urbanization following the coming of the djinn had only accelerated matters, as middle-class Cairenes flocked to new developments with modern conveniences. The influx of farmers, peasants, and immigrants into the city meant a fresh set of inhabitants for the necropolis—mostly impoverished. The mausoleums had fallen into disrepair, many crumbling—some no more than rubble. There was no running water, no gas lines or steam-run machinery, not even paved roads. Still, people made do, building small dwellings; others even taking up residence inside the tombs. It was as if this place constructed for the dead couldn't help drawing the living.

"Nothing like a trip to the slums," someone muttered.

Fatma turned to see Aasim beside her. No one made a trip to the City of the Dead a regular habit. Maybe pilgrims looking for blessings from the Sufi mystics who still dwelled in the monasteries, though their schools were long closed. There were festivals at some of the more well-kept mausoleums. But most Cairenes steered clear.

"Think of it as you getting out more." Fatma looked to a nearby building. From behind a curtain on a second floor, a woman watched the caravan of police assembling at the outskirts of her home. Beneath her, two young boys jostled for a view.

Aasim grunted. "Say that when one of the little slum rats lifts away that shiny pocket watch you're fond about. You know what they say—something goes missing, chances are it'll turn up in el-Arafa."

An exaggeration. Many here worked in greater Cairo. Or

engaged in the informal economy that sustained this city within a city. Most people in el-Arafa weren't thieves or criminals. Just poor.

"We're not here to stop fencers dealing minor goods," Fatma replied.

"Minor goods? They say the Forty Leopards are headquartered in this place. Nothing *minor* about what those lady thieves pilfer. You know the last time we were here, I had more than this." His white-gloved hand touched the handle of a wood baton at his side.

"No guns," Fatma reiterated. "We're dealing with people. Not a legion of flesh-eating ghuls." She suppressed a shiver that came at the memory of their prior visit to the Cemetery, investigating the machinations of a mad angel.

Another grunt from Aasim, and his overwrought moustache twitched with unease—no doubt also having vivid recollections. "Hope you're right." He jerked a chin into the distance. "Because that doesn't fill me with confidence."

She followed his gesture to a pack of makeshift houses set among gravestones and mausoleums. Somewhere just beyond, a bright glare lit up the sky, illuminating the rooftops. It reminded Fatma of an open-air night market. Only there were no night markets in the City of the Dead. And the raucous chants and cheers that erupted now and again didn't sound like dickering.

"Is everyone in place?"

Aasim looked back to assess his ranks. The wagons had emptied, leaving policemen standing in two lines shoulder to shoulder. He frowned. "I think you've got company."

Fatma turned, not understanding—and caught sight of someone hurrying past the policemen. Hadia? The woman reached them, breathing calmly despite her swift gait.

"What are you doing here?" Fatma asked. "Did something happen?"

Hadia shook her head. "Nothing happened. I'm just being your partner." She smiled, but the words were tight.

"I expressly forbade you from coming here tonight!"

"I know." Hadia lost the smile. "Only you can't. That rule you quoted me, about ordering a recruit to stay behind. It doesn't exist. You made it up."

Fatma felt her face flush. Beside her, the other Ministry agents bit back smiles.

"You made up a rule?" Hamed chuckled. "And left her with Onsi?"

"He knows the Ministry Code of Conduct by heart," Hadia affirmed. "I mentioned your *rule* to him in passing, and he alerted me immediately there was no such thing. So, I hopped onto a police wagon and made it up here. Where I belong."

"I did it for your own good," Fatma grumbled. "This might get dangerous."

"I realized things might get dangerous when I went to the academy," Hadia retorted.

Their gazes locked into silence.

Aasim cleared his throat. "You two need a moment?"

"No." There wasn't time for this. "Hadia, you're with me. If this turns bad, you get back behind police lines."

"I can handle myself—"

"With what? Your hands?" Fatma turned to Aasim, trying not to let her irritation boil over. "Are we ready to do this?" The inspector looked between them, but nodded. "Good, then." She shrugged, pulling her bowler tight, and stepped out with her cane. "Let's go."

The small army marched down the Cemetery's narrow streets. Fatma walked at its head with Aasim—and now Hadia—flanked by Hamed and the other agents. Behind them followed lines of police. At least forty. Aasim wanted more, whole contingents to encircle the place. But Fatma objected. They were already descending on people in the middle of the night. No need to make things tenser than they already were.

Not all of el-Arafa's residents had gone to the rally. They sat in windows and doorsteps, watching the procession snaking between stone tombs with raised markers—sometimes ducking beneath laundry lines and navigating around brick ovens. Most faces regarded them blankly. Some were anxious. One woman let out a set of panicked "Ya lahwy!" as they passed. Others, however, gave hard stares. Once or twice came a whispered curse.

Aasim leaned over. "Did I mention that police aren't well liked in the slums?"

Fatma didn't doubt it. From reports she'd heard, and with good reasons too. Their march continued in relative quiet, though the sounds from ahead grew louder as they approached. There was cheering. And someone was speaking. She could make out a few words echoing through the narrow passages of the necropolis. But it wasn't until they cleared the settlement of buildings that she got a full measure of what lay beyond.

A packed crowd filled a clearing. More people stood or sat atop buildings that rose up on the other side. Fatma had expected high numbers. But this looked to be a few hundred. Much more than the last gathering. Lamps with glow gas had been strung up, and their glare basked the entire area, bringing to mind an outdoor amphitheater or opera house. The stage here was a towering mausoleum. Its crenellated walls had probably been smooth once, though the mud brick showed numerous cracks. Wooden scaffolding surrounded the sides, where someone was making repairs. The structure was capped by a grandiose pear-shaped dome, its surface decorated with indented lines that ran from base to tip—a pinnacle rising to end in a crescent. Just in front of the dome, in an opened-up space where a section of triangular, honeycomb-patterned merlons had crumbled away, stood the speaker.

Fatma frowned. Not the man in the gold mask. Someone else—dressed in a blue gallabiyah and a white turban. He held up both hands, shouting into the night. ". . . and I saw with my own eyes, the wonders performed! He called upon those made of smokeless fire and destroyed the foreigners! I had once helped them carry out their theft and desecrations! But he has guided me proper! He has returned so that we may all see and know the truth! He has returned so that he may teach us, as he did before!"

New cheers went up in a roar that was deafening this close.

"Who is that?" she asked, leaning close to Aasim.

"From what we've been told, all of this imposter's speeches are preceded by people like this. They go on about what they claim they've seen al-Jahiz do."

"Bearers of Witness," Hadia added.

Fatma was familiar with the title. It was said when the real al-Jahiz walked the streets of Cairo, he often had men and women who preceded him—bearing witness to his teachings and wonders. This imposter *had* studied well.

The crowd's roaring grew louder. Along the rooftops, people stood in expectation. The man atop the mausoleum was yelling now, though only bits of his speech traveled through the din. ". . . The Traveler of Worlds! The Father of Mysteries! The Knower of the Mystic . . . !"

Aasim said something that was impossible to hear. But Fatma's attention was fixed atop the mausoleum. The speaker finished, stepping to the side. She felt herself tense as the man in the gold mask made his entrance.

He looked just as before—tall and draped in flowing black robes. Even from here, she could see the etchings on his mask, moving as if alive. To his right was another familiar figure, a slender man in black billowy breeches and a shirt of heavy cloth. As the imposter took his place, the crowd chanted: "Al-Jahiz! Al-Jahiz! Al-Jahiz!" He stood, hands clasped behind his back—while his companion stood on his right, an immobile statue. The praise only died down when the imposter held up his hands—which Fatma only now noticed were covered in dark chain mail. In the quiet that descended, he spoke.

"You have come here tonight, seeking wonders."

Gasps went up, and Fatma knew why. Unlike the last man, this imposter didn't need to shout. His words came in a perfect pitch that made it seem as if he were speaking right beside her. This was a new trick he hadn't used the other night.

"You have come tonight, seeking great wisdom. To hear me tell of what sights I glimpsed as I walked between worlds. You have come because your eyes and minds ache with hunger, the same one in your bellies, and those of your children. You have come because your souls are thirsty, dry as the dust at your feet. You have come because even in this age where wonders are so abundant"—he gestured into the distance, toward greater Cairo—"there is yet emptiness, a hole at your center. This new world has failed you. This claimed 'modernity' has left you unfulfilled—like a man adrift in an ocean without a drop of water to drink."

He took in a deep breath, as if drawing in life—then let his voice explode.

"I have returned to you, my people lost!" he thundered. "I have returned to you, my people abandoned! I have returned to you! Not to the powerful, the wealthy, not those who misuse my teachings to live in decadence! To raise up a great city for the high while so many yet live so low! Who dare proclaim an age of wonders, on the backs of those who build and work their factories! Who must bake their bread as they gorge on the sweat and toil of your hands! Who must live in squalor while they build, and build, and build as if wishing to listen in on the heavens! Masr has strayed far from the path I set! Together, we must set it right! Even if that means bringing down all they have built upon them so that we may start anew!"

The shouts in response became almost earsplitting. Fatma shared a look with Aasim. It was time. What she was about to do was genius, or the worst idea in the history of worst ideas. She mouthed a silent Bismillah. Then, before the imposter could start up again, she shouted.

"Is al-Jahiz a murderer?"

Fatma didn't have one of those voice transmitters, like singers used. No nice tricks either, to be heard inside everyone's ears.

What she did have was a smooth intonation that didn't tremble. And a quiet lull that made her words echo. Every head turned, followed fast by a buzzing murmur. For once, she doubted it had much to do with her suit. More likely, it was the armada of police who stood behind her. From atop the mausoleum, the man in the gold mask looked down—that burning gaze latching onto her. Steeling herself, she spoke again, and walked forward—her retinue following.

"I asked, is al-Jahiz a murderer?"

The crowd parted at their approach. Some with children began leaving the gathering entirely, likely fearful of a coming conflict. But that wasn't going to happen, because she was going to end this imposter here and now. She never let her eyes stray from him long, where he glared from his perch.

They reached the front of the gathering. Those here, mostly younger men with heated gazes, had to be pushed to gain passage. One—with a chin that grew sparse hair—planted his feet in challenge. She put her shoulder down and casually bodychecked him, sending him stumbling back. Regaining his footing, he lunged but ran up against Aasim, who returned a glare over a moustache that twitched. "Try me." Fatma ignored them, fixed now on the figure above.

"You haven't answered my question," she shouted again. "Is al-Jahiz a murderer?"

The imposter remained quiet, and she thought she might have to repeat herself again. But then he spoke. "You ask riddles. Speak plain so that all can understand." There were murmurs of assent from the crowd.

"The al-Jahiz I've learned about was a teacher," Fatma called out. "A thinker. An inventor. A man of righteousness, of truth, and of justice. A man who spoke of freedom. God as my witness, in nothing I have read, has he ever been named a murderer."

"Then why do you name me so now?" the imposter asked.

That's it, Fatma thought. *Take all the rope you need.*

"Last week over twenty people were killed, murdered," she

shouted. "Burned alive. Their bodies reduced to ashes. One man was seen fleeing the crime, like a common thief, a coward attempting to cover up his deeds. A man wearing a gold mask."

Shouts of anger went up. Fatma's eyes strayed to the policemen, whose hands hovered above batons. She shot a meaningful look to Aasim, who turned to hiss something to his men. Whatever he said was carried down the line, and their hands relaxed. Atop the mausoleum, the man raised a chain-mailed hand, and the crowd quieted. Fatma didn't let the silence go wasted.

"I do not name the great al-Jahiz a murderer," she said, addressing the crowd. "I name this *charlatan* a murderer who has chosen to carry out this fraud upon you, this falsehood. A man who would kill so many cannot be trusted. A man like that does not deserve your praise." A few faces looked troubled. Good. She whipped her head back to the imposter. "I ask you again, is al-Jahiz a murderer?"

There was a long quiet. It seemed everyone was now waiting on an answer, eyes fixed on the figure above. At last, he replied, "I am many things to many people. Teacher. Thinker. Inventor. I have been called other things. Saint. Madman." He paused. "And to those of whom you speak, who perished in fire, I was vengeance."

Fatma released a breath. There it was. Beside her, Aasim cleared his throat and shouted: "Sounds like a confession to me."

"I confess only to doing what had to be done," the man replied. He turned his burning gaze on the crowd, who stared back uncertainly. "What they do not tell you is who died that night. Right here, on the very earth I once walked, foreign men create a mockery of my name. They do not tell you, that one of these men, the claimed English Basha, formed a deceitful cabal of other Englishmen, who poisoned my teachings. They do not tell you that these men practiced foul arts—even daring to call themselves the Brotherhood of Al-Jahiz. That they consorted with idolaters! Worshippers of false gods!" New murmurs, and Fatma looked to find more than a few scandalized faces. Still, that wasn't enough. Doubt still filled the air.

"That is no reason to murder!" someone shouted.

Fatma looked about, searching for the voice. Another spoke. "We are a nation of laws!"

"There is no call to kill even idolaters!" came a third shout.

"Or foreigners!" said another. "We are not to kill those who do not make war against us!"

More voices now. Even arguments. Breaking out here and there among the crowd. One old man was quoting hadith on nonviolence to a knot of young men who listened respectful even while disagreeing. Others looked as if they were making to leave, returning to their homes. Fatma looked up to the imposter with triumph in her eyes. If he thought he could wrap his crimes in some sense of righteousness, he'd been sorely mistaken. *Your move*, she thought silently.

"War has been made against you," the imposter thundered, cutting across the din. He waited for silence to settle again as all eyes returned to him. "What they will not tell you, is that these foreign men committed theft. Pilfering what they would from our land. They seek to take what was yours by right, to make themselves a new power. They seek to corrupt our country, corrupt your children, debase our society—using my name, and perverting my teachings for their own greed! Their aim is nothing less than to weaken Egypt, to make us once again a vassal to Western powers! To place us under the rule of the very tyrants from whom we escaped!"

New gasps now. And true looks of alarm. Fatma frowned. What was he getting at?

"Tell us!" someone shouted. "Who would do this?"

"The very ones who keep you in this slum," the imposter answered. "Those who call themselves your leaders. Who sit in the halls of government." His arm shot up, gesturing down toward Fatma and the others. "And they knew! These authorities, charged with protecting you, they allowed this desecration! Why? Because the English Basha walked with the wealthy, the powerful, who use their influence to bribe the quiet of your statesmen, to even silence your newspapers to keep you blind!"

He paused, waiting for his words to sink in. And to Fatma's discomfort, she could see that many were listening. Not all were convinced, but they seemed open to hearing more.

"Traitors!" a voice shouted. She thought it was one of the young men. It was quickly picked up, buzzing through the crowd like a set of wasps.

"Traitors!" the imposter pronounced in unison. "Traitors in league with these idolaters and Englishmen, conspiring to allow the foreigners to take root again on our soil! To undo the work I had done to help free Egypt! So yes, I burned them! I let the fires consume them! To end their plot to once again shackle our land and bind us all in chains!"

A chorus of assent from the crowd rang out in the night.

"That was actually good," Aasim admitted. "I'm hoping you have a rebuttal?"

"Of course she does," Hadia said. Her eyes flicked nervously. "You do, don't you?"

Fatma set her jaw. This wasn't going as she'd planned. She'd gotten a confession, but he'd turned it into a badge of honor. And weaved the most ridiculous conspiracy. The Egyptian government was part of a plot to help make the country a colony of England? Preposterous! Yet she could also see that it struck a chord, with people who had little reason to trust authority. There were some in the crowd who looked genuinely shocked, even worried. What he was playing at here was dangerous, *very* dangerous. Fortunately, not all were swept up by that speech. Open skepticism played on many faces. A few even glanced her way, waiting, as if willing her to make a worthy rebuttal. Well, time to give them the full show.

"Take off your mask!" she shouted. That cut through the exultation, which slowly faded away. "Al-Jahiz never wore a mask. He never concealed his face from his followers, like some criminal or robber. So why one now? I've found that men who hide behind masks do so to shroud their lies. If you are the great al-Jahiz, then work this one wonder. Remove the mask. Show us what lies beneath."

A stunned quiet fell over the crowd, and then a voice called: "Yes, take off the mask!" It was followed by another. "Let us see your face! Take off the mask!" Fatma allowed the barest smile as more demands came. That was the thing about Cairenes. They'd listen to you. But if you wanted them to follow you, if you wanted to gain their confidence, they had to feel they knew you. They had to look you in the eyes and read your heart. Going around in a mask was a good gimmick. But lots of people here had come more out of curiosity than anything else. She'd taken hold of that curiosity and given it a good shake.

"Why do you take so long?" she mocked. "Is this feat beyond the great al-Jahiz? Or are you better at giving speeches? My mother always says that beneath the nice and unassuming exterior are often catastrophes. Maybe you're hiding a catastrophe under that mask? Maybe your eyes are as big as your name implies?" There were peals of laughter. That was the other thing about Cairenes—give them a reason and you could go from serious to laughingstock, the butt of jokes traded on street corners and in coffee shops.

"Come on, great shaykh," Fatma added for good measure. "Take off your mask!"

The imposter held up a hand, bringing renewed silence. "I have never claimed to be a shaykh," he spoke in that soft voice. "That is a title you have placed upon me. I am but a revealer of truth. I speak these truths to those who need hear them— Muslim or Copt or disbeliever. When I first walked the streets of Cairo, I came only as a teacher and no more. As one whose face could be lost among the many. I did not wish for my likeness to be remade, to become an idol for misunderstanding men to venerate. I did not want to be used by the deceitful to lead the people astray."

Fatma gleefully readied more gibes. He wasn't going to just talk his way out of this one.

"But I am not without understanding, that eyes must at times see to strengthen truth."

The words on Fatma's tongue evaporated as the man did the unthinkable—placing his fingers to either side of the gold mask and prying it away. The gasps that rose around her cut through the stillness like a knife.

Beneath the mask was a face that staggered, and she had to fight not to take a step back. It was a face of deep angles, sunken in about the cheekbones and elongated to the chin. The skin that covered that face was as dark as any Soudanese, contrasting with the matted peppered locks of hair that fell about it. And those eyes! If it were possible, they burned even fiercer—as if unveiled in all their severity. It was not that this was truly al-Jahiz; for that her mind wouldn't allow. But if ever she imagined what the man whispered of in stories and legends would look like, stepped back into their midst, this was the face she would conjure to stare back at her.

The awe that came from the crowd was palpable, rising up amid exclamations of "It is him! He has returned! Al-Jahiz!" That last one was picked up by new voices that blended into one constant chant. "Al-Jahiz! Al-Jahiz! Al-Jahiz!" If there were still doubtful out there, they were drowned out by these more fervent cries.

"This isn't good," Hadia said.

Fatma looked around. She had hoped to unmask the imposter, show him for a fraud. Instead, she had given him validation. There was a sinking feeling that this had been a trap. And she'd walked right into it.

"What now?" Aasim asked.

Fatma pushed away the dread and self-doubt. "I remember him admitting to murder. We take him, before he riles up everyone further."

"They seem pretty riled already," Hadia pointed out.

Not the only ones either, Fatma noted. Hamed and the other agents had their black truncheons clutched tight. The police had hands on their batons, shoulders tensed like men ready to spring. This could explode. "Aasim! We arrest him now or make a retreat!"

The inspector's moustache actually went stiff. "The Cairo police don't retreat," he said bitingly. Pulling out a whistle, he blew it twice. His officers drew their batons and formed up ranks like a battalion. "I am authorized to place you under arrest!" Aasim shouted at the imposter. "For the murder of Lord Alistair Worthington and his known associates! Anyone who impedes will be arrested for interference in the carrying out of the will of the state!"

He was answered with eruptions of anger, jeers joining the chants.

"The will of the state." The imposter's voice came from the rooftop in mockery. "Do you see now of what I speak? Where are Cairo's authorities when you are sick? Or need clean water? Or the price of food goes high? They cannot be bothered. But now, to protect these scheming foreigners, they will send an entire army of police. And against who? The poor and downtrodden. Invading your homes and dwellings. All to apprehend one man? I will go willingly, my people, if you so wish it. So that this shameful betrayal goes no further."

Cries of defiance went up along with raised fists. As Fatma watched, a group of thirty or more broke from the main crowd. She recognized their leader: the young man she had pushed earlier. He led his group directly in their path, urging on their shouts and profane gestures. She cast a glance back to the police. There was anger on their faces but fear too at understanding they were woefully outnumbered. Things had escalated and now balanced on a knife's edge. The slightest nudge could send them tumbling over. No, this *couldn't* happen. She glanced up to the imposter, whose impossibly aged face now seemed content. She wouldn't *let* this happen! She called out to Aasim, thinking to tell him to pull back—when the nudge arrived, in the form of a shoe.

CHAPTER ELEVEN

Fatma watched the shoe fly—a sandal thrown by unseen hands. It fell at an arc and couldn't cause real injury. But the policeman it struck in the face roared—perhaps more offended than hurt—pushing forward and setting off a chain reaction. Police in the front charged, carried by the momentum of those behind them. When they met the crowd, everything exploded.

Batons lay about backs, arms, and legs. People went down, screaming as they were hit. Some fought. Others ran, police chasing them further into the crowd. The melee spread as new combatants joined the fray. In a flash, they were in a pitched battle.

Fatma dodged a man aiming for her. She jabbed him with the pommel of her cane, forcing him back. Another appeared, this one more agile. Fatma barely missed a fist swung inches from her nose. Then the figure spun and leaped up to smack Aasim flat across the face. He yelped, clutching his cheek, free arm reaching futilely at his attacker, who was already zipping away.

"Was I just slapped by a girl?" he asked, incredulous.

Fatma eyed the lithe figure disappearing into the crowd. It *was* a girl. Couldn't be out of her teens, tall with dark skin. But what stood out were her garments—a bright red kaftan and blue Turkish trousers.

"Forty Leopards!" she shouted in warning. "There are Forty Leopards in the crowd!"

Now that she looked, she could spot the lady thieves dispersed through the mayhem—snatching away batons or taking policemen's legs from under them. Others used slingshots to hurl rocks that knocked men out cold. A few were arranging the disorganized crowd to make strategic hit-and-run attacks along Aasim's officer line.

"Forty Leopards!" he spat, working his jaw. "Why are they even involved?"

Fatma had no idea. But it only made things worse. Another set of attackers charged, separating her from Aasim. She was left with Hamed, and one other agent, working hard to keep the angry crowd at bay. A sudden alarm went off in her head. Where was Hadia? She spun, finding the woman on her right.

"Get away! Find the back ranks and have them escort you out!"

"There are no back ranks!" Hadia retorted.

"You can't stay here! You'll get—"

Fatma's words were cut off as someone pushed her. She went down, looking up to find a large man looming with a stick. He raised it up to bring down on her—when a fist caught his side. The man squealed, dropping the stick and spinning to his attacker. Hadia. A moment of surprise registered on his face, before he lunged. Fatma watched open-mouthed as the woman coolly evaded his reach. Grabbing his arm, she used his momentum to send him flying—crashing back into his companions. He righted himself and came at her again. This time, she swung up a leg, her boot connecting solidly with his chin. His meaty head snapped back, and he crashed in a heap. His friends looked to his unconscious form, before fleeing after easier pickings.

Hadia offered a hand. "I told you. I can handle myself."

Fatma was lifted to her feet. She was seriously beginning to question her judgment of character. Above them, the imposter stared impassively at the chaos. At sight of her his gaze lingered. He had donned the mask again, but she could imagine the twisted smile it hid. The thought filled her with fresh anger. She lifted her cane to him and shouted: "I'm coming for you!" He answered with a perfunctory wave of his hand—and the figure at his side came alive, leaping to the ground below.

Fatma pulled back. Damn! She'd forgotten about that one. As

before, he landed easily on his feet, as if he hadn't just jumped from a height of several stories. Before she could blink—there were two. Hadia gasped. But Fatma had seen this trick and come prepared.

"Hamed!"

He ran up, the other agents in tow. "They don't look so bad."

"Looks can be deceiving," Fatma warned.

Hamed ordered his men into a semicircle. "There's still four of us. And only—" He broke off. An agent cursed. The two figures in black had become four.

"You were saying?" Fatma asked.

His answer came in a set of quick commands. His men flipped the levers on their truncheons. There was a humming whine, and the bulbous heads crackled with electricity. It was a Ministry weapon—carrying a battery that produced a powerful jolt. When your job called for confronting supernatural beings often much stronger than humans, you needed an advantage.

In a blur, the four figures were on Hamed and his men. Their billowy breeches flapped as they threw jabs and kicks. Fatma squinted. They seemed slower than the other night. Not by much, but enough to allow the agents to hold their own. Hamed pressed the fight, taking a glancing blow off a shoulder to strike one in the arm. The jolt should have knocked him unconscious. Instead, he shrieked a high-pitched scream—and his right arm fell off. Fatma blinked. No. *All* their right arms had fallen off, to similar shrieking. She watched as before her eyes, each append-age turned to black ash.

Hamed grinned as the four injured figures slinked back. "Think we found a weak spot. This might go easy after all!"

A ghul! Fatma recalled the black mist from the wound she'd delivered. The man was some kind of ghul. When you cut off a part of the undead, it turned to ash—just like this. But what ghul was this agile? Or could replicate itself? Before she could complete the thought, the ash on the ground stirred. It flew up, attaching at the shoulders of each figure and forming solid regrown arms—down to the black clothing. One of Hamed's men uttered a prayer.

"Keep them busy!" Fatma said. "I'm going after their master!"

Hadia grabbed her arm. "I'm coming with you!"

It was more statement than question. The woman had even gotten hold of a police baton.

The two made their way through the mass. Most people were too occupied to get in their way. The few that did were pushed aside until the agents reached the mausoleum. The only way up was to scale the scaffolding built up along its side. As they climbed, Fatma caught a glimpse of a shadowy form moving up an opposite row of scaffolding. Reaching the top placed them on the narrow walkway of the mausoleum's square base. They ran, turning a corner, and—

The imposter stood with arms behind his back, staring down contemplatively. "Glory be to God," he intoned. "It is an amazing thing, how words can so move men."

Fatma pulled up short, stopping Hadia. "Charlatans have a way of twisting people's heads," she retorted.

The imposter looked up, his gold mask alive with shifting patterns. And those eyes!

"Still an unbeliever. Even after what you have seen."

"When you're in my line of work, tricks aren't so impressive."

"Is that what I am? A trick? Of the eyes? Of the senses?"

"Don't know and don't care. I'm here to arrest you. Let the courts handle the rest."

"Where I would, no doubt, get a fair trial," he mocked. "In these courts of men."

"You murdered more than twenty people. Burned them alive. You expecting a parade?"

"They might give me one." He gestured below. "The people do not judge me so harshly. They understand why I carried out my deed. To save this land from traitors and—"

"Right," Fatma cut in. "Nice conspiracy you've concocted. You're still a murderer!"

"I will be a hero by dawn. My name on a thousand tongues. Do you not hear them now?"

Fatma's jaw tightened. "Your name will be remembered for sowing discord and dissent."

The man cocked his head. "You think I've sown this strife on my own? Look at how people live, in squalor and ruin. The world moves swift in its boasted modernity, forgetting those it leaves behind, or grinds beneath the gearwheels of progress. This is greater than me. The fitna that comes, has been long in the making."

"Fitna?" Hadia asked, perplexed. "Fitna is just a word. A feeling of disorder or unrest, facing difficulties, differences of opinion, learning something that compromises your thinking. What does it have to do with whatever you've concocted here?"

"Ah." The imposter held up a finger. "The great philosopher Ibn al-A'raabi also described fitna as a testing, a trial, to burn with fire. I see it similar to the ways of alchemy. To melt to such a heat as to separate the elements, much as one distinguishes the oppressor from the oppressed. That is what I bring to this city, to expose what ugliness lurks beneath this age of wonders. So that all with eyes and heart may see. And what will be left, once the adulterations and pollutions are cast away, will be clean and pure."

Hadia grasped for words. "You're twisting things around!"

"Or perhaps I am giving them meaning."

"Thought you said you weren't a shaykh," Fatma spat.

The imposter shrugged. "I reveal truth in whatever language is needed."

"Well, save the lectures for your trial. There, you can play the learned philosopher or revolutionary all you want." She lifted her cane, sliding the sword free.

"Is this what I will face? A woman with a sword and another with a police stick?"

"You're forgetting the third one." Fatma relished the confusion in those eyes. Even as she spoke, a form detached from the shadows on the other side of the imposter, catching his attention—a woman garbed in black.

"Hey, Uncle," Siti greeted, waving gloved fingers tipped with silver claws. She sauntered over, leaning against the mausoleum wall. Her eyes—the only features visible on her wrapped face—narrowed. "You're looking good for . . . what? A hundred? Getting in a lot of exercise? Drinking plenty of water?"

The imposter took her in. "The idolater from the other night."

"We have to stop meeting like this. Sekhmet sends her regards."

A gasp from behind said Hadia just figured things out. Fatma had arranged for Siti to be here, but to only get involved if her plan went bad. It had gone bad.

"So are you going to come with us?" Siti asked, extending fingers to nonchalantly eye her claws. "Or do you plan to make things interesting?"

The imposter looked over the three, before reaching his right hand into the air—where a sword suddenly materialized out of nothing. It was long, with a slightly curving blade, and made of a black metal that rendered it almost invisible against the night. A quiet humming emanated from it, like a song.

"I'm going to take that as a no," Siti growled, and ran forward, claws bared.

He raised his sword to meet her attack, and the sound of metal striking metal rang out. The blade released that odd humming as he wielded it with one hand. Where it met claws, sparks flickered like fireflies. Siti slashed in wide punishing arcs, grinning in barely restrained delight. Fatma took that as her cue and rushed in from the other side, hoping to overwhelm the man's unprotected flank. She'd had her blade specially made, with the lion pommel balanced for her weight. It had one sharp edge to inflict cuts that, if not fatal, forced an opponent to surrender—or bleed out. She planted her feet and aimed for a slashing maneuver.

But the man whipped his sword about in a blur, the twists and flicks of his wrist almost imperceptible. He turned aside her thinner blade with ease and flowed back, readying for either of their attacks. They all stopped, assessing. Siti went down to her haunches, balancing on her toes like a cat, dark eyes reflective.

"This sword," the imposter said, almost touching the humming blade to his mask. "It was forged by a djinn. They say when it takes a life, the last thing the dying hear is its song."

"You always this chatty?" Siti asked. "Or is it my perfume?"

"I only wanted you to know. So when you hear singing in your ears, you will know why."

Siti narrowed her eyes and bounded at him, claws first. Fatma moved in to help. But it was hard to fight on the narrow walkway. Each attempt to strike, she was met with a frustrating parry before he returned to dealing with Siti.

Loath as she was to admit it, he was good. Very good. He moved the blade as if it were an extension of his own arm. She couldn't hope to match him, and he knew it. His main concern was Siti, who was relentless. She was forced to back off as the two drove toward her, rounding the corner of the walkway. Hadia kept her distance but followed, baton held ready.

Fatma stayed on the edge of the fight waiting for an opening. The man couldn't keep this up. He must have realized as much, because as they reached the rear of the mausoleum, he unexpectedly hopped onto the honeycomb-patterned merlons lining the walls—then jumped away. She ran to peer over the edge to find he'd landed atop a building below. He stood there, sword raised and expectant.

Siti gave a yell and then, before anyone could stop her, leaped from the mausoleum, landing with a roll and coming up on her feet. Fatma moved to follow, but Hadia caught her arm, shaking her head. "That's impossible!" She was right. Whatever sorcery the imposter held, and whatever strange magic surrounded Siti, she'd break her legs at the attempt—or worse.

They were forced to scale the mausoleum wall to get down, dropping onto a rickety bit of scaffolding. Fatma ran along it, Hadia following close, before jumping across a wide gap to more scaffolding—that shook until she was afraid it might tumble. But the thing held. One more climb down and she could see the building, where the clang of claws meeting steel sounded. Another jump, and she was there. The effort winded her, but she ran straight for the fight, taking up a place at Siti's side.

"Glad you could make it," the woman huffed.

Fatma didn't have breath to waste on words. Together, they pressed the man. His blade still met their attacks, but he gave up ground. Even better, labored breaths now came from behind the gold mask. He'd make a mistake eventually. Tiring fighters often did. She thought she could see it happening, legs almost tripping on themselves, buckling. Siti saw it too and dove to get inside his guard. But suddenly his legs turned sturdy and he balanced low, before his sword inexplicably vanished. A feint! Before Fatma could call a warning the sword rematerialized in the man's other hand just under Siti's exposed side. Thrusting, he sent the blade sliding into her ribs before twisting and pulling it back out. Siti gasped as blood spurted, and crumpled.

Fatma rushed to her as the man backed off to watch at a distance. Siti's breaths came hard, and she clutched at the wound before staring in disbelief at the crimson staining her claws.

"You're out of this fight!" Fatma told her.

The woman's protest came out in a cry of pain.

Hadia ran up, kneeling to look Siti over. "Glory be to God! If you're not spitting up blood, it hopefully missed a lung! But this wound needs stanching!"

"Do it," Fatma said, her eyes on the imposter, who stood watching—waiting.

"You're not trying to take him yourself?" Hadia asked, tearing strips from Siti's garments.

"Something like that," she answered. Her body ached from all the jumping and fighting. But the heat building behind her eyes made it distant. Standing, she peeled to her waistcoat. She hadn't bought her gun, but she had her janbiya—a gift from a foreign dignitary during her first months in the Ministry. Her hand drew the double-edged knife from a silver-worked sheath fitted to a broad leather belt. Balancing it in one hand, she held her sword in the other and stepped forward.

"Just you?" the imposter asked. He flicked droplets of blood from his blade.

"Just me."

They stood staring at each other for a long moment. The gold mask wasn't carved in any expression—just the visage of a man with down-turned mouth. So it was hard to know what he thought as he eyed her, until he spoke.

"That idolater. She means something to you. Interesting."

Fatma felt her anger flare. She was going to fight this man. Not to kill. But to maim, and hurt very badly. Her vengeful thoughts were broken by the clang of sirens. She turned to look into the distance, where lamps announced approaching police wagons. Aasim had gotten word out. Called in the whole force.

"It appears we will have to do this another time," the imposter said. He shouted in a language she couldn't place. Some djinn tongue.

Four figures scrambled hurriedly onto the rooftop. The men in the black masks. They ignored Fatma, walking toward one another, and it seemed she only blinked before there was just one. He stood in front of the imposter, staring through her and then quite suddenly exploded into billowing black ash, skin and flesh, clothing and all—becoming particles that swirled about in a swarm. The imposter spread his fingers wide, and the cloud drew into his open palm until it was gone. He lowered the hand and stared with eyes that burned anew.

"The great and celebrated Ministry. You think yourselves so grand. With your secrets and petty magics. Do you even understand what you are dealing with?"

There was a blast of wind—hot and fetid, with a burning stench. It washed over Fatma with such force she thought she might choke, and she covered her mouth, gasping.

"I will teach you," the imposter said. "I will make you hurt. I will make you understand. And drag your secrets into the light."

Without warning, the world behind him erupted into flames.

To Fatma, it looked at first like a wall of bloodred fire. But what she'd mistaken for a wall soon coalesced into another shape: a body like a man formed from an inferno, with a head crowned in curving horns and bright molten eyes. The being stood behind the imposter, a giant thrice his size that burned in the night like a beacon. She didn't have to look down to know that the melee below had gone still, as every gaze locked on this wondrous and terrible sight.

An Ifrit.

The djinn roared, causing the very air to ripple in a haze. It bowed down to reveal something tied across its back—a leather harness that somehow didn't burn, with long encircling straps. The imposter climbed and settled into it, the licking flames not touching him. Pulling on reins looped around the Ifrit's horns, he stared down at Fatma.

"All of Cairo will speak of what they see here tonight. All of Cairo will know that I am al-Jahiz. And I have returned."

He spoke another command in that tongue, and great wings of fire sprouted from the Ifrit's back. It lifted into the air, the hot wind from its flapping bearing down on Fatma, sending her to her knees. From there she stared up, shielding her eyes and watching the fiery djinn soar through the sky, streaking away like a blazing star, and carrying its rider with it.

CHAPTER TWELVE

Fatma wanted to hit something. To say that the past two and a half days had been terrible didn't do justice to the meaning of "terrible." The fallout from Sunday night—"fallout" was another understated word—seemed to arrive by the day.

She'd spent Monday morning in a meetings with Amir, Ministry brass, and representatives from the bureaucracy administering Cairo's many districts—all demanding reports on what the papers were already calling the Battle of el-Arafa. Scores arrested or hurt. Rights activists charging police heavy-handedness. The police union charging they'd been sent in unprepared. Threats of lawsuits and counter lawsuits. She'd been grilled for hours, then forced to spend more time filing paperwork. In triplicate.

Monday evening was worse. The newspapers officially ended all embargo on the Lord Worthington story, revealing everything they knew about his death and the Brotherhood of Al-Jahiz. That turned out to be facts mixed with half-truths. The more sensational penny presses spread salacious stories of indecency, indicting politicians and even insinuating Egypt's monarchy as coconspirators. The papers had gotten hold of the guest list from that night, publishing every victim's name—including the two Egyptian dead outed as idolaters.

That paled to the buzz on al-Jahiz, which left el-Arafa and hit every street corner and gossip mill by morning. Fatma had gotten an earful from her bewab. Al-Jahiz had returned! Had she heard the news? Had she been at the Cemetery? Had al-Jahiz truly called down lightning upon the police? Did he and the head of the Forty Leopards really duel atop a mausoleum? She got the same on her way to work. From her shoe shiner to chattering on the trolley. Al-Jahiz—the imposter—was on everyone's lips.

Then there were the sightings. Scores of witnesses had seen the man ride off on the back of an Ifrit. She was still trying to process that memory in her own head. More outside the Cemetery had seen a fiery *something* flying across Cairo's skyline. Now fresh reports were flooding the Ministry and police, of reputed sightings. Al-Jahiz was flying over Bulaq in a chariot pulled by djinn. No, he had been seen over Old Cairo on a rukh. Others claimed he walked the back alleys of the Khan. And he'd reopened secret schools, performing wonders. The words *Al-Jahiz Has Returned* covered whole walls—alongside claims of the government and monarchy in league with some foreign cabal to reduce the country to a colony. Each time cleaners scoured them away, they reappeared elsewhere. She doubted most believed such fanciful tales. But people whispered about these odd events all the same. Many feared they could only portend some great misfortune or calamity, and there was real concern hysteria might grip the city.

Do you even understand what you are dealing with?

Fatma's mood darkened as she walked the block to the Ministry. Other than chasing phantom sightings, she had no good leads. They knew now who had killed Lord Worthington. But not much else. Was this imposter just some fanatic? Or was this all a ruse for something bigger? And what kind of sorcery made him master over an Ifrit—riding one of the most powerful and volatile of djinn like some tamed hound! *I will make you hurt. I will make you understand. And drag your secrets into the light.*

The one saving grace was that despite everything, she'd been kept on the case. Amir argued to brass and the city's administrators that she was still the best hope to solve this. They'd agreed. What choice did they really have? Next week was the peace summit at the king's palace. There were going to be foreign rulers, dignitaries, and ambassadors in the city. The intent was to project a modern Cairo that could be a broker in world affairs—not a city caught up in fear and hysteria. They wanted this thing out of the papers as soon as possible.

"A moment of your time, agent," someone called.

Fatma stopped mid-stride, turning to settle on a figure in dark brown robes with frayed ends, his head hidden in a cowl. He stood beneath the awning of a gramophone shop, blending into the shadows. She took him at first for a beggar and fished into her pockets—until he lifted his head. She walked up to grab him by the arm, dragging him to a nearby alley.

"Ahmad! What are you doing here?"

The man pulled from her grip, letting out a stream of cigarette smoke. When he looked directly at her, she almost stepped back. His face had changed further since she'd last seen him. His gray skin looked rougher, with dark splotches—though the front of his neck was pale and smooth, almost rubbery. His nose had vanished completely, replaced with nostril slits on a protrusion that reminded her of a snout. Both his eyes were still green, but his pupils were strange—as if they were elongating.

"I wanted to know," he rasped, "how you were getting on with the case."

Who didn't? Fatma wanted to tell the man to pick a number and get in line. But somewhere in those inhuman eyes was a sadness. And she remembered he was here out of love. How did you begrudge someone that? "We have a suspect. The same one you led us to."

"This claimed al-Jahiz." He gripped the cigarette between pointed teeth as he spoke. "I've seen the . . . trouble you've had since our first encounter."

That was one way to put it. "We're doing what we can, but we still haven't got a motive."

He shrugged, flicking the scarab lighter and moving to his second Nefertari. "It matters?"

"Aywa. When twenty-four people are burned to death, it matters."

Ahmad grunted. "What the papers are saying about Nephthys. How they are painting her." Anger trembled his voice.

Fatma could understand. The penny presses had gone overboard, doing extensive write-ups of Ester Sedarous. They hounded her family, called her a witch, some even implying she had something to do with the murders. One tabloid named her "the Madame of Death."

"Her parents buried her yesterday," Ahmad continued. "I was told not to attend."

"I'm sorry. How are your people? I know things have gotten . . . bad."

The outing of the temples was another casualty. People who had practiced in secret now found their names splashed across the front of dailies. There were threats against establishments or meeting places suspected to house them. In the worst ugliness, a reputed "idolater" had been chased from his home by angry neighbors. *Seeing someone else's problems makes your own problems seem smaller*, her mother's voice intoned.

"The House of Sobek is strong," Ahmad declared. Then, more measured: "How is Siti?"

"She's well." Fatma was still surprised even as she said it. Siti had refused to be taken to the hospital—insisting that she depended only on the blessings of the entombed goddess. Whether by a goddess or some other magic, a day later there was nothing but a scar where she'd been run through. She spent her time at Merira's now, watching over the fortune-teller's shop.

"I can be of help," Ahmad said, taking a drag. "I'm not Siti, but I have contacts."

Fatma shook her head. "This man, whoever he is, he's dangerous. He can do things that I can't explain. You or your people get in his way, and you could be killed. There are enough dead to deal with. Let the Ministry and the police handle it."

Ahmad appeared skeptical. "The police's hands appear full at the moment."

He was talking about the protests. Most of those arrested in el-Arafa were just locals who'd gotten overzealous. People didn't like police running about their homes. One had been a prize, however. The alleged Bearer of Witness who'd introduced the imposter. His name was Moustafa. He'd actually been in the employ of one of the members of Lord Worthington's Brotherhood—a Wesley Dalton, who, from what they'd discerned, was none other than the corpse with its head twisted about. This Moustafa had worked odd jobs for Dalton—a mix of a manservant, bodyguard, and guide. He'd also been a witness to the murders. Told them as much openly—that al-Jahiz appeared and slew the Englishmen. It had impressed him enough to become an acolyte. Claimed al-Jahiz spared him to go out and bear witness to what he'd seen. Since Monday, crowds gathered every morning outside the police station, demanding his release. She shook her head. What a mess.

"We've got enough hands. Let it alone, Ahmad. I mean it. And stop skulking about!"

"It's creepy?" he asked, a cigarette perched on his lips.

"Yeah. A little bit. Creepy." She took in his strange face again. "Are you okay?"

"Never felt better. Go in peace, Agent Fatma."

"Go in peace, Ahmad," she said, watching him disappear down the alley—a cloud of smoke hovering. It was telling that he was probably the least strange thing she'd deal with today.

Fatma quickened her pace, reaching the Ministry. She made her usual glance up to the spinning mechanical gears of the building's brain and tipped her bowler in a silent good morning. She gave another to the guard on duty, in that too-big uniform. He *really* could use a tailor. An empty elevator was already waiting, and she hopped in ready to call out the fourth floor—but hesitated. She still felt like hitting something. To clear her head. She knew just the remedy.

"Top floor." The elevator closed, taking a lurch before ascending.

Fatma began undoing the buttons on her jacket. By the time the elevator stopped, she was down to a black silk waistcoat stitched with Persian buta motifs. Stepping out, she loosened her tie along the way until coming to a set of doors.

The Ministry had its own gymnasium. But that was for men. She'd petitioned to get in when first arriving. But while brass wanted to boast of hiring its first woman agent in the Cairo office, they didn't want a full-blown scandal. So they'd built an entirely separate gymnasium for women. It was smaller and not as well equipped. But it had the basic needs and amenities, including a bath. Best of all, she mostly had it to herself.

At least, she usually did.

There was surprise at opening the door to Hadia. She wore a white shirt with bulky, loose-fitting gym trousers. In a gloved hand she wielded a wooden practice sword, swinging it at a mechanical training eunuch. The machine-man only had a torso that extended from a pole in the floor. But it twisted its body this way and that, to wield a wooden blade held in one arm.

At seeing Fatma, Hadia straightened, calling the training eunuch to a stop. She tucked a stray curly strand back into her hijab. "Good morning, Agent Fatma."

"Agent Hadia," she returned, stepping inside. Since Sunday night, they'd been formal in their interactions. And the woman seemed sullen. "Didn't know you were in here."

"Just came to practice. I'll bathe and leave the room to you."

"You don't have to go. Room's big enough for both of us."

"Yes, well, you'd think so. But I wouldn't want to get in your way."

Oh yes, definitely sullen. "I think you should stay. I could do with a sparring partner. Unless a training eunuch is more your style."

That last part came out a bit mocking, and Hadia's eyes narrowed before she nodded.

Fatma wasted little time donning gym clothes from a closet. She was overly eager for this. Grabbing a practice sword, she walked to the center of the room.

"How are we going to keep score?" Hadia asked. She flowed

into position, her wooden blade held out as she balanced on her feet.

Fatma did the same. "We stop when we're tired of hitting each other."

Hadia's reply was a quick set of attacks, her taller body lunging forward. Fatma's own sword darted up, and the strikes came as light batting to the middle of the blade—as if testing. Hadia changed angles, this time aiming low. Fatma met them again, stepping to the side as she knocked them away without allowing an opening. The two paused their attacks, continuing to circle.

"Where'd you learn to fight? Another cousin?"

"Father, actually," Hadia answered, blade up and making small lazy loops. "He got beat up a lot as a kid. Turned soldier, learned how to fight, and came back to teach his bullies a lesson. He insisted his five daughters would never be intimidated. You?"

"My father's a watchmaker. But when I was small he'd take me to Tahtib matches. Back then no one was going to train a girl to stick fight, though. Had to teach myself."

"Hmm. Probably explains why you like to go it alone."

Fatma frowned. She was getting psychoanalyzed now? She initiated the advance this time, with swinging strokes that rapped hard on her opponent's blade. Hadia gave ground, but quickly rebounded, blocking Fatma's attacks with sharp striking motions. This went on for a while, and when they disengaged again, both were breathing heavy.

"You give away your feint too easily," Hadia huffed.

"What?"

"Your feints. You squint." She imitated the action. "It's an easy tell on when you're not going to follow through on an attack. A bad habit. I used to bite my lip. Had to break it. But it's hard, when you're stubborn."

Fatma's jaw tensed. "You have something to say, agent?"

Hadia's face went flat in return. "Permission to speak freely?"

"This look like the army to you? Say what you have to say."

Words spilled out: "Do you know how embarrassing it was to

learn you made up a rule to keep me away Sunday night? That I had to confront you about it in front of other agents?"

So that's what this was about? "I told you, I was trying to protect you."

"I don't need protecting!" Hadia shot back. "I can—"

"—handle yourself," Fatma finished. "I've seen. How was I supposed to know you were some kind of . . . ninja?"

"You could have asked! You could have let me be your partner, instead of replacing me with the first great big man you could find." She made a frustrated sound, dropping her sword to her side. "I was the only woman at the academy. You, of all people, know what that's like. Other than Onsi, most of my class barely interacted with me—as if just being courteous was somehow eib, or worse, haram. The unsolicited lectures from male teachers on the dangers of women in the workplace were my favorite—as if their own grandmothers weren't probably selling goods out at market or helping with the farming. I expected when I got assigned, I'd have to deal with people who didn't think I could measure up. Who thought I was in the wrong place. Who only saw some *girl* they'd stick behind a desk. But, wallahi, I didn't think one of them would be you!"

Fatma flinched. That stung. Her own sword fell. "I'm not used to doing this with others."

"You seem fine working with tall Nubian women with claws," Hadia remarked.

"That's different. Siti's . . . she's just different."

"Not some sheltered hijabi, you mean? Concerned with etiquette and propriety? Who frets at missing salah? Who you think is too delicate to deal with the harder parts of this job? So what, you just put me up on a shelf?"

Fatma felt her cheeks heat.

Hadia made a face, like someone who knew the answer to the question they asked—but hoped to hear different. "I thought so." She stood erect suddenly, shoulders forward. "But too bad for you. I trained to be an agent of the Ministry, knowing all the danger it might bring. I made it through the academy and graduated at the top of my class, because I'm *incredible*, because I earned the right to be here, because there is no end to God's Barakah upon me. So you're going to have to deal with the fact that I'm your partner. That you're not doing this alone any more. That I'm here to watch your back. When you're ready to get on board with that, you let me know!"

Fatma stood quiet, meeting Hadia's large dark brown eyes. They practically quivered, and her beige cheeks were flushed. "That was bold. You practice that?"

The other woman swallowed. "Maybe. A few times. In a mirror."

Fatma snorted, unable to hide the laugh. Hadia's mask faltered, and she laughed as well.

"You're right," Fatma admitted. "I'm sorry. I hated it when agents did that to me when I first got here. So I went out of my way and took all kinds of risks to prove them wrong."

"I've heard about them," Hadia said. "They sound pretty brave."

"No, lots of times they were just stupid. Nearly got myself killed. Wouldn't have needed to do any of that if people just treated me as an equal. You shouldn't have to relearn my mistakes." Her tone turned serious. "But I'm going to need you to trust me. I've been doing this longer than you. Sometimes, I'm making the call that'll get you home at night. Even if you think it's the wrong one. You have a problem with my decisions, you take it up with me after. Don't sneak behind my back just because you think you're right."

It was Hadia's turn to flinch. She nodded, lifting her blade. "Still want to hit each other?"

"Not until I work on my squinting. Ever thought of carrying a sword? Maybe a cane?"

"That's more . . . your look. Goes with the suits."

"You know, you've never asked me about that. My suits."

"Should I? You've never asked about my stunningly modern hijab."

Fatma smirked, enjoying the brief reprieve. "We'd better get on to work. There's probably already a stack for us to go through."

"Another day hunting down sightings of al-Jahiz," Hadia sighed. "I'm beginning to suspect that brass and the city administrators just want to keep things quiet until the king's peace summit. They're thinking if we don't go disturbing the wasp's nest, maybe it'll stay hidden."

"You're not so wrong."

"Wouldn't mind a turn with that ash-ghul, though."

Fatma arched an eyebrow. "Ash-ghul?"

"It's what I'm going with. Can't we go talk to that Moustafa again?"

"For him to go on for about the tenth time about the wonders of al-Jahiz? I don't think he has any real connection to the imposter. He's just being used."

"This imposter," Hadia said. "He's good at that. Using people. What he was saying Sunday night, about how things are. He wasn't lying. He was just twisting it, picking at all our raw places. He knew how to turn that crowd against us, and how we'd react."

Fatma shared the concern. Whoever this imposter was, he'd studied this city. As well as he'd studied al-Jahiz. He wasn't going to just go away like brass and the administrators hoped. He had a plan. And they needed to figure it out.

A knock came at the door. Fatma moved to open it, finding of all things a courier eunuch. It did its usual greetings and verification, handing her a message before running off. Didn't anyone just make phone calls anymore? She opened the note, surprised to find it printed in English.

"It's an invitation," she read. "From Alexander Worthington. He's agreed to an interview. I think we just got a chance to find some real clues."

CHAPTER
THIRTEEN

They reached the Worthington estate by mid-morning. The sprawling mansion was more arresting by day as the automated carriage pulled up along the driving path. Several cars were already parked, with well-dressed drivers who lolled about—men accustomed to long waits between jobs.

"We should have talked to him a week ago," Hadia grumbled, following Fatma out.

"Worthington name has its advantages."

"Wonder why he decided to meet with us?"

"Can't say. But the invitation is just for us—not the police. Talking to Aasim makes it look like there's some criminal mischief. Talking to us—"

"—just makes it look a bit spooky," Hadia finished.

Fatma eyed her sideways. Siti was such a bad influence.

When they knocked on the door, they were greeted by a man with the bearing of someone who worked for the wealthy. The day steward, it turned out. They were ushered across the large parlor, passing through a bulbous pointed archway.

"This place looks like something from stories I used to read," Hadia whispered, eyeing the patterned rugs and mashrabiya latticework. "With spoiled princes and enchanted storks."

"Might get to meet at least one of those."

The day steward stopped at the library doors, bidding them enter. There were no windows, and a hanging gas lamp lit up the room. But what made Fatma blink were the people.

The stocky man with golden hair, she recalled, was Victor; the dark-haired one, Percival. They wore full-length black kaftans with red tarbooshes. Seated on the modish moss-green divan were three women, each dressed in a black sebleh and wrapped in a milaya lef. Their faces were hidden behind matching bur'a, though their heads were strangely uncovered.

"Agent Fatma," one called in a familiar voice. Abigail Worthington. The red hair should have been a giveaway, and her still-bandaged left hand. She held an open book in her right—titled in English *Mysterious Tales of the Djinn and Orient*. One page bore a scantily clad veiled woman, arms up in distress at a menacing djinn with fire emanating from his mouth.

"Aass-a-lamoo Ah-lake-um!" she greeted.

Fatma winced. How did anyone speak Arabic that badly? "And unto you peace," she replied, in English. "Abigail, this is Agent Hadia. My partner at the Ministry."

Abigail's blue-green eyes widened above the bur'a. "Partner? How splendid! Good morning to you, Agent Hadia. As I've told Agent Fatma, simply Abbie is fine."

"Good morning, Abbie," Hadia replied.

"Oh! Your English is as remarkable as Agent Fatma's! Is that accent . . . American?"

"I spent some time there."

Abigail let out an astonished breath. "Another woman at your Ministry. And well traveled! I was just relating with Bethany and Darlene how advanced your country has become for women—practically leaving us English behind! We're all *féministes*, you know. Hardly Pankhursts by any means. But we are fellow travelers in the sisterhood."

Bethany and Darlene, Fatma recalled, putting names to the brown-haired women flanking Abigail. The Edginton sisters. Their hazel eyes carried that same appraising measure, like cats sizing up a rival.

Victor guffawed. He was drinking again, sipping from a crystal glass. "Give women the vote in England, and soon they'll have us in the dresses and them in the suits." He gestured a meaty hand to his gallabiyah and then to Fatma's attire, before flashing a toothy smile. "No offense meant. Just a bit of English humor."

"Poor humor," Percival murmured, burying his moustache in his own drink.

Abigail's eyes fixed sharp on Victor, and the man turned crimson, downing his glass hurriedly and going into a coughing fit.

"I'm sorry," Abigail apologized. "Victor inherited the famed Fitzroy tongue. Whole family is forever tripping after their own words. You might recall the more refined Percival Montgomery. Percival, be a dear and help poor Victor. He might choke to death the way he's going on." The smaller man sighed, delivering hard slaps to his friend's back. "Victor's just sour because he's not used to the garment."

Fatma couldn't resist the question. "Is there a reason for your . . . garments?"

Abigail blinked. "I thought it obvious. We're in mourning. My father's funeral was yesterday. He was so in love with your land, we wanted to honor him by taking on native dress. We've even adopted mourning veils."

"Mourning veils?" Hadia asked.

Abigail pulled down the bur'a, confused. "Isn't that what they're for?"

"You mean we don't have to wear these?" Darlene Edginton asked, ripping hers off.

"Thank God!" her sister followed. "How do you even breathe?"

Hadia stared open-mouthed. Fatma headed things off with a question. "We've come at the invitation of your brother?"

Abigail nodded. "Alexander's upstairs. I'll take you." She stood, wrapping the milaya lef awkwardly over one arm before turning to her friends. "Go easy on the scotch. We've a long day ahead."

She led them from the library and down the hall. As they walked, a faint clanging came to Fatma's ears, conjuring images of a hammer striking metal. She remembered hearing it on her last visit. She'd thought her mind was playing tricks, but it was clearer now. Then it was gone. Maybe there were workers on the premises?

"Have you read this book, Agent Fatma?" Abigail asked. She held up the text she still carried. "It's written by one of England's foremost Orientalists. With stories of djinn and magic and the like. Quite informative!"

Fatma glanced to the book, remembering its sensational content. It looked like utter nonsense. Most of these "Orientalists" thought their bad translations and wrongheaded takes might help them better understand the changes sweeping the world. It seemed reading from *actual* Eastern scholars was beneath them.

"From what I've heard," Abigail went on, her tone darkening, "that dreadful man in the gold mask I encountered has been causing mischief all through Cairo. There was a riot of some sort? And he's calling himself after that Soudanese fellow."

"Al-Jahiz," Fatma affirmed as they began climbing the absurdly long set of stairs. "Is your hand better?"

Abigail flinched at mention of her bandaged appendage. "The doctors say I've sprained it with my clumsiness. May take weeks to heal." Her tone shifted. "The papers claim this man killed my father. And all those poor people."

"He's confessed to it," Fatma confirmed.

Abigail stopped, leaning against the railing and swaying as if she might faint. She caught herself, shaking her head at their concerns. When she spoke again, her voice was strained. "Why would he do this? What did my father do to him?"

"We don't know," Fatma answered truthfully. "We're hoping your brother might be able to help." She paused before making her next statement. "You told us your brother was overseas, the night of your father's murder. But he was here in Cairo."

Abigail's blue-green eyes glazed in confusion. "Alexander arrived the *next* day. True enough, he was already en route to Cairo, unbeknownst to me. But he wasn't here. Not that night. I'm afraid you're mistaken."

Fatma searched her face. "Perhaps we are. Thank you." They resumed their walk, and Hadia shared a critical glance. So much for needling a different story from the woman.

"This man in the gold mask," Abigail said shakily. "Do you think he might return here? To come after my brother and me?"

"It's possible," Fatma conceded. "We don't know his motive. If you'd like, we can see about having the Giza police provide a guard for your estate."

"Yes. That's a splendid idea. I'll bring it up to Alexander."

She fell into idle chatter, pointing out the ornamentations of the house. It turned out the estate had been the hunting lodge of the old basha, sold to Alistair Worthington back in 1898.

"That's around the same time the Brotherhood of Al-Jahiz was founded," Hadia noted.

"Four years after my mother passed away," Abigail replied. "I was seven when she died. Alexander was ten and remembers things better than me. He says it was her death that drew my father's interest in al-Jahiz. Father believed that had England taken the mystic arts more seriously, my mother could have been saved from the consumption that claimed her. He bought this lodge and had it refashioned toward that goal. He liked the view." She gestured with her book to a window, where the pyramids loomed.

"Is that where he got the design for his brotherhood?" Fatma asked. "The six-pointed star. Two interlocking pyramids." She sketched the symbol with her fingers.

"Clever of you to notice. He claimed it came to him in a vision. That it held some great meaning that evaded him. Together we would stare at it, hoping to puzzle it out."

"But you weren't a member of his organization?"

Abigail let out a light laugh. "Heavens no. My father didn't take the term 'Brotherhood' lightly. He might talk to his daughter of his explorations while thumbing through old books. But the Brotherhood was for men. Though in the end, I understand he allowed a native woman to take part. My brother fears his mind was slipping."

"Your brother, however, was a member," Hadia said.

"At Father's insistence." There was an awkward pause. "Alexander and Father didn't see eye to eye on such things. After acquiring the estate Father w ɔ often here in Egypt—half the year at times. Alexander went off to boarding school at a military academy. I was left with nursemaids and tutors back in England. But Father started sending for me to spend time with him as he built his brotherhood and hunted after relics. When he moved here permanently, I stayed a year or two off and on. He confided in me about his quest, as if I were Mother. I even helped read through his strange books and manuscripts. It's why I'm so well acquainted with the native culture."

Not acquainted enough, Fatma thought. She held her tongue, though she wasn't certain how many more times she could stomach the word "native." They reached the top of the stairs, turning left.

"I'm afraid it wasn't the same for poor Alexander," Abigail continued. "He only visited infrequently. Egypt's still all a foreign place to him. And he never took to Father's society. I'm sure he only joined to receive his inheritance. But look at me going on about my brother's business. I'm certain he can speak for himself."

She led them to the place Fatma had visited previously—the ritual room of the Brotherhood of Al-Jahiz. The wood doors that hung off their hinges had been removed altogether, leaving an open stone archway. The smell of burning flesh was scrubbed away, replaced with the lingering fumes of disinfectant. With its rounded water-blue walls of flowering gold and green patterns, rows of curving arches, and honeycombed muqarnas, the space exuded tranquility—belying the horrors of a few nights past. Perhaps the only reminder was the white banner at the room's rear: star, crescent, sword, and fiery serpent. Beneath, at a black half-moon table with one high-backed chair like a king's throne, sat a solitary figure. Unlike the men downstairs, he wore a black suit with a white starched collar. He bowed his head, scribbling on a sheet, and only looked up when they'd come to stand right before him.

Alexander Worthington wasn't precisely what Fatma had expected. She thought to find someone with the common Edwardian look: a trimmed moustache and a clean-cut visage. This man had long pale gold hair that fell to his shoulders. And a beard—just short of unruly. With his pointed nose and angular features, she imagined he favored a younger Lord Worthington. When his sister moved to stand beside him the resemblance was unmistakable.

"Alexander, these are the agents from the Ministry you requested to speak with," Abigail introduced with a smile. "Agent Fatma and Agent Hadia."

Alexander's blue eyes roamed slowly to his sister. He removed a brown cigar held between his lips, resting it in an ashtray fashioned like a turbaned figure holding a dish. "That *you* requested I speak with," he remarked in refined English.

Abigail flushed. "And you agreed it was a good idea. Please, Alexander, don't be rude."

Her brother sighed, before turning to a large book on the table—bound in brown leather and with yellow parchment. He tucked in his pen as a marker, then closed it, before looking up. His eyebrows rose as if only truly noticing the two women for the first time. He didn't get up, though Fatma estimated he'd be considered tall. She filed that observation away.

"You two are from what ministry, exactly?"

Fatma showed her badge. "Alchemy, Enchantments, and Supernatural Entities."

His lips pursed into a smirk. "I'd expect this country to have such a thing. And run by women no less. How can I be of assistance to you?"

Fatma kept her smile as slight as possible. "We'd like to talk about your father's death."

His blue eyes turned hard. "Have you come to tell me you've arrested the murderer?"

"Not yet."

"Then I'm uncertain what we have to talk about. Your papers

say he's running about your city with reckless abandon. Some Mohammedan fanatic astounding the crowds with tricks? I'd think you'd be out there hunting him down, not taking up my time."

Fatma compressed her lips. It turned out that Alexander Worthington, despite his looks, was precisely what she had expected after all. Hadia stepped into the breach.

"We know you've just buried your father and are still in mourning. We don't mean to take up your time. But any information you can offer would be helpful."

Alexander studied her appraisingly. "Your English. It's almost American."

"Agent Hadia spent time in the States," Abigail added. She had taken to standing behind the table, holding her book close.

"I've visited the States," Alexander said. "A country still in need of taming, particularly in the west, where the native tribes are again giving trouble. But the Americans, I believe, have the right idea of how to succeed in this age, with these untoward occurrences that have led to so many uprisings. England would be wise to follow, if she's ever to regain her footing. Chasing after primitivism will do us no good."

"Alexander has been serving with the colonial armies in the East Indies," Abigail put in. "Commanding a whole regiment! He's even been made an officer! Can you believe such a thing? Going around with a rifle and sword!" she added with a self-deprecating laugh. "I've taken up a bit of fencing myself."

"A *captain*." Her brother folded his arms self-importantly. "I wouldn't compare the delicacy of a lady's fencing with our work in India—trying to aid Britain in holding on to what's left of her raj."

Which wasn't much, Fatma recalled. India had its own djinn, and even older magic that was said to flow with the Ganges itself. Open rebellion had reduced the British to just a few garrisoned cities—all that was left of the onetime jewel of an empire. Score one for "primitivism."

"Alexander's made quite a few daring exploits," his sister

fawned. "And with his long hair and beard, come back to us something of a nabob!"

Her brother scoffed, but puffed out his chest, stroking the pale gold hair on his chin. "I studied the natives of India. Hunted tigers at their side. Their ways are backward, certainly, but something of the long hair carries a wild nobility I imagine was held in my own English forebears. Therefore, I believe you mistaken, sister. I've gone more Saxon than nabob." He turned to address Fatma. "So then, what is it the two of you want to know?"

"The man in the gold mask," she said. "He's admitted to your father's murder. He's also an imposter who claims to be al-Jahiz. We believe there's a connection."

"Because of my father's . . . peculiar habits."

"Anything you might tell us about the Brotherhood of Al-Jahiz?"

Alexander rubbed his temples with his hand. "My sister has probably told you of my father's fanaticism with that Soudanese magician. Our mother's death broke his mind. His little order spent a great deal of money, time, and effort seeking 'the wisdom of the ancients.'" The last came with biting sarcasm.

"Doesn't sound like you believed in your father's mission," Hadia assessed.

"I'm not a man of superstition. I understand that sorcery and cavorting with unnatural creatures is germane to the Oriental cultures. But rationality is the only means to true progress. In the West, we look forward. My father, on the other hand, was seduced by these backward-looking notions of the East." He held up a placating hand. "No offense to you and yours, of course."

"None taken," Fatma replied evenly. "But you were a member of his 'little order.'"

Alexander's face went taut as he played with a band of silver on his pinkie finger. Fatma recognized it right away—the signet ring bearing the Worthington seal, last worn by his father.

"I was a boy of ten when my mother died. I watched my father slowly descend into his madness. All along, I played the part of a dutiful son. Went off to school. Served for crown and country, became learned in the ways of business, and everything necessary to take control of the Worthington name. But for my father that wasn't enough. He insisted I join in his delusions, making me promise to dedicate myself to finding the secrets of the heavens and the like."

He took a stilling breath, as if trying to hold back his anger.

"So I submitted to his request. Then I got as far away from him and his madness as I could. I ended up in India, because in England I was tired of hearing whispers of the crazed Alistair Worthington. The men he kept about him called him 'the old man.' My father found it endearing; I think they believed he'd gone senile. Now I return to find him murdered. I buried him yesterday, and I couldn't even look into his face, because there was nothing but charred remains. So yes, I was a member of his brotherhood. But I never did more beyond stating so for his benefit. Because I knew it would one day be his ruin."

Beside him, Abigail Worthington wept silently, clutching her book and using the bur'a to wipe her tears. Her brother looked to her, his voice not rising but cold. "Now you cry. Did you shed tears when he was making a mockery of our family name back home? Or spending our money on his meaningless ventures and building this ridiculous place"—he gestured about the room—"that would only serve as his tomb?" His sister cried harder, and he sighed lengthily.

"My sister is given to tears, but I can't spare them. Do you see this?" He placed a hand atop the book on the desk. "A ledger of my father's businesses in the past sixteen months. I've been trying to make sense of bizarre transactions he or his hangers-on were making with the company—selling off some industries, investing recklessly in others, large sums of money simply gone. An entire shipment of Worthington steel—enough to construct a building—vanished! I came up here, hoping that in his treasured sanctum I might find some enlightenment. You see, I'm left to get my family's affairs in order—while my sister spends time playing dress-up with that lot of sycophants downstairs."

"They are my friends." She tried to sound firm, but it only came out as a petulant sob.

"They're your friends as long as you fly them to Egypt and put them up in fancy villas about the city." He shook his head. "Fitzroys, Montgomerys, Edgintons. All *recent* money. They latch onto my sister and the Worthington name. More hangers-on at the trough. I swear, you're as bad as Father."

Fatma coughed. She wasn't here for a family squabble. "Is there anything else you can tell us about your father's brotherhood?"

Alexander gave her a flat look. "That they're all dead."

"What about enemies? Someone who might want to do it harm?"

"A Mohammedan who took my father too seriously, it seems. Are we finished here?"

"Almost." Fatma met his irritated glare. "We're trying to clear up some discrepancy on your arrival into Cairo. You say you got here the day after your father's murder."

"That's seems apparent."

"We've heard claims you were here that night."

"Whoever told you so is obviously wrong."

"So you're saying you weren't here that night? You weren't the one who asked the newspapers to quiet news of your father's murder?"

This made him frown. "What? Where did you hear such a thing?"

"I'm sorry," Fatma told him. "I can't speak on an ongoing case."

They stared at each other for a moment before he threw up his hands. "I can assure you I arrived in the city when I said I did. Check my travel documents if you'd like."

"And why did you come back?" Fatma pressed. "Right now? All the way from India?"

He frowned. "If you must pry into my personal business, I received a letter from my father requesting my presence. He didn't write often. So I obliged his request."

"The dutiful son. Are you the new Lord Worthington now?"

He gave a wry expression. "My father was the third son of a duke, hence a lord. The title he takes with him to the grave. All I'm left with is the Worthington name, which I must now rehabilitate."

"You could be the English Bey—the son of a basha," Hadia put in, her tone sarcastic.

"I think I've had enough of Oriental decadence," he replied flatly.

Fatma thought she'd had enough of him. "Are you going to stay in Cairo?"

"Only as long as it takes to put my father's business in order and sell this monstrosity of an estate. He loved this country so much he insisted on being buried in it—like the great conqueror Alexander of old, his will claimed. Well, not *this* Alexander. *I* plan on returning to England. My sister will be coming with me. Where she can find better uses of her time than frivolities with her so-called friends." Abigail looked as if she wanted to protest but swallowed the words.

"And your father's collection of relics?"

"Worthless heirlooms," he answered sourly. "Before I sell the estate, I'm going to have this room demolished. They can go with it. When I return to England, I want all memory of this brotherhood business put behind us. Anything more, agent? Perhaps you could spare some time to find out which local has pilfered an entire steel shipment? Maybe one of your Forty Leopard hooligans. I hear they've fallen in with this crazed Mohammedan."

"I'll pass it on to the police," Fatma replied. She tapped the tip of her bowler. "Thank you for your help. We'll get back to you should we have more questions."

He gave a weary wave of acknowledgment, bowing his head and reopening the ledger—not even watching them go. Abigail led them out and downstairs in silence back to the parlor. When they'd arrived, she turned to them apologetically.

"I know my brother probably wasn't very helpful. But I so do want to help you find my father's murderer." She opened up her book and, to their surprise, pulled out another book. Thin and bound in black leather, it was small enough to fit in one's palm. Fatma accepted it, opening to the first page. Handwritten words in English read: *The Vizier's Account*.

"It's a notation book of some sort," Abigail explained. "I found it here in the house. It belonged to a man who worked close with my father—Archibald Portendorf. If you want to know more about the Brotherhood of Al-Jahiz, perhaps it might be useful?"

◆   ◆   ◆

"April 14, 1904. Procured for TOM, one scrap of tunic claimed to have belonged to al-Jahiz, £2,900," Hadia read aloud as they rode the automated carriage back to Cairo. Her fingers flipped to another part of the journal. "December 1906. Procured for TOM, pages reputed to have come from a Koran touched by al-Jahiz, £5,600." She turned the small book about, displaying its contents. "I don't think Alexander Worthington was exaggerating about his father's spending. There's years of information in here."

Sitting opposite, Fatma scanned the page. Handwritten English script wasn't her forte. Some things she could make out, but it was slow going. Luckily Hadia seemed at ease with it. She remembered the name Archibald Portendorf listed among the murdered members of the Brotherhood of Al-Jahiz. He'd been one of those at the table with Worthington. She distinctly recalled his charred hand clutching a kerchief marked with the letter G. His wife, it turned out—Georgiana. She wondered what his last thoughts of her had been as he died.

"This is more than a ledger," Hadia said, flipping through the small book. "He jotted down notes alongside his expenses. Here's one: 'September 13, 1911. Wired to that young idiot WD £200 emergency funding for latest venture. Claims to have encountered sand trap. Pity it didn't swallow him.' Exclamation point, exclamation point, exclamation point."

Fatma looked down a small list naming members of the Brotherhood. They'd been using it to decipher the journal's coding.

TOM had stumped them until they remembered Lord Worthington's nickname and reasoned it out in English: *The Old Man.* "Wesley Dalton," she said. "He's the only WD."

"Nearly every mention of him comes with a biting comment," Hadia noted. "Doesn't seem Archibald liked him very much."

"Wesley Dalton was the corpse whose head was on . . . backward," Fatma remarked.

Hadia's eyebrows rose. "I guess he had a way with people. Look here." She pointed at the journal. "Beside a lot of these entries is written the word 'archivist' followed by 'Siwa,' in parentheses. Maybe he had to visit there? With an archivist?"

Siwa was an oasis town in the far west of Egypt. Fairly remote—some nine hours' travel by the faster airships, and only if they weren't stopping to fuel. "That's a long way. How many times is it mentioned?"

"Often. Especially the more expensive purchases. Why go to some archivist in Siwa, though, for"—Hadia stopped to read—"a sebhah rumored used by al-Jahiz to perform dhikr? I don't recall al-Jahiz being in Siwa."

Neither did Fatma. This wasn't making sense.

"You have that look on your face," Hadia observed. "The frustrated one."

"I was hoping we'd come away with some leads. Instead we get puzzles. Not to mention we still can't nail down basic facts—like when precisely Alexander Worthington arrived in Cairo."

The clear contradiction between his and Madame Nabila's account had taken up much of their discussion since leaving the estate. One of the two was clearly wrong or lying. The documentation was in Alexander's favor. But it seemed an odd mistake on Madame Nabila's part. And why would she lie?

"This is interesting," Hadia murmured. "The last entry. It's dated November 6."

"The day of the murders. What does it say?"

"November 6, 1912. After two weeks of haggling, procured for TOM from the list, the reputed sword of al-Jahiz, for agreed upon price, £50,000. Archivist (Siwa)." Hadia gasped. "That's a lot of money! Do you think it's the same one the imposter has?"

Fatma shifted uneasily, reliving that singing sword skewering Siti. "What else?"

"There's a long notation: 'Encountered difficulty gaining the item in Red Street. Inquired on discovery of second wire transfer to archivist (Siwa) for £50,000 from AW.'" Hadia raised her head quizzically. "Alistair Worthington?"

"No. He's TOM. AW is someone else."

"You're not thinking . . . ?"

"Alexander Worthington! Keep reading!"

"'Informed Siwa that I was the only one authorized to speak for TOM. Became erratic and unhinged. Has left me shaken. Will suggest to TOM no further transfers to archivist (Siwa) until matter sorted. Will not support his habit, even if he holds the list over us.' Exclamation point."

Hadia stopped. "It seems there were two transfers to the same archivist in Siwa for £50,000. One was on the night of Alistair Worthington's death—for a sword. The other transfer was two weeks earlier, from AW. Perhaps Alexander. But for what? And what's this business about a list or Red Street? I thought the money was wired to Siwa?"

Fatma shook her head slowly as understanding set in. "Red Street. He means Red Road. The artisan district. Siwa isn't a place. It's the name of the archivist. A djinn." Not wasting another moment, she shouted a new set of directions for the carriage, holding to the inside railings as it banked hard to the left and set out for Al Darb al-Ahmar.

CHAPTER
FOURTEEN

The Red Road was dotted with buildings, monuments, and masjid dating to the Fatimids and as recent as the Ottomans. The famed artisan district was a labyrinth of winding alleys lined with endless shops, where craftspeople preserved techniques passed down through the ages.

Fatma and Hadia hurried past thread-dyeing houses where women huddled over large stone baths, drawing out bundles of cotton from the black ink. Elsewhere, apprentices painstakingly stitched together tasfir under the watchful eye of a master bookbinder. Al Darb al-Ahmar was one of the few places in modern Cairo where steam or gas-powered machines were rare, its artisans preferring tradition to mechanized production. It meant slower going, but there were people who paid handsomely for such handcrafted creations.

They turned a corner to the Street of the Tentmakers, facing the old Bab Zuweila, with its impressive twin minarets. They'd had the carriage drop them at the newly reestablished Al-Azhar University, where they queried two students who sat drinking coffee. The women weren't familiar with a djinn named Siwa, but suggested a carpet-maker they claimed knew every part of the district. It turned out he was indeed the person to ask. As he and his eldest daughter sat at an old-fashioned vertical loom weaving silk into prayer rugs, he related precisely where to find Siwa—down to the façade on the building.

"We're lucky he's the only djinn archivist in Al Darb al-Ahmar that goes by the name Siwa," Fatma said, eyeing the print on a set of tents. The Street of the Tentmakers was aptly named, where artisans stitched by hand colorful geometric styles from local architecture across massive cloth canvases. Every shop belonged to a tentmaker, and they advertised with banners promising even more tantalizing craftsmanship inside their stores.

"I'll never get used to that," Hadia said, stepping aside as a flatbread seller pedaled past on a three-wheeled velocipede, a basket of rounded aish baladi stacked on his head. "How do djinn even tell one another apart?"

Fatma shook her head. Given that djinn called themselves mostly by geographical spaces, it was inevitable many ended up sharing the same name. She'd come across a dozen Qenas and scores of Helwans. How they distinguished one another by name was a mystery. They just . . . did.

"Here it is." She motioned to a sign that read *The Gamal Brothers*, just above a drawing of three men stitching. The four-story building was made of brown stone broken by red swaths and windows framed in green. Like most of the block, an awning stretched from its roof to across the street—a tan canvas with mahogany stripes—shading all beneath.

Inside, they found Gamal—a man with curling gray whiskers—and his equally graying brothers. The three worked on a majestic tent of red, blue, and yellow designs with green calligraphy. A gramophone belted out music—surprisingly one of the songs made popular from the Jasmine. Never stopping their needlework, the three directed the two women upstairs when they inquired after a Siwa. As narrow as the passage was, Fatma thought it a wonder a djinn could fit the tight space.

"You'd think with all the money this Siwa's been paid," Hadia mused, "he could afford a bigger place."

"Maybe he's the frugal type," Fatma muttered.

They stopped at a door on the third floor, which looked recently painted over a bright yellow. Before they could even knock, it opened. Djinn had a habit of that.

"Ahlan wa Sahlan!" he greeted.

"Ahlan biik," Fatma replied.

She was taken aback at the warm welcome, as well as the djinn. He wasn't small after all—just slightly less massive than Zagros, in fact—though his voice was higher than his size might predict. Beneath a black velvet kaftan embroidered in gold, his skin was dark red with thin curving lines of ivory. They formed swirling patterns that moved continually. The effect was hypnotizing, and she had to look away—though his yellow-and-green eyes did much the same. "I'm Agent Fatma, and this is Agent Hadia, with the Ministry of Alchemy, Enchantments, and Supernatural Entities. We're looking for Siwa?"

The djinn inspected their badges, then touched the tips of his looping blue horns in some gesture she didn't quite understand. "I am Siwa." He smiled. "As I've already welcomed you to my home, please enter at your leisure."

He guided them inside, and Fatma stopped in her tracks. Beside her, Hadia released a stunned breath. Like most djinn dwellings she'd visited, this one mimicked a museum: with antique furniture, statues, paintings that had the appearance of another time—and books. Endless books. Everywhere. In shelves. Stacked onto tables. In towering piles that looked like orderly mounds of art. But it was the size of the room that stood out. The apartment was immense, with archways and columns, and a wide stone floor. She looked back through the still-open doorway that showed the narrow stairs and then to the scene before her.

"It's bigger on the inside than the outside?" Hadia whispered, incredulous.

Apparently so. Djinn magic was sometimes perplexing.

"I beg your pardon for the great mess," Siwa said.

"You certainly like to read," Hadia remarked.

"I'm something of an archivist. Of rare texts—both ancient and medieval, by mortal reckoning. Most of these are works of literature, from my personal collection."

Hadia examined a thin volume written in Greek. "Have you read them all?"

The djinn beamed. "Several times! Will you take tea with me in the sitting room?"

He led them across the apartment—and Fatma tried not to gawk when they entered another room with a towering water fountain, made up of white marble camels balancing a bowl upon their humps. Paintings in gilded frames lined the walls—most depicting camels galloping across sweeping desert vistas.

When they arrived in the sitting room, the djinn offered them space on a plush purple divan while he sat in a wide chair large enough to fit his frame. On either side of him were tall gold carvings of camels. The detail was exquisite, down to the fur on their flexed muscles imitating movement and bright red rubies meant for eyes.

"Definitely not the frugal type," Hadia whispered.

A small wood table was set up between them that held a gilt bronze pitcher carved with Persian designs and a spout like a camel's mouth. Beside it were three cups of tea, with fresh mint leaves. They were invited to drink, and Fatma took her cup, sipping in surprise. This might have been the best mint tea she'd ever tasted.

"Now, how might I help the Ministry?" Siwa asked, a pleasant smile on his large face.

"We're looking into the death of Lord Alistair Worthington," Fatma said. "We understand that you knew him?"

The djinn blinked as Fatma moved to set her cup down. She fumbled, almost dropping it as she missed the edge of the table. Had the thing grown smaller?

"The papers say it was a terrible tragedy," he answered. "But I did not know the English Basha, not personally."

"You did do business with him. Through an intermediary—Archibald Portendorf?"

"Yes. The Wazir and I did business together."

Fatma took note to better phrase her words. Djinn weren't inherently deceptive. But they were at times direct, answering only precisely what you asked.

"This business. It was for the Hermetic Brotherhood of Al-Jahiz?"

Siwa blinked again. His smile wavered, lips trembling before going still. Fatma took note of that, breaking her concentration as her eyes flickered to the dark wood walls. She'd already noticed the mural that hung behind the djinn, displaying more camels on a gold background. Seemed to be a theme. Only now the camels that had been running right appeared to be running left. Her eyes went to her cup. What was in that tea?

"Yes," Siwa answered finally. "My business was with the organization founded by Lord Alistair Worthington."

"You helped them procure items."

"Such was I was tasked, by the Wazir. We did good business together."

"Why do you call him that?" Hadia asked. "The Wazir?"

"The members of the Brotherhood of Al-Jahiz often held titles. Lord Alistair Worthington was known as the Grand Master. Archibald, the Wazir, his second."

That explained the journal. "Were you a member of the Brotherhood?" Fatma asked.

Siwa's smile broadened, and he chuckled. "No djinn belonged to Lord Alistair's Brotherhood. Not that he didn't try."

"He tried to recruit you?"

Siwa's smile wavered. Fatma glanced to make sure Hadia was writing this all down, but found her contemplating the teapot—which had oddly become brass instead of bronze.

"He made the attempt," the djinn said. "But I declined. Such intimacy in mortal affairs can bring . . . problems." For the first time his smile shrank to nothing, and his eyes took on an inward look, before his pleasant demeanor returned.

"How do you know so much about the Brotherhood, then?"

Siwa shrugged. "The Wazir was nervous around djinn. I would try to settle him with tea, and he would chatter on—I believe to cover his discomfort."

"The things you procured for the Brotherhood," Hadia asked.

"They came from a list? Were they authentic? Because you were paid a lot for them."

The djinn's smile remained, but his answer was stiff. "I only deal in authentic items. My list is sound. My word is my reputation."

"Of course," Fatma jumped in. Djinn were sensitive to the insinuation of lying—even when they were. "You know, then, that Archibald died alongside Alistair Worthington."

"Again, a terrible tragedy. May God show them His mercy."

"You might have been one of the last people to see him, outside of the Brotherhood. He came to collect a sword from you, for £50,000. What kind of sword was that?"

"A blade that once belonged to the man you call al-Jahiz," Siwa replied. "Forged by a djinn. A black blade that sings."

So that explained how the imposter had gotten it. "Where did it come from?"

Siwa sighed regretfully. "Forgive me. But such secrets of my trade, I cannot divulge."

She'd expected as much. "One last thing. Archibald claimed the night he came to get the sword there was an argument over money." The djinn's lips did that trembling thing again, and he blinked rapidly. "It seems someone else had already wired you £50,000 from Worthington's account, two weeks prior, for unknown services. Someone with the initials AW."

Siwa emitted a strangled noise. His lips compressed tight, as if holding something back, before he bellowed: "Ethiope! A cursed land indeed! The blackamoors from there are in his keep! Broad in the nose they are and flat in ear! Fifty thousand and more in his company!" The djinn clapped a clawed hand over his mouth, shaking his horned head.

Fatma, startled, looked to Hadia and back to the djinn. "Are you well?" When he didn't answer, she tried again. "I only wanted to know about the second wire of money. What was it for? And who made it? The initials AW—was it Alexander Worthington?"

She'd barely finished speaking before Siwa let out a howl. No, not a howl, a stream of words without end. "Have the bards who preceded me left any theme unsung? What, therefore, shall be my subject? When the gods deal defeat to a person, they first take his mind away, so that he sees things wrongly! Nothing can be revoked or said in vain nor unfulfilled if I should nod my head!" Then without warning, the world rippled.

Fatma jumped to her feet.

"What just happened?" Hadia stood as well.

Before she could answer, the world rippled again. Not Hadia, not herself. But the djinn and the entire room shifted about, undulating like the swirl patterns on the djinn's skin. She thought she might guess what was happening, when Siwa gave a gurgling scream. His mouth opened wide, unhinging until his jaw gaped, and a dark blue tongue lolled out—so long it fell to the middle of his chest. He pulled something from his kaftan: a long knife with a serrated blade. Fatma reached for her pistol. But the djinn put the sharp end to his tongue. With a fevered look in his eyes, he began to cut.

Fatma heard Hadia gag as blood spurted. Without another word, the two hurriedly backed out of the room, watching the apartment heave in sporadic spasms as the djinn's screams filled their ears. They didn't stop until they'd gotten out the front door, down the stairs, and past the three tentmakers—who still worked studiously at their stitching. Only when they reached the sidewalk did they speak.

"Ya Satter ya Rabb!" Hadia gasped. "What was that?"

Fatma had no answer. A djinn cutting out his own tongue was a first. "Didn't the journal say something about him turning erratic when asked about the wired money? I'd call that erratic."

"What was he yelling? It sounded like literature or—?"

"—poetry," Fatma finished. "I didn't know the first bit. But the second, it was Antar."

"The medieval poet? So am I crazy? Or was that apartment . . . jumping about?"

"You're not crazy," Fatma answered. "He's an Illusion djinn."

Hadia blinked, then widened her eyes in understanding. Fatma should have caught it right away: an apartment too big on the inside; items changing one moment to the next. All djinn were gifted with illusion. The strongest ones in stories made entire cities appear in the desert and could fool each of your senses.

"But I *felt* like I walked a whole way to that sitting room," Hadia insisted.

"That's what makes Illusion djinn so good at what they do."

"Did we even see the real Siwa? Did I really drink mint tea?"

"I doubt his apartment is as opulent as it seems. I also have a guess where his money's been going. Did you notice all the camels? Almost always running?"

Hadia frowned quizzically, but Fatma let her work it out. "We won't support his habit!" she said, catching on. "From the journal. He's a gambler! Camel races!"

Fatma nodded. Camel racing had always been more popular out in the eastern desert, or back home near Luxor. Anywhere with flat wide spaces, which were hard to come by in Cairo. That was, until the djinn created their mechanical steam-powered camels, which could reach breakneck speeds. A track sat outside the city, and the high bets on riders and their clockwork mounts were notorious. Nothing emptied pockets faster.

"That explains why he needs so much money," Hadia deduced. "But why rip out his own tongue? Unless that was an illusion too."

"That felt *too* real," Fatma said. "He seemed genuinely upset. Every time we asked him anything that came close to touching on the Brotherhood, his illusion slipped. When we asked about that night with Archibald, the argument over the money, it started falling apart."

"Not just the money," Hadia noted, frowning. "It was when you mentioned Alexander that things got bad. He really didn't want to talk about that."

Or couldn't. Fatma gazed back up to the tentmaker's shop. She'd heard of spells that could stop someone from revealing secrets, rendering a person unable to form words, sealing their lips tight. A spell that could reduce a djinn—a Marid no less—to spouting random lines of literature and force him to cut out his own tongue was strong magic.

"One more question," Hadia said. "Is it darker out than usual?"

Fatma broke from her contemplations to follow Hadia's gaze. The sky *was* darkening, the blue obscured by a growing yellowish haze. A warm strong wind picked up, buffeting them and fluttering the awning above. All along the street, canvases were tossed about in the growing gale—a few becoming unmoored and flapping wildly. The bread seller they'd seen earlier sped by, still holding loaves atop his head. He shouted as he went: "Sandstorm! Sandstorm!"

Sandstorm? This time of year? But as Fatma watched, signs of a brewing storm mounted, as sunlight dimmed and the wind intensified. People hustled to get indoors, closing shops and pulling down barricades. She could already feel the dust in her nose, making it hard to breathe.

"We need to make it back!" she told Hadia. Holding her bowler tight and putting her shoulder against the wind, she set out, hoping to beat the storm before it arrived.

Fatma sat in the automated carriage, stringing pieces together in her head. First, Alistair Worthington and his brotherhood were all killed by a man claiming to be al-Jahiz. That same night, it appeared his own son wired money to a djinn behind his back. Now some sorcery was preventing that djinn from revealing more. Alexander had, at best, a troubled relationship with his father and bore no love for the Brotherhood. With both gone, he was free to inherit the Worthington name and scrub it of his father's influence. People murdered for far less.

Still, none of this explained the magic this imposter wielded. Certainly not the Ifrit. Could this false al-Jahiz be someone hired by Alexander? The man seemed to hold disdain for anything related to sorcery. Yet here he was transferring large sums of money to a djinn with a penchant for gambling. She'd have to do some digging on counter-spells, see if there was some way to get Siwa talking. Something in her gut told her the answers were there. *What is hidden is still greater,* her mother often said.

"That's strange."

Fatma looked up to find Hadia staring out the window. But she didn't appear to be looking at anything. Instead her head was cocked—more so like she was listening. The storm had worsened, making it hard to see. It howled over the city like an angry child. "What's strange?"

"I can't tell the direction of the storm. We get sandstorms in Alexandria. They blow from one direction. You can't tell by seeing it, but you can certainly feel it in the wind. This one though sounds like it's blowing from, well, every direction."

Fatma frowned. "This *is* an odd time of year for sandstorms." And they hadn't gotten any of the usual warnings. Was it even hot enough for a sandstorm?

"I might have something odder," Hadia choked. "Is that the Ministry?"

Fatma squinted to where the woman indicated—a dark shape in the distance. No, that couldn't be the Ministry. She squinted harder, tracing the shape's rectangular outline. It *was* the Ministry! Only shrouded in a thick yellow haze that swirled about the building.

"No wonder we couldn't tell the storm's direction," Hadia said. "It's centered on the Ministry!"

Looking to the sky, Fatma made out veins of blowing sand, all streaking toward the Ministry building. They merged with the churning cloud as if eager to join a dance, growing thicker by the moment. This didn't look good.

"You have your sidearm?" she asked.

Hadia's dark brown eyes showed alarm, but she nodded, pressing at a place beneath her coat. "You think it's that bad?"

Fatma checked her own pistol. The service revolver was standard Ministry issue, nothing fancy: silver plated, a thin long barrel, and a six-shot cylinder. "When there's a strange, unknown disturbance centered around the one place meant to investigate strange, unknown disturbances—yeah, I think it might be that bad. How are you with that?" She jerked her chin at Hadia's pistol.

"Good enough, I suppose. But I don't like guns."

Fatma sympathized. Carrying the thing always felt like an extra weight about her neck. "Think of it as insurance. We won't use it unless we absolutely have to. You ready?"

Hadia nodded. "Wait!" She pulled a hijab from her satchel. Handing it over, she began loosening her own headscarf to fit over her mouth and nose.

They stopped the carriage a short distance from the Ministry, as the vehicle threatened to tip over in the increasing winds. When they stepped out, those same winds hit them. Fatma hunched her shoulders, one hand gripping her bowler, the other clenched to her jacket. She had to walk at an angle, as the storm batted at her much as Hadia had suspected—oddly from every direction at once. Fine grains found any bit of exposed skin. Usually this was more an annoyance than anything else—but for some reason this sand actually stung!

Hadia wasn't faring much better—her long skirts flapping wild. The two moved more on instinct than sight, and they had to be careful not to lose one another in the gloom. Reaching the front of the Ministry felt like they'd trekked a mile rather than a block. The glass doors didn't open at their arrival, and they were forced to pry them apart before squeezing inside one at a time.

Fatma grunted with exertion as they pushed the doors closed again, shutting out the storm. She shook herself, stripping the hijab from her face and letting sand spill across the floor. Beside her Hadia unwrapped her mouth and nose, pulling in breaths. The normally well-lit foyer was dark. Partly it was the sandstorm. But there didn't seem to be a light on anywhere.

"The power's out," Hadia noted.

Fatma peered into the black. Where was that stationed guard? "The building has backups. Its brain should send out repair eunuchs to fix whatever's wrong."

At her words a loud rumbling came, like metal creaking and grinding against itself. There was an almost mournful cadence to it, and the building shuddered with its passing.

"What was *that*?" Hadia asked.

"The building's brain." Fatma craned her neck, trying to glimpse the iron gears and orbs beneath the glass dome. "Something's wrong. Listen. Doesn't sound like it's even spinning."

"Maybe sand somehow got into the gears?"

"Maybe. Can't make out anything. Wish I had a pair of spectral goggles right now."

"I have mine," Hadia said, fumbling in her pockets. "I know

most agents only take them out on crime scenes and the like, but guidelines say keep them on you so . . . I do."

God's blessings for the eagerness of rookies, Fatma thought.

"I've got them on," Hadia said. "And I'm looking up . . . but . . ."

"What?"

"I don't know what I'm seeing. There's movement up there, but it doesn't look right."

"Let me try." Fatma took the goggles, fitting them on. The dark turned into a luminescent jade—bright as day but filtered through the spectral world. Everything was vivid here. Even the storm outside was a set of intricate patterns that broke apart and re-formed again. Gazing up at the domed ceiling, she adjusted the rounded green lens and focused.

Viewing the building's mechanized brain through spectral glass was usually breathtaking—a cascade of light that made each rack and pinion glow, the many orbs awash in brilliance. But none of that was visible now. Instead, a dark accumulation obscured everything. She adjusted the lenses again. Now she could see bits of light, but buried beneath clumps of shadow. Shadows that moved and writhed. What in the many worlds? One of the shadows lifted up as if stretching, before falling back into the larger mass. In that brief moment Fatma glimpsed its shape—humanlike, long limbed with an elongated torso. The sight turned her insides to ice. Reaching for Hadia, she gripped the woman's arm and pulled them flat against a wall, then whispered one word filled with urgency.

"Ghuls!"

Hadia's face showed all the shock and revulsion expected at hearing that word.

"Ghuls? You're certain?"

Fatma nodded grimly. She'd know those twisted bodies and limbs anywhere.

Hadia cast her gaze upward and shrank—as if expecting the creatures to fall down on them any moment. "There is no God but God," she whispered. "What are ghuls doing in the Ministry?"

"Stop asking me questions I can't answer!" Fatma snapped, frustration getting the better of her. "But they're all over the machinery up there. No wonder the building seems out of power." Another grinding rumble came, likely the gears struggling to move beneath that mass of undead. They sat on the mechanical brain like a disease, infecting it, draining its magic.

"First a storm," Hadia said. "Now ghuls. Odd coincidence, don't you think? This feels purposeful."

"Like an attack," Fatma finished.

"But who? You don't think . . . him?"

The imposter's words sounded in Fatma's head. *I will make you hurt.* "We have to check the building. People could be injured."

"Or worse." Hadia swallowed.

Fatma didn't want to think that out loud. Ghuls were ravenous, and ate anything. She'd seen one chase a butterfly once for almost a mile. People trapped in this building wouldn't last long. "You remember your training against ghuls?"

"Sort of?"

Fatma frowned. "What does 'sort of' mean? Didn't you train at the Settlement?"

The Settlement had been part of a government project to create new towns in remote places, irrigated by djinn machinery. This one was built in the western desert, east of Dakhla. No one was certain what happened exactly, but the settlers all disappeared within months, and the town was overrun with ghuls. The Ministry cleared it out, declaring it ghul-free. Yet after just a year, it was thick with them again. More tries yielded the same results. A bizarre phenomenon.

"No cadets have gone gardening at the Settlement for two years," Hadia said. "Gardening" was the euphemism for the yearly culling of ghuls, carried out by academy instructors and trainees. Like a field trip. But with guns, sharp things, and lots of undead. "Not since that one class was nearly overrun and eaten. Didn't you read about it in the alumni newsletter?"

Fatma shrugged. Who read alumni newsletters? "So how are you 'sort of' trained to fight ghuls?"

"Simulations. One group of cadets dressed like ghuls, and chased the rest of us—"

Fatma held up a palm, not wanting to hear any more. Even in the dark, Hadia's unease was plain. Understandable. Ghuls weren't to be taken lightly. "You don't have to come with me. If we're at the storm's epicenter, it might be lighter in other parts of the city. Maybe you can find a phone, get help—"

"I'm coming with you," Hadia cut in. "I'm a Ministry agent. This is what we do."

The resolve in the woman's voice, even in the face of her fear, said the matter was settled. Fatma reached to her waist, pulling free the janbiya from its sheath. "Since you're not fond of guns."

Hadia accepted the knife, looking quizzical. "What are you doing with a janbiya?"

"Present from a Yemeni dignitary. Ministry did his clan a favor. He thought it a fitting gift for such a brave and 'pretty young man.' Didn't bother to correct him. And kept the knife."

Hadia balanced the weapon between her hands, testing its weight. "Oh, I like this!"

"I'll expect that back." Fatma glanced at the undead above. "Elevator's out. We'll have to take the stairs. This way."

They made it to the stairwell, Fatma taking point with her gun drawn. Making a sign to indicate it was all clear, she led them up. It was darker here than in the foyer, and they slowed at every bend, to avoid running into anyone—or anything—by surprise. Somewhere in the back of her mind lurked the question of how exactly ghuls got into the Ministry. But she tamped it down. Time enough for that later.

They made it to the fourth floor without incident. There'd been more rumbling from the building's infected brain—but no ghuls, praise God. Fatma felt guilty for not stopping at the other floors. But the people she knew and worked with were up here.

She'd see to them first. Just as they reached the door a loud banging came from the other side.

"When we get in, keep low," she whispered. "Remember ghuls are stronger than us. Fast too, but not very bright. Aim for the head. Got it?" Hadia gave a firm nod, eyes set—one hand on her pistol, the other on the janbiya. Together, they opened the door and stepped inside.

The office was dark—the only light coming dimly from windows where the sandstorm churned. But by now Fatma's eyes had adjusted. There'd been a struggle here. Papers lay strewn about along with knocked-over chairs. But no people. Hadia tapped her shoulder, pointing to bullet holes in a wall. Must have been some fight.

Crouched low, Fatma led them down a side aisle toward the sound of the banging. Spilled cups of tea and a half-eaten bo'somat indicated people had been taken off guard. But gone where? The banging. That would tell her. As they got closer her nose picked up rotted flesh and earth turned sour. The unmistakable stench of the undead. Snatches of snarls and snapping teeth confirmed it. She was set to turn and warn Hadia when an arm shot out from the other side of a desk—brandishing a pistol. Fatma did the same on instinct, heart hammering. But wait, ghuls didn't use guns. She made out a face.

Hamed?

The man let out a relieved breath. He was crouched as well, awkward for his big frame, and beckoned them to follow. He led them to where a long table had been turned on its side. Someone else was there, hunched down. Onsi. A smile lit up his round face at seeing Fatma and Hadia. But it vanished at another loud bang. They gathered together, backs to the table.

"Some weather we're having," Hamed half joked. Behind them the banging and snarling grew. Fatma needed to see. Turning, she lifted her head just over the edge and peeked out.

Ghuls. Their naked pale-gray bodies were visible in the dim

light—misshapen mockeries of men with elongated limbs. She took a quick count. Twelve. No, one more clung to the ceiling, in their unnatural way. A whole pack, then. They massed about Director Amir's office—some on two legs, others crawling on all fours. One wielded the back of a broken chair, hurling it against the office door. Every bang was followed by muffled cries from the other side. Human cries.

She sat back down. "What happened?"

Hamed's expression turned dark. "Our friend from Sunday night. In the gold mask."

Fatma's hand tightened on her pistol at the confirmation.

"First the power went out when that storm hit," he related. "Then the ghuls were just here . . . in our midst. It got crazy." For the first time Fatma noticed the man's usually pristine uniform was disheveled and he was missing his tarboosh. "We were fighting hand to hand. Amir got as many as he could into his office, where they've been holed up. Onsi and I have been trying to find a way to break them free. Now that you're here—"

"Where is he?" Fatma more hissed than spoke. "The imposter?"

"He left. With several ghuls and that odd man who can . . . duplicate himself."

"The ash-ghul," Hadia put in.

Hamed eyed her dubiously. "If that's what we're going with . . ."

"Where did they go?" Fatma pressed.

"Don't know. Said something about dragging our secrets into the light."

I will make you hurt. I will make you understand. And drag your secrets into the light.

Fatma played the words over in her head. Their secrets. Where did the Ministry keep its secrets? "The vault!" she breathed. "He's heading for the vault!"

"The vault?" Onsi asked. "What would he want there?"

"Whatever it is, we can't let him have it!" Fatma said.

Another set of bangs came alongside frustrated snarls.

"He can't open the vault," Hamed assured. "It's locked. The building's systems—"

"—are compromised." Fatma finished. She related the current situation.

"The entire brain machinery?" Onsi whispered in disbelief. "Covered by ghuls?"

"We're on our own," she told them. "We have to protect the vault!"

"The door to Amir's office won't hold," Hamed warned. "A lot of people in there are secretaries and clerks. They're not armed. If the ghuls get in, it won't be much of a fight. Two of us going it alone wasn't looking so good. Four stand a better chance."

Fatma looked to the stairs longingly. Every minute they spent here gave the imposter more time. But more banging came, followed by cries from Amir's office. For a moment she was ready to abandon those cries to their fate. She'd hate herself, but she'd do it. A hand fell on her arm, and she looked up to see Hadia's dark brown gaze reading the warring notions within her.

"I think we can do both," the woman said. Her eyes looked to the ceiling, and everyone followed—tracing a series of thin pipes.

"The sprinkler system?" Hamed asked. "That idea that ghuls won't cross water is a myth."

"But they hate it," Hadia countered. "Get that going, and it'll be enough to distract them—we put them down quick, get everyone out, then make it to the vault."

Fatma met her partner's expectant look, then slowly nodded, warming to the idea. She'd seen ghuls struck by water. It sent them into fits. This could work. Then to the vault. "The sprinkler's run by the building, but there's a manual crank near the door. Somebody will have to get to it, quiet. When it's on, we hit them hard."

"I'll loose the sprinklers!" Onsi volunteered. "I can be very quiet."

Fatma eyed him skeptically, but Hamed agreed. "He's unnaturally good at it, actually." He paused, his face going grim. "There's one other thing. The man in the gold mask. Before he left, he said there was a bomb. Though we don't know where."

Fatma swallowed down that bit of news. A bomb. Why not? Could this get any worse? "Then we move fast. Onsi, get going!" He actually gave her a salute, of all things, eyes stern behind his spectacles, then made off. The banging came again. "You two ready?" Hamed and Hadia gave firm nods and thankfully didn't salute. "Then I'm going up top. Take your shots when you can!" Drawing a deep breath, she rose up, her free hand gripping the table's edge, and hurled herself over it. She landed with her pistol already raised and let out a shrill whistle.

The ghuls turned as one to regard her with sightless faces. A dozen lips peeled back to bare black gums and teeth that snapped, wrinkling the pale gray skin that sat where eyes did not. The one that had been banging on the door stood in their center, and it stretched a long neck, jaws unhinging to emit a high-pitched shriek. The sound cut off abruptly as a bullet lodged square in its forehead. A croak escaped its throat, before it flopped to the ground, going still.

And that made eleven.

Fatma peered around the smoking pistol barrel to appraise her shot. First rule of dealing with a ghul pack. Establish the leader and take it out. That usually enraged the rest. As expected, they were working themselves up now—snarling and snapping—to do some truly murderous violence. But enraged was better than co-ordinated. Still, as they launched at her, she wondered what was taking Onsi so damn long!

A deluge of water came in answer as the sprinklers above hissed to life. The ghuls broke their charge, some tripping and sliding on the slick floor, others beating at their heads to deflect the downpour and screeching in panic. One just whimpered and ran about in a circle. They really *did* hate water!

Fatma took aim and fired into the disarray, counting as she went. Ten now. Nine. New gunshots rang out beside her. Hamed. Eight. Seven. Six. They were down to half. But a few of the creatures collected what sense they had, breaking from their companions and galloping in a mad rush. They zigged and zagged in their run, and Fatma cursed as her bullets glanced off shoulders or went wide. Damn, the things were fast!

In seconds, one of them was in front of her, teeth snapping. She didn't have time to get off a shot, so she kicked the thing in its chest. The blow would have sent a regular man to his back. But ghuls were strong enough for two men. It only stumbled, snaking out an arm and reaching elongated fingers for her face—when a knife suddenly slashed, severing the limb clean at the elbow. The appendage fell away, smacking the wet floor and transmuting to ash. The ghul turned its head to this new threat and was rewarded with a janbiya—Fatma's janbiya—pushing straight through where a left eye should have been. Its body dropped like an automaton with an off switch. Hadia pulled the knife free and spun in one motion to slice right through the leg of another ghul, sending it sprawling. She didn't give it time to get back up, burying the janbiya into the base of its skull up to the hilt.

Fatma looked on appreciatively. Guns were definitely wasted on the woman. No more ghuls were standing. What was left of them lined the floor in still heaps. For reasons never understood, appendages separated from their bodies always turned to ash—but never the bodies. Those were always left for cleanup.

"Think we got them all," Hamed panted. "I count twelve here."

"Good work." Fatma moved to put her pistol away. "Now let's—"

A snarl came before she could finish, and she looked up in time to see the ghul on the ceiling—that they'd completely forgotten about. It landed in front of Hamed. He lifted his gun, but the thing swatted the weapon away before knocking the man aside. It turned to Fatma, reaching her in a bounding leap. She squeezed the trigger of her pistol—to find it empty. That wasn't good.

Bracing, she put up an arm as the ghul landed atop her, tumbling them both to the floor. It took all her strength, as she lay flat, to keep her palms against the thing's neck, to stop those snapping teeth from reaching her. The stink of its breath—rot and death—nearly choked her, but she strained against it. From the corner of her eye she caught sight of her janbiya coming in to end the creature. *Hadia!* Unfortunately, the ghul saw it too. It turned at the last moment, and the knife missed its temple, instead going through its jaw.

The ghul shrieked, flinging back from atop Fatma as it gripped the knife lodged sideways in its mouth. Bullets struck its flank. Onsi. The short man was firing. But he had terrible aim, his shots hitting mostly in the body. He was empty in moments and had done little but slow it. Fatma scrambled to her feet, fumbling to get bullets into her own gun.

But Hadia was already moving. In something Fatma would not have believed had she not seen it, the woman leaped onto the ghul's back, putting an arm around its neck and clinging there. Pulling the knife free from the thing's jaw, she turned it over in her hand and drove the blade up through its chin. That wasn't enough to kill it, but the janbiya had managed to lock its jaw, and it now clawed at its mouth in confusion. Hopping off its back, Hadia walked around, eyes searching for the right spot, then delivered a swift kick to the hilt—sending it home. The ghul's body went stiff, then dropped, landing on its face.

Quiet descended as they surveyed the carnage. After a moment the door to Amir's office cracked open. The director peeked out, then opened it fully. He was holding a pistol, and behind him were frightened-looking men and women, mostly office staff. "Got them all?" he asked matter-of-factly.

Fatma nodded, helping Hamed to his feet. The ghul had almost struck him unconscious and he was just recovering. She handed him over to someone else, her mind already on their second task. "The man in the gold mask. He's heading for the vault. I need to get down there."

Amir took in what she was saying. "Right. Take some men with you. We have to get everyone else out. You might have heard, there could be a bomb."

"If you don't mind, director, Agent Hadia would be fine." She looked to where the woman was turning over the dead ghul, retrieving the janbiya, now covered in black blood.

"No, that's alright," Hadia called back. With a grunt, she yanked the knife free. "I'll help clear the building. Take care of any more of these things. You—" She waved the bloodied blade at two agents armed with black truncheons. "Help her out. And make sure you watch her back!"

The two men regarded her oddly, but—perhaps it was the bloodied knife—didn't argue. Fatma gave her a look of unspoken thanks, then sped for the stairs, not slowing for the men following. What if she was already too late? What if the imposter had made his way to the vault and gotten whatever he came for? *I will make you hurt. I will make you understand. And drag your secrets into the light.* She sped up her strides.

When she reached the library, she had the presence of mind to stop at the entrance. The two agents emerged soon after, black truncheons at the ready, and she motioned at them to keep quiet. The way both were huffing, you'd think they were the ones who'd just fought a pack of ghuls. Pulling her gun, she took the lead, and led them inside.

The library was dark, even more than other parts of the building. There was a silence to the emptiness that made her uneasy. Not that it was ever a noisy place. Zagros made sure of that. But not to hear the absent cough, the sound of pages turning, or books being set down, made it feel almost lifeless. And she'd had her fill of dead things today.

Every few steps she stopped at the edge of shelves, prepared to meet whatever may come. In the distance came a steady familiar ticking accompanied by spinning gears and the low thrumming whoosh of a swinging cable. The great clock timepiece had been a gift to the library, and operated separate from the building. Its pendulum hadn't been affected by the power outage and kept up its rhythm. Behind it lay the Ministry's vault—which secured items of immeasurable importance. She ought to know. She'd help put some in there.

Her eyes adjusted as they drew closer, and she made out the pendulum—a giant bob like a golden sun disc inscribed with geometric patterns. She squinted, trying to glimpse the door to the vault between the swings of the cable. But a shadow blocked it. She stopped, holding up a hand. Someone was there. Someone big, in long purple robes of velvet embroidered in white that stood out even in the dark. They turned, and Fatma released a breath, lowering her gun.

Zagros.

The djinn librarian struck his usual regal pose, that half-lidded gaze staring down at her from behind a pair of silver spectacles. He held the biggest book she'd ever seen, thick with pages and covers that looked made of gold. If he still stood guard at the vault, that meant they weren't too late. Maybe the imposter had tried and learned the hard way not to tangle with a centuries-old Marid.

"Zagros!" she called in a low voice. "You don't know how happy I am to see—"

Her words broke off as someone stepped from behind the djinn. Her breath caught. The man in the gold mask! He stared at her with those intense burning eyes, before tilting his head up to whisper in Zagros's ear. The librarian listened silently.

Fatma tried to make sense of what was happening. Now that the djinn had moved, she could see the vault door was indeed open. Behind the imposter, a figure in black stood holding rolled papers. The ash-ghul. Several duplicates followed, carrying some metal items. They were raiding the vault. Taking what they wanted. And Zagros was letting them!

"What are you doing?" she cried in alarm.

The usually composed librarian drew himself up, a low rumble emanating from his thick throat in what she realized was a growl. His jaws suddenly opened wide—baring tusks long as her forearm—and he roared! The sound shook the empty library. The only thing that came close to matching it were his feet thundering on the floor as he ran toward them.

Fatma had seen some nasty brawls involving Marid djinn before. Like watching giants battle. She'd often compared Zagros to a rhinoceros. But as he bore down on them, his golden horns bent low, she knew no rhino could look this frightening.

She recovered from her initial shock in time to throw herself to the side. Her two escorts weren't so fortunate and took the brunt of the djinn's charge. He swung that hefty tome like a battering ram, knocking both men from his path before they could bring their truncheons to bear. Fatma didn't stop to see where they landed. She was running, turning down a corridor to seek shelter between a set of shelves. The maddened djinn gave chase, squeezing his bulk between aisles, splintering wood and sending books flying as his claws reached to grab her. She managed to break free of the corridor, with him plowing after in pursuit— sending pieces of shelf raining.

Fatma leaped, sliding across a wooden table, just as the djinn brought the heavy book down. There was a sharp crack, and the table buckled, one of its legs snapping as it toppled. She barely made it down another corridor, turned a corner, and crouched down to hide. Her heart pounded, her mind now on survival. There was no time to question why the normally prudish Marid librarian was unmistakably trying to kill her. She just needed to get out of this alive!

From where she huddled, she could still see the imposter. He was leaving, strolling casually from the library as the ash-ghul and its duplicates followed with their arms laden. He caught a glimpse of her where she hid, and put a chain-mail finger to his lips for quiet. The sight made her buzz with anger, and for a moment, all thoughts of self-preservation fled. Until a shadow came to loom above, and she looked up to see the djinn's lavender-skinned face contorted in senseless rage—his roar setting the tiny bells on his tusks tingling.

She rolled, narrowly missing a fist that sent stone chips flying from the floor. Reaching her feet, she ran back the way she'd come, toward the vault—throwing down chairs and books and whatever else to slow the murderous djinn. She could lock herself in if need be. But a swiftly closing roar told her she wouldn't make it.

She almost ran past the thing on the floor just ahead—long and black. One of the truncheons! She scooped it up, not stopping her stride. New plan! She banked toward a set of tables that had been tossed on their side. Setting herself up behind them and bracing her back against the wood, she cranked the lever on the truncheon to its highest setting and listened for the low humming whine. Above her, two giant hands gripped the table's edge, and the djinn's horned head soon appeared, golden eyes wide on her. Eyes that despite their brightness looked dead inside. He opened his mouth to roar, but she didn't give him a chance—stabbing the underside of his neck with the bulbous end of the truncheon.

Blue bolts crackled, lighting up the dark. The librarian howled. The truncheons were made to handle creatures like djinn. At this setting, it would kill a human. It should have at least incapacitated a Marid. But he fought, digging his claws into the table and pressing toward her, mouth gaping, so that hot saliva splattered her hands. She didn't stop, even as she was forced down by the weight of him, her back pushed against the flat of the table. At this rate, he might just crush her outright. Then, mercifully, his push slackened. He seemed to grow sluggish before his eyes rolled back. He rose up to his feet, stood a moment, then fell with a tremendous crash.

Fatma lifted up, peeking over the table edge. Zagros lay on his back, chest heaving. Alive, but unconscious. She staggered up, forcing her mind to refocus on her earlier goal.

The man in the gold mask.

She picked up her pace, running for the stairs. Or tried. Somewhere along the away she'd hurt her leg. And all she could manage was a jogging limp. She spied the two downed agents rising shakily to their feet and called for them to follow. Reaching the stairs, she took just a few steps up—before a deafening boom shook everything. Her hands gripped the railing, holding tight as the building swayed. Thick billowing dust rolled over her. She choked in it, and realized she couldn't hear herself coughing, because her ears were ringing.

The bomb.

Two figures were quickly at her side. The other agents. Together, the three of them climbed the stairs. When they reached the top, the door was already open—blown off its hinges.

The foyer of the Ministry was unrecognizable. Beneath a haze of dust, the floor was strewn with masonry and shards that crunched under their feet. Meaty pale-gray bodies lay everywhere, charred and torn to pieces. Fatma now understood. The explosives had been *inside* the ghuls. The ones massed under the dome. She walked around twisted giant iron gears and dented orbs, and it took a moment to recognize what they were. Her eyes went upward. The storm had passed, leaving behind a clearing blue sky. She could see it plain—because the bits of machinery littering the ground had been the building's brain. All that was left was a gaping hole.

By the time Fatma made it outside, she was bent over, trying to expel dust and smoke from her lungs. Somebody took her arm, leading her away. Hadia. Someone else had her other arm. Hamed. She stumbled between them, thinking she must be in some state for him to actually hold her up as he did. The man was usually very proper about such things.

The two led her a safe distance. Here people milled about, their faces distraught. A few held hands over their mouths. Others openly wept. She turned to what they were looking at. The Ministry still stood, but it had been struck a severe blow. The glass dome was gone—blown clean away—and black smoke poured from a smoldering fire.

I will make you hurt. I will make you understand. And drag your secrets into the light.

The imposter's words echoed with the ringing in her ears, given new awful meaning. She turned to Hadia and Hamed, trying to get her mouth to work. They sought to calm her. Hadia was saying she was in shock. Amid their chatter came the distant clang of sirens. No! They needed to listen. She'd *seen* what the imposter took from the vault. She'd recognized it.

"Plans and pieces," she stammered. "He took plans and pieces."

Both only stared in confusion. She gritted her teeth, pushing away the ringing and the world, willing the words to come.

"Listen! I saw what he took! Plans and pieces! They were from the Clock of Worlds. He took plans and pieces from the Clock of Worlds!"

Hadia still looked confused. But seeing the blood drain from Hamed's face told her she'd gotten her point across. Closing her eyes, she let the ringing and the world flood back in, trying not to let the terror she felt consume her.

CHAPTER
SIXTEEN

T he night air was cool on Fatma's skin, stirring her from a fitful sleep.

She'd been dreaming. Of the man in the gold mask. Ghuls and roaring djinn. Ifrit that flew on wings of flame. She pulled free of Siti, and rose from the bed. Slipping on a gallabiyah she walked to where Ramses lay on her high-backed Moroccan chair—a ball of silver fur atop cream-colored cushions. She thought to sit, but remembered her mother's claim that the Prophet—peace be upon him—had once cut his own cloak rather than move a sleeping cat. Instead, she stepped past fluttering curtains to her balcony, and looked out at the city below.

When she was younger, her family spent summer nights on the house roof to avoid the heat. They'd sit sharing coffee and what news of the day. She slept peaceful there, preferring the expanse of open sky to closed walls. A part of her toyed with going to the roof of her apartment. But it wasn't the same. Besides, getting lost in memories of home was usually her way of trying to escape the now. Too much at stake to lose herself in that kind of reverie. It had been three nights and two days since the attack on the Ministry.

And Cairo was in shambles.

The city's administrators and Ministry brass had come by the day after to assess the damage and present a strong front to the public. But people could see the wreckage. Photographs of the Ministry building pouring black smoke were splashed across all the dailies. And everyone knew who was responsible. If the streets had been abuzz about al-Jahiz before, now they were on fire.

Ask the average person what it was the Ministry did, and you got all sorts of answers—much of them fanciful. But people understood what the Ministry stood for: to make some sense of this new world; to help create balance between the mystical and the mundane; to allow them to go on living their lives, knowing someone was there to watch over forces they barely understood. To see that institution laid low was like taking a hammer to the collective psyche of the city.

Riots erupted that first night and continued into the second. Some of the unrest came from Moustafa's sympathizers, who took the attack as a sign to demand the release of the alleged Bearer of Witness. It got ugly. Almost a repeat of the Battle of el-Arafa. Scores arrested. More police injured.

And that was only the beginning.

Protestors calling themselves Al-Jahiz's Faithful demonstrated outside state offices—even showing up in front of the bombed Ministry. They called on the government to stop hiding the truth, accused authorities of outlandish conspiracies to strip Egypt of its sovereignty, and demanded acknowledgment of al-Jahiz's return. More violent elements attacked anyone denying their claims. There'd been beatings and at least one fire-bombing at an aether-works shop. This wasn't some extremist religious sect. Al-Jahiz's followers included Sunni and Shia, Sufi and Copts, fervent nationalists, even atheistic anarchists and nihilists—all united in their dedication. To an imposter.

I will make you hurt. I will make you understand.

Fatma realized her hands had balled into fists. Her eyes ran back to the bed, and some measure of her tension eased. Even sleeping, Siti had that effect. It was hard to believe the woman had suffered a grievous injury just days past. Even the scar was gone. Whatever magics she and the Temple of Hathor dabbled in, it was potent. Her gaze left the bed, falling on a bit of gold that sat on a nearby table. Her pocket watch.

She picked up the timepiece, turning it over. The back was fashioned like the tympan of an old asturlab—with the coordinates of the celestial sphere engraved in a stereographic projection, overlaid with an ornate rete. Depressing a latch, she flipped the watch open to reveal a glass casing covering bronze wheel gears, plates, pinions, and springs. A silver crescent moved along an inner circle ticking down the seconds, with a sun and star keeping the hour and minutes.

Her father was a watchmaker, a skill that yet proved resourceful in this age. In the industrial world everyone needed a watch, if only to keep up with airship and railway schedules. Her father crafted beautiful timepieces, no two the same. His creations were commissioned in nearby Luxor and as far south as Aswan. This one, he'd made for her. She still remembered his words when offering it.

Old travelers and sailors used the asturlab to tell their place in the world. So that no matter where they went, they could locate the Qibla for prayer or know the proper time of sunrise. I made this watch for you, light of my eyes, so that you can always know where you are. Cairo is a big city—so big, you can get lost if you're not careful. If things ever get too fast, and you feel as if you don't know where you're going, remember this gift. It will always lead you back where you need to be.

"Counting down the hours?" a voice purred in her ear.

She jumped slightly as Siti's arms wrapped around her waist. She hadn't even heard the woman stir, much less cross the room. "Still can't sleep?"

Fatma closed the pocket watch. "Can't keep my mind quiet."

"Been a busy week. You're lucky to be alive."

That was true. No one had died in the attack, praise be to God. The ghuls, it seemed, were meant to keep people out of the way. Even the missing guard had turned up, in his oversized uniform. But they weren't without casualties. The building's brain had been destroyed. For all intents and purposes, the imposter had murdered it.

Zagros was another troubling matter.

That the imposter was able to turn one of their own damaged morale more than any bomb. The djinn librarian hadn't put up resistance when arrested. He was a traitor for certain. But an oddly quiet one. He spent his days in a cell, refusing to speak to anyone. She still saw his golden eyes as he tried to kill her. Empty. Dead.

"Come back to bed," Siti urged, nuzzling her neck. "Worry about tomorrow, tomorrow."

Fatma leaned back, wishing she could. But her mind wouldn't stop working, like her watch. She and Hadia hadn't been able to do much on the case since the attack. Between sweeps for traps, leftover ghuls, and repairs, the building wouldn't be habitable for days. They'd been working out of makeshift offices, but things were no longer solely in their hands.

Brass had stepped in, pulling in agents from as far as Alexandria. It was a manhunt now. Find out where the imposter would strike next. Chase down every sighting. Arrest anyone involved. The leads she and Hadia had dug up, the investigation around Lord Worthington's death—all of that had been mostly abandoned.

"It's like they don't even care about solving the case," she grumbled.

"The imposter's admitted to the crime," Siti said. "Added a bombing to the list."

"But there's no motive!"

"I thought we were just going with criminally insane?"

Fatma cursed silently. "We were getting close. I know it. Alexander Worthington. He's involved somehow!"

Siti shook her head. "No one's going to let you go after Alexander Worthington. Not on the eve of the king's peace summit. The one his father put together. It would be a scandal. And, no offense, but you don't exactly have much to go on."

Fatma exhaled wearily. Not from lack of sleep but exasperation.

Siti was right. Brass had commanded her to stay away from the Worthingtons. Not to question their associates, or take any action to embarrass them. They couldn't even subpoena business records. Aasim had similar orders. Finding the imposter and making certain the king's summit went off without a hitch was now top priority. She and Hadia had even been put on assignment that night, in an attempt to make the palace an impregnable fortress.

"I told you what he took from the vault," Fatma whispered. "You know better than anyone what that could mean."

The two of them had been the only ones to see the Clock of Worlds set into motion. The machine had been built by a rogue angel named Maker—based on the Theory of Overlapping Spheres, the very one al-Jahiz used to open the portal to the Kaf forty years past. Using blood sorcery, the angel had unlocked a doorway to some nether-realm—part of a mad plan to cleanse humanity and start anew. She and Siti managed by the skin of their teeth to stop him, closing the portal, and sealing away the terrible things within.

She'd explained all this to the higher-ups at the Ministry, begging them to take seriously the threat of the Clock of Worlds in the imposter's hands. Amir backed her up. But their concerns were waved away. No madman and imposter would be able to re-create the work of an angel, they reasoned. She was certain more than a few doubted her account of what the machine was capable of doing. It was all so maddening.

"It's getting dark out there."

Siti looked out onto the city, understanding she wasn't speaking about the night. "All the temples are worried about these Jahiziin."

Fatma rolled her eyes at the term, cooked up by the dailies to describe the imposter's followers. There couldn't be that many. Most Cairenes were too sensible for that. Probably fewer than a thousand. But a loud and determined minority was all you needed to sow chaos.

"That firebombing last night of the aether mechanic," Siti went on. "That was actually a Temple of Osiris. The head priest was only saved because some Forty Leopards intervened—chased the Jahiziin off."

Fatma met that with surprise, recalling their run-in with the Forty Leopards at el-Arafa. "So the lady thieves are on our side now?"

"Be thankful someone is," Siti remarked playfully. Her tone turned sober. "Merira's shop window was smashed last night. But I think it was just random vandalism, not an attack on Hathor. We've been careful."

Fatma was reminded of their argument about whether the temples could come out into the open. She didn't bring it up.

"It might all unravel, you know. The whole city. Come apart like a cheap suit."

Siti rumbled a low laugh. "Like you know anything about cheap suits." Then hugging Fatma tight: "Whatever comes, we'll meet it. We've done it before. Now get back to bed. Not taking no for an answer."

Fatma finally allowed herself to be led back. Curling about Siti, she took a deep breath, drinking in the woman's scent, and finally drifted away. Her dreams now were pleasant, even peaceful. And she tried to hold on to them for as long as she could.

The summit took place the following week.

On a Wednesday.

CHAPTER
SEVENTEEN

The king's palace was a wonder of the times: a synthesis of Persian, Andalusian, Ottoman, and Neo-Pharaonic styles. It was built for the current monarch—who ascended the throne during the nationalist upheavals in the wake of al-Jahiz's disappearance. His predecessor, the very same Khedive that had attempted to arrest the Soudanese mystic, had been deposed upon demands of the British. They ordered the new king to denounce the nationalist movement and all "superstitious" claims of djinn walking Cairo's streets.

To his credit, the young ruler carried out these acts half-heartedly while secretly signing a treaty with the djinn: allowing them to live out in the open and become Egyptian citizens. After the British were routed, the new republic retained the monarchy, though most governing power resided with an elected parliament. For his role in the so-called Stable Revolution, the djinn constructed the king a grand residence—meant to demonstrate their skill and affirm their place in the new Egyptian society. They named it al-Hadiyyah, the gift.

Fatma walked the garden of the palace paying little attention to its many wonders—not the marble domes that shone like gleaming clouds in the night, or topiaries of fantastic beasts that dotted the grounds. Her job tonight wasn't to gawk. She was part of a silent army of guards, soldiers, police, and agents—tasked to assure the imposter calling himself al-Jahiz didn't mar the king's summit.

She stopped to allow servants in royal livery passage—each

escorting mechanical gold and purple ostriches on thin leashes of glittering pearls. The clockwork gears of the avian automatons ticked rhythmically, glimpses of machinery visible behind their amber eyes.

The actual summit began tomorrow, where leaders and diplomats would attempt to prevent the growing prospect of conflict in Europe. Egypt sat as one of the great powers now, and there was a fearsome possibility it could be drawn into any conflagration.

But that was none of her business. Her duties were on the festivities tonight—held in the sprawling palace gardens to welcome foreign dignitaries, both human and otherwise. They arrived by the hour from where they were housed at Abdeen Palace, departing chauffeured automobiles and gilded steam carriages.

The men wore Western suits and decorated martial uniforms, alongside kaftans and modish Turkish coats with gold epaulets. For the women Parisian styles with Cairene influences dominated, with floral hijabs and intricate embroidery.

Some opted for more traditional dress. Soudanese fakirs stood out in green gallabiyah, with scarves bearing the tricolor of the Revolutionary Republic. A dignitary from one of the liberated Indian states was draped in a stunning lapis-blue sari with gold accents. She stood conversing with a boy in his teens, wearing a long white shirt over loose trousers, and a striped shawl. Likely the Abyssinian heir—come in place of his ill emperor. This didn't account for the djinn, whose fanciful garb defied imagination. One Marid dazzled in robes of shifting hues, while a watery Jann clothed herself in a gown of fine mist.

Fatma had chosen a dark suit for tonight. It balanced a black striped waistcoat and white shirt with a silver tie pinned in place by a blue bauble that matched blue-on-silver cuff links. The bowler was new, its velvet covering catching more than one eye. Especially the Englishmen, with their drab Edwardian attire. Jealous, no doubt. She put an extra swagger in her stroll as she passed them, eyes pretending to follow a set of colorful gas lanterns floating above the gathering like jellyfish. A marker for Hamed. He stood across the garden directly beneath, his Ministry uniform traded in for a stylish kaftan, with stitching along the sleeves and collar. Hadia was at his side, in a burgundy gown with beaded embellishment that followed up to her hijab. The two looked the part of a wealthy and modern married Cairene couple, as was the entire point. The king had no intent of giving the appearance his palace was under siege. Agents and police were to be as inconspicuous as possible. Hamed gave a slight nod. She returned a flick of her bowler. Another circuit of the garden complete and no signs of anything amiss.

She should have been relieved. There'd been no sightings of the imposter since the attack, much to the content of the city administrators. But she was reminded that he'd done the same just before unleashing a sandstorm and ghuls on the Ministry. A part of her was itching to face off with him again. They'd be ready this time. *Eat your enemy for lunch, before he can eat you for dinner,* her mother's voice urged.

A commotion caught her ears, and she gripped her cane, heart quickening. But it was only applause. Not hard to make out the reason. The king and queen were walking out among the crowd, surrounded by a swirl of attendants, royal guards, and clerks. The king was an older man, the hair under his velvet red tarboosh more gray than black, as was the moderately sized moustache on his aging face. He wore regalia common to monarchs of the day—a military suit garlanded with gaudy gold stars and medals, and an embroidered sash that ran crosswise over his chest.

Beside him, the queen wore a red gown that cascaded to flow along the garden. She was younger, and it showed on her plump face. His second wife, who was remarkably of common birth—a trait that endeared her, and thus the monarchy, to the people. A shrewd-faced man in a black suit shared the space with them. The prime minister. The power structure that held together modern Egypt, all gathered in this one place.

Keeping a short distance behind the entourage was a djinn,

almost lanky and somehow familiar. His dark suit brought out his milk-white skin and midnight blue horns. It took a moment to place him. From the Jasmine. How could she forget that unnaturally handsome face? One of the king's advisors perhaps? Another stipulation in the treaty signed with the djinn. She wondered if they knew of his late-night exploits?

"Agent Fatma?"

Fatma turned to find a tall woman striding toward her. Abigail Worthington—who'd thankfully decided to not make mockery of local customs. She wore a rose-colored evening gown that flowed with the airy feel of chiffon and satin. A black silk sash finished with silver and pearls cinched at the waist, and purple lilacs were worked onto the shoulders. It was eye-catching enough to almost miss the bandage still covering her right hand. Behind came the usual retinue—Darlene and Bethany, in matching wine-hued gowns, their hazel eyes judgmental. Broad-chested Victor and the ever-smirking Percival brought up the rear, in black tuxedos.

"Good evening, Abigail," Fatma greeted. Then remembering, "I mean, Abbie."

"I hadn't expected to see you here!" She used her uninjured hand to pat dark red tresses piled into a fanciful pompadour, then leaned in to whisper. "I heard of the attack on the Ministry! Horrid! Do you expect that . . . madman . . . to appear here?" Fear tinged her voice.

"We're here to make sure that doesn't happen," Fatma assured. She looked over the small group. "Where's your brother?"

Abigail sighed, making a face. "Alexander shall be a late body. Spent all day again with his head in the company books. I'm sure he'll be along presently."

Fatma frowned. "I'd think he'd want to be here. This summit was your father's doing."

Abigail gazed about with a fond sadness in her blue-green eyes. "Father would have been so proud. He very much wanted to see more peace in this world."

"We all do," Fatma replied.

A cough came from Victor—who was eyeing a boilerplate eunuch with a tray of drinks.

"That, I believe, is my cue," Abigail said. "Victor feared this entire event would be dry. Or worse, only stocked with wine. I think he's happy to see stiffer refreshments provided for we Occidentals. If you will excuse me, agent." She turned, leading her troupe in search of likely mischief. Fatma shook her head. What it would be like to have no responsibility beyond her own whims. Speaking of which, it was time to start up her rounds again.

She began her way through the garden, eyes sharp. She hadn't gotten a quarter of the way before someone tapped her shoulder.

"Pardon me, zir."

Fatma turned to face a tall woman in a long white gossamer dress. Her face was hidden behind a cloud of a veil strung with pearls and capped by a broad white hat. She spoke English, but with a strong French accent.

"I wuz wondering where I might find ze powder room?"

Fatma gestured to the palace. "There's a place to freshen up in there."

"Ah! *Magnifique!* And tell me, how might I get you out of that fabulous zoot?"

Fatma started—then noticed the silver brooch pinned on the right side of the woman's gown. A carving of a snarling lioness. Dark smoky eyes stared back. Familiar eyes. One winked.

"Siti?" she blurted out.

A chuckle came from behind the veil. "Had you going there."

Fatma was at a loss. "What are you doing here? *How* are you even here?"

Siti tapped the lioness brooch. "Merira knows . . . people. Got an invitation." She produced a small letter between white-gloved fingers, addressed to some woman Fatma never heard of, with a French name.

"Siti, you can't just crash a royal event!"

The woman waved the invitation about. "Not crashing. Invited."

"That's not you."

"*Non?* But who elz would it be?" Siti asked, that silly French accent returning.

Fatma released a breath, trying to keep patient. "I'm working here."

"I'm working too," Siti replied, shifting back to Arabic. "Merira wants me here. In case our *friend* shows his face. He's decided to take on the temples. Set people after us. Well, we're not taking it lying down."

"If you're found out—"

Siti scoffed. "Found out? As if it's hard to play and act among this lot. Look at them. That's all they do—play and act. Not a real face in the bunch." She laughed throatily. "In a crowd like this, I can fit right in."

As if to prove her point, she whirled to a passing man and rattled off something in that French-accented English. He appeared startled, but stammered back in what she thought was German. In moments he was escorting her to a waiting boilerplate eunuch offering drinks. Siti laughed richly with him, turning to spare a winking glance.

The woman is incorrigible, Fatma thought. *And she looks good in that dress too.*

"I think that German will propose marriage before the evening is through," someone assessed. A woman stood near, watching Siti's antics with amusement. She looked in her thirties, with a plumpness that extended to her round cheeks. Her English carried inflections from the western parts of the continent. Her dress—with its bright greens and blues—bore the same. But what stood out was her company.

Standing beside the woman was a djinn. Tall and striking, her deep blue skin was wrapped in robes as gold as her twisting horns, though her face was a stark chalk white—so that it looked as if she wore a mask. Dizzying scents surrounded her—frankincense and cracked shea nuts, fragrant peppers and sweetened coconuts. She peered down imperiously with bright silver eyes, and Fatma pulled her gaze away, feeling flustered.

The woman, not appearing to notice, still stared after Siti—head cocked beneath a sun-yellow hijab that seemed more an elaborate crown. "I wager she's very interesting to be around. I saw you talking. You are a friend of hers? But forgive me my manners. I'm Amina."

"Fatma. Happy chance at meeting you."

"I'm happier." The woman smiled. She gestured to the djinn. "This is Jenne."

Fatma turned back to acknowledge the djinn, then did a double take. Jenne was now a man—no less imperious or striking, and with those same intoxicating scents. Those silver eyes regarded Fatma briefly, then took to inspecting a set of manicured claws.

"I must apologize again," Amina said, abashed. "Jenne doesn't mean to be rude. But you know how Qareen are. This one has been with my family for ages."

A Qareen. That explained things. Well, somewhat. True Qareen were said to be personal djinn tied to individuals: a type of life-long companion or shadow, even perhaps one's spirit double. This particular type of djinn, however, did far more—attaching to whole lineages, like living heirlooms that passed themselves down through time. While they were popularly referred to as Qareen, the Ministry officially listed them among the unclassifiable djinn. As a rule they could be troublesome, flighty, or fiercely protective of those they bonded with—one never knew.

"I've been eyeing that man over there in the silk clothes," Amina said. Her chin motioned to the figure in question. "An advisor and consort of the late Chinese empress dowager. Rumor claims he's actually of dragon blood, and over a hundred years old."

"Two hundred," Fatma corrected.

The woman's eyes widened. "We have dragons in my country. Temperamental beasts who will drink up rivers if given the chance. Are they very different in China?"

"No one's actually seen a Chinese dragon," Fatma related. "People claiming their blood, yes. But actual dragons remain elusive."

"Well," the woman murmured, eyeing the advisor with interest. "I'd like to know what a man with dragon blood is like. Are you one of the dignitaries?"

"I'm with the Egyptian government."

"A local. I thought by the suit you were English. Do you know many people here?"

"I'm not that high in the government. Just with a particular agency."

"Agent Fatma, then. I haven't yet met many Egyptians, sequestered as we are at Abdeen Palace. Odd housing us in the very place al-Jahiz bored into the Kaf—as if to make certain we understand Egypt's place in the world."

Fatma didn't doubt the intent. It was said that Abdeen Palace still bore the residue of the formidable magic al-Jahiz had wrought—and that it could be felt, like a shiver on your soul.

The woman assessed her, pursing a set of full lips. "You don't look like a bureaucrat. They don't dress near as well." She plucked a glass from a passing boilerplate eunuch, offering another to Fatma—who declined. The Qareen took two, and downed them in one gulp. "I've often wondered, with your modern city, why you don't just put these machine-men in charge? I'd give anything for a handful, over the men who govern us."

"Boilerplate eunuchs generally don't have much in the way of thought," Fatma explained.

The woman chuckled. "And how is that different from men?"

That actually made Fatma smile. But she wasn't here to socialize. She was set to excuse herself when several new figures stepped up to join them.

One was an older man with white whiskers on a ruddy face, and fitted into a double-breasted suit that looked stretched to its capacity. The second was short, in a plain black suit and in his middling years. His expression was serene, his mouth all but buried within a peppered beard. The third was taller, wearing a blue imperial uniform with gold about the collar and broad cuffs of his coat. His trimmed moustache swept across his upper lip, and he regarded them all with the eyes of someone accustomed to giving commands.

"Let the people replace us with automatons," the ruddy-faced man huffed in English, "and the rascals will be calling to overthrow them within the year!"

Amina turned to him, arching an eyebrow. "You think they will do any worse?"

The man snorted. "We at least share with the commoners the consanguinity of tissue, bone, heart, blood, and passion. Not the cold unfeeling will of a machine."

"And yet here we stand," Amina mused. "Set to decide whether we will be sending those people into war—to shed their tissue, bone, heart, and blood. Perhaps we could use less passion, and more cold unfeeling will."

The man raised bushy eyebrows, addressing his companions. "Did I not say the fairer sex will soon overtake us in politics and philosophy? Mark my words, our days are numbered!" He turned back good-naturedly. "My apologies, my lady, we overheard your commentary and wished to engage on the matter." He regarded the Qareen uneasily before returning to Amina. "Pray tell, are you not the princess of Tukulor?"

"There is no more Tukulor," Amina answered. "But I am a granddaughter of the empire."

Fatma's eyes widened. Princess of Tukulor! This was the granddaughter of al-Hajj Umar Tal, the wandering West African mystic who prophesied al-Jahiz's coming! He had returned to conquer his homeland in a self-proclaimed jihad, until nearby states united to stop him. Tukulor hadn't survived its founder. What remained knitted into a confederation of caliphates, which together with Sokoto and the help of djinn repelled Europe's armies. Umar Tal's legacy was complicated, to put it lightly. Though his descendants, like Amina, were all but revered.

"Allow me to make introductions," the Englishman said. "I am Lord Attenborough, a representative of His Majesty. This is President Poincaré of France." He indicated the short man in the plain suit. "And the big brooding fellow is General Zhilinsky, representing His Excellency of all the Russias."

"May I inquire, madame," Poincaré asked genially, "the purpose of your presence here? Surely the West Soudanic caliphates would not become involved in any conflict that might take place in far-off Europe."

Amina returned a diplomatic smile. "Conflicts have a habit of spreading—like fires in the brush. The caliphates would not want any . . . stray embers tossed our way."

Fatma parsed her words. Both England and France had been routed in their attempts on her homeland. Now the French were struggling with the Algerian territories, and it was no secret the caliphates openly supported the independence movements. If war came, it would extend to those colonies. Stray embers indeed.

"Let us hope, then," Zhilinsky spoke, "to find a way to resolve our differences without taking to the field. I do not relish sending cavalry to help our French friends fend against caliphate sorcery."

"What's this?" a voice broke in. "Yakov, are you going on about your cavalry again?"

A man strode into their midst, wearing an all-white military suit with white epaulets and festooned with medals and emblems. If there was a competition for such things tonight, he was the clear winner. He stood shorter than the other men. But his brashness more than made up for it.

None of that gave Fatma pause. Not even the man's moustache, brown like his trimmed hair but turned up at the ends in a way that reminded her of her uncles. Nor the small group of men trailing him like dutiful attendants. What startled her was the creature perched on his shoulder: short and squat, with dark green skin, a pencil nose, and long pointed ears. Dressed to mimic the man—down to the medals—it looked like an ugly doll. The name of the thing came to her then. A goblin. Beside them, the Qareen gave a low hiss.

The man looked them all over, his blue eyes taking in everything in one sweep, before turning to address Amina. "Are these men boring you with their talk, Frau? They can go on so." His English bore a German accent, unsurprising given the goblin. At the moment the eyes on the creature's wrinkled little face were shut tight. From what Fatma recalled, they spent most of their time in this realm sleeping.

The French president's face tightened at the gibe, and the Russian general's turned to stone. Only Attenborough seemed unfazed. He bowed to the German. "Madame Amina, may I introduce His Excellency, Kaiser Wilhelm II of the German Empire and Prussia."

Now the goblin made sense. It was Germany that had called a conference of European nations in 1884—two years after the routing of the British at Tell El Kebir. They met in Berlin and decided colonization was the only way to confront "the menace of magic," lest another Egypt take root. That mission proved harder than expected. A German-Italian force sent to take Ethiopia was wiped out utterly at Adwa in 1896. In 1898, the British were again spectacularly defeated at Omdurman. Maxim guns, it turned out, were no match for what al-Jahiz had released back upon the world.

Germany learned its lessons from those humiliations. While other European nations balked at magic, the new kaiser embraced it. German folktales were collected and scoured for any practical use. Djinn were not native to the country, but there were other creatures—chief among them goblins. Unlike his predecessor, Wilhelm II made open overtures and entreaties to the Goblin Court, allowing Germany to rapidly grow in its magical and industrial expertise—perhaps Egypt's only true rival in that regard. That bargain required the German leader to keep a goblin advisor. Though Fatma hadn't known the agreement demanded so literal a reading.

"When I saw this gathering," Wilhelm remarked, "I knew it would be the liveliest in the place. Yakov! I see Nicholas has sent you in his stead." He leaned in to Amina, feigning a whisper. "I hear the tsar can barely leave the country, with all the uprisings and peasants in the streets." He turned jovially to the French president. "Always good to see you, Poincaré. How are things with the colonies?" Leaning in again, he added: "Another beating like the one you gave them, and I don't know that they'll have much of an empire left."

Amina only sipped from her cup, making eye contact with Fatma. She didn't need to speak to be understood. Men. They could be such children.

"Why does everyone look like someone died?" Wilhelm demanded.

A set of shouts suddenly rose up—followed by a scream. Every head turned.

"Maybe someone *has* died," he concluded.

Fatma went on alert, scanning the crowd to see what the matter could be. People were scrambling back, their faces stunned. She struggled for a glimpse, bracing for what might come. Several dignitaries stumbled away, finally clearing a path. Her heart skipped. There, in dark robes, stood a figure in a gold mask.

The imposter was here.

CHAPTER
EIGHTEEN

Fatma watched as the man in the gold mask walked the palace garden with a casual air, hands behind his back. A silence followed in his wake. He stopped once, turning to look at someone. Abigail Worthington. She stood rooted to the spot, eyes gone round. When their gazes met, her body went limp—just managing to be caught by the young Abyssinian heir. Fainted. At least she hadn't landed on her hand again.

Fatma hadn't a clue how the imposter got past all the security, but he'd made a mistake. There were enough agents and police to take him. No riot would save him this time. She already had her pistol drawn, prepared to hold him until help arrived, when a new commotion came. Someone else pushing through the crowd, which parted a second time. The king, followed by his guards—the queen and prime minister hurrying behind.

"This man is a terrorist and a murderer!" he shouted. "Place him under arrest!"

The imposter didn't flinch as royal guards surrounded him, rifles raised. Instead he glanced over their heads, addressing the crowd. "I come to you tonight with no weapon in hand. All I have are words. Does the king of all Egypt fear a man and his words?"

The question was a challenge. And Fatma could see eyes shifting to the king. Before he could answer someone else spoke.

"I have no fear of words." Wilhelm shrugged, managing not to unseat the sleeping goblin. "Your Excellency, you have invited us to your country and kept us well secluded in your palaces and gardens. Yet we all know what has been happening in the streets of your city. It is on every tongue, even if others are too polite to make mention. Now the man himself has come. I would like to know why."

The imposter turned to the kaiser. "To bring truths that others may keep from you."

This elicited murmurs that rose through the garden in a low hum.

Amina scoffed. "What truths can a man hiding behind a mask reveal?"

The king seized the moment to reassert himself. "He is a fraud. A charlatan. He claims to be who he cannot. Nothing he says is worth listening to."

"Pardon, Your Excellency. But perhaps we should be the judge of that." This time it was the French president who spoke. He bowed but kept his eyes on the imposter.

The king frowned. "I assure you. Whoever this charlatan claims to be, he speaks lies."

"And who is it you claim to be?" Wilhelm asked.

The imposter stood straighter, his eyes burning. "I am al-Jahiz. Returned."

Gasps went up all around. Rumors were one thing. To hear it spoken, another. Some gaped. Others looked uncertain what to think. One voice rose to speak over them.

"You are not al-Jahiz." It was the unnaturally handsome djinn, the king's advisor. He pressed forward from the crowd, taller than the humans about him, black eyes smoldering against milk-white skin. "You are not fit for his shadow. A pretender who dares to wear the title—"

"Silence," the imposter commanded, waving his hand.

To Fatma's shock, the djinn's head jerked back as if struck. His mouth snapped shut, the sound of his teeth meeting reverberating with a crack. He stood confused, gripping and pulling hard at his chin. But his jaws would not open, as if they'd been welded and sealed. His dark eyes quavered, and he stepped back, a look of horror marring his perfect face.

The crowd grew silent at sight of the cowed djinn. Beside her, Fatma heard Amina mouth a prayer as her Qareen flowed to stand before her protectively. Even the king went quiet, staring as if he couldn't believe his own eyes. His guards stood their ground. But their faces showed uncertainty. The imposter paid none of them any mind, his gaze fixing on Fatma. No. Not her. The leaders and dignitaries about her.

"You are as remarkable as the rumors claimed," Wilhelm voiced in the quiet. He sounded both impressed and cautious. His attention went momentarily to Amina. "What do you say, Frau? Your grandfather prophesied the coming of the Soudanese mystic. Is this truly him returned in the flesh?"

Amina stared out from behind Jenne at the imposter, still shaken. She composed herself, however, and addressed the German kaiser. "As I must often remind others, I am not my grandfather. You will have to make that assessment yourself."

Wilhelm chortled, running fingers over his upturned moustache. "I suppose power doesn't flow in the blood." He turned back to the imposter. "So then, what words do you need to speak?"

"I must ask the same," the French president added, eyes inquisitive. "What words are so important that you make yourself an uninvited guest and risk your certain capture?"

The imposter spread long arms, letting his gaze wander over them. "Why are all of you here? Why has the king of Egypt sought this audience?"

"To bring about a lasting peace," Lord Attenborough answered succinctly.

"Peace." The imposter repeated the word as if it were a curious fruit he'd plucked. "You think Egypt can bring you peace when it cannot bring peace to itself. When its people cry out against its own injustices. When its corruption and decadence devour it from within."

"Let nations govern their personal affairs," Wilhelm retorted. "I am not here to judge how a sovereign rules his people. If you have come to persuade me on such matters, you are wasting your time." He gave a gracious nod to the king, who replied in kind.

"But Egypt is not concerned with just its own affairs," the imposter countered. "Egypt has involved itself in all of your affairs. It believes itself now a great power, who meddles far beyond its borders. Certainly, the sultan knows this."

All heads turned to a man who stood among the kaiser's entourage. He wore a Turkish suit with a red tarboosh, and his lightly bearded face was pensive. The Ottoman sultan. Fatma hadn't recognized him, behaving more like an attendant to the German emperor than his equal.

"The once magnificent Ottoman Empire," the imposter said. "Now beset by rebellions on all sides. Unable to gain back territories lost and losing more by the day. It sits weak and humbled, waiting to be picked apart by its foes." The imposter gestured to Lord Attenborough, the French president, and the Russian general Zhilinsky. "Does Egypt come to its aid? Does Egypt help mend these wounds? No, it only plunges the dagger deeper."

"This is outrageous!" the king bellowed. "Egypt has attempted at every turn to maintain the integrity of the Ottoman Empire. We have sought amenable solutions to all sides."

True as that was, the Ottoman Empire was in trouble. The return of djinn hadn't bestowed upon them the same gifts as Egypt. They were stretched too thin across too many continents, with subjects who held no abiding loyalty to the sultan. Nationalists rose up in every corner, making claims to sovereignty, drawing on magical traditions of their own. Meanwhile, Britain and France refused to return territories forcibly ceded near a century ago. The Russians openly encouraged independence movements in the East. Maintaining the empire was untenable; but no one wanted to see an utter collapse. Egypt had been working to avoid complete chaos.

"Was forcing you to grant Armenian independence one such amenable solution?" the imposter asked the sultan. "What has been the result? More of the empire, believing they can do the same? Believing that if they fight, Egypt will arrive to provide an . . . amenable solution?"

The sultan's face grew dark, and he turned to the king. "You did promise us that granting independence would alleviate grievances. Show that the empire could be reasonable. Now every nationalist clamors for a state, and my people whisper of my weakness." A bold admission—though nothing anyone here didn't know. The reputed plots and coups against the sultan were common knowledge. "Yet when we call you for aid in the Balkans, you say you cannot come. You say it is not a matter for Egypt."

The kaiser clapped his hands together. "Now things have become interesting!"

At her side, Fatma felt Amina grip her arm and lean in close. "He will turn them against each other! Like a snake let into your house. Stop him!"

That was going to be harder than the woman realized. So many here were looking for a reason to be at one another's throats.

Before the king could offer a rebuttal, the French president spoke. "I admit we found the calling of this peace summit odd, given Egypt's current support for the upheavals in Constantine and Algiers. You may not send troops or weapons, but your djinn are there. They and local djinn offer support to the rebels and Egypt does nothing to curtail them."

The king looked exasperated at this line of questioning, and the queen stepped in for him. "Surely, President Poincaré," she said with a stately grace that belied her common roots, "you do not think we must answer for every djinn in Egypt. Many do not recognize borders drawn on human maps, when they have walked these lands for centuries."

Poincaré bowed deep. "Your Highness knows the ways of djinn better than I." He paused, looking back up. "Yet how is it Egypt believes she can be an arbiter of peace among nations, if she cannot contain her own citizens?"

The imposter watched silently—like an assassin who had

plunged his knife into a weak spot, and waited for blood to flow. Fatma never took her eyes from him.

"I, for one," Wilhelm mused, "find it a curious thing that Egypt can be so magnanimous in providing a path to peace, yet so miserly with its wonders." There were new grumblings among the foreign dignitaries in the crowd. "Germany had to forge its own way. While Egypt refused to share its secrets. Well, that isn't true, is it? Some nations are more deserving than others, it seems. Yakov! How are those new gas lines getting along? And soon I hear an airship construction yard?"

Zhilinsky returned a stare. "It is no business of yours what we do and with whom."

"Those are developmental programs," the Egyptian prime minister explained, loud enough so that all could hear. "They don't include any machinery that could offer a nation an advantage over the other. Egypt is committed to its neutrality."

"And what of the work you are doing in Armenia?" the sultan pressed.

"More of the same, Imperial Majesty," the prime minister answered. "I assure you."

"Assurances," Wilhelm repeated, smoothing his whiskers. "I would not want to look up one day to find a fleet of heavy air cruisers decorated in pretty Russian designs flying over the Balkans, come to help their Slavic cousins." His tone turned sharp, like a blade drawn slightly from the scabbard. "It would be unfortunate if Germany had to help our friend the Sultan shoot such a fleet down. Even a very pretty one."

Zhilinsky glared. "Only if you want a million Russian soldiers on their way to Berlin to avenge their mother country!"

A sudden movement caught Fatma's eyes. The goblin on the kaiser's shoulder was stirring awake. It opened dull yellow eyes and yawned wide to show sharp teeth. Settling, it turned to the Russian general and spoke in a croaking voice: "The Goblin Court would not stand by and allow such an invasion. Doubtless it would include filthy rusalki and bagiennik, and lowly peasant

magic. We would consider that an act of war." It swiveled a baleful gaze to the French president. "Do not think us unaware of
the overtures you have made to the disgusting Fae. We would be
forced to act against any provocative alliance with such treacherous creatures."

Poincaré's face turned crimson. "You dare threaten us? Wretched
beast!"

Everything erupted after that.

What had been bared teeth turned to shouting. A nearby
French diplomat shoved his German counterpart, and a scuffle
ensued. The king's guards pulled him back, even as he pleaded
for order. Wilhelm and Poincaré traded insults only feet from
one another, while Zhilinsky looked ready to brawl.

In the midst of it all, Fatma struggled to keep track of the
imposter. She hadn't looked away, even as the exchanges grew
heated. But now there were tangles of people. Some grappling
with one another. Others trying to separate them. Amina was
loudly calling for calm, though Jenne looked ready to sweep her
away if need be. Fatma pushed people out of the way that blocked
her view, to find the place where the imposter stood—empty.

She cursed, spinning about and searching. He couldn't have
just disappeared. He had to be here! Her desperate eyes caught
sight of him, and she stared in disbelief. The imposter stood clear
across the garden, surveying the scene like a spectator. How did
he get there so fast? It was impossible! His eyes locked with hers
across the distance, before he turned and walked away.

Fatma was off, squeezing past people, knocking others aside.
When she finally broke free, she took off in a sprint. The gardens
about the palace were immense. The night's festivities were only
being held in one portion, and she had seen him moving into
the unlit portion—where palm trees and topiaries formed a small
dense forest. She was halfway there when someone pulled up
alongside.

"I figure wherever you're going," Siti called, "must be the right
place!"

Fatma glanced the woman over—running while holding up the hem of that white dress. She'd hoped for Hamed or Hadia or some of the other agents. But Siti was never the wrong person to have on your side in a fight.

"He went that way!" Fatma huffed, gesturing with her cane.

They reached the trees, stepping into shadow and looking about. Siti inhaled, as if testing the air. Then pointed with her chin. "This way." Fatma didn't argue, knowing by now to trust the woman's oddities. They ran, passing topiaries of beasts set up like a maze, turning this way and that before finally sighting their quarry.

"Stop!" Fatma shouted.

The imposter never broke his stride, hurrying for the shelter of some trees. Pointing her gun into the air, she pulled the trigger. The gunshot would send guards and soldiers descending on this area. Good. It also had the desired effect, forcing the imposter to turn about. He stared at them from behind his gold mask, before lifting a hand and throwing out what looked like a spray of sand in the dark. No, not sand. Ash. The flecks swirled through the air, fast resolving into a solitary masked figure garbed in black. The ash-ghul. In a blink there were two. They stalked forward as their master stood back to observe.

Fatma had no intention of letting them get close. She took aim. Beside her, Siti pulled hard at the bottom of her dress—tearing it away to reveal white breeches fitted into boots. Strapped to her legs were metal pieces which she pried off and began fitting together. Fatma waited until the two ash-ghuls were close enough to hit in the dark—and fired.

She'd learned two things that night in the Cemetery. The more divided the creature was, the weaker its duplicates. Also, what you did to one affected the other. Her bullet struck the one on the left, and it shrieked, bleeding black ash. Its doppelganger jerked, spilling ash from the same wound. She fired again, just at the one. Each mark hit home, slowing their advance.

"Here!" Siti stepped up. "Let me try."

Fatma looked to find her holding a blunderbuss with a flared muzzle. She'd been carrying that in pieces under her dress this whole time? The gun went off with a terrific boom, tearing through an ash-ghul and sending whole appendages flying. Siti walked forward, reloading and firing as she went. After four shots, there wasn't much left but a stumbling torso attached to two shattered legs. She swung the weapon like a club, smashing it to dust.

"Impressive," the imposter called. "But we have unfinished business." He reached out with his right hand, pulling his humming blade from nothingness and pointing it at Siti. "I recall putting this through your side. Yet here you are. How is that possible?"

Siti bared a sharp grin. "I have a lot more surprises."

Fatma had her own blade out. "We know what you took from the vaults."

The imposter waved the sword tauntingly. "There are no secrets kept from me."

"What do you want with it? What are you planning?"

He raised a finger to the lips of his gold mask in a hushing motion. "The Nine Lords are sleeping," he whispered.

Fatma frowned. Nine Lords? What was he going on about now?

"The Nine Lords are sleeping," he continued in singsong. "Do we want to wake them? Look into their eyes and they'll burn your soul away!"

Fatma gritted her teeth. For once, could villains stop being so damned cryptic?

Beside her, Siti growled. "Are we going to keep talking, or are we going to do this?" She had donned her claws and was all but dancing with anticipation.

"Now!" Fatma cried, charging.

They met the imposter at a sprint. Fatma pressed the attack, parrying the singing blade, then following with her own swings. Siti slashed, her claws raking the sword to send up blistering sparks. Something new drove them, different from that night in the Cemetery. Siti had seen her friends slandered and attacked.

Fatma had watched the Ministry burn. The memories fed their determination. This was going to end tonight!

With a sudden surge of strength Siti went hurtling toward the imposter. Her claws reached inside his guard, tearing through the front of his robes. He lowered his defense and backed away only to take a fast kick to the chest that sent him sprawling. There was an audible grunt as he hit the ground, and the black sword vanished into mist. Siti cried in victory, crouched and readying to leap when he held up a chain mail–covered hand.

"No!" His word was sharp, like a command.

And quite unexpectedly, Siti went still.

The imposter exhaled a surprised breath. "Of course! I thought I sensed it. But I couldn't be certain. How else could you have survived my blade?"

Fatma stared at Siti, not understanding. What was happening? The woman just stood there, muscles strained and poised, ready to attack. But she seemed unable to move, like a statue locked in place. Was this some new sorcery? She lifted her own sword and pointed the edge down at the imposter. "Undo whatever you've done!" she demanded.

He laughed. The first time she'd ever heard him do so. And his eyes burned bright. Dangerous. He uttered a word. Something in the djinn tongue. She thought it might have meant "unveil" or "become." Siti's eyes turned to Fatma, filled with something she'd never before seen in the woman—fear. Then, she changed.

It seemed to Fatma that Siti simply vanished. In her place stood a woman whose face still bore some resemblance. But she was taller, unnaturally so, with black skin like liquid ink. Two crimson ram horns curved up from her head into jutting points, and her eyes were those of a cat—bloodred pupils forming vertical slits that sat on beds of iridescent gold. It took a moment for Fatma to make sense of what she was seeing. Though it still made no sense at all. Siti hadn't become some other woman. She had become a djinn.

"You did not know." Fresh mirth tinged the imposter's voice.

"That will make this even sweeter." He turned to Siti. This time speaking in Arabic. "Kill."

Fatma was on the ground before she could think. The air ran from her lungs in a rush as her body was crushed by the weight bearing down on her. Someone was atop her, their knee pressing hard onto her chest, holding her down. She struggled to breathe. But someone had hands about her neck, choking her. Not someone. Siti. It was Siti who was choking her.

Fatma's legs kicked frantically, trying to escape this nightmare. But if Siti was stronger before, she was inhuman now. Between the pain Fatma tried to focus, looking into that strange but familiar face—filled with rage and teeth bared, showing sharp long canines. Her gaze swept up to find Siti's eyes. Djinn eyes. Opening her lips, she struggled to breathe, fighting to call the woman's name.

"Siti."

The sound was so weak, Fatma barely recognized her own voice. She hoped hearing the name might break the murderous trance that had come over the woman. Cut through whatever power now held her. But there was nothing. She fought for another free breath and tried again.

"Abla."

Still nothing. Not even the barest hint of recognition. As if the woman hadn't heard. And she remembered now where she'd seen such eyes before. Zagros. This was just how the djinn librarian had looked when he'd tried to kill her. A face like a mask of rage with dead eyes. Lifeless eyes. Like nothing lived behind them.

Fatma gagged as the breath was squeezed from her. Even as she struggled, there was a competing desire to just let go. To not fight. To let herself drift into a calm sleep. Just for a moment. Her eyelids were now so very heavy. The world grew distant and even the pain dulled to a numb ache that seemed someone else's concern.

No! Some stubborn part of her screamed defiance, jolting her into awareness. The world crashed in around her again in a wave of senses. The weight of Siti atop her. The pain. The inability to breathe. In her head, that stubborn voice persisted, urging her on. *Fight!* it demanded. *You're not going to die here! Like this! Fight for your damned life!*

Fatma forced her eyes back open—and found herself not staring into Siti's lifeless gaze but instead at a carving of a snarling lioness dangling from what remained of the woman's gown. Extending a hand she reached out for the silver brooch. It was a measure of her desperation that she even thought this might work. Her fingers grasped the bit of jewelry, ripping it away with the last of her strength and bringing it before those dead djinn eyes.

"Sekhmet."

Her voice was even weaker than before, an almost inaudible croak when she uttered the name of the entombed goddess. But the desperate answer she sought was immediate. Someone else's eyes suddenly looked out from behind Siti's gaze. Not dead at all but beyond life. Not ancient but ageless—as if it had seen the stars born and burned away. They stared down with the curiosity of a lioness inspecting a mouse, or the vast fiery desert contemplating the existence of a droplet of rain. Fatma felt as a speck beneath that glare, a mote of dust caught in a raging storm—and she thought she might wither away beneath its intensity, that beat down with the fierceness of a hundred suns. Then as quick as they came, those terrifying eyes vanished, leaving behind djinn eyes. No longer lifeless. No longer empty. And filling with utter horror.

Siti—or the djinn she had become—yanked her hands from around Fatma's neck. In one movement she bounded up, stumbling back and away, her body trembling. She shook her head wildly back and forth as if trying to dispel something, before an anguished scream escaped her throat. Unexpectedly a set of broad feathered wings unfurled from her back and spread wide.

They beat frantically, lifting her off her feet and into the air. In moments she was high into the sky, soaring away into the night.

Fatma watched it all, turned on her side, trying to breathe. How long had all of that been? Minutes? Seconds? Lights swam in her head. Once again she had to force herself not to black out. There would be time later to try to put together what had just happened. There would be time later to think after Siti. There would be time later to try to mend the pieces of her life.

Her eyes instead searched the dark. She found the imposter, standing and watching the skies after Siti, before turning to walk away. Something inside Fatma snarled like an animal. She rose on weakened legs and stumbled forward, grabbing for the first thing she could find. The abandoned blunderbuss. Out of ammunition. But still useful. Breaking into a stuttering run, she got as close to the imposter as possible and let out a shrill whistle. He turned in surprise, and she swung.

He never saw it coming. Had likely thought her dead. Or incapacitated. His mistake. She heard a satisfied crunch as the gun's barrel connected solidly. The gold mask cracked on one side, spinning away. He stumbled back, a tumble of black locks flying from beneath his hood—before his face *rippled*.

Fatma's eyes went wide, watching as the man's dark skin undulated like water. He clutched where he'd been struck, either in pain or to smooth out the distortion. Too late! Dropping the blunderbuss, she reached to grab at a fistful of locks, her other hand going for her janbiya. She only managed to get hold of a strand as he pulled away, the knife slicing down. Something struck her hard, and she went flying, tumbling end over end— before the night erupted in fire.

The Ifrit.

It seemed to materialize out of darkness, a living bloodred inferno in the form of a giant, with glowing horns and molten eyes. A torrid wind buffeted the trees and topiaries—turning them all into pyres. Still clutching his face, the imposter scrambled onto the djinn's waiting back. His mount spread fiery wings and in one leap soared into the sky, bearing its master away.

Fatma watched them disappear, before limping over to where the gold mask lay. Picking it up, she found the dark lock she'd managed to cut away. Her hands tightened on both as one thought filled her head.

His face had rippled!

CHAPTER NINETEEN

Atop the stage at the Jasmine, a lone trombone player belted out a solo. Frog, as Alfred was better known, hadn't gotten the sobriquet for his short stature. Or his gravelly voice. But instead for the sounds he forced from his trombone—something between a croak and blare, inspired, he claimed, by the nighttime bayou in his native New Orleans. Tonight, he played a somber tune, with long drawn-out notes as his cheeks puffed and blew.

The spot was less crowded than usual—a by-product of the unease in the city. The djinn proprietor stood dejectedly among his idle servers, eyes fixed on the door for patrons.

Well, Fatma thought gloomily, they had her.

She didn't remember deciding to come here. Things were a bit fuzzy after the police and palace guards found her among the burning topiaries. She recalled handing over the cracked gold mask and lock of hair to Hadia. Then she'd wandered off, her mind set on one thing—Siti transforming into a djinn. Make that two things. Siti trying to murder her. When she closed her eyes, she saw that inhuman stare—lifeless, as Siti choked the breath from her. She should have felt sick. Angry. Hurt. But she was just numb. In that dazed state, she'd ended up here.

"You better slow down."

Fatma turned to find Benny. His silver cornet sat between them, like a silent customer. He scowled at her cup.

"You need a real drink to drown your sorrows. Can't do nothing on sarsaparilla!"

"With mint leaves and tea," she muttered.

He shook his head, glancing her over. "Must have had some night."

Fatma looked down at her suit, which bore scorch marks and a tear along one shoulder. She'd lost her bowler too, letting her cropped black curls hang messily.

"Been a long two weeks, Benny."

He threw back a glass. "Work or personal?"

"Both." She finished her cocktail and motioned to the bartender for another.

"Them the worst kind. This have to do with Miss Trouble? You two have a fight?"

Fatma almost laughed, eyes darting to the door. A part of her wanted Siti to stroll in, wearing some outrageous gown. As if that would make everything that happened tonight disappear?

"Whenever me and my lady had problems," Benny related, "seemed like the whole world was on fire. No one or nobody could hurt us the way we hurt each other."

Fatma resisted the urge to ask if this lady of his ever transformed into a seven-foot djinn and tried to break his neck.

"I'd try to remember the good times then," he said. "Not let this one hump break us. Sure enough, we'd be back together right as rain."

"Did your lady ever keep secrets, Benny? About herself?"

He put a finger to the tip of his nose. It took a moment for Fatma to catch his meaning, until she rubbed her own nose and a bit of soot came off on her fingers.

"Usually the secrets we keep deep down, ain't meant to hurt other people," he said. "Not saying they won't, but not through intentions. Those deep secrets, we hide away because we're afraid what other people might think. How they might judge us, if they knew. And nobody's judgment we scared of more than the one we give our hearts to. Besides, everybody got secrets. Even you, I'm betting."

He sat with his drink then, polite enough to leave her to her thoughts as the trombone wailed its lament.

She walked out of the Jasmine after about an hour. There was only so much sarsaparilla a body could take. Buttoning what was left of her jacket, she made her way through the backstreets near Muhammad Ali Street. Head down, she tucked her cane under one arm and hunched her shoulders, hoping to broadcast that she wanted to be left alone. She especially hoped whoever had taken to following behind her—their heavy footsteps unmistakable in the quiet—would get the hint. Sighing, she stopped under an archway near a set of short steps and spoke in a clear no-nonsense voice.

"Look, I've been having a rough go of it. In the past week I've fought ghuls, a sorcerer, a maddened Marid, and stared down an Ifrit. You think you want some of this, then go ahead and try me. Just wanted you to know what you're getting yourself into."

There was silence followed by a familiar guttural rumble.

"Your days have been quite full, agent."

Fatma turned around, shoulders slumping. "Evening, Ahmad."

The self-proclaimed god of the Cult of Sobek skulked from the shadows. It seemed he'd undergone more changes. He was bulkier, and moved with an odd gait. Beneath his brown robes, she caught snatches of pale gray skin and a protrusion on his face like a muzzle. His penetrating dark green eyes looked more crocodilian than ever. What was the man doing to himself?

"Evening, Agent Fatma," he returned in a raspy hiss.

"Didn't we talk about you following me around? I thought we agreed it was creepy?"

He spread his hands apologetically—both now webbed, with black claws.

"Malesh. I just want to talk."

Fatma squatted on the steps, her back to the archway. She didn't feel like going home yet anyway. "So talk."

Ahmad squatted opposite her, though he seemed to have a rough time at it. He pulled out a Nefertari, his inhuman face asking, *Do you mind?* She waved her consent. He made an elaborate show with the silver scarab lighter before taking a drag and cocking his head. "Are you well, agent?"

"Do I look that bad?"

His green eyes studied her. "Yes."

"Thanks."

"I mean to say, you don't seem yourself. I see beyond flesh and bone to spirit. Yours looks . . . wounded. I am here, if you need someone. To listen, I mean."

She stared at him. He thought she wanted to unburden her problems on him? A man who thought he was an ancient god and was now disfiguring himself? What gave him the nerve?

"You want to know what's wounding my spirit?" she asked hotly. "Fine! I'll tell it all to you, until you choke!" That's precisely what she did. She told him about the fruitless quest of her case. Of the attack on the Ministry. Of what had happened tonight. And about Siti. Of those lifeless eyes that sought her death. When she was done, she felt wrung out. But at least she wasn't numb.

"That . . ." Ahmad began. He cleared his throat. "I thought you were going to tell me about your self-doubts or maybe about some interpersonal conflicts with your coworkers. I wasn't quite expecting so much. You *do* have problems!"

"You've been a great comfort," she told him wryly.

"I'm sorry all of this has happened to you, agent." He offered his cigarette.

Fatma hesitated, then accepted, taking a long pull. The tobacco smoke swirled in her nostrils, reaching her tongue—and she gagged. She could probably count the times she'd ever smoked a cigarette on one hand. But this was by far the worst. "This is awful. It tastes like . . ."

"Stale feet?" he suggested.

"Why do you smoke them if they're so bad?"

"They don't call it a habit for nothing."

She handed back the Nefertari. "Did you know? About Siti?"

He shook his head. "Though I myself am no stranger to . . . transformation. I hope the two of you can find a path forward. I am also no stranger to love and loss."

His words struck her, as they always managed to do. She fought to rise above her own problems and grief, imagining the pain he carried. "I haven't given up on the case, Ahmad. I'm going to find this imposter. I'm going to bring him in. Your . . . Nephthys will receive justice."

His reptilian eyes searched her. Whatever he saw there appeared to bring satisfaction.

"Justice comes for the wicked in time. The scales of Thoth demand it." He came to his feet, dropping the spent cigarette and stamping it out. "Thank you, agent."

"For what?"

"For trying. For deciding that Nephthys mattered."

He turned to walk away.

"Wait," Fatma called. He swiveled his head around, fixing her with green baleful eyes. She searched them, trying to see if there was anyone else—anything else—staring back at her. "You really believe there's a"—she fumbled at the word—"god, living inside you?"

"A bit of a god. A drop, to an ocean." He squinted curiously. "And what is it, agent, that you have seen this night?"

Fatma fidgeted at the question, unnerved by his odd perception. She didn't answer, instead posing another query. "What's happening to you now, is it your choice? Or something being done to you, by your"—she fumbled again—"god?"

Ahmad seemed to contemplate this, before rolling his shoulders in a shrug. "When you have faith, it really doesn't matter." With those final words he left her there, his odd gait carrying him into the shadows like a god back to his realm.

It was near midnight when she reached her apartment. *You have to go home eventually,* her mother often said. She caught sight of two figures in blue gallabiyahs standing at her door, in heated discussion. One was the bewab, Mahmoud. The second one was . . . Fatma frowned. The second man looked remarkably like Mahmoud as well. Same portly build. Same receding graying hair. As she came close, both turned to her, surprise on their faces, and she stopped in her tracks. There were two Mahmouds.

That same red-brown face, bushy eyebrows—even that look that could weigh and judge in a moment. She blinked, and wondered whether this night had finally taken its toll on her mind.

"Good night, Captain," one of the Mahmouds greeted.

"We know how this might seem," the other said.

"But we can explain," the first finished, palms open.

Fatma looked between them. "Are there two of you?" She needed that confirmed first.

"Yes," both replied.

That was a relief. "Which one of you is Mahmoud?"

"I am Mahmoud."

"And I am also Mahmoud."

Seriously? "Then which one of you is my doorman?"

The two exchanged an awkward look. "Both of us."

She nodded, though that made absolutely no sense. "You were going to explain . . . ?"

"My brother and I are both the bewab of this building," one Mahmoud said.

Twins. She'd already deduced as much. "This whole time, there've been two of you?"

"When we came to Cairo, it was not easy finding work," one spoke. "Everyone wants mechanics for the factories or expects you to have skills in machinery. What do old men like us know of such things? This was the best work we could find."

Fatma listened, things falling into place—the way Mahmoud seemed always on duty, or didn't appear to sleep, or how he knew everything that was going on. "Does the building owner know?"

A Mahmoud shook his head. "And we would keep it so. We have traded shifts quietly, outside of everyone's view." The two put on identical sheepish looks. "We were careless tonight. Brothers will argue."

"The owner's only paying one of you? Why do double the work if not double the pay?"

"It's more complicated than that," one answered. "We are offered a place to sleep and live, so long as we mind the building."

"We mind it so well," the other picked up, "we're paid more than most bewab in the city at comparable places, wallahi."

"More than twice as much, wallahi!" the first exclaimed. "The owner does this because he believes one man is doing such tremendous work. He feels good in knowing that he is so generous in his rewards. If he were to find out there are two of us . . ."

Fatma thought she understood. It was the perfect racket. Sort of. Maybe? She was a bit perturbed they'd fooled her for so long. What kind of investigator was this unaware of what was going on right in front of her eyes? Thoughts of Siti flashed in her head, knotting her stomach.

"Your secret's safe with me," she told them.

"God keep you, Captain," a Mahmoud said thankfully. "We Sa'idi can always be counted up to keep each other's secrets."

He looked over her disheveled clothing. "The Ministry is working you even harder than usual." His tone went low as if he were delivering some secret information. "We hear the palace was attacked!"

Of course they had. Fatma just nodded, not wanting to get into it.

"You catch that son of a shoe making these troubles!" the other Mahmoud exclaimed as he ushered her inside. "We do not believe his lies! I do not care if he is al-Jahiz returned twice over, wallahi!"

"Wallahi, he belongs in a prison!" his brother finished.

She walked through the open door, then stopped to peer back at them. "How do you keep it up? Pretending to be one person? Knowing that you have to hide what you are?"

Both men shrugged. "We already know who we are," one answered.

"We all do what we must do," the other said. "The first lesson we learned in Cairo."

Well, she couldn't fault them there. You made a place in this city however you could.

She took the elevator up. When she got to her door, she

fumbled for the key before opening it and stepping inside. The place was dark. Just as she'd left it. But not empty.

Siti sat in the chair by the balcony with her head in her hands, Ramses lounging in her lap. At seeing the door open she lifted the cat away and stood, coming forward. Fatma stepped back, more by instinct, and Siti broke her stride, going still, hands clenched at her side. Neither spoke, until Fatma closed the door. Siti took a few tremulous steps, bringing them closer. Her dark eyes held worry, and streaks on her face showed where tears had left their mark.

"Are you . . ." she began, voice tremoring. She reached out a hand, and Fatma tried not to flinch. Siti's fingers pulled back before trying again, touching at the cloth Fatma wore about her neck. Hadia had given the hijab to her, when she'd seen the wounds. Siti's hands shook as she unwrapped the fabric. When she saw the deep bruises beneath, her face seemed to break. "I'm sorry," she whispered.

Something about the statement sent a spike of anger through Fatma, and she fought to control her roiling emotions. Pulling away, she wrapped the hijab back about her neck and sat down heavily on the edge of her bed.

"You're a djinn," she said. A declaration rather than a question.

"Yes," Siti answered, her voice low. Even after seeing it with her own eyes, the admission still staggered Fatma, and she took a deep breath to steady herself.

"And no," Siti continued. "I mean, I'm a half-djinn. Or however that works out."

Fatma looked up sharply. By "half-djinn," people often meant a nasnas, a troublesome creature that was literally as its name described—with a half a head, half a body, and even only one arm and leg. She'd been gifted her janbiya for banishing a particularly nasty nasnas troubling the clan of a visiting Azd dignitary. But that's not what Siti meant. She was speaking to something even more fantastic, of which even the Ministry knew little.

"One of your parents was a djinn," Fatma reasoned. It was the

only thing that made sense. If any of this made sense. "Your father."

Siti's face tightened. She walked back to the chair, making
space besides Ramses and wrapping her arms about herself. "I
don't really know much about him. My mother claims he came to
her the first time as a laughing breeze, while she was out tending
goats. The second as a shower of coins that fell from a clear sky.
The third time, he was a man—tall and beautiful, with golden
horns, skin that shone like polished ebony, and eyes that twinkled
with starlight." She scoffed. "Or at least, that's how my mother remembers it. She was just a girl. Not even fifteen. He had probably
lived hundreds of lives. Their tryst was short, just long enough to
keep his attention before he wandered off to whatever new fancy
caught his eye. Long enough to leave me in her belly."

Fatma took it all in. The Ministry had been dwelling on this
probability. Djinn hadn't only come back into the world, they'd
become part of it—working, living, and interacting with humans.
Sex was a foregone conclusion. Rumors of the carnal insatiability
of some djinn were the stuff of bawdy jokes and songs. But there
were also relationships, some serious. Djinn procreation, at least
with other djinn, remained shrouded in mystery. No one had ever
seen a djinn infant or child. Half-djinn, however, were popular in
old stories and folklore. Bilquis, the queen of Sheba, was claimed
to be a half-djinn, among other famed personages—all reputedly
gifted with supernatural powers. With the return of djinn, the
Ministry predicted the world would once again enter an age of
people who could no longer merely be called human—born to
magical lineages and with unpredictable, unknowable capabilities.

"Which one are you?" Fatma asked. "The person sitting here
now, or . . ." An image of the inhuman being she'd seen tonight
flashed across her thoughts: those curving ram horns, sharp
teeth, and feline eyes.

"Both are me. I'm exactly who you see now. How I see myself
most of the time. And sometimes . . . I'm who you saw earlier. I
know, it's hard to understand."

That was an understatement. Fatma had an easier time understanding the two Mahmouds. She was reminded of Siti's aunt,
Madame Aziza. What was it the old woman had said? That Siti
was like the wind. *Too much of her father in her.* Those words took
on new meaning. So much did now. Siti's seeming abilities—the
magic that granted her speed, allowing her to scale walls, or leap
distances humanly impossible. The question of that magic had
always nagged at Fatma's mind. But she'd never asked. *Maybe
you didn't really want to know. Maybe you knew the answer would
lead to something like this.* Another thought wormed its way into
her head. The dizzying high she felt around Siti. The woman's
almost electric touches. No, the thought had been there all night.
She was just finally confronting it.

"Did you ever . . ." It took a hard swallow to continue. "Did
you use djinn magic on me? Did you make us happen?"

Siti stared as if she'd been slapped. Shock morphed into hurt,
and then into anger that flashed in her eyes. "I would never do
that. I'm not my father. I didn't think you would have to ask." Her
voice tremored again, this time with all the emotions that passed
across her face.

"Didn't you?" Fatma shot back, her own emotions seizing her.
"You lied to me. How do you expect me to react?"

"I didn't lie. The person who laughs with you, who dances
with you, who shares your bed, who washes your hair. That's me!"

"But that other person is you too. You said as much. They're
both you."

Siti didn't argue, going silent. "I wanted to tell you," she said
at last. "There were so many times I came close. But how could
I speak about what I am to Agent Fatma, at the Ministry of Alchemy, Enchantments, and Supernatural Entities? I'm right there,
in the last word of your damned title. All I saw was you regarding
me as some curiosity. A specimen to study. Just another *thing* that
needed minding."

Ramses meowed, a warning they were getting too loud, and
Fatma felt her face flush. Would that have really been her reaction?

Was it part of her reaction now? She recalled Benny's words on secrets. *Usually the secrets we keep deep down . . . we hide away because we're afraid what other people might think. How they might judge us, if they knew.* Maybe that was worth considering. But there was more at stake here.

"That other you tried to kill me tonight." Her hand went reflexively to her neck. "Is it something you can't control? When you're . . . a djinn." The word was still hard to say.

Siti closed her eyes, as if facing the memory was too much. "When I'm my other self, I feel . . . free. Everything is just— *more*. Every sensation. Every awareness. And I love that." She opened her eyes again, fixing on Fatma. "Do you know where I go at night? When I leave your bed before dawn? To fly. To soar above the city. If you could see it the way I do—like a glittering jewel to snatch up!" Her hand reached to mimic the motion, a moment of joy lighting her face.

"I don't have sad tales to tell you. I'm not some tragic character from a story, lost between two worlds. I revel in who I am. What I am." Her voice hardened. "That monster, he took that from me. Took away my freedom." She tapped a forefinger to her temple, face contorting as she searched for words to explain. "I could hear his voice. In my head. Like he was inside me, shouting, so I couldn't hear anything else. The part of me that's me, got lost in that voice. I tried to fight, but he just pushed me aside. I was there but not there—buried somewhere deep, sunken away, while my body did what *he* wanted. What *he* demanded. Do you understand what I'm telling you?"

Fatma searched Siti's face, and what she saw there left her shaken. The most daring and reckless person she'd ever known was terrified. She remembered staring into her lifeless half-djinn eyes. Zagros had that same empty look as he tried to murder her. She recalled the king's djinn advisor, forced into silence. And an Ifrit, tamed into a faithful hound.

"The imposter . . . he can control djinn," she said breathlessly. The revelation chilled her.

Siti nodded grimly. "He's more dangerous than we ever thought. Far more."

That was putting it lightly. It wasn't just dangerous, it was a disaster! Worse, this imposter had a plan. Everything he'd done was methodical, with purpose. And now he'd stolen the means to re-create the Clock of Worlds. None of this was good. In fact, it was terrible. They had vastly underestimated what they were up against.

Fatma looked to Siti, tracing the outline of her face, which had taken to stare out the balcony, imagining her fingers running along its curves.

"What stopped you, then? From killing me?"

Siti looked back solemnly, then gave a surprising laugh, wiping a tear from one cheek. "You did. That beautiful voice of yours, calling out my name. It was like throwing a rope into a dark hole. I grabbed it and climbed up, until I could get out."

Fatma was quiet. Siti may have heard her voice, but it wasn't her name that had broken that trance. "You didn't answer when I called your name," she said finally. "You only answered to this." She fished a piece of jewelry from her jacket, fashioned as a snarling lioness. She hadn't discarded the brooch since ripping it away. Siti accepted the silver carving, her face bemused. So she had no idea, then. No memory of what actually happened.

Fatma's immediate instinct was to say nothing. Yet weren't there enough secrets between them? She sighed inwardly and, taking a breath, began to explain—as best as anyone could explain—what she'd called forth and what she'd seen behind the woman's eyes.

When she finished, Siti whispered an unfamiliar prayer. "Blessed Lady of Flame, Daughter of Slaughter. She for whom the two skies open at once after she shows herself in splendor!" Her wide eyes fixed on Fatma. "You were blessed to have looked into the Eye of Ra!"

"I tell you I saw . . . something . . . lurking inside you, and that's your only response?"

Siti gave a slight shrug. "I'm a child of the goddess. She does with me as she wishes."

Fatma couldn't say why, but for some reason that answer rankled.

"Besides," Siti went on. "She came to you."

"What does that mean?"

"I've spoken prayers to the Blessed Lady. Given offerings. Praised her many names. Yet she's never shown me her face. You called her and she came." Siti paused in thought. "Perhaps you and the goddess share a special bond. One of which until now you were unaware."

That, Fatma decided, was absolutely terrifying. She whispered her own prayer and changed the subject.

"You fled," she said, her tone accusatory. "When you came back to yourself. You just . . . left me there."

Siti lowered her eyes. "I had to. Seeing what I'd just done. Knowing I could be used, like a *thing*. I didn't trust myself. I needed to get as far away from him as possible."

Fatma ran a hand through her hair. "I don't blame you for what happened tonight," she said at last, surprised that she meant it. "You were being used, and I know you wouldn't do what you did, intentionally." The relief that stole over Siti's face made it hard to say the rest. She plowed on anyway. "But I can't just make things go back to how they were. You kept a part of yourself from me. Even if you had good reason." She'd always felt she was only getting pieces of the woman, what she wanted to share. Now she knew it was true. And that hurt. More than she cared to admit. "It's going to take time for me to work through all that." Her hand touched the scarf at her neck. Some wounds healed slower than others.

Siti looked back up. "Time is something I have a lot of," she replied soberly.

Fatma started. "Are you saying you're immortal?"

"What? Gods no! I'm being metaphorical."

"That's a relief. I don't think I'd be able to stand you at all if

I found out you were going to live forever." Technically, djinn didn't live forever. Still, they counted centuries the way people counted decades.

"Well I'm not going to live a whole millennium," she amended. "Maybe I'll see a hundred years. Or two? No one's really certain."

Fatma gawped. Then she recalled something suddenly, another oddity from that night.

"When I asked the imposter about the Clock of Worlds, he answered with a song. Something about Nine Lords."

"Nine Lords who are sleeping," Siti recalled. "Who would burn your soul away."

"You know what that's about?"

Siti thought for a moment. "Sounds like some djinn tale. There are lots of them. Always about more awful djinn we should be thankful didn't come through the Kaf. But I don't recall anything about Nine Lords. Maybe it's another story of djinn rulers?"

There were certainly enough of those. Most were fables, or distorted versions of the truth. Popular folklore, for instance, told of a legendary djinn king who ruled over Mount Kaf, a land of fantastic wonders at the edge of the world. Al-Jahiz had shown that the Kaf was in reality another realm—or realms—rather than some hidden mountain.

"I want to see you," Fatma said. "The other you."

Siti's eyebrows rose at the request. "You're sure about that?"

Not really, Fatma thought. She'd only decided moments ago. But it felt like something she needed to do.

Seeing her resolve, Siti stood and walked over, extending a hand. "I'll do it slow."

Fatma took her fingers and felt a small tingle. Then, before her eyes, Siti transformed. Her dark skin turned black until it glinted. Horns a deep red erupted from her head, bending and curving upward while her body grew taller. Slow or not, it was over in several heartbeats. At Siti's feet, Ramses purred. He'd hopped off the chair, and now nuzzled her legs.

Fatma stood, tracing fingers along Siti's new hands, the ones with real claws, trying hard not to remember what they'd done tonight. She moved to Siti's arms, feeling the taut muscle beneath black smooth scales—each so miniscule it was hard to see where they fit together. She had to go up on her toes to touch the horns, sliding fingertips across the ridges.

Siti hummed low in her throat, tossing her head slightly before staring down with crimson cat eyes that shimmered on gold.

Fatma pulled back. "Did I hurt you?"

"Not that." Her voice was almost the same, just deeper. "The horns have certain . . . pleasure spots."

Pleasure spots? That was new.

"Didn't you have wings?" Fatma almost jumped back as in answer, two enormous black and red wings unfurled from Siti's back, their crimson tips brushing the ceiling. For the first time she noticed they matched the tuft of curly hair that sat nestled between the horns on her shaved scalp. Ramses stood on his back legs to swat at her feathers, but they were out of his reach. He jumped up onto the bed, hoping to get at them from a better angle.

Fatma let out a small laugh.

Siti frowned. "What's funny?"

"You. You're damned beautiful. Even as a half-djinn, you're still as beautiful as ever."

Siti smiled. Touching Fatma's chin lightly, she bent until their lips met. *Definitely electric*, Fatma thought, falling into the kiss. She had to will herself to pull away and stepped back, almost stumbling.

"Sorry," Siti winced. "I said I'd give you time. It's just . . . you touched the horn and . . ."

Fatma caught her breath, shaking off the rush. "I know you said you never did anything to make us happen. But you're not the first woman I've ever kissed. And none leave me dizzy."

"I was born, in part, of magic," Siti answered.

"Meaning? That's how you can do the things you do?"

"It makes me stronger. Faster, more agile. And when I really care about someone, that magic works on them too. Maybe you find you heal faster. Or you wake up rested like you've had ten hours of sleep, when it's actually been two." There was an awkward pause. "I might also be able to feel or know where you are at any given time." Fatma's eyes widened at that, and Siti added hastily, "None of it is meant to deceive you. It can't make you behave in ways you wouldn't otherwise. It's just nothing I can help, any more than I can how I feel about you."

There was so much she was going to have to reevaluate about these past months, Fatma sighed. Another thought. "How are your clothes still intact?" She motioned to the black outfit Siti still wore—the one she usually did when running about at night. "There's a lot more of you like this. Not to mention the wings."

"Half-djinn can't do a lot of complex magic. Not like full djinn. But shifting our garments so that we're not ripping out of them and standing around half-naked is pretty standard. Took a while to perfect it, of course. I went through so many clothes when I was younger my mother—aay!"

Ramses had launched from the bed, and now clung to the underside of one of her wings. She transformed back, and he tumbled to the floor in a furry ball of silver. Scooping him up she wagged a scolding finger, which he batted at playfully.

"You're *sure* he isn't a djinn?" Siti asked.

Fatma sat back down, watching them. "We have to stop him. The imposter."

Siti joined her, Ramses in her lap. "We will."

The three of them sat there—a Ministry agent, a half-djinn, and a cat (likely), staring out past the balcony to the sleeping city they somehow had to find a way to save.

CHAPTER
TWENTY

T he Abyssinian coffee shop was fairly empty for ten in the morning on a Thursday. But that wasn't too surprising. The city was beset with fresh new fears once word got out about the peace summit. Cairo's rumor mill was working overtime: al-Jahiz had descended in a fireball, slaying everyone with his sword; no, he'd soared in on the back of an Ifrit, raining fire; the king had fled the country, and would return with an English army; no, it was the king that slew al-Jahiz with his own sword, and now the Jahiziin sought vengeance.

Fatma read over the morning papers as a boilerplate eunuch delivered coffee, setting down a white porcelain cup with a mechanical "Buna tetu." The Amharic phrase, literally "Drink coffee," had joined the lingua franca of Cairo as Ethiopian brews grew more popular. It was now a polite comment and even a greeting among the more modish that frequented coffee shops. A few of that sort were here now, in their telltale black coats and black tarbooshes—the women with stylish black dresses and bright white hijabs. They threw around words like "post Neo-Pharaonic" and "epistemologies of alchemic modernity," eyes veiled behind dark glasses and lips pulling leisurely at thin cigarettes—perhaps meant to show their defiance to the panic gripping the city.

Or they were just being weird. Good for them either way, Fatma decided.

She turned back to the papers. The summit was still on. Despite last night's debacle, none of the delegates or leaders had departed—each playing a game of one-upmanship and bravado. The king would have his hands full. Well, that was his problem. She had enough to deal with.

The door opened, and Hadia walked in, taking a seat across from her. They greeted each other good morning and called the boilerplate eunuch over for another order. When the machineman walked away, Hadia looked Fatma over with a scrutinizing gaze.

"You going to tell me what happened to your neck?"

"No," Fatma replied, sipping her coffee. She'd not bothered with a scarf, opting for a striped blue shirt with a high collar. But it couldn't hide everything.

Hadia scowled like a disapproving grandmother. "You look rested. So that's good." She squinted. "Even your neck looks better. I can barely see the bruises. How's that possible?"

Fatma shrugged, a hand rubbing where the soreness had mostly vanished. No way to properly explain having a half-djinn lover. She'd slept soundly too, waking to find her weariness gone and her mind alert. For once, Siti had been there, curled up and asleep on the chair. Sharing a bed right now was awkward. But neither had wanted to spend the night alone.

"After you wandered off," Hadia continued. Was there a reprimand in her tone? "I didn't expect to see you this morning. Why'd you leave a message to meet here and not the office?" She took a cup offered by the boilerplate eunuch, tasting it and wrinkling her face before scooping in more sugar.

"We still have a case to solve," Fatma reminded. "After last night, brass is throwing every resource at hunting down the imposter."

"So I've gathered. There are new agents all over the office. Requesting our files—well, demanding them, really. I spent the last two hours recounting everything we have. Though I think they'd prefer to talk to you."

"Bet they would," Fatma grumbled. Likely agents flown in from Alexandria, here to muscle her off her own case. "That's why we're not meeting at the office. I have information that I don't want to share just yet." She leaned forward, and in a low voice told what she knew. Hadia's eyebrows climbed with each revelation.

"He can *control* djinn? How is that even possible?"

"Don't know," Fatma answered.

Hadia shook her head in wonder. "And I thought when you explained this Clock of Worlds, that was going to be the worst of it. So an Ifrit as tame as a horse. Zagros trying to kill you. The king's advisor having his mouth welded shut. All of it, the imposter controlling djinn. How did you even figure this out?"

"Can't say." She'd omitted references to Siti, of course. "It's . . . complicated."

Hadia studied her again, those calculating brown eyes shifting to her neck and narrowing.

"Let it go," Fatma said. "We need to focus. And we're mostly on our own."

"You're thinking if the Ministry gets wind of this, it might cause a panic."

"I *know* and it *will*. Word hits the streets that this imposter can control djinn, and the city will explode. I also know how brass works. They're spooked as it is and embarrassed about last night. They'd push to have djinn rounded up—claim it was for public safety."

Hadia looked horrified. "That's a bad idea! There are thousands of djinn living in the city. Dozens more passing through at any given moment. Not to mention, most are Egyptian citizens. They have rights. They're not going to take being rounded up quietly."

Fatma knew that for certain. "We had to take in a Jann once—an earth elemental. Evacuated a city block to be on the safe side. Contracted two Marid to help us. Got him in the end. But half the block was reduced to rubble. Government tries rounding up a few thousand djinn, and we won't have to worry about this imposter destroying Cairo. We'll have done it for him." She set down her cup. "One other thing . . ."

"Nine Lords?" Hadia asked incredulous when Fatma finished. "Who burn away souls?" She slapped her palms to her cheeks, shaking her head. "Do you ever have good news?"

She did actually. "Last night when I broke the imposter's mask, I saw his face."

"How is that good news? We've seen his face. Soudanese. A bit fanatic."

"Yes, but this time, it rippled."

Hadia frowned before understanding played out on her face. "An illusion!"

Fatma smiled triumphantly. The moment she'd seen that ripple, she'd known. Of all the miserable things gone wrong last night, that one glimmer sustained her. "He's a fraud! Hiding behind an illusion!" She leaned in. "Did you notice? Alexander Worthington wasn't at the summit."

Hadia nodded slowly. "You really still think he's the imposter?"

"He's where our investigation left off."

"But why disrupt a peace summit his father helped plan?"

Fatma didn't have an answer. Why disrupt the summit at all? It was one thing to sow chaos in Cairo, but an international meeting of world leaders and dignitaries? That was upping the stakes considerably. Then there was the Clock of Worlds. It still bothered her that the one thing they lacked for this imposter, whoever he might be, was a motive—or an endgame. Still . . . "Alexander Worthington's absence at a moment al-Jahiz makes an appearance is at least suspicious," she noted.

Hadia chewed her lip. "Checked on that. It was one of the things you mentioned last night before disappearing. Turns out Alexander did try to attend, but had car trouble. His driver confirmed it."

"Convenient," Fatma huffed.

"There's more." Hadia pulled a folder from her satchel, placing it onto the table. "I had some research done on Alexander last week. Results came back this morning."

Fatma raised an eyebrow. "You mean you did what we were expressly forbidden to do?"

Hadia blushed. "I have a cousin who works in Immigration and Customs. I merely suggested it might be good to look into Alexander Worthington as a foreign national. Standard background review."

Fatma opened the folder. "I'm really liking your cousins. What am I looking at?"

"Military school records. Turns out Alexander isn't exactly what he seems—but not in the way you might think. See his graduation?"

Fatma scanned the page. Alexander did attend military school as he claimed. Only his marks were less than stellar. Dismal in fact. "Bottom percentile," she read. "He barely passed."

Hadia handed over another sheet. "You know how he went on about serving in India? He spent most of his time game hunting sacred Makara. The one battle he did lead was a disaster. He and his men had to be rescued. My cousin claims his commanding officer wouldn't stop talking about how useless he was as a captain. Was relieved when he left for Egypt." She shook her head. "Alexander doesn't strike me as some great mastermind. More a mediocre Englishman."

Fatma looked over the file. It seemed the Worthington name, rather than merit, had bought him the rank of officer. She closed the folder, unsure what to make of it. Alexander was still their best lead. He *was* involved. Somehow.

"You're not the only one who went digging," she said. "Contacted a bookie I know about that Illusion djinn Siwa." Khalid confirmed the djinn was well known among the betting circle—for placing hefty wagers, making fantastic winnings, and then losing it just as fast. "Siwa's in debt, like we thought. The money wired him went right into paying some of that off—and placing new bets. But it's a long way from proving anything."

"So how do we get proof?" Hadia asked.

Fatma finished her cup. "We start with what we have and work from there. Did you get the items I gave you last night to forensics?"

"Dropped them off before I went home. Told the clerk on duty we needed a quick turnaround."

"Good. Let's see what they've found." She stood up, adjusting her bowler. "Then we need to have a talk with our librarian."

◆   ◆   ◆

Entering the Ministry after the attack was surreal—like walking in on a patient undergoing surgery. The debris had been cleared, and masons were recasting the emblem—laying down fresh blue quartz where the stone had been chipped away. High above on scaffolding, a blue-skinned djinn with black curling horns barked out commands to a crew of harnessed workers dangling by ropes. They worked fitting together gears under the djinn's frantic instructions, calls of "Yes, ya bash-mohandes, right away!" ringing out. She heard the djinn architect had cried when he saw the destroyed clockwork brain. Their old building was dead and gone, but he'd construct a new brain to make it live again.

The elevators at least were working, operated for the time by boilerplate eunuchs. She signaled to the machine-man they were headed to the third floor, and watched the doors close, dulling the cacophony of the workers.

"I'm hoping Dr. Hoda can give us some clues," she told Hadia.

"Dr. Hoda? The chief of forensics is a woman?"

"You didn't know? Been with the Ministry since the beginning. Kept it quiet, though, so as not to cause a scandal. Was easier when headquarters was stuck out in Bulaq. Ministry tried to keep her there when the new building opened in 1900 and hired a forensic paranormalist to be the public face. Only he wasn't very good. Agents bypassed him, sending everything to Dr. Hoda. He got upset, I hear, insisted either she'd go or he would."

"Guess we know how that ended," Hadia deduced as the doors opened.

Supernatural Forensics took up the third floor—a maze of desks topped by laboratory equipment and gadgets. Men in white coats bustled about, peering through spectral goggles at specimens or taking measurements with calipers. The laboratory had taken damage during the attack, as rampaging ghuls smashed instruments and overturned tables. They were beaten back by Dr. Hoda, who whipped up an alchemical concoction that melted the undead to soupy puddles. You just didn't mess with her lab.

They found the chief of forensics in a room with darkened windows, sitting before a large glass orb filled with clear liquid being heated under a burner. Dr. Hoda peered at it through an odd contraption covering half her face—with about eight lenses of various sizes, some retracting or extending at the tap of a finger. Her hair was a frizzy gray mass like a halo, with some strands dangling heedlessly close to the open flame. She paid no mind to that, studiously holding a dropper to a spout at the sphere's top.

"Mind your eyes," she remarked, not looking to them, and let a tiny globule fall from the dropper. It landed in the clear liquid, which swirled a bright luminescent white, before releasing a sharp burst of light.

Fatma blinked away the sparks dancing in her vision. When she could see again, the air about them had changed, bathed in iridescent swaths that vibrated and hummed. Beside her, Hadia was a silhouette of shifting colors in the shape of a woman. Then with a suddenness everything snapped back to normal.

Dr. Hoda tapped a pen to her chin before scribbling in a notebook. When she finished, she stripped off the contraption about her head, replacing it with a pair of regular glasses. Her eyelids fluttered as she took them in, brown skin wrinkling about prominent cheekbones.

"Agent Fatma. Haven't seen you in my lab in a while."

"Good morning, Dr. Hoda. Thought I'd make a personal visit. This is Agent Hadia."

Dr. Hoda's black eyes glittered. "A new woman agent? I hadn't even heard. I should get out more, I suppose. Is that the right thing to say?" She shook Hadia's hand enthusiastically. "When are they going to see about getting me a woman in here? They keep sending me more men. Pretty little things, but I've got maybe five more good years in me before retiring, and I want to leave my lab in capable hands!"

Fatma suspected the doctor was going to be here much longer than five years. They'd probably be wheeling her from the lab straight to her own funeral. "You'll have to take that up with Director Amir. He seems keen on getting more women into Cairo headquarters."

"I'll have a talk with that young man, then." Dr. Hoda nodded.

Oh, Amir was going to *love* that. "Agent Hadia dropped off some specimens last night. Hoping you've had a chance to look at them?"

Dr. Hoda's eyes widened, and she hopped up from her chair. "Yes! Yes! You left me quite a project. Come." She led them out and into another room. Inside was a table atop which sat two familiar items. One was the gold mask. A jagged crack extended where Fatma had struck it, though the etchings still slithered across its surface. The other was the lock of black hair she'd sliced away, its wiry fibers binding it together.

"What do you see?" Dr. Hoda asked.

"A mask?" Fatma answered.

The doctor returned a flat stare. "I'm going to need you to be a bit more observant."

"A gold mask. With etchings that move across it. Some kind of magic."

"Better. A gold mask with magic etchings. Pick it up. How does it feel?"

Fatma sighed inwardly and picked up the mask. Was it too much to get a straight answer for once? "A bit heavy. Smooth. Except for this crack running—" She stopped, frowning as her fingers traced the fracture.

"Is there a problem, agent?"

"I used a gun to hit a gold mask, and it cracked. Gold shouldn't crack that easy."

"Very good," Dr. Hoda commended. "Look back at the mask."

Fatma did, and almost dropped it. The crack was gone. The mask's surface was unblemished—except for a slight dent where the fracture had been.

"What's going on?" Hadia asked, equally stunned.

Dr. Hoda chuckled. "Denting a gold mask seems more reasonable, doesn't it? Lay the mask flat on the table. Good. Now, I don't believe this is gold. I'm going to show you. When I do, you won't believe it's gold either." She took a small hammer from a set of nearby tools and, with a firm swing, brought it down on the edge of the mask. A piece broke away, and she followed up by smashing it to gold dust.

"That's impossible," Hadia breathed.

"That's an illusion," Fatma rejoined, understanding dawning.

"An illusion," Dr. Hoda agreed. "Whose magic works by getting you to play a part in your own deception. When you first struck the mask, you probably weren't consciously thinking of it being gold and all the properties that should entail. So it cracked. However, I asked you to identify it as gold. That even made it feel heavy like gold. When you realized that cracking a solid gold mask was unlikely, the illusion rearranged into a dent to make more sense in your mind. Now, I've sowed new doubts, breaking off a section of a supposedly gold mask and grinding it to dust." She leaned forward, tapping a forefinger beneath one eye. "Do you still believe it's gold that you're looking at?"

Fatma shook her head. "It can't be. So why do I still see gold?"

"Because you're stubborn," Dr. Hoda snapped. "Keep telling the mask what it should be and it will keep trying to meet your expectations. Stop expecting anything. Just let it be what it really is."

Fatma looked at the mask. Let it be what it really is. How exactly was she supposed to do that? She stared at it for a long while. Nothing. She scowled at it. Still nothing. She picked the mask up. Still heavy. No, gold felt heavy. Only this wasn't gold. It was just a mask. That's all she really knew. It could be made of anything. *It was just a mask.*

The change happened quickly.

One second, she was holding a broken gold mask. The next, something else—dull and gray, with the crack again running along its length. Hadia's gasp told her she saw it too.

Dr. Hoda whooped a triumphant laugh. She took the mask from Fatma and turned it over, running careful fingers along its underside. "Clay." She gestured to the table, where the gold dust had turned into bits of broken earth. "It's just clay."

Fatma stared in disbelief. "Did you know all along?"

"Not exactly. When I saw the crack, I knew it couldn't be gold. But it wouldn't change for me. This illusion appeared attuned to you—making your perception the focal point. Perhaps because you were the last to see it woven around the person meant to be concealed."

"But the mask appeared as gold to us as well," Hadia put in. "You're saying that's because Fatma believed it was gold?"

"Illusion magic often works by creating a mass shared delusion," the doctor explained. "Some people in a crowd see a man in a gold mask. Then, like a contagion, they spread the deception to others. Soon, everyone sees a gold mask."

"Who would be able to create that type of illusion?" Hadia asked.

"Why, only a djinn. This imposter has djinn allies, I hear."

More likely under his control, Fatma corrected quietly. "Could an Illusion djinn do this?"

The doctor pondered the question. "Unlikely," she concluded. "Illusion djinn are able to change their appearance or that of a place they inhabit—where they're strongest. They're likely behind stories of thirsty people seeing water in the desert that isn't there. Or the man granted riches, only to later find the glittering jewels are rocks. Notorious tricksters. Their illusions vanish as soon as they're no longer in proximity." She gestured at the clay mask. "This illusion carried on long after it was separated from its weaver. That's potent magic—beyond an Illusion djinn."

Fatma shared a disappointed look with Hadia. Not Siwa, then. "What about an Ifrit?"

Dr. Hoda's eyes widened. "Oh yes! Fire magic! Very potent!"

It made sense, Fatma reasoned. If you could control djinn, go with the more powerful. She turned to the lock of hair. "What about this? Can I try what I did with the mask? Maybe it's an illusion too."

"Definitely an illusion," the doctor confirmed. "I put it under spectral analysis. It's drenched in djinn magic. But a mask is one thing—a created object. Hair is a different matter. It belongs to this imposter, a part of him. He's woven that illusion tightest of all. You'll have to try very hard."

She did. A few times. But the hair remained as it was.

"Don't blame yourself," Dr. Hoda soothed. "We're dealing with very strong illusion magic. Your mind doesn't have the first hint on how to see past it. I can use an alchemical treatment to make it easier for you."

"How long will that take?" Fatma asked.

Dr. Hoda bent to scrutinize the piece of hair. "Days. Weeks."

"We don't have that. We need it done immediately."

"Winds often blow against the way ships want!" the doctor snapped, sounding uncannily like Fatma's mother. "The solution to loosen up magical bonds could also dissolve the hair itself. Go too fast, and you'll end up with nothing." Seeing Fatma's insistent stare she rolled her eyes. "I think I can make something that speeds up the rate of magical decay but won't cause physical erosion. That will still take many, many hours."

"How many hours is that exactly?"

"'Many' means 'many,'" Dr. Hoda reiterated testily. "It's your illusion. If you want to unravel it sooner, find a way for your mind to see past it. Go hunt some clues or something. Isn't that what you do?"

"Thank you, Doctor," Fatma said appreciatively, knowing well enough when not to push.

They left the lab, letting the doctor get on with her work. Boarding the elevator, Fatma gave an order she hadn't in a very long time. "Floor Zero."

When the doors opened again, it was to a hallway lined with arched wooden doors inscribed with red calligraphy. Floor Zero was the official designation for the Ministry's holding cells, created with the help of djinn. There were no guards here; the calligraphic inscriptions served as wards against even the most powerful magic. Today there was only one occupant. She stopped at a door and fished out a gold key, fitting it into the lock.

"You sure about this?" Hadia asked. "What if he's still . . . how he was?"

"I don't think it works that way. The control wears off once the imposter's gone."

"Let's be on the safe side." She unhooked a black truncheon hanging from the wall, priming the lever until the bulbous end crackled. Fatma couldn't begrudge her caution. She turned the key, pushing the door open.

Zagros sat on a cot that looked far too small for his bulk. The djinn librarian was dressed in his usual long-sleeved khalat, his back to them. He faced a blank wall, not bothering to move at hearing the door. A bowl of uneaten food sat in the corner, alongside a jug of water.

"Good morning, Zagros."

The djinn stiffened at Fatma's voice. His horned head turned slowly about, golden eyes taking her in from behind silver spectacles. There was nothing dead in that gaze now. Just resignation. Neither had seen the other since the day of the attack. This first meeting was as awkward as expected. His stare lingered awhile before returning to the wall.

"I'm sorry for what happened," he rumbled, the bells on his ivory tusks tingling.

At least he was talking.

"Why don't we discuss that." Fatma pulled up a stool and sat. Hadia shadowed her, eyes wary and black truncheon at the ready. "You're facing serious charges. Besides trying to kill me, the Ministry thinks you helped break into the vault. That you're in league with the imposter."

Zagros gave no response. He'd gone still again, a rock carved in the shape of a djinn.

"But we know that's not true, is it?" Fatma asked. "So why do you let people believe that? Why not defend yourself?"

More silence.

"The Ministry could keep you here for a long time. With nothing to do but stare at that wall. Probably hire someone else for the library. Let them rearrange all your books. Maybe create an entirely new ordering system."

Her words elicited the smallest tremor, but the djinn returned to his stoic pose.

Fatma frowned. He must really be far gone to shrug that one off. Might as well lay her cards on the table. "I know about the voice. The one in your head. That made you want to kill me. I know how you heard it not just in your ears but everywhere." That certainly got his attention. He turned back to her, eyes rounding. She went on, remembering Siti's description. "I know when you tried to kill me, it wasn't really you. That the real you was buried somewhere deep inside. That you had to watch yourself do all those things, helpless to stop it."

Zagros's jaws went slack. A thousand questions seemed poised on his tongue as his eyes searched her for answers. Then something seemed to close within him. The light in his gaze faded back to dull resignation. Slowly he turned to the wall, resuming what he seemed intent on making his eternal stare.

"This is ridiculous!" Fatma snapped, losing her patience. "I know you didn't try to kill me. I know that the imposter can somehow control djinn. Why are you set on letting everyone think you're a traitor? Why don't you exonerate yourself?"

There was a long stretch of silence before he uttered in a rumbling whisper, "I cannot."

"What do you mean you can't? Are you protecting someone?"

"I cannot." The words were still a whisper, but more insistent.

"Or are you just ashamed to admit what happened to you?"

"I cannot!" His voice came strained.

"That's not good enough!"

Zagros turned, and when she saw his face, she started. It had gone a pale lavender—coursing with sweat and contorted in pain. His lips worked, fighting to squeeze out the smallest sounds.

"He can't answer you!" Hadia said, recoiling. "Don't you see? He's choking! Make him know he doesn't have to answer!"

She was right! The muscles in the djinn's neck bulged, and his golden eyes rolled back as he sputtered. Fatma jumped to her feet. "I'm not asking you anymore! Stop!"

Zagros let out a lengthy wheeze, clutching his throat. He heaved in great ragged bellows, before his shoulders slumped and his breathing returned to normal. Fatma looked in bewilderment to Hadia, who just shook her head. What in all the worlds was that?

"You work so hard," Zagros's voice came quietly. "To perfect yourself. To cultivate an impeccable air. And in the end, it can all be taken away from you. In an instant." His gold eyes rolled up to look at them. "Do you know that I am, in truth, a half-djinn?"

Fatma's eyebrows rose. Another half-djinn? She took in his massive size. "Half of what?" she blurted out before she could stop herself.

"My mother was a daeva," he intoned.

Ah. That she could see. Daeva were distant cousins of djinn from Persia and its neighboring regions—though some djinn balked at claims of kinship. Highly reclusive, what little the Ministry knew of daeva came from Zoroastrian writings and oral folklore. One thing the sources all agreed upon, was that as a class of beings they were highly disagreeable. And that was putting it lightly.

"I grew up with all the stereotypes of being half-daeva," Zagros continued. "That our daeva blood made us quick-tempered. That we were wild, untamed—prone to violence and destruction. My father's family warned him my mother might tear him limb from limb on their wedding night. In truth she only tried to do so once. Perhaps twice."

Right, Fatma thought. *Definitely disagreeable.*

"I worked hard to counteract that bias. I became the most dignified of djinn. I carried myself with grace. So that none could cast aspersions on my lineage. All of that taken from me now—at last reduced to the half-civilized daeva prone to murderous rage." He released a weary sigh. "It is a terrible thing, this politics of being perceived as respectable. To be forced to view your frailties through the eyes of others. A terrible thing."

Fatma wondered at that. She hadn't asked Siti how djinn treated those of partial blood. But from what she knew of immortals, they could be as foolish on such matters as humans.

"Then let us help you," she urged. "Let us clear your name!"

Zagros opened his mouth only to have it snap shut again, seemingly against his will. He hung his horned head, shaking it in submission. Fatma realized it was futile to ask again. This wasn't obstinance. There was magic at work here. He was being prevented from talking.

"Just like Siwa," Hadia whispered, sharing her unspoken thoughts.

Fatma ground her teeth in frustration. Someone was throwing roadblocks in their way, whenever they got close. At this rate this case would never be solved. She motioned to Hadia that they should go. There was nothing to be gotten here. They'd made it to the door when Zagros called out.

"Have you ever read *One Thousand and One Nights*?"

Both women turned back to him.

"A very influential set of tales," he went on, gaze still on the wall. "The Ministry library has several bound versions. But don't bother with any of those. There's a bookseller. Rami. In Soor al-Azbakeya. He's the one to buy from." He paused, as if choosing his words delicately. "Ask him to show you what you cannot see."

Fatma exchanged a curious glance with Hadia. "Thank you," she said uncertainly. Though confused at his advice she decided to push further. "One other thing. Have you ever heard of the Nine Lords?"

Zagros turned to her now. She thought there might actually be surprise in those eyes. "Where did you hear this?"

"The imposter. He sang a song. 'The Nine Lords are sleeping. Do we want to wake them? Look into their eyes and they'll burn your soul away.'"

The librarian looked at her with bewilderment before answering. "An old djinn lullaby. My father sang it to me. It tells of nine ancient Ifrit. There's a fuller rendition: 'The Nine Lords are sleeping. In their halls of fire. Do we want to wake them? No, we dare not wake them! Look into their eyes and they'll burn your soul away! Go to sleep, my children, or they'll burn your soul away!'"

"The imposter has an Ifrit," Fatma said. "Could that be one of these Nine Lords?"

Zagros shook his head. "The Nine Lords are *great* djinn. Some of the first formed of smokeless fire. A few blasphemously and boldly claim to have created themselves, pulling their fiery forms from the void. Any Ifrit you have encountered would be as children to them. These Nine Lords were once masters of djinn."

"Like the stories of djinn rulers and kingdoms?" Hadia asked.

"They were our enslavers," Zagros growled. "Djinn were held as thralls to their power. Forced to proclaim them our Great Lords. To fight in their ceaseless wars. To raise up monuments in their honor. To toil building them palaces to house their thrones."

Fatma could hear the ire in his voice. Djinn didn't appear too fond of these past kings. "What happened to them?"

"These are only stories," Zagros rumbled. "But it is said that djinn rose up, fought for our freedom, trapping the Nine Lords into an endless sleep and burying them deep within the Kaf. They exist now only in lullabies sung to unruly djinn children as a warning. Be good, heed your elders, or the Nine Lords will awaken—and come for you!" He shrugged heavy shoulders. "But again, these are only stories."

"You know what the imposter stole," Fatma said. "The secrets to the Clock of Worlds. Could he be trying to awaken these Nine Lords?"

Zagros raised a bushy eyebrow at her. "How can one awaken a story?"

With those last words he went silent and spoke no more.

CHAPTER
TWENTY-ONE

Soor al-Azbakeya sat in the very heart of Cairo. Books were what was sold here—piled on tables, stacked in stalls, sometimes assembled on the street itself. The best places to explore were the shops dotting the buildings—some so small, only their owners could fit inside to grab out what you wanted. More enterprising vendors took up several floors and housed everything from medieval manuscripts on alchemical mathematics to manuals for barometric steam mechanics—not to mention the new rage for trashy western romance novels.

Rami's Books & Assorted Ephemera was a medium-sized affair. Bigger than the small shops, yet only taking up the second floor of a building—its sign visible from the street below. Fatma and Hadia crossed toward it, pushing through yelling vendors all looking to attract buyers. Being there were few of those, they were especially forceful—thrusting books right under your nose and promising good prices. Fatma almost rapped one man with her cane to get him to step aside. There was only one book she was interested in right now, and one seller.

She and Hadia had stopped to eat, reviewing Zagros's cryptic remarks over a plate of kofta atop fragrant arugula. Neither had the first idea where to start seeking these Nine Ifrit Lords. But they'd both read *The One Thousand and One Nights*.

The stories had been popular in Egypt for centuries. With the return of the djinn, they were now treatises for academics to pore over, trying to separate possible truths from fancy. What those tales had to do with all of this, however, was hard to imagine. But they couldn't afford to turn up their noses at possible leads. Reaching the building, they climbed the stairs to Rami's.

True to its name, the shop was filled with books. Most were old, bound in worn leather whose scent hung in the air. Gilded brass lamps descended from the ceiling to provide illumination, joined by tallow candles in bronze holders. A surprising extent of antique clocks lined the walls, all synced to the same time. Altogether, the place carried a rustic feel detached from Cairo's modernity.

Fatma surveyed the shop and caught sight of a small man perched on a ladder and stuffing books onto an upper shelf. Seeing them, he ambled down and walked over, baggy trousers swishing.

"Welcome to Rami's Books and Assorted Ephemera," he greeted warmly, the white curling hair on his face moving in time with his speech. "Is there a text you are looking for that I can help find?"

"*The One Thousand and One Nights*," Fatma answered, her eyes roaming. There was one other person in the shop—an old woman, Abyssinian by the look of her, not to mention the white woven dress and colorful sash about her waist. She sat bent over a large tome, turning pages gingerly before inspecting them with a magnifying glass.

"I have many of those!" the bookseller beamed "Most are in Arabic and include the over one thousand stories. I have others in the original Persian or Sanskrit, though the stories are fewer."

"How about the ones that might interest a Persian djinn who goes by the name Zagros?" Fatma displayed her Ministry badge. Hadia followed.

The bookseller's smile slid away, and his aging face furrowed. He licked his lips for a moment, reaching up to scratch his head and pulling back at remembering he wore a tarboosh. "Zagros sent you?"

"Big djinn. Purple skin. Ivory tusks. Something of a snob."

The small man chuckled. "That's certainly Zagros. Is there

a particular reason he asked you to come to me? To find that book?"

"He said you could show us what we can't see," Hadia answered.

The bookseller straightened, his face turning eager—as if he'd been waiting for just this moment. "Well, then. We'd better have a talk." He turned, calling out to the Abyssinian woman. "Tsega! Brew some tea while I close up the shop. We're having company!"

Sometime later, Fatma sat with Hadia at a small table. Above hung a brass lamp that poured down light that glinted off a banner with a gold Star of David. The old woman was setting down small cups of tea in front of them, while the bookseller inspected the spine of a bound volume. Both spoke as they worked.

"I was alone in the shop after my first wife, Magda, died," Rami related. His short fingers ran along the book's covering as if they could suss out its contents. "Then about ten years ago Tsega wandered in and promptly started an argument over how I'd arranged some Sassanid texts. I knew right away I had to marry her."

Tsega sniffed, pushing back her braided hair. "I worked at the royal library at Addis Ababa," she said proudly, sitting down and taking up her tea. "His arrangement was all nonsense. It took me this long to get it right. Only reason I stayed and agreed to marry him."

The bookseller offered a sly wink. "As you see, I'm a very fortunate man. A practicing Egyptian Karaite marrying a Haymanot from Abyssinia. And both unabashed bibliophiles. Where else but Cairo could such love take root and bloom?"

"How do you know Zagros?" Hadia asked, smiling, seeming to have already taken a liking to the couple.

"I was always able to get old manuscripts for him when no one else could," Rami answered. "That djinn might have a rough tongue, but his heart's soft for books." His tone became worried. "Is he alright? I know the Ministry was attacked. I can't imagine he would send you to me unless something had gone wrong."

"And why would he send us to you?" Fatma asked. She wasn't

trying to be rude, but she really needed this to move along. Besides, the public didn't need to know about Zagros. The bookseller seemed to sense her mood.

"Right, then. Let's get to it." He set down the book. "*The One Thousand and One Nights*. A common enough book. Really a work completed over time, by many authors. The first tales came from Persia and India and weren't translated to Arabic until the eighth century. Sometime later, probably in Baghdad, a new set of stories joined the first along with some older folklore."

His eyes took on a storyteller's twinkle, and Fatma sighed. This was going to take a while.

"It wasn't until the thirteenth century that stories from Syria and Egypt helped swell the number to a thousand," he continued. "Some stories were only added recently—like the one about Ali Baba and the thieves. The conjuration of an imaginative Frenchman likely. Though these Forty Leopards I read about in the papers appear inspired by the tale, which itself drew inspiration from older stories. Since the arrival of the djinn, newer tales are being spun within coffeehouses and in backstreets. Probably some right here in Azbakeya. I suppose when it comes to *The One Thousand and One Nights*, we are ever swelling its pages."

There was an impatient click of the tongue from Tsega, and Rami shook himself from his reverie.

"At any rate, you're likely familiar with the more traditional tales. You probably even have favorites."

Of course, Fatma thought. She'd known them since she was a girl. "The Merchant and the Djinn." "Abdullah the Fisherman." "The Ebony Horse." When she got older she read the more frightening ones—like "Gherib and His Brother Agib," filled with ravenous ghuls—or downright bawdy ones, like "Ali with the Large Member." There were stories about mansions on the moon and mermen or talking trees, each more fantastic than the next.

"I always liked 'The Three Apples,'" Hadia related. "And 'The Tale of the Murdered Girl.' Things like that. About mysteries that had to be solved."

"Seems fitting." Rami nodded. He tilted his head to the side. "What about 'The City of Brass'? What do you remember about it?"

"The one with King Sulayman, yes?" Hadia asked. "About some people on a quest?"

"Looking for a lost city," Fatma added. The story had been a favorite as a child. "There were brass horses, people who had been petrified, a mummified queen . . ."

"Oh! I remember the mummified queen!" Hadia added briskly.

"Do you remember what it was the quest was searching for?" Rami asked.

Hadia opened her mouth, then frowned. Fatma did the same. She recounted the story in her head—so vivid with its living marionettes and humanlike machines, which many scholars now thought were early djinn-created precursors to boilerplate eunuchs. But she couldn't recall what the quest was about. And that was odd—as it was the whole point of the story.

"I don't remember," she admitted.

"Perhaps this will help." Rami opened the book to a page, tapping it with his finger. "Go ahead. Read. What the quest was about is right there."

Fatma's eyes scanned the text. It read easily enough, written in that old style and rhythm typical to these stories. It started with a king and a discussion over the prophet Sulayman. A sailor landing in a strange kingdom with black-skinned people who were naked and walked around like wild beasts, without speech. She frowned. Had that part always been so uncomfortably racist? There was something about a djinn she couldn't quite grasp. Her mind seemed to slip around the words. Putting it out of her head, she continued searching. The quest was begun by a character named Talib. Only she couldn't see exactly why. She tried again, reading slower, ignoring the places where the words appeared to just skate out of her vision. Shaking her head, she slid the book toward Hadia who was craning to get a view.

"I didn't find anything," she said. "What was I supposed to see?"

The bookseller smiled, exchanging a knowing look with his wife. "Stop playing with them, Rami, and just explain," she chided. Then to Fatma, "With his dramatics, sometimes I think he should have gone into the theater. Back home, he might have made a good Sulayman in the staging of the *Kebra Negast*. Or maybe one of the debating Coptic orthodox fathers in the overture."

Rami snorted at the remark but answered. "What you aren't quite seeing is where the purpose of the quest is mentioned. The seekers were attempting to find a set of brass vessels that once belonged to King Sulayman. It was said he trapped djinn within, using his seal, before throwing them into the sea." He tapped the book again. "Do you see it now?"

Fatma took another look—and saw what he was talking about immediately. The words were right there, plain as day. Talib had learned of vessels of brass used to house djinn, who had been trapped there by King Sulayman using his signet ring. He had gone on the quest, searching for them. There was even a symbol drawn to the side of the text—a hexagram made of two interlocking pyramids embedded in a circle. Where had she seen that before? Something was written beneath the symbol, in djinn script.

"The Seal of Sulayman," Hadia translated, eyes fixed on the hexagram. She frowned, looking to the bookseller. "What's that? And why didn't we see any of this a moment ago?"

Rami pointed a finger upward, wagging it tellingly. "Two questions of the same kind. Like either side of a coin. The Seal of Sulayman is many things. Sometimes it is a six-pointed star, or a five-pointed star, or eight, even twelve. At other times it's the symbol on the page, often enclosed in a circle. The image became popular in Renaissance Europe and with later believers in the occult, who likely adopted it from far earlier esoteric Judaic, Byzantine, and Islamic traditions." At those words, Fatma remembered where she'd seen the symbol—on the banner of the Brotherhood of Al-Jahiz! Only the circle was a fiery serpent devouring its tail.

"No one is exactly certain what the seal looked like," Rami went on. "But there is a very interesting account in 'The City of Brass' about the djinn said to be trapped by Sulayman. It tells of a ring. Some say the ring is engraved with the seal, placed there by God. Others, that the ring itself *is* the seal. The one claim they all agree upon is that the ring granted Sulayman power over spirits. In Islamic tradition, that meant control over the djinn!"

Fatma glared at the bookseller. A ring that could control djinn! A ring that would make one the Master of Djinn!

"Why haven't we heard of this before?" Hadia asked. Fatma wanted to know that as well. It seemed impossible the Ministry could have overlooked something so important.

"The other side of the coin," Rami pronounced. He looked intently at Hadia. "That is a beautiful hijab. So very modern. Forgive an old man for being so forward, but it goes well with your eyes." He next turned to Fatma. "I could say as much for your tie. That color is red?"

"Magenta," Fatma replied, looking as uncertain as Hadia. What was he getting at?

The bookseller leaned forward. "What were we just talking about?"

Fatma opened her mouth to answer. Then stopped. Her mind had gone inexplicably blank. She quickly recounted the past few minutes. They'd sat down to talk about *The One Thousand and One Nights*, he mentioned "The City of Brass," asked them to read a page and . . . and . . . She looked to Hadia for help, but the woman seemed equally perplexed. Fatma's eyes went down to the book, scanning the page. Just the story. And those words her mind slipped around that she ignored.

"We were talking about the Seal of Sulayman," Rami said helpfully. "A talisman with the power of control over the djinn."

Memories flooded back in an instant. As Fatma watched, the

blurring words on the page turned firm. And the symbol reappeared. She almost jumped from her chair.

"What just happened?" Hadia whispered, looking like she might also bolt to her feet.

"Drink your tea," Tsega told them, waving her slender fingers encouragingly. "The leaves it's brewed from bring calm. You'll need a bit of that for what comes next."

Fatma had only taken slight sips, because the tea was actually rather bitter—with a nutty taste. She found herself now, however, downing a whole gulp. After she'd swallowed, she eyed the bookseller firmly. "Explain."

The small man sat back, choosing his words before speaking. "You know, they call al-Jahiz the Master of Djinn. But it's a misnomer. He never used such a title. It was given to him after he disappeared—part of the myths and legends that swirl about him." He moved a hand as if clearing the stories away. "In truth, al-Jahiz was known to abhor slavery. He himself may have once been a slave and preached against it at every turn. So I cannot believe he would ever own a ring that would rob from djinn their free will. That would make them little more than slaves."

"But you said the ring was given to Sulayman by God," Hadia countered.

Rami held his palms open before him. "So the stories say. Sometimes gifted to him for his wisdom. In other accounts to bind and punish disobedient djinn. But it later became a talisman to be wielded over *all* djinn. That hardly seems fair, or just. I'm sure djinn might tell their own version of events. Who can even know if it was first held by Sulayman. Or if it is a thing far older, perhaps not even of this world. Whatever the truth, if I were the djinn of today, returned, would I want anyone to know of a ring that could grant power over me? That could once again make me a slave?"

Fatma stared, incredulous. "You're saying that someone created a type of magic, a spell, to make everyone *forget* about this Seal of Sulayman?"

"Not just forget," Tsega corrected. "To hide it from our eyes in books. To banish it from our histories." She tapped her temple. "To make it slip from our very minds."

"All our books," her husband added. "All our writings. Anywhere the Seal of Sulayman is mentioned, it becomes hard to read. We are left with gaps we aren't even aware are there. Do you understand what I'm saying? This magic doesn't just conceal the truth, it makes us accept the absence! The silence! It forces our minds to work to make those gaps make sense!"

Fatma looked to Hadia, who appeared just as stupefied. The type of magic required to accomplish such a thing was mind-boggling. It staggered any concept of sorcery they understood. It made the Ministry and all their studies seem like the tinkering of children in the face of forces that defied comprehension.

"Then how did you know?" she asked the bookseller. "How did you see it?"

He put on a smug smile. "I'm a very curious man. It has gotten me in more than a bit of trouble in life. But it has its uses. When I encountered those gaps, they bothered me. It was as if the silence they were trying to create was too loud."

"He's just stubborn," Tsega interjected tersely. "A head like stone."

The bookseller ignored his wife, continuing. "I would go back to read a page again and again, feeling I was missing something. Then one day, I caught a peek. The magic, it turns out, has its own gaps—spaces that can't account for every mind. Once I was given that glimpse, it was only a matter of time before I could perceive it all."

"Why didn't you come to the Ministry with this?" Hadia asked. "We needed to know!"

Rami's eyebrows rose. "Tell the Ministry about a sorcery grand enough to confound the entire world? And what would happen when whoever performed this all-powerful magic found me out? I said I was curious, not suicidal!"

"But you did tell someone at the Ministry," Fatma said. "Zagros."

"My djinn friend," Rami confirmed. "And a fellow bibliophile. Surely, if anyone knew of this, I was certain it would be him." He frowned. "But when I asked, he began to act . . . strangely. Not as if he wouldn't answer me but—"

"—as if he couldn't," Fatma finished. It's why Zagros had sent them here. The bookseller was the one person capable of telling them what they needed to know.

"The magic works differently on the djinn, I think," Rami pondered. "They appear to know but cannot speak it. It ties up their tongues."

"When we stopped talking about the seal we forgot about it," Fatma said. "Will that happen again?"

He nodded. "The magic is potent. But I have devised my methods to take advantage of its gaps." He gestured at the clocks about the shop, where the hand was just close to the hour. "Give it a moment."

They did, waiting as the seconds ticked down and the hour struck. Every clock in the place erupted in chimes and bells, even whistles—alongside automata that beat drums or danced and sang. In the midst of the clamor the bookseller and his wife took out folded sheets and began to read. He handed an extra copy to Fatma. It read simply: *Remember the Seal of Sulayman, and the ring to control the djinn.*

When the clocks stopped, he slipped the sheet back into his vest, patting the pocket. "I think of it as a kind of medicine. Take it every hour or when needed. That way, the memory doesn't fade."

Fatma gave him her appreciation, folding away her own note. "Have you ever heard or read anything about Nine Ifrit Lords? A djinn lullaby? Maybe Zagros mentioned it?"

Rami shook his head. "Zagros never talked about djinn lullabies."

Well, it was worth a shot. "Could you give us the names of books with any mention of the Seal of Sulayman and a magic ring capable of controlling djinn?"

The bookseller nodded eagerly. "That I can do! I've put together a list!" He got up, talking to himself as he began rummaging through his holdings. Fatma moved to follow but was stopped by a hand on her arm. Tsega bid her and Hadia to stay a moment, her voice low.

"Rami will not tell you this. More than once, he has disappeared from the shop. Sometimes for a whole day. He does not remember leaving or where he's gone. But when he returns, it is as if he has to relearn all he knew about the seal."

Fatma read her naked concern. "You think someone is taking him? Making him forget?"

She answered with a solemn nod. "I fear what toll it will take on his mind."

"Do you know who's doing it?" Hadia asked.

The woman's lips drew tight. "I cannot say with certainty. But once I hid, and watched him close, to see when he might be taken again. I never saw the kidnapper. But I heard him!" She spoke the last words with a hiss. "It was the sound of wings! Mechanical wings!"

Fatma inhaled sharply. "An angel," she whispered.

Now what in the many worlds did one of *them* have to do with all of this?

I t took another day to get a meeting with the angels.

Fatma was surprised they'd even agreed to see her. Angels hardly deigned to answer the request of mortals—even government officials. The Ministry usually had to draft repeated missives before getting, at most, a brief, perfunctory response.

So imagine her shock at not only being granted an audience but with the Angelic Council no less. True, the letter she'd gotten was authored more like a summons—*Your presence is required before the Grand Council of Higher Angels*... and so on. But when was the last time any agent met with their ruling body? She guessed the words "Seal of Sulayman" written in her request did the trick.

"You think they were expecting us?" Hadia asked. She kept adjusting her hijab as they walked—a swath of white silk, patterned in gold leaves.

"With them, who knows," Fatma replied. "Let's do another one."

They stopped under the shade of a building, and she reached into her light gray suit jacket to draw out a bit of paper—the same one Rami had given them. She read the contents before passing it to Hadia. Since yesterday, they'd made certain to check the note frequently—to thwart the confounding spell.

Halfway back from the bookseller, they'd completely forgotten what they were doing or why. An hour had passed before Fatma, by chance, pulled the note from her pocket and read it with curiosity—sending everything flooding back. Now they kept a schedule. They'd even made copies, tucked into pockets or anywhere they might look. It was tedious, but they couldn't afford to lose more time.

Though the imposter hadn't been seen since the king's summit, his effects were still felt. Friday wasn't a workday, but the streets were emptier than usual. Even the Jahiziin were lying low. Many feared this was a calm before the storm. Rumors circulated that al-Jahiz was readying to attack the city, whipping an army of ghuls before him. City administrators appealed for calm, lest mass panic trigger an evacuation. Fatma didn't even want to imagine that traffic nightmare.

"I wonder what they want?" Hadia asked, still fidgeting with her hijab. "The angels."

"You ever met one?" Fatma asked as they ascended a lengthy set of steps.

Hadia shook her head. "I caught a glimpse of one once in Alexandria, soaring far away."

"Not the same up close. When you're in there, try not to look them in the eye. It helps."

"I should be fine. These aren't true angels after all. True angels reside in heaven with God, having no free will. These things are something else entirely."

Fatma knew the recitation. But the woman's words sounded rehearsed. And she was still fidgeting. "I've dealt with them before, so let me do most of the talking. Keep the note ready. If I start straying or looking confused, make me read it."

"I can do that," Hadia assured. "I hope they have a way of removing this thing." She motioned a hand about her head at the unseen spell. Fatma hoped so too. It was impossible getting anything done like this. Arriving at the top of the stairs, they stopped to stare at the structure looming before them.

The citadel. It had been built in the twelfth century and had since seen numerous additions, the last under Muhammad Ali Basha, the Great. It was one of the oldest medieval buildings in Cairo, joined to several masjid—including one named for the basha. That had been its greatest claim to fame, until the angels arrived. They'd established their leadership here immediately, in Al-Gawhara Palace. No one had objected. One rarely did when angels were concerned. Since their arrival sometime after the djinn, they'd commandeered numerous such historical buildings, often paying the government large sums for their lease.

Al-Gawhara had been built by Muhammad Ali, on the same avenue where he'd invited several hundred Mamluke leaders to a feast—only to slaughter them all. It was widely believed the basha's secret djinn advisor played a decisive role in this consolidation of power, rendering the Mamlukes' weapons to sand in their very hands. It was an odd choice for the supposed angels to make their sanctum, but who ever knew their reasoning. The palace was rebuilt yet again to house them, refitted with floors that towered near as high as the masjid named for Muhammad Ali, and several rounded domes that took up most of the southern enclosure.

Two big men in white robes and turbans stood guarding an entrance. Each held long lances ending in a gold crescent and Star of David crowned by a pointed cross. Angels liked to cover all their bases. The men inspected Fatma and Hadia with dazed expressions on their beefy faces.

Fatma handed over their invitation to one of them. He took it, letting out a sigh of wonder at the scripted fiery holy tongue that moved and writhed about. Returning it, he stepped aside, opening the door to let them pass through.

The inside of the onetime palace had been transformed into a place of angels. One or two very small ones—no bigger than children—flitted through the air on mechanical wings to the accompaniment of music: Gregorian chants, lilting nasheeds, and odes to whirling dervishes. Beneath, human and djinn workers in all white went about their businesses of maintaining the domicile. All shared the same dazed expression as the guards.

Fatma looked to Hadia, who wasn't that far off. She was staring at an angel walking the hallway. He was more like the ones she was used to—a giant in a clockwork construction resembling a man, with four long arms and great wings of jade and cobalt. His true ethereal body was ensconced within the machine framework and glowed like light become flesh.

"Are you going to be alright, Hadia? Hadia!"

The woman turned sharply at her name, looking unsettled.

"Do you remember why we're here?" Fatma asked. Now she had a confused look on her face, which didn't disappear until shown the note.

"Sorry," Hadia said, color tinging her cheeks. "I just hadn't realized they were so . . . I mean they're not real angels, but . . ." She glanced about. "Aheeh! This place. It's just a bit overwhelming. So massive. Bigger on the inside. Another illusion? Like Siwa's apartment?"

Fatma shook her head, taking in the towering columns and high vaulted ceilings. "Angels don't do illusions. This is magic of the very high kind. The Ministry believes the inside of the building functions as extra-dimensional exponential space. Technically, we may not even be in Cairo right now."

"Technically, agent, you aren't," someone confirmed.

They turned to find a djinn with ridged ochre horns striding toward them. She wore a slender white gown and a pleasant silver smile on her ebony face. "Good morning, Agents Fatma and Hadia. I'm Azmuri, your escort to the Council."

They returned the greeting. "I didn't know we needed an escort," Fatma said.

"We've found this space confounding to mortals," Azmuri explained. "We've had, ah, incidents, where some have become lost for days. Sometimes weeks. You have your letter of summons?"

Fatma held up the invite. So she'd been right about that.

"Excellent," the djinn pronounced. "If you could spare a moment, there are the necessary forms." She motioned to another figure they hadn't even noticed—a short man with that same dazed look on his face. He held a stack of papers in one hand and a set of pens. Fatma grimaced.

Angels were notorious for their bureaucracy. They required every little thing be recorded, signed, stamped, and reviewed—often in triplicate. Cairenes joked that they must have invented paperwork. Taking a pen, she looked over the first form, getting almost dizzy at the printed blocks of legalese before scribbling her name in five places. Eight more forms followed. By the time it was done, her hand was cramping.

"I hope I'm not signing away my free will or fondest memories," Hadia muttered.

"Oh no," Azmuri replied. "Those forms are much longer." Hadia stopped her signing midway at the remark, before seeing the smirk on the djinn's lips. A joke. At least, Fatma hoped so. When they'd finished, Azmuri dismissed the man and turned back to them.

"Now that's out of the way I'll take you to the Council. Follow me, please."

They set out, the djinn leading them through the cavernous hall and down one of the many corridors. As they walked, Fatma noted the large open rooms—where people performed odd labors. One was filled entirely with veiled women, seated at desks in orderly rows and using brushes to scrawl out fiery holy tongue onto parchment. As they passed, one of the women began laughing uncontrollably, falling out of her chair. She was picked up and led away, another woman assuming her place and taking up her work. A second room displayed whirling dervishes in colorful dress, all chanting a dhikr and spinning longer than should have been possible. A third held a great machine of rotating gears with men and women moving about frantically to maintain it. Fatma stopped to watch, the Clock of Worlds coming uncomfortably to mind.

"What does that do?" she asked.

"Hmm?" Azmuri glanced distractedly. "Oh, that's the machine that keeps the world going." At seeing their stunned faces, the djinn smiled. "A joke, agents. Please, come."

"Is there really such a machine?" Hadia asked, catching up. "Keeping the world going?"

To Fatma's discomfort, the djinn's only answer was another silver smile.

They turned down more corridors to finally stop at a set of tall gold doors with more guards. These were djinn, scaled and bearing sharp weapons.

"We've arrived, agents," Azmuri said. "I'll wait here to escort you back out."

She spoke to the djinn guards in another tongue, and the two pulled open the doors to allow admittance and reveal what lay inside.

Seated about a wide round table in chairs carved for giants were four angels.

Their clockwork bodies were sculptures of art more than machinery, with gears that ticked like hearts and steel fibers mimicking muscle. Each turned at once to regard them, with four sets of brilliant gazes. Fatma choked back a gasp and instead stepped forward, pulling out her badge and introducing herself. She waited for Hadia to do the same, but the woman just stood stupefied again, staring up into those brilliant eyes. She'd distinctly told her *not* to do that. She gave Hadia a hard nudge that sent her fumbling to lift her badge. But all that managed to escape her throat was a small "urk."

"We know who you are, agents," one of the angels spoke. His voice was a melodic rumble: a beautiful song mingled with thunder. Like all angels he wore a mask with oval cutouts for eyes. This one was made of glittering gold, as if dipped in starlight. It matched his body, wrought of black iron except for the tips of his wings that also shimmered gold. "I am called Leader here."

Of course he was. As with djinn, angels didn't share their true names. They instead took on titles related to their purpose. Fatma followed a gesture from one of Leader's four arms toward two chairs small enough to fit them. She took one, leading a dazed Hadia into another.

"We are still awaiting another of our number," Leader said. Two of his hands sat folded on the table near a folder that looked far too small for them to handle. Fatma only now noticed there was a fifth giant chair left empty. The angel's words carried a tinge of annoyance, which seemed to fit his mask—with its flat expression and set lips. "While we wait, perhaps it is best you meet the others."

"I am Harmony," another angel greeted warmly. This one had a voice like a woman and wore a mask with a fixed pleasant smile. Her full rounded body was the color of an ever-shifting rainbow, so that no place stayed the same hue.

"I am Discord," a third stated brusquely. His body was sharp and angular, looking as if you might cut yourself at a touch. It was bone white, down to the wingtip, with not a hint of color. He stared out from behind a scowling black mask.

"I am Defender," a fourth boomed. He appeared aptly named, with a bulky clockwork body and six thick arms—two more than she saw on most angels. He was silver and crimson, with a mask that looked carved for a hero's statue.

No sooner had he finished than the gold doors parted and another angel bustled in. Like the others, this one towered at least twelve feet. Four mechanical arms extended from bronze shoulders, while shiny platinum wings tinged by dashes of crimson and gold sat behind a broad back.

At the sight, Fatma felt her body seize up. It was an involuntary thing, which she could no more control than a sneeze or an itch. She was on her feet in an instant, drawing her pistol, heart thumping until the sound filled her ears.

"Maker!" she growled. It should have been impossible. She had seen this angel die—plunge knives into his own flesh in sacrifice. Yet he was here now, alive! She'd recognize that translucent alabaster mask with its permanent faint smirk anywhere. It haunted her nightmares. She didn't know what a bullet could even do to one of these creatures. But she'd find out.

The angel stopped, cocking a head at the gun—more curious than afraid.

"You are late," Leader admonished.

"Apologies," Maker said, surprisingly with a melodic woman's voice. "I think this mortal wishes to do me harm. Fascinating!"

Leader turned to Fatma, only now noticing her standing there with the gun. Hadia never even broke from her awe.

"Please stop her," Harmony moaned. "It will make things disagreeable."

"No," Discord countered. "I want to see what happens."

Defender only rumbled his mechanical throat.

"I wanted you here on time so I could explain," Leader chided. "She believes you to be the *other* Maker, with whom she had an . . . unpleasant . . . experience."

"Can she not see I am not him?" Maker asked.

"As I have told you on several occasions, mortal perception is limited," Leader replied.

Fatma listened, the bits of information forcing her to reassess. This Maker spoke with a woman's voice. Younger too. And talked as if they'd never met. Slowly, the pistol lowered.

"Another Maker?" she asked. "Why?"

"To replace the last Maker," Leader answered. As if that should explain everything.

Fatma felt her heart slowly return to normal, accepting that this wasn't the rogue angel after all. She sat down again, putting up her pistol yet too shaken to feel shame at her outburst. Her eyes lingered on Maker, following the angel's every move.

"Now that we have all arrived," Leader spoke, "to the matter at hand." He addressed Fatma. "We know why you are here."

Fatma turned to stare up at him, a bit confused.

"The Seal of Sulayman," Harmony mentioned helpfully.

The memory came rushing back, to Fatma's embarrassment. She was getting distracted.

"You know of the ring," Leader continued. "You've either reasoned it out for yourself, or visited the bookseller. We suspected you might in due time."

"I told them so!" Maker added. The angel's face was impassive, but her words rang with excitement. "When I learned of how you handled my predecessor, I was certain you would figure this out as well! You are quite a remarkable mortal!" She turned to the stunned Hadia and added hastily, "Oh, I am sure you are remarkable too."

"It seems we and Agent Fatma are fated to cross paths," Harmony mused.

"Or she insists to tread where she should not," Discord quipped.

Defender, again, rumbled.

Fatma fixed on Leader. "It was you. The ones who erased all traces of the Seal of Sulayman."

"Erased from human understanding, yes," the angel affirmed. "And memory. It was quite a feat of intricate magic, but we strive to be thorough."

Fatma's anger flared at the casualness of his tone. "What gives you the right to play with our heads? Who left you the arbiters of what we can and can't know?"

The angels all regarded her in silence, as if perplexed.

"She believes we acted on our own," Maker commented. "Fascinating!"

Fatma frowned. "What does that mean?"

Leader opened two of his four palms in a placating gesture. "We did not take the initiative of removing your knowledge of the Seal of Sulayman. It was at the request of the djinn."

That actually left Fatma speechless.

"The djinn," Hadia murmured, like someone slowly emerging from a dream. "The bookseller said as much. They didn't want us to know about the ring."

"They believe such knowledge in your hands is a danger," Discord affirmed. "Your kind are so wonderfully unpredictable after all."

"The only way to be safe, they decided, was to rid you of temptation," Leader continued. "To that end, they contracted us to weave a grand magic. One that would expunge what you knew and conceal that wisdom from your eyes going forward."

"It also stopped the djinn from speaking about it," Fatma added.

"Magic abhors imbalance," Harmony said. "The djinn could not ask for this thing and be exempt. The price exacted for balance was their own silence."

"As I have said," Leader noted with pride, "we strive to be thorough."

So that bit hadn't been intended, Fatma noted. The Ministry regularly released public announcements warning people against making unwise compacts with djinn. Bartering with beings who counted centuries of experience almost always put you on the losing end. Maybe they should have given similar warnings to the djinn about contracting with angels.

"Your grand magic has some gaps," Fatma said. "Some people can see through it—like the bookseller. You've been abducting him, trying to erase his memories. But he keeps coming back to it. He keeps finding a way around the magic."

Sets of mechanical wings shifted awkwardly. Defender did his usual rumbling. Fatma had seen another of those gaps yesterday. She'd told Siti about the ring. The woman had never heard of it, the magic seeming to do its work on her human side. But after Fatma explained it to her once, she didn't need reminding. Her djinn side also had no problem speaking on it.

"This is correct," Maker said. She turned to address Fatma directly. "I saw the structural dangers in the weaving as soon as I arrived on this plane. The magic is like the fabric about your airships. Attempt to wrap it around too big a frame, and it becomes taut. Weak points develop, and soon you are in danger of an unraveling! I warned of this, but would they listen to me, whose very essence is that of constructing—"

"Enough," Leader ordered firmly, brilliant eyes fixed on Maker. "We shall have a talk about your penchant for speaking more than you should at the wrong moments and among inappropriate company." The younger angel shrank back, her wings going limp. Leader returned to Fatma. "What is important is that someone other than the vexatious bookseller has a will strong enough to evade our concealment. And now they wield the ring as well."

"The imposter who claims to be al-Jahiz," Hadia said, seeming herself again.

Discord hissed. "A miscreant. Who has taken the ring from our safekeeping!"

Fatma gaped. "You've had the Seal of Sulayman? All this time?"

"Part of our agreement was to secure the ring," Leader explained. "Each day this imposter holds on to it, we are in breach of contract."

"Why did you even keep the thing?" Fatma asked. "Why didn't you destroy it?"

Gasps went up about the room. Even Defender's rumble seemed offended.

"To destroy such a holy relic would be desecration!" Harmony melodically lectured.

"How did anyone even steal it from you?" Hadia asked. "Who's bold enough?"

"The same ones seeking after items associated with al-Jahiz," Leader answered.

"Lord Worthington's Brotherhood," Fatma reasoned.

"The late Lord Alistair Worthington and his quaint obsession," Leader affirmed.

"The seal," Fatma said. "It's part of the Brotherhood's insignia."

"Another unfortunate evasion of our magic," Harmony sighed. "Though only a partial one. Lord Worthington's mind conjured up the seal's likeness, but he never truly understood what it was. We long ago assessed the matter as harmless."

"More vexatious were his dealings," Leader said. "His Brotherhood had in their hire a certain djinn who once worked here as an archivist, until we terminated him for unethical practices."

"That would be an Illusion djinn named Siwa," Fatma said, putting the pieces together.

"Before he left, he pilfered a listing of the holdings in our vaults," Discord said. "He employs thieves of rare skill to make their way inside and take what he instructs. These items are then delivered to Lord Worthington for a price."

Hadia turned to Fatma. "Portendorf's journal! It mentioned a list!"

Fatma nodded, remembering. "Was al-Jahiz's sword on that list?"

"The blade," Leader confirmed. "Pilfered on the same day the seal was taken."

"Why not just do away with Lord Worthington and his Brotherhood outright?" Hadia asked. "I'm guessing that's in your power. Why play this game?"

The gathered angels all exchanged glances before answering.

"It was not our intent to make a fuss," Harmony said delicately.

"You don't want the attention," Fatma deduced. "Let it be known that Lord Worthington was breaking into their vaults, and soon every thief in Cairo would be trying to do the same—just to see if they could."

"You see, then, our predicament," Leader said. "When the ring first went missing, we suspected Lord Worthington, thinking perhaps he had finally puzzled out the meaning of the seal on his insignia. Then he and his Brotherhood all met an untimely end. It left us puzzled. So we began to look into matters." He placed a large steel thumb upon the folder on the table—nudging it toward them. Fatma opened it, shuffling through the contents. Financial accounts by the looks of it. She passed several to Hadia.

"Lord Worthington's company's holdings," Leader informed. "Over the past year there have been some interesting investments and acquisitions."

"Armament holdings," Hadia read. "Weapons industries. Airship bombers. Maxim gun and gas canister manufacturers."

"Strange assets for a man touting peace," Discord quipped.

It was more than that, Fatma assessed, flipping through the pages. The shares and sums here were astronomical. As if Alistair Worthington was trying to convert over his entire company to profit from war. No, not him, she realized.

"You don't think Alistair Worthington was making these decisions, do you?" she asked.

"An irksome mortal, certainly," Leader complained. "But this seems unlike him. Someone else in Lord Worthington's house was making these changes."

"Someone who held him and his Brotherhood in clear disdain," Discord said.

"Someone who had access to Siwa and the list," Harmony added.

Fatma parsed those words carefully. "Who are you talking about?"

The angels all shared another of those infuriating glances, before Leader shook his masked head. "We are not investigators. That matter is left for you. Whoever this imposter is, they now hold the Seal of Sulayman—an instrument of immense power."

"Immeasurable power!" Harmony wailed. "Too much for a mortal to wield so willfully. So often. Even Sulayman knew better. It will take its toll on them, body and spirit!"

"It is why we have consented to bring you here," Discord spoke. "Why we have shared what you should not be privy to."

"You must retrieve the ring, agent," Leader said, his tone insistent. "You must take it from this imposter before more damage is done and return it to us. So we may fulfill our contract."

Fatma didn't respond right away. These angels didn't know who the imposter was. But they had clear suspicions. Someone in the Worthington household. She and Hadia had been on the right track all along. There was vindication at least in that.

"We'll find the ring," she said finally. "But only on the condition that you answer two more questions and grant two demands."

Leader didn't appear to like this bargain, but he dipped his head in agreement. "Speak your words. We will answer or meet them, within reason."

Fatma spoke carefully. "What does the imposter want with the Clock of Worlds?"

Another awkward shifting of wings.

"That machine should have been destroyed," Leader said flatly.

Fatma had said as much to the Ministry, to no avail. "Yes, but that wasn't my question."

"No one knows," Maker put in. "My predecessor had nefarious designs for its intent. I fear little else from this imposter. Leader is correct, the machine should be . . . unmade." The last word sounded almost foreign to her.

"Second," Fatma began. "What do you know of the Nine Lords?"

"Djinn superstition," Leader dismissed idly. "Their kind are prone to such delusions."

"But the imposter would have the power to control them, with the ring?"

"That is a third question," Leader replied. "Our bargain only allowed for two."

Fatma moved on to her demands. "My first demand: stop abducting the bookseller. Either work better magic or undo it altogether. You don't understand humans as well as you think. You can't hold knowledge from us. We'll find out somehow, someway. It's who we are. Let the bookseller be."

There was a bout of silence, before a rumbling voice said, "Done."

Fatma looked to Defender in surprise. The others all seemed to take his word as final, however, stating their assent.

"Second request. Release Hadia and me from this confoundment magic of yours. We'll work faster without it about our necks."

"Oh, that we cannot do," Leader said, shaking his head.

"Why not?" Hadia asked. "It's your doing."

"Not just ours," Maker explained. She glanced to Leader, who gestured to continue. "The means to creating the concealment of the Seal of Sulayman involved angelic powers, and that of *others*, beyond this realm, as silent partners. To willfully release you from the confoundment would place us in violation of our contract with them." Her voice lowered to a whisper. "One does not break obligations to them. Ever."

Fatma had no idea who these "others" were. But the ominous

finality in the angel's tone made her uncertain how to argue the point.

"There is a way that will not cause imbalance," Harmony offered. "The sleeping djinn."

"The sleeping djinn," Leader repeated wistfully. "That would not violate the contract."

"It might disrupt the spirit of our agreement," Discord warned.

"Our partners are not so slavish as to start a blood feud across the realms over wording," Harmony countered. "At least, I hope not." She turned to Fatma. "Our contract with the djinn at once bound each of their kind to its tenets, forcing their consent by mere existence. The only exceptions were any djinn who may have at the time been unable to grant consent on account of their incorporeal inert state. As they exist outside of the contract at its making, they are unbound and as such can, at their choosing, renegotiate how the contract is applied and to *whom* it is applied—as long as it meets our approval."

"So . . ." Hadia began, slowly turning things over in her head. Angels could be taxing with their legalese. "We can be released from this spell without causing any . . . inter-realm conflicts. But who's this sleeping djinn?"

At the question, the angels all turned to Fatma. She sighed, already knowing the answer.

"A very unpleasant Marid. Who I promised never to bother again."

Angels. They were going to end up being the death of her.

CH PTER
TWENTY-THREE

For the second time in two days, Fatma walked the cells beneath the Ministry. Zagros was still here, but she hadn't come to see him. What she intended was more dangerous than questioning the librarian—even if he'd tried to murder her. She understood now he had been under the control of the imposter. The djinn she would encounter today was far less predictable.

"You're quiet," she remarked, eyeing Hadia who walked beside her.

The other woman nodded. "Visiting with those . . . supposed angels. Just has me thinking."

"It can be a lot—even knowing they're not really angels."

Hadia shook her head. "It's not that. Well, not that alone." She stopped to look at Fatma, who stopped in turn. "They changed our minds around. Got into our heads. And we had no idea. What else might they have changed or hidden from us? Our writings? Our histories? Our holy books? What else might we no longer know? How can we be certain of anything?" Her eyes closed and she released a lengthy sigh before opening them. "How do you deal with the crushing weight of it? Knowing that we're just people and there are these vast powers pulling strings we may not even know about? I'm supposed to be helping plan my cousin's wedding next month. But that just all seems so meaningless in the face of this." She frowned. "I wonder if this is what it must have been like back when al-Jahiz opened the Kaf? To suddenly learn the world you knew wasn't quite so real. I'm picking an odd time to be philosophical, I know. Maybe I'm having a mental breakdown. . . ."

Fatma shook her head slowly. "You're not having a mental breakdown. Every agent has this moment. More than once. This is what it means to work for the Ministry. To understand more than the average person just how strange the world around us has become. It's what we signed up for. And why it's not for everyone. But yeah, I sit down and think about it hard sometimes—then I go out and buy a new suit. Because those little things, like planning your cousin's wedding, that's what keeps us grounded." She winked. "Maybe you could expand your hijab collection."

Hadia laughed slightly and they started up their walk again.

"Remind me what this Marid said again?" she asked.

This was her fifth time asking, but Fatma answered anyway. "That he slept in the hopes of outliving humanity. Also, he granted the last person who woke him the chance to choose their death."

"And you gave him your name and word?"

"Both." She'd felt the pact settle into her skin.

"Doesn't that make it unbreakable?"

"Anything's breakable. Just means there'll be a cost."

Hadia recited a quick dua for her protection, the worry on her face plain. Her gaze wandered to the object Fatma clutched in one hand—a tarnished, pear-shaped bronze bottle, inlaid with gold floral patterns. "They just let you walk out of the Ministry vault with that thing?"

"I was the one who brought it in. Told them I needed to correct the paperwork. No reason to think I'd do something absolutely foolish—like open it."

"Of course not," Hadia muttered. "Not unless you had some sort of death wish."

They stopped at a cell, the furthest down the hall.

"You don't have to come in," Fatma said. "If something goes wrong, the wards of the cell should hold him."

Hadia reached up and took both black truncheons off the wall this time, hefting one in each hand. That was answer enough.

Fatma opened the door to the cell, and they stepped inside,

shutting it again behind them. Moving to the center of the room, she knelt and stood the bronze bottle up on the floor.

"We're really going through with this?" Hadia asked.

"We have to."

Hadia looked perplexed. "Why do we have to again?"

Fatma handed over a copy of the bookseller's note, and the woman winced as her memory returned. "Precisely why we need this magic on us broken. We can't keep this up forever." She pulled free her janbiya. "Ready?"

Hadia clutched the black truncheons tight and nodded. Fatma pressed the knife to the dragon-marked seal about the stopper and held her breath—before drawing the blade across the wax covering, breaking the reestablished wards.

There was barely time to jump back as bright green smoke burst from the bottle like a geyser. The swirling gas fast took shape, knitting into a broad form somewhat like a man—only far bigger. The cloud coalesced, becoming firmer until it was made flesh. In moments, a full-grown djinn towered before them.

The Marid was as terrifying now as he had been that night—a giant covered in emerald scales, his bared chest heaving, with smooth ivory horns grazing the ceiling. For a moment he stood, silent, coming out of his slumber. When his three eyes opened—a pyramid of burning stars—they took in the cell with one imperious glance, before settling and narrowing on Fatma.

"Enchantress." The word rumbled in the small space.

Fatma forced herself to meet that scouring gaze. "Great One, I say again, I'm no enchantress."

The djinn's green lips twisted. "Yet twice I have been summoned into your presence. Who but an enchantress would dare such a thing? Not that it matters. You have broken your word. Sworn to me by your name. You are already dead."

He spoke that last sentence as if relating the weather. Fatma steeled herself. "Great One, I would not have awakened you, if not for dire cause."

The Marid actually yawned. "You mortals always have reasons

for breaking your oaths. Excuses for your filthy ways. For your very existence. Just listening to your inane chatter is vexing to my ears." He raised a clawed hand twice as large as her head, palm open and fingers spread. "Should I remove your bones so that your frail body collapses into pulp? Perhaps replace your blood with scorching sand? Or make you cut out your own entrails and choke yourself with them?"

"I see you've given this some thought," Fatma said. Her voice came firm, but her insides quivered.

The djinn grinned sharply. "When I sleep, all I dream of is how to slaughter mortals. I could slay every last one of you, like so many sheep."

"That's enough!" Hadia said. She activated both truncheons until they crackled hot with blue bolts. "No one's slaughtering anyone today. If you'd just listen—"

The Marid casually waved in her direction. Stone arms suddenly erupted from the wall behind Hadia, each with hands bearing seven fingers. They grabbed hold of the woman, pulling her into the wall. Her shocked cries cut off as her body became stone—a statue trapped halfway in and halfway out. The black truncheons she dropped had not hit the floor before it was over. Fatma stared, janbiya in her hand. She rounded on the djinn.

"Let her go! This is between you and me!"

The Marid snorted. "It is between whomever I wish it to be. Let apprentice and mistress suffer."

"She was just trying to get you to listen! So that I could tell you . . ."

Fatma's words trailed off. Tell him what? Whatever had seemed so important had vanished. She looked up to see the Marid with his arm still extended. Those fiery eyes flared into hot white flames. In the palm of his hand a jade glow emanated. Inexplicably, a ringing bell went off. The djinn frowned, looking to her jacket. It went off again.

"Are you going to get that?" he asked. "It's irritating."

Fatma drew out her pocket watch. Why had she set an alarm?

Flipping the timepiece open, she found a bit of folded paper inside and unwrapped it. As she read, her mouth worked in a rush.

"The Seal of Sulayman!"

The Marid cocked a horned head. His fiery eyes dimmed to a simmer, and his arm lowered slowly to his side. "What," he asked coldly, "do you know of that?"

Fatma released a breath. "I know that it's a ring created to control djinn. One that robs you of your free will. A mortal holds that ring now. He bound an Ifrit. He'd think nothing of tearing you out of that bottle and making you a slave. I just thought you might want to know."

The djinn said nothing for a while, only stroking his curling white beard. Finally, he flicked a wrist—and Hadia fell out of the wall, her body made flesh again. Her interrupted cries finished in a wail as she landed on hands and knees. Fatma bent down to help her up.

"An abomination," the Marid murmured, distracted. "We were fools to think its forging a wise thing." Fatma's eyebrows rose at that. He turned back to look at her, dismissing Hadia, who swayed unsteadily. "What do you want of me, not-enchantress?"

"There's magic woven around the ring. It makes us forget. We need that removed. The angels said you could do that."

The djinn rumbled in his throat. "Angels. Is that what those creatures are calling themselves now?" Sniffing a sharp nose, he made a bitter face. "The stench of them is thick about you."

Fatma really preferred he stop smelling her. "Well, the angels—or whatever they are—said you could remove the spell. When you do, we can find this mortal who stole the ring and return it to their keeping."

The djinn rumbled again, louder this time.

"What?" she snapped.

"A mortal," the Marid drawled mockingly. "Stole the Great Seal. From one of them? Is that the story they told you?"

Fatma frowned. "What are you saying?"

The djinn rolled all three eyes, as one would to a baffled

child—or dog. "You believe that beings able to traverse planes of existence, who wield sorcery potent enough to confound an entire world, who can bend space and reality to their will, were swindled—by a mortal thief?"

"They said the ring was stolen from their vault . . ." Fatma managed.

The djinn sighed. "Did that pathetic organ you call a brain never stop to think the power that emanates from those creatures might allow them to make you believe what they wish? Or what you want to believe?"

Now Fatma's head swam. She ran through their meeting with the angels. The awe they naturally induced. The idea of thieves breaking into one of their vaults had seemed far-fetched. Yet they'd provided an answer she'd wanted to believe. So she'd accepted it, without another thought. But what this djinn was saying spoke to her buried doubts. It could only mean one thing.

"They allowed the ring to be taken!" Hadia exclaimed. The shock of the realization appeared to bring her back to her wits, though her voice shook. "They *wanted* it to be taken!"

The weight of it staggered Fatma. "Why?"

"To have its power wielded, one must assume," the djinn answered matter-of-factly.

"Why not just use it themselves, then?" Hadia asked.

"The seal cannot be wielded by djinn or any other magic-touched creature. It is meant for mortal hands, provided it finds one worthy."

Fatma frowned. "Finds worthy?"

The Marid looked ready to throw up his hands. "Do you know nothing of the properties and laws that govern near-sentient magical objects?"

"Pretend we don't," Fatma snapped. "We're just pathetic-minded mortals after all."

At this he gave an agreeable snort. The son of a dog!

"The seal has its own mind," he told them. "Only a mortal of exceptionally strong will could call it master. It would not allow itself to be revealed to any other. Though it seems it yet keeps the greater part of its power veiled. That you believe the seal's true form is that of a *ring* is proof enough."

"Is that supposed to make sense?" Fatma asked, not masking her annoyance.

The djinn leaned forward, his words crisp. "The seal is no more truly a ring than you are a creature approaching even middling intelligence. Its most potent power and true form are revealed only to one whose want is pure—a quality its present wielder appears to lack. As is the way with most mortals."

"The bookseller said that no one really knows what the seal looks like," Hadia murmured.

Fatma recalled as much, but it hardly seemed relevant. Besides, her mind was busied trying to untangle the various strands the djinn laid before them. "It was all arranged," she thought and spoke at once. Her eyes met Hadia's. "The list getting to Siwa. The Brotherhood's thieves. Taking the seal. Every piece carefully put together, so that the ring could end up in the hands of someone able to wield it." She turned back to the djinn. "But why would they want a mortal to wield the ring?"

The Marid shrugged hefty shoulders, to say that either he did not know or did not care.

"Whatever the reason," Hadia said, "they lost control. They hadn't prepared for the ambitiousness of this imposter. Who can't be reined in. Now they want us to clean up their mess."

"The greed of mortals should never be undervalued," the Marid intoned.

Angels. Fatma shook her head. Whatever machinations were at work, none of it changed that the ring had to be retrieved from this imposter. "They said you could remove the confoundment spell. That there's a contract you can renegotiate by—"

The Marid waved her off. "I understand how magical contractual bindings work, mortal. Please do not insult me by trying to explain it with your inarticulate speech."

"Will you do it?"

"What will I gain in return?"

Fatma gaped. He wanted something in return? After putting Hadia in a wall? "How about making sure this imposter doesn't turn you into their personal puppet. That good enough?"

"Magic exacts a price," the Marid insisted. "What will you give?"

She clenched her fists. Djinn could be insistent about contracts. There wasn't going to be a way out of this. Or, it suddenly dawned on her, was there? "Do Nine Ifrit Lords mean anything to you?"

Alarm crossed that ancient face. It was both satisfying and frightening.

"So they're real, then," she pressed. "The imposter plans to awaken them. Bring them here. With the Seal of Sulayman, he'll have control of the most powerful of djinn. You want a trade for your magical contract? We stop that from happening."

The Marid scowled. "You wish to keep them from this world as much as I."

"Think of it as a mutual benefit," Fatma retorted. "Do we have a bargain or not?"

The Marid's three eyes burned angrily, not caring for the offer. But he seemed to like these Nine Lords less. "We have a bargain," he decreed. "But know this, not-enchantress. If ever you awaken me again, there will be no bargains to make. I do not care if the heavens are falling."

"Whatever," Fatma bit back. "Now fulfill your side and remove the spell."

The djinn extended a hand, and Fatma felt suddenly like she was on fire—as if she had been thrown *into* fire. The pain was so intense, she couldn't even scream. When her vision cleared she found she was sprawled on the floor, writhing as the agonizing sensation faded to a dull sting. She could see Hadia beside her, similarly incapacitated. Neither of them looked to be physically hurt. But Merciful God, the pain! As she lay on her back, the Marid's horned head loomed above.

"The magic is removed," he rumbled. "I could have done so

without pain." His mouth broke into a wide toothy grin. "But you didn't make that clear in your request."

Fatma lifted a trembling hand to form a rude gesture. She *really* did hate this djinn.

◆   ◆   ◆

She was still grumbling about haughty djinn and conniving angels as the automated carriage sped through Cairo, to their next destination. At least the confounding magic had been removed. They'd tested it out, including opening up texts to find whole passages now viewable. The Marid had been as good as his word. She'd taken his bottle back to the vault and put in an expedited request to have a safe place found for it—hopefully a chest weighted down to the deepest part of the sea.

"You sure you're okay?" she asked Hadia.

The woman sat across from her, busily reading through Portendorf's ledger. She'd made notations of the words "the list," affirming much of what they now knew. Siwa had been making good use of his pilfered register, marketing and then retrieving items to the highest bidder—which turned out to be Alistair Worthington. The angels had probably assumed someone in that arrogant circle of Englishmen would be willful enough to come across mention of the ring. Hadia looked up at the question.

"A djinn put me into a wall. I think for a while, I *was* the wall. Then he tried to singe my skin off. So no. I'm not okay. But, God willing, I'll be alright."

Fatma didn't press the matter.

"One question we haven't asked," Hadia said, changing topics. "Why are angels—or whatever they are—collecting and hoarding things associated with al-Jahiz?"

Fatma shook her head. If there was one thing they'd learned today, when it came to angels, who knew their motives. The carriage jostled as the streets turned rough, and she pulled back a curtain to look out. "We're here."

"Again," Hadia added.

The Cemetery didn't look too different in daylight. Except maybe the night obscured some of the squalor—where crumbling bricks littered the ground, and makeshift wooden shacks barely held together. Not every place was like that. Some mausoleums were well kept by their occupants, and there were graves both freshly cleaned and painted. In other places new construction went on, and vendors sold plaster vases—as if it wasn't a Friday. Children played about the stone markers, amid lines of clothes drying under the midday sun.

"Do you think any of them recognize us?" Hadia asked as they stepped from the carriage. She'd opted not to wear her Ministry jacket, given recent events.

Fatma noticed a woman glancing at them through her kitchen, where she cooked at a stone oven right beside an elaborately carved tomb. "Maybe. Easy to stand out, when you're not from here." Not to mention her light gray suit, matching vest, and red-on-white pin-striped shirt. Not exactly discreet.

"That's it coming up." She nodded at a tall mausoleum in the distance.

It looked almost like the one they'd fought the imposter on that night. Four figures lounged about outside—young women. No, girls. In bright red kaftans that ended at their knees, over baggy tshalvar. The Turkish trousers were deep blue and tucked into laced black boots. The girls leaned against the mausoleum entrance, idly chatting. One practiced spinning a dagger along the back of her hand, while the others all wore theirs openly at the hip. At seeing Fatma and Hadia approach they stopped their talk, fixing the new-comers with hard stares.

Fatma bid them greetings, then said, "We're here to see the Leopardess."

A tall girl with Soudanese features ran Fatma up and down. "Back for some more? Where's that fat policeman? I'd enjoy slapping his face again, wallahi!"

The other girls barked laughter. So this was the one who had delivered that five-fingered palm to Aasim's face. And, as Fatma recalled, taken a swing at her. Probably best to let that go.

"She knows we're coming. So just take us there."

Another girl said something rude, setting her friends to renewed laughter. But the first one shot them a look that brought silence. She glanced again at Fatma, before turning and beckoning to follow. They were led into the mausoleum, where more people stood about. All women, all wearing the same red kaftans and Turkish trousers, with the older ones in matching red hijabs. Some kind of rank perhaps. From somewhere nearby came the unexpected sounds of children's laughter.

The girl stopped to confer with one of the women, who eyed both Fatma and Hadia. When they finished, the girl left, presumably returning to her post. Someone from their cluster came forward—a woman in a white dress and black hijab, wearing of all things a brilliant necklace of sapphires and rubies. Her brown skin bore creases and slight bags about her curving eyes, while her body had the stoutness of a grandmother. There was a discomfiting cast to her gaze, however, almost predatory. That was fitting as well, for the leader of the Forty Leopards.

The moment the angels said Siwa hired thieves bold enough to break into their vault, Fatma had known it could only be them. Who else would be that brazen? The lady thieves had started out as shoplifters, often wearing full bur'a, sebleh, and milaya lef to hide their ill-gained goods. They'd gone on to ransack homes of the wealthy, posing as servants and maids, then to heists that made off with jewels, art, and once an entire armored carriage carrying casks of gold coins. To this day, no one knew what had happened to it. Their members went in and out of prison, usually for the smaller crimes. But none revealed a word, serving time in silence. Their leader remained untouched and un-betrayed. People claimed she was as hard to catch as the feline moniker associated with her gang.

"Peace be upon you, Leopardess. I'm Agent Fatma, this is Agent Hadia. Thank you for meeting with us."

"And upon you peace, agents," the head of the Forty Leopards replied. "The Usta said to expect you."

That would be Khalid. The bookie was Fatma's best tie to Cairo's underworld. She'd contacted him straight after meeting with the cursed Marid. To her surprise, he'd said the leader of the gang was willing to meet with them—today.

"Tell me, agents," she went on, "why shouldn't I have some of my daughters bind the two of you right now and seal you up in one of these mausoleums—where not even someone in your vaunted Ministry will hear your screams?"

Fatma tensed. The words were offered idly, as if asking how much honey they wanted spooned into their tea. But it held the promise of a drawn blade. Beside her Hadia went rigid, eyes scanning the room. No girls like the ones outside, but grown and fit women—very much like leopards. So it was going to be *that* kind of meeting.

"We didn't come here to threaten you," Fatma said. "Or to be threatened by you."

The Leopardess's tone went cold. "The last time agents were in el-Arafa, you caused a riot."

Fatma felt her indignation rise. "Your people were the ones stirring up the crowd. Working on the side of the man in the gold mask."

The woman's dark eyes drew to slits, her voice tight. "We are only on el-Arafa's side. Do not place us in league with that foul man. You came in as an army onto our land, among the people we protect and who protect us in turn. We would have fought you to the end."

Alright, then, Fatma conceded. One question answered—even if not how she'd planned going about it. Time to de-escalate.

"That night," she said with regret in her voice. "It was a mistake."

The Leopardess seemed to weigh her sincerity. She finally

gave the apology the barest nod of acceptance. "People in el-Arafa are bad off enough without all of you making things worse. It seems the only time we see the police is when there's some crime in the more respectable parts of Cairo. People here distrust authorities, and with good reason. That night didn't help."

"I don't think the man in the gold mask helped either," Hadia put in. "He's the problem."

The leader of the Forty Leopards looked to Hadia—who actually took a step back under that hard gaze. But the older woman dipped her head appreciatively.

"He is a problem," she agreed. "No one who lives here is stupid or gullible. They're just tired of the exploitation. Tired of being ignored. Desperate ears will listen to anyone offering up others to blame. What do you want of me?"

"Khalid said you'd be willing to tell us about one of your contracts," Fatma said. "For a djinn named Siwa."

The older woman eyed them both now with scrutiny. The uneasy quiet that followed was broken by a lilting adhan.

"Time for prayer," she remarked. "You'll join me. And you may call me Layla."

That wasn't a request. So after performing their ablutions, they prayed.

When they'd finished, the Leopardess—Layla—led Fatma and Hadia through the mausoleum to an entrance in the back, her entourage trailing like bodyguards. Outside was a surprising sight. A set of sky-blue tents had been set up. Beneath them were rows upon rows of wooden tables seated with children—likely the ones they'd heard before.

"I grew up here," Layla said. She took a white apron embroidered with colorful flowers from someone, wrapping it about her dress. "There was a woman who took care of one of the tombs. It was not her family but the family her own had worked for. I thought her a fool. Taking care of the dead of someone who had likely treated her family as servants for generations? But every day after Friday prayer, she would come around and give all of us children loaves of bread and cheese. I later learned she was taking what monies the tomb owner's family gave her and using it on us. It was a lesson not to pass judgment so quickly. She's gone now, but I carry on her tradition."

Fatma stayed quiet. If the woman wanted to claim her band of lady thieves were actually philanthropists stealing from the wealthy to feed the poor, she wouldn't argue. But she doubted anyone else in this slum could afford fancy aprons. And the red ruby that extended from the woman's necklace—the size of a hen's egg—could probably feed all these children for a year.

"You'll need aprons as well," Layla remarked. "And ladles."

Someone stepped forward to offer both.

"I don't think you understand why we came," Fatma began. "We don't have the time—"

"You had time to come in here and disrupt these children's lives," Layla countered sharply. "Some of their parents are still in jail. Others saw their brothers or family beaten by police. I think you have time, agents. Unless your apologies are just words."

Fatma looked at the children. None paid her much mind in their chatter. But she felt the guilt all the same and slipped on the apron without further protest. Hadia joined her. In short order, the two were serving rounds of baladi bread along with bowls of chicken and mulukhiya—the latter filling the air with the fragrant scent of fried garlic and coriander. Sometime in the middle of this, Layla spoke.

"I am at times contracted by a djinn named Siwa."

Well, that was one confirmation. "To break into the vault of the angels," Fatma said.

"That is where he sends us." Layla paused to scold two children fighting over some bread. "It pays well. Though not as thrilling as my girls hoped."

Fatma exchanged a look with Hadia. "Oh? How's that?"

Layla shrugged. "One would expect breaking into the vault of angels would carry more danger. Or greater difficulty. Not to say it was easy. But . . ."

"It seemed just dangerous enough to navigate for your girls," Fatma guessed. "Just difficult enough for them to overcome. And tended to work out in their favor. Without fail."

The older woman paused, inspecting them with hard eyes. "Odd, that, don't you think?" She turned back to her work. "When Usta Khalid told me you wanted to ask questions about my contract for Siwa, I agreed. Because something has been troubling me these past few weeks. The last time he hired us, it was to steal two items. Said it was very important that I go myself. I did." Seeing their surprised looks, she frowned. "Don't let these old bones fool you. I'm quite agile. I retrieved the items with the information he provided—telling me precisely where to find it in the angels' vault. But a strange thing. I recall stealing a sword—a blade dark as midnight that sings. The other item, however." She frowned deeper. "When I try to remember what else I stole—"

"—you can't," Fatma finished.

Confusion creased the Leopardess's sharp eyes. "I can't remember anything from that night other than retrieving the sword. Like a hole in my memory. I don't know what else I came out with from that vault. But then this man in the gold mask appears on Cairo's streets. Wielding that very black blade. Claiming to be al-Jahiz. Riding on the back of an Ifrit!" She shook her head at the implausibility. "We were paid handsomely. But I cannot help but feel I played a hand in the wrongness that has gripped the city. And every night since coming out of that vault, I dream ill omens. Something terrible is coming." She paused. "I'm telling you this because I believe you are trying to stop that."

"We are," Fatma assured. "You've been a great help. Now we have to visit—"

"All well and good," the older woman cut in. "Once you finish here." She gestured pointedly to an empty bowl. A small girl with a bit of dirt on her nose sat behind it, looking up expectantly. "Now keep spooning out food. These children are hungry."

CHAPTER TWENTY-FOUR

Fatma and Hadia arrived at the Street of the Tentmakers in early afternoon, heading directly to the Gamal Brothers shop. With business slow, the three proprietors sat about drinking tea. Two played a board game while a third watched, the gramophone sounding a scratchy recording of horns and darbukas. She and Hadia flashed badges, and the men absently directed them toward the narrow stairs. Reaching the top, they rapped on the door. Siwa opened with a warm smile—which evaporated upon seeing them. The Illusion djinn moved to shut the door but Fatma rammed her cane between.

"We know you're involved with this imposter. So you can talk now. Or we can have the Ministry bring you in with every agent I can round up. What's it going to be?"

The djinn glared with those swirling yellow-green eyes, looking the part of a menacing Marid. Then, realizing she wouldn't back down, the fight seemed to go out of him. He slumped and let them inside.

"You can also stop with the illusions," Fatma said, gesturing at the opulent space.

The djinn made a face, waving a hand in the air as if cleaning it. Instantly, the illusion vanished. They stood in a small room with faded walls lined by worn and chipped shelves stacked haphazardly with books. The once neat mounds of texts were disorderly piles. Murals of camels still remained—cheaper paintings depicting races and their riders. Strewn across the floor were discarded betting slips in the hundreds.

The change in the towering djinn was no less startling—now a squat figure dressed in rumpled robes. Still bigger than a human, but nowhere the size of a Marid. His orange-striped overly large head resembled a cat's, with a broad down-turned mouth that made him look petulant. With an undignified huff, he waddled over and promptly fell into a rickety worn wooden chair, resting his chin in his hands and whimpering.

Fatma and Hadia exchanged a look and moved to where he sat, trying not to stumble over the mess.

"Siwa," Fatma said. "We just want to talk."

The djinn whimpered harder, burying his face in his hands and shaking his head. Beside him, a rounded woven basket rattled—as if something were alive inside. She and Hadia stepped back, uncertain they wanted to find out what that might be.

"We know about the Seal of Sulayman," Fatma said. "We know what it does." That only made Siwa release a long terrible moan. "We also know that you had it stolen by the Forty Leopards."

Siwa's wailing cut off, and he looked up with eyes no longer hypnotizing but filled with fear. "The sweetest way of life we have experienced is one spent in indulgence and wine drinking!" he blurted. "For we are the lads, the only lads who really matter, on land and sea!"

Fatma sighed. This again. "We asked before about the money wired to you from this AW in Portendorf's ledger. That's who has the ring, isn't it? The imposter calling himself al-Jahiz."

Siwa shook his head harder now, his words choking. "He was all black, even as I tell ye! His head! His body! And his hands were all black! Saving only his teeth! His shield and his armor were even those of a Moor! And black as a Raven!"

"Who is this AW?" Fatma pressed, getting annoyed. "Who was it that asked you to steal the ring? Was it Alexander Worthington?"

Siwa emitted a strangled cry, pulling a knife from his rumpled kaftan. Before Fatma could stop him, he extended a long dark blue tongue and in one quick swipe—cut it off. Beside her, Hadia made a heaving sound.

The djinn slumped back into his chair, his ruined tongue bleeding messily onto his clothing. Then, as they watched, the blood stopped. The wound amazingly healed, and before their eyes, the tongue began to grow back. It took perhaps a minute, but at the end it had grown back fully. The djinn still held the severed organ in one hand, which jerked about—still alive. He moved to the woven basket and lifted the lid. Inside sat a mass of blue fleshy things that jumped around like fish. Only Fatma knew that's not what they were. They were tongues. A mass of severed tongues.

"Ya Rabb!" Hadia croaked weakly. "Now I'm definitely going to be sick."

The djinn closed the basket and looked at them with sad resignation. Fatma met his gaze. The magic that prevented djinn from talking about the Seal of Sulayman was one thing. But he'd cut out his tongue again at the mention of Alexander Worthington, not the ring. The angels' magic was exacting, but this was different—cruel and sadistic.

"It's another spell," she realized. "On top of the one that already binds you not to talk about the seal. Any mention of al—" Her words cut off as Siwa tensed, gripping the knife with pleading eyes. "Any naming of the imposter," she amended, "or talk of the theft, forces you to spout gibberish."

"Not gibberish," Hadia corrected, eyeing the thumping basket. "You said before it was literature, from his books. I recognized that first bit. It's from one of the Maqāmah."

Fatma hadn't heard that term since university. "Aren't they collections of stories from the ninth or tenth century?"

"That's right. We had to read them to pick up the rhythm of the prose, which is also used in some Basri incantations. 'The sweetest way of life we have experienced is one spent in indulgence . . . For we are the lads, the only lads who really matter.'

It's a boast of one of the leaders of a group of thieves. I think he was responding to you about the Forty Leopards. He's actually trying to talk."

The thought that the djinn might be communicating with them hadn't even occurred to Fatma. "'He was all black . . .'" she quoted, recalling his frantic words. "'His shield and his armor were even those of a Moor . . . black as a Raven.' I don't know where that's from. But he must be speaking about al-Jahiz. Or the imposter's illusion."

Siwa relaxed the grip on his knife, exhaling lengthily. He reached again into his robes, this time pulling out a set of folded papers and offering them with a shaking hand. Fatma took the sheets, smoothing back their wrinkled surfaces. The first was filled with almost unreadable scrawling. Djinn script. Just two words.

"I told," Fatma translated. The rest was erratic scribbling amid a red smear.

"I think that's blood." Hadia grimaced.

Fatma went to the next page. "Seal." That was all, before the markings became obscure.

She shuffled through the rest, as Hadia read. "Spoke of . . . Gave . . . Wrong . . . Tricked . . . Messengers . . . Slavery . . . Damned. Damned. Damned." That only word on the last few sheets grew more indecipherable between splatters of blood.

"An attempt at a confession," Fatma worked out. She looked to Siwa, who covered his eyes with one hand, then to the basket of quivering tongues. "You tried to write what you'd done. But even the smallest bit cost you. This whole business of cutting out your tongue, the imposter did that to you." She was struck with pity. How many times had he painfully maimed himself? Grabbing a nearby stool made for a djinn—which meant it was large as a bench—she pulled it close and sat down. Hadia joined her. Perhaps there was another way.

"You like the races," Fatma said, gesturing to a mural.

Siwa lowered his hand and looked to the painting. "They are

beautiful when they run," he replied. So he could still talk normally. As long as it wasn't about the imposter.

"I have a cousin who bets on camel races," Hadia said. "Too much. Like you. It's not your fault. It's a sickness."

Siwa's face crumpled. "I should have just been an archivist. It was my passion. Until the races. Then that became my passion. I lost my employment to it and turned to any means of getting money—so I could keep going to the races." He motioned to the betting slips across the floor. "I do not know how to stop!"

Fatma could only imagine. Djinn were like people in a way, in picking up vices or habits. But it was worse for them. Their passions truly became just that—insatiable and unquenching. Almost as bad as golems.

"You took the list from the angels to fund your gambling," Fatma said. "Finding Alistair Worthington's Brotherhood must have been a gold mine."

"It was only supposed to be a few items," Siwa said sorrowfully. "But it became more."

"When did you realize the angels were using you?" she asked. "In your confession. You wrote the words 'Tricked.' And 'Messengers.' They're the ones that let you take the list. You must have figured it out. Known it couldn't be so easy to steal from them. But you kept doing it. For the money." If the djinn's orange face could blush, it would. He hung his head. "We're not here to judge. But we need to know about the one thing you didn't steal for Alistair Worthington. That you stole for someone else."

Siwa's face immediately seized up, the magic taking hold.

"We won't say anyone's name directly," Fatma added hastily. "Maybe we can talk without making you hurt yourself."

The djinn looked her over before acquiescing. "I will try. To help undo what I have helped unleash." It seemed that like the head of the Forty Leopards, he too needed some absolution.

"Can you nod or shake your head at questions?"

"Not if they are about . . ." His lips drew tight, unable to finish.

Of course it wouldn't be that easy. Magic never was.

"The imposter asked you to steal the Seal of Sulayman," she began.

Siwa visibly struggled before speaking. "Indeed, each one says: 'My faith is right, and those who believe in another faith believe in falsehood, and are the enemies of God. As my own faith appears true to me, so does another one find his own faith true; but truth is one!'"

"I think that's a long way of saying yes," Hadia reasoned.

One down, Fatma thought.

"Was it you that told the imposter about the ring?"

"Soul receives from soul that knowledge," the djinn answered curtly. "Therefore not by book, nor from tongue. If knowledge of mysteries come after emptiness of mind, that is illumination of heart!"

"I think he's saying the imposter learned it on their own," Hadia translated. "The angels told us as much. That some people were just strong-willed enough to see through their magic. And that Marid, he said the ring had its own mind. That it would only reveal itself to someone it believed could wield it."

"Aywa," Fatma commended. She was good at this. "The imposter saw the ring on your list and came asking after it. You probably refused at first. But you needed the money."

The djinn scowled in self-recrimination, his down-turned mouth spreading wider. "The learned man whom you accuse of disobeying divine law knows that he disobeys, as you do when you drink wine or exact usury or allow yourself in evil-speaking, lying, and slander. You know your sin and yield to it, not through ignorance but because you are mastered by concupiscence."

Hadia frowned in concentration, deciphering. "He's admitting his weakness?"

"Last one," Fatma said. "The money wired for the ring. It came from the imposter?"

Siwa's face strained as he fought to speak, guilt plain on his face.

"You have an illness," Hadia said gently. "The person who

knew this took advantage. Those . . . angels . . . knew this and took advantage as well. That is the true wickedness." She looked to Fatma. "I think that's confirmation enough."

Fatma agreed. No need to agitate the djinn further. "Now we know for certain. The imposter is one and the same as the AW from Portendorf's ledger. We know who that is. He had the ring stolen. And used it to make himself the Master of Djinn. All the things we've seen this imposter do, his mysterious powers, come through that ring—willing djinn to use their sorcery as his own."

"God protect us," Hadia whispered, hand to her heart. "How do we stop evil like that?"

"We get the ring back," Fatma insisted. "If we have to take his hand to do it."

She stood up, her mind already on what they had to do next, when Siwa unexpectedly grabbed her arm. The djinn's face was a mass of frustration.

"So you did not care for full-bosomed companions?" he bellowed. "How does it suit you to be tested by the lion of the forest?"

Fatma looked to Hadia, who this time seemed equally baffled. "I don't understand," she told the djinn.

"How does it suit you to be tested by the lion of the forest!" he repeated. He said it several more times, growing more frustrated. When he started reaching for his knife, Fatma held out her own hand to stop him.

"Maybe you could show me," she suggested.

Siwa's large eyes widened. He jumped up, almost knocking her over to get to his books. In a frenzy, he tore into them, tossing texts into the air as he searched. Fatma exchanged another look with Hadia, who shook her head. There was a cry of triumph, and the djinn ran back to them, a bound leather tome in his hand. Turning to the first page, he displayed the words: *Sirat al-amira Dhāt al-Himma.*

He thrust it at Fatma. "I'll read it," she assured, taking the text. A look of relief washed over his face, and he returned to slump into his chair.

"*The Tale of Lady Dhāt al-Himma*," Hadia noted, inspecting the title. "Do you know it?"

Fatma shook her head. "I'm sure there's somebody at the Ministry who does. We're heading back there now. Time to see Dr. Hoda. Think I'm ready for another try at my illusion."

♦ ♦ ♦

"Are you concentrating? Don't think about what you want the illusion to be. Let it reveal itself. Remember, empty your mind. Empty your—"

"I got it." Fatma cut off Dr. Hoda. This was trying enough, without her hovering and giving instructions. The chief of forensics shrugged, pushing back her glasses and folding her arms. But she barely moved to give any space.

Fatma returned her focus to the lock of hair sitting on a large petri dish and soaked through in liquid. Dr. Hoda claimed the alchemical solution had done its work, breaking down the bonds binding the magic about it. Now she had to do the rest.

Only that was proving difficult. She'd been staring at the lock of hair now for almost a half an hour. Nothing had changed. Not a single strand.

"Maybe it needs more solution," Fatma suggested.

The doctor shook a head of frizzy hair. "Do that, and it might dissolve away."

"Great," Fatma grumbled. She could go to Amir with everything they had now. But the cryptic words of angels, the head of a notorious thieving gang, and an Illusion djinn with a gambling addiction weren't the most convincing sources. They needed this last piece to tie things together—something Amir and the higher-ups couldn't ignore.

"Just show yourself," she muttered to the lock.

"You can do this." Hadia spoke confidently. "Think about everything we've learned in the past two days. Trust in that. It's gotten us this far."

Everything they'd learned, Fatma considered. Parts of the

puzzle had been coming together. A ring that could control djinn. Kept by angels and stolen from them. All tying back to the Brotherhood of Al-Jahiz. It was all there. She just needed to make the pieces fit. Focusing, she let her mind empty of everything else and took her lead from all she now knew. The picture it painted was easy enough to see. It had always been there, right in front of her.

The change wasn't as quick as the mask—as if the magic fought her. But once it began, it didn't stop. The dark fibers of knotted hair untangled, becoming straight and less wiry. As she watched, once black strands turned a familiar pale gold. Dr. Hoda clapped while Hadia stared in wonder.

Fatma picked up the pale gold lock and held it up triumphantly. "Got you!"

CHAPTER
TWENTY-FIVE

B y late afternoon, papers had been sent for the arrest of Alexander Worthington.

Fatma read the list of charges—terrorism, inciting civil unrest, use of illicit magic, disturbing the king's peace. News of the ring—which they'd had to repeat over and over again—had caused alarm enough to get the warrant. Turned out the Worthington heir wasn't above the law after all, not when it came to a threat like that.

They'd even established a motive: an ambitious son who resented his father's eccentricity; who felt he should be heir sooner rather than later. Masquerading as al-Jahiz seemed right in line with making a mockery of all the Worthington patriarch held dear. The sudden investments into weapons contractors, the interruption of the peace summit: all attempts to undo his father's legacy. They'd even resolved the discrepancy over his arrival in the city. A man able to control djinn could easily forge travel documents. It all fit.

So then why did she feel she was missing something?

"Are you ready?"

Fatma looked up at Hadia's question. They both stood outside the Ministry, where an armada of police wagons gathered. This was going to be a joint arrest. She and Hadia were backed up with ten more agents and perhaps four times as many police. The plan was to take Alexander and remove the ring before he could summon help. If it came to a fight, they were authorized to use lethal force. Dead men couldn't wield magic rings.

"Ready."

Hadia studied her face. "You seem bothered."

"Still working some things out."

"What you've done so far is pretty impressive. I admit, I wasn't too certain it was Alexander. But the hair . . ." She indicated the pale gold lock Fatma held. "You were right!"

"Still the business with the Clock of Worlds. We don't have a good answer for that."

"Well, hopefully we'll get one as we cut that ring from his finger," someone put in.

Aasim joined them wearing his usual khaki uniform and Janissary-esque moustache.

Fatma shook her head. "I don't understand how of all people, you're the least affected by the angels' magic." She'd told him about the Seal of Sulayman once, and he'd not forgotten yet. That was hours ago. Was he really all human?

Aasim smugly tapped his temple with a thick thumb. "Strong-willed. Don't be jealous."

She rolled her eyes. Should have never mentioned that.

"How did you never come across it in any books?" Hadia asked.

"I don't read much. Not ashamed to say it either."

"That I absolutely believe," Fatma retorted.

The inspector gave her an admonishing look. "And wish not for the things in which God has made some of you to excel others," he said, quoting the familiar ayah. Then followed up by flashing an open palm, as if to ward off her envy.

"Did you bring him?" Fatma asked, changing topics.

"In there," Aasim said, nodding at a wagon. "If you're done brooding, I'm ready to go round up this Englishman. Be nice if we can get it done by sundown."

As everyone piled into vehicles, her eyes searched about—and stopped when she realized she was looking for Siti. She'd grown accustomed to the woman showing up out of the blue during times like this. No sign of her today. Good. If this came to a fight, who she was—*what* she was—would prove a liability. But she still felt a pang of disappointment at not seeing that confident smile and unmistakable swagger making its way between the assembled agents and police. Pushing the idea from her head, she was about to climb into a wagon when someone called her name. Turning, she found Onsi running after her. When he reached her, he took out a kerchief to mop his face while regarding her cheerfully. Did the man ever stop smiling?

"Agent Fatma!" he huffed.

"Agent Onsi. You're in another wagon, with Agent Hamed."

"Yes! And my thanks again for including me on this mission. I hope—"

"You don't have to thank me, Onsi." Admittedly, he wasn't the first person she had in mind for the field. But he'd been handy during the ghul attack. "Is there something else?"

Onsi nodded vigorously. "I wanted to tell you, I read over the book you gave me!"

Fatma blinked. "You read *The Tale of Lady Dhāt al-Himma* in the past few hours?" Normally, she'd have taken it to Zagros. But the djinn hadn't been released yet, even after what she'd told Amir. Not with the ring still being unaccounted for. Onsi was the next natural choice. But this had to be some kind of record.

"I picked up speed-reading at university," he said. "It doesn't allow for detailed understanding, but I've found you can gain a fairly good summary. Why, once I finished the complete thirteenth-century volumes of the Timbuktu esoteric philosophies in—"

"Onsi," Fatma gestured to the wagon. "We're in the middle of something?"

"Ah! The book! A fascinating read. One I hadn't come across, though I hear it's very popular in the kingdoms of Western Sahara. It tells of Lady Fatma Dhāt al-Himma."

"So we share a name. Could that be what Siwa wanted me to know?"

"That's hardly the most remarkable thing. In the literature she's a princess who becomes a warrior-queen. Some uncomfortable events occur with her husband, and she bears him a son with black skin. This alarms the father, who refuses to grant the child legitimacy—though physicians confirm the boy is his. Quite a scandal."

"I'm certain," Fatma replied impatiently. "Is there more?"

"Oh yes!" He pushed up his spectacles. "Lady Dhāt al-Himma is forced to become her son's sole parent. She takes him under her wing and teaches him the art of a knight. To test her son, she would often dress as a man and attack him. He grows to be a great warrior, but also arrogant. In one story, when his mother warns him off entering into battle with the Byzantines, he rebukes her—tells her to go back to spinning with the women and leave it to him to fight."

"That's ungrateful," Fatma noted.

"Quite. Lady Dhāt al-Himma takes her vengeance by masquerading as a Byzantine knight and defeating her son in front of whole armies, before pulling back her veil to reveal who she was—a woman, and his mother."

"Sounds like something my mother would do. What's the point?"

"It's what Lady Dhāt al-Himma says to her son after lifting her veil: 'So you did not care for full-bosomed companions? How does it suit you to be tested by the lion of the forest?' Those are the same words spoken by this Illusion djinn. Perhaps you can find meaning in them?"

Fatma looked at him for a long while. At last she said, "You're a treasure, Onsi." His round face beamed as if she had pinned a medal on his chest.

◆　◆　◆

The sun slunk low by the time their caravan rumbled down the road to the Worthington estate. The sky began to fade from blue to a hazy shade of yellow, and Fatma could make out the pyramids standing their ceaseless watch. They had been joined by Giza police, swelling to almost as large as the company that entered the Cemetery. She hoped this wasn't a repeat of that disaster.

Hadia sat beside her, forced to endure Aasim recounting stories of his strong will—inherited, he believed, from his grandfather. He sat close to two other men in police uniforms. The one in the middle Fatma glanced to every now and again. He returned her stares, with black eyes as unreadable as his set face.

In reality, she wasn't paying much attention to him. Or to Aasim's bragging. Siwa's parting words lingered, and she mouthed them like some mantra. *How does it suit you to be tested by the lion of the forest?* She twisted the strands of the pale gold lock between her fingers, probing them with the proficiency of a seer.

Hearing her name pulled her from contemplation. Hadia was gesturing to the wagon door—where Aasim and the others were already making their exit. She hadn't even noticed they'd stopped.

"Are you alright?" Hadia asked, face showing concern. "You didn't talk the entire way."

"Aasim talked enough for everyone. Did he compare you to his daughter yet?"

"Inspector Moustache? About three times." She dropped her voice. "But really, what's going on? I thought you'd be ecstatic. We're about to arrest our imposter."

"Just some things on my mind." Fatma looked down to the lock of hair, then drew out her pocket watch, holding it up. "My father gave me this when I came to Cairo. Made it like an old asturlab. Said to look to it whenever I feel lost, so I can find my way."

"You feel lost now?"

Fatma met Hadia's eyes. "Do you trust me?"

She seemed taken aback but nodded with certainty. "Yes."

Fatma tucked the watch back into her jacket. "When we get in there, follow my lead. I can't explain. Still working through things. But just bear with me. No matter how crazy it looks."

Hadia raised a curious eyebrow. "Crazy comes with this job."

They stepped out of the wagon, joining Aasim. He stood in

front of the Worthington estate, giving orders. "I'm stationing most of my people around the estate. In case the Englishman tries to find another way out." He touched a whistle hanging from his neck. "One blow, and they'll swarm the house. If that Ifrit shows up . . ."

"Let's not let it get to that," she told him. "But don't try putting on the cuffs until I give the go-ahead."

Aasim regarded her quizzically. "Fine, as long as he doesn't do one of those villain rants—they love hearing themselves talk."

In the end, it was him, herself, Hadia, and four policemen that knocked at the entrance of the estate. Hamed took charge of the other agents, each armed with specialized weapons to take on supernatural entities. Though none had ever been tested on an Ifrit. When the door opened, it was the night steward. His eyes turned to full circles at seeing the police wagons.

"Peace be upon you . . . Steward Hamza, is it?" Fatma greeted.

"And upon you peace, daughter," the older man returned uncertainly. "How may I help?"

"Is Alexander Worthington in the residence?" Aasim asked.

Hamza took in the inspector's uniform. "Master and mistress are in the upstairs rooms."

Aasim motioned at his men, who pushed past the steward. They took up places in the parlor while the rest of them followed. "Could you fetch *Master* Worthington for us?"

More a demand than a question. The night steward bowed slightly. "Of course, inspector." He turned to go but Fatma stopped him.

"Fetch them both," she said. Then more gently. "Uncle, are there others in the house?"

"Myself, a cook, some of the evening staff."

"When you're done, gather them and leave. Get as far away from here as you can."

To the old man's credit, he didn't question her or look to Aasim for confirmation. When he disappeared down a corridor, she took in the wide rectangular parlor, with its antique silver

Mamluke lamps, Safavid murals, and star-tiled floor. Walking to one side, she stopped near the set of swords she'd noticed her first day. Their rounded pommels sported black tassels dangling from hilts in decorated silver trim sitting above iron cross-guards. She pulled one halfway from its leather scabbard. A straight double-edged blade. Kept sharpened by the looks of it. She could just make out inscriptions from the Qu'ran etched onto the surface. Hadia watched her curiously. Before either could speak, their hosts arrived.

Alexander Worthington strode from one of the bulbous pointed archways. He sported gray pants and vest, beneath a dark evening jacket. Fatma noted the silk blue neckwear with feathered patterns that garnished his high-collared white shirt. A cravat. She'd often wondered if she could pull off one of those.

Beside him walked Abigail Worthington, as elegantly garbed. She wore one of the more modish Parisian-Cairene gowns: black and gold silk, beads and lace, worked into masterful floral patterns that mimicked henna on skin. A necklace of black and ruby sapphires hung just above her square neckline, with matching earrings and wrist pieces—even about her still bandaged hand. With those dark red tresses piled into high elaborate curls, she and her brother looked the same height side by side.

"What's the meaning of this?" Alexander demanded without the bother of a greeting. His face looked as annoyed as when they'd first met, framed by a length of pale gold hair. "Hamza tells me there are police wagons on the estate?"

"Alexander Worthington." Aasim stepped forward, holding up the writ. "I am Inspector Aasim Sharif with the Cairo police here to deliver a warrant for your arrest." Aasim's English was poor, at best. But he got that line across well enough because Alexander looked as if he'd been slapped. He opened his mouth dumbly, and his eyes roamed over the assembled faces until landing on Fatma.

"The warrant is for your father's murder," she said, answering his questioning look. "And twenty-three others, including members of the Brotherhood of Al-Jahiz and two Egyptian citizens."

Abigail's loud gasp echoed through the parlor, a hand clutching her chest as her mouth gulped for air. She looked ready to faint.

"Is this some kind of a joke?" Alexander glared, incredulous. "A sick gag? Where you barge into my home and accuse me of murdering *my own father*?"

"Yes." Abigail let out a nervous laugh. "This is some bit of native humor. They're having sport with you, Alexander."

"Hardly sport," Fatma continued. "Inciting a riot, committing a terrorist attack on an Egyptian civil institution, endangering the life of the king. It's all in there." She gestured to the writ. "We made one in English to look over if you'd like." Aasim held out the paper, and Alexander snatched it out of his hand, reading furiously. Fatma watched him, her eyes meeting Abigail, who still seemed in shock.

"What nonsense!" Alexander thundered. "These charges are one and the same for this miscreant running about your city claiming to be the Soudanese mystic! The very one who my sister encountered, who as I understand has admitted to my father's murder!"

"Who is also you," Aasim got out in stilted English.

Alexander practically sputtered. "Me? You believe that madman is *me*? Do I look like some black-skinned turbaned Mohammedan? Are you people blind?"

"The imposter uses a disguise," Fatma said. "An illusion of illicit and stolen magic." Her hand fished into one pocket, pulling out the lock of pale gold hair. "I cut this off him the night of the king's summit. Not very common among 'black-skinned turbaned Mohammedans.'"

Alexander stared and a hand absently went up to touch his own hair. Realizing what he was doing, he lowered it and shook the writ angrily. "Is this what passes for justice in this country of superstition and charlatanry? My father is murdered, then I am accused of his crime? What follows now? Some grand extortion for money, I must assume?" His voice grew louder, and he shook as he spoke. "You are mistaken if you think I will pay any brib-ery! I'll have my solicitors ring the English embassy at once! You won't get away with this . . . this . . . outrage! I'll see every last one of you jailed before the night's done!"

Abigail put out her hands pleadingly—one for them and one for her brother, whose face was steadily turning a violent shade of purple. "This has to be some mistake. I'm sure Alexander can ex-plain . . . that." She motioned at the lock of hair. "You can, can't you?" Her blue-green eyes regarded him with clear uncertainty.

"Why are you looking at me like that?" he demanded. "You believe *them*?"

"Of course not! I'm sure you have a good answer." She put a hand to her temple. "This is all just so unexpected. I'm not cer-tain what to think."

"Do you see what you've done? Addled my sister's easily impres-sionable mind. This is an assassination upon my very character!"

Fatma looked the woman over. "Are you well, Abbie?"

"Just a bit light-headed. This is all so sudden."

"Were you two going somewhere?"

Abigail blinked, then looked down at her dress. "To a dinner engagement."

"With one of your family's powerful friends, likely." Fatma turned back to Alexander. "We have one of them on record, who can identify you in Egypt on the night of your father's murder."

"I have documents showing my time of arrival!"

"Not hard to forge for someone who uses illusion," Hadia put in.

Alexander threw up his hands, then began to laugh, shaking his head. "You're all mad. This entire country is mad. It claimed my father, and now it wants to claim me." His voice dropped to a hiss. "But it won't! It won't take me like it took him! I won't let it!"

Fatma searched his hard blue eyes for signs of that burning she'd seen in the imposter. There was arrogance certainly—the self-importance of men who thought too highly of themselves. But none of the intensity. She looked to his fingers. All bare, save for the one adorned with his father's silver signet.

"It does seem like madness, doesn't it?" she asked. "When the first clues led to you, I thought I was mad too. But it began to make a sort of sense. You appearing to lie about when you arrived in the country. Your unwillingness to talk to us. You even have a motive for getting your father out of the way. And you certainly didn't think highly of his Brotherhood. You're also very unlikable." His lips tightened at that.

"But it wasn't enough," she went on. "What finally led us to you were the more recent happenings. First you don't appear at the summit your father helped put together, while the imposter does. Then we learn about a money transfer to the djinn Siwa bearing your initials—AW. By the time we visited the angels about the ring, it all painted a picture—straight to you."

"What are you talking about?" Alexander was beyond frustration. He looked to Aasim and then Hadia. "What is she talking about? Who is this djinn, and what monies did I send him? Angels? Why would I have anything to do with those . . . creatures?"

Fatma walked back to the wall with the swords. "Investigations can have their own life. If you go in wanting to believe something, the clues take you right there. They'll line up just like you want them. Paint you a convenient picture." She pulled out a sword fully, feeling the textured grip. "Your father built this entire estate after al-Jahiz and the so-called Orient. This sword, it's Soudanese, I think?" She turned to Hadia, offering it.

The woman accepted the weapon without question, looking it over. "It's a kaskara. Soudanese, or maybe Bagirmi."

"Agent Hadia's good with swords," Fatma explained. She drew the other blade, then looked to Alexander. "I bet you're good with swords. Had to be, as a captain." She met Aasim's questioning look, motioning for patience, before tossing the sword to Alexander.

He caught it in surprise. But awkwardly. Managing to get a hand on the tassel, before gripping the hilt. He glared at Fatma. "What do you think—?"

"Fight him!" she said.

Hadia didn't miss a beat, moving into a fighting stance and rushing him. Alexander yelped as he brought up his sword to block. It was clumsy, and he almost dropped the weapon when their blades met. She quickly sent him shuffling back, trying to defend as the flat of her sword penetrated his guard repeatedly—catching him on the arm, hip, and leg.

"That's enough," Fatma called. Hadia fell out of her stance, stepping back.

"What the devil are you about?" Alexander roared, apoplectic.

"My apologies," Fatma said. "You're not very good with a sword."

Alexander turned a shade redder. "We don't use Oriental blades in His Majesty's army!"

"Of course," Fatma said. Hadia walked back, handing over the kaskara. "It's just that the imposter is a very good swordsman. He also favors his right. You fight with your left. That's odd." She hefted the sword, then threw it hilt-first.

Abigail hadn't been expecting the weapon to be hurled in her direction, but she caught it smoothly—snatching it out of the air with one hand.

Fatma didn't waste another moment. Drawing her sword from her cane, she rushed the woman—who flowed surprisingly fast into a defensive stance, bringing her blade up to meet the attack. Fatma pressed with quick, even strokes. Each was deflected by well-executed parrying strikes. She pulled back, nodding. Abigail stood, body poised and balanced beneath her evening gown, an all-too familiar fire in her blue-green eyes.

"Oh my!" she exclaimed, the intensity flashing away. She handed the sword back, giggling nervously. "I suppose those fencing lessons have paid off."

"That was a bit more than some lessons," Fatma remarked, returning the blade to the wall. She glanced to Hadia, whose knowing gaze said she had caught on. "You're good. And you favor your right. But that's not all you're good at, is it, Abbie?"

Abigail looked puzzled. "I don't think I know what you mean?"

"You were the first one to tell us about the imposter—the man in the gold mask. Your brother seemed to have all the motive for killing your father. But what about you? The daughter who he brought to Egypt, spending months, then years at a time. Who he confided in about his obsession, who helped him look through books and manuscripts—while your brother's off playing at being soldier."

"See here!" Alexander began. Fatma held up a hand for quiet.

"What else did you help your father with? Maybe the secret hand growing the Worthington fortune while he chased after esoteric antiques? Then in the end, you don't get anything. Your father doesn't let you join his Brotherhood, though he invites some 'native' woman. Your brother gets to join even though he doesn't want to. Not only that, but he's the heir. You were there when your father needed someone, and you're just left to be the idle daughter. If anyone had a motive to kill Alistair Worthington, wouldn't it be you, Abbie?"

"Preposterous!" Alexander blurted out. "First you accuse me of being this Soudanese madman. Now you imagine it's *my sister*? Who next? The servants?" He looked to Aasim. "Inspector! How long will you allow this farce?" This time Aasim held up a hand for silence.

"Is that how you came across a passage about the ring?" Fatma continued. "Not in one of those silly books you'd read in front of us. In one of your father's manuscripts. You saw it, didn't you? Someone with strong will. Maybe even driven by anger. You knew all about the Brotherhood's dealings with Siwa. You went to him, asking. He couldn't tell you, but you'd seen it on his list, perhaps when your father and no one else could. And you wanted it so badly. With it, you'd have the power to take vengeance on your father and his Brotherhood. Power to do whatever you wanted."

She held up the lock of pale gold hair again. "Ifrit magic, that's how you created your illusion. How you became al-Jahiz. I'm told it's a special kind of deception. It makes us see what we *want* to see. I thought I'd solved it. But I just traded one illusion for another—like when you think you've woken from a dream, but you're still dreaming. AW was never Alexander Worthington. It was Abigail Worthington. That's how I know this hair I'm holding isn't really gold."

Fatma looked to the lock in her hand, and finally, emptied her thoughts—free of expectations and wants, letting it simply be. The gold coloring of the strands vanished, leaving behind a familiar dark red. The room went absolutely still.

"All of you must be out of your minds," Alexander spoke into the quiet. He laughed openly. "My sister? A sorcerer right under my nose? A master swordsman? Look at her! She sheds tears if you speak too harshly, or faints at the sight of blood. I hardly think the poor creature could even dream up so many fanciful notions and schemes!"

Fatma held up her hand again to quiet the man. But someone else beat her to it.

"Do shut up, Alexander," Abigail said. She twisted her slender neck to fix her brother with a stare that could have burned through a wall—and he swallowed his laughter. Her eyes returned to Fatma. "I suppose that's that, then," she commended in fluent Arabic. Her brother gaped as if he'd been slapped a second time, which just about matched Aasim's face. Even Hadia, who by now had seen it coming, let out a low breath.

"No more playing the part of the wide-eyed Englishwoman?" Fatma asked.

Abigail chuckled. Her puzzled expression was gone as if she'd torn off a mask. "Play the part people expect, and they'll accept it every time." She switched to English, gesturing to her brother. "He believed it. Not all illusions require magic."

"But magic helps," Hadia put in. "It was you who went to Madame Nabila on the night of your father's murder, wrapped in the illusion of your brother. Begging her to keep things quiet in the newspapers."

"Amazing what a well-placed word here or there can do to sow confusion," Abigail said. "The trick is knowing what people want to hear. Maybe it's an appeal to their fears, their prejudices, their hunger, the natural distrust between empires. Or it can be as simple as a haughty Egyptian woman who delights in seeing a young Englishman grovel at her feet."

"Or leading two agents to chase after your brother," Fatma said. "Throwing us off your scent so that you can go about your deeds, unmolested. You sent the letter luring him to Cairo. Then planted clues for us—even handing us Portendorf's journal. The spell on the Illusion djinn. The one that makes him cut out his tongue at the merest mention of your brother's name. Very incriminating."

Abigail performed a slight curtsy. "That one was my special touch. Reciting from all his books. Does he still keep those tongues in a basket? Absolutely wretched!" She narrowed her eyes. "But how did you reason it out?"

"How does it suit you to be tested by the lion of the forest?" Fatma recited. "Ever read *Sirat al-amira Dhāt al-Himma*? It's about a queen who goes into battle dressed as a man—hiding herself like a lion in the forest. The quote is her boastful taunt, admiring her own wit and deception."

Abigail nodded appreciatively. "Oh, I like her!"

"One trick I haven't figured out," Fatma said. "I'm guessing you were behind your brother's car troubles to keep him from the summit. Make him look guilty in our eyes. But I saw you faint when al-Jahiz appeared. How?"

Abigail broke into a wolfish smile. "Al-Jahiz. Prophet. Savior. Madman. So many things to so many people. Whoever he truly was, all we have now is . . . illusion." She waved her bandaged hand, and the imposter was there—garbed in black and with the dark-skinned face of al-Jahiz. About the room, gasps went up. One of the policemen, Fatma noted with satisfaction, gasped loudest of all.

"Al-Jahiz is no one person," Abigail said, shrouded in illusion. "He is here."

"And here," a voice came as another al-Jahiz walked from a corridor.

"And here," twin al-Jahiz echoed, emerging from a second.

"He is everywhere," yet another al-Jahiz spoke, entering from a third.

Four replicas of al-Jahiz moved to stand beside Abigail. She waved her hand, and their illusions faded. One al-Jahiz became Victor Fitzroy, with a sneer on his square jaw. The Edginton sisters, Bethany and Darlene, stood where the twin al-Jahiz had been. The ever-smirking Percival Montgomery accounted for the fourth.

"So which one of you gave that speech at the summit?"

Percival sketched Fatma a bow to which Abigail clapped delightedly.

"Abigail," Alexander said hoarsely. "Are you saying you truly did all these terrible things? That you murdered our father?"

For a heartbeat the hard mask the woman wore slipped. But it reappeared just as quick. "It was time for Father to step aside," she said stoically. "You saw what he was doing to our family name, to our wealth. Who do you think was running things while you were gallivanting about India being a poor soldier? Those doddering old men he encircled himself with? I was the one making sure the Worthington name survived in good standing another generation."

"All those business deals you couldn't understand," Fatma said to Alexander. "The ones with weapons contractors and buying up munitions factories? That was your sister. It's why she tried to ruin the peace summit. She wants a war. All to make profit."

Alexander glared at his sister, aghast.

"Profit?" Abigail scoffed. "You think this is about money? Or to get back at my father for not inviting me into his little club? Retribution against my brother as heir?" She gave Fatma a disappointed look. "If I were a man. If it was my brother as you suspected. What would you think my motive?"

Aasim leaned in close to Fatma. "I feel a villain rant coming on."

"Power," Hadia answered. "It's what men usually want."

"What else is there?" Abigail asked. "Egypt has that now. Thanks to al-Jahiz. You once held the scepter thousands of years past. Now you've become a new power. While you build fantastic wonders of mechanics and magic, the old powers are in retreat, or squabbling among themselves. England is barely an empire at all. The Union Jack routed by mystic Hindoos in the Punjab and Ashanti queens with talking drums in the Gold Coast." She huffed. "My father was right about one thing—failing to embrace this new age has left Britain faltering, while the darker races rise. But why create when we can simply take? The heart of Egypt's power is its djinn. And I will take them from you."

Abigail lifted her bandaged hand, and the wrappings vanished—another illusion. Beneath, the skin was pale and withered almost to the bone. On the fourth finger sat a plain gold band, adorned with fiery script. Fatma knew it at once—the Seal of Sulayman.

"I will make Britannia rule again," Abigail pronounced. "Egypt will be the first to fall, its djinn under my control. Then I will set about taking back everything we've lost, making the empire whole again. Making us great once more. Perhaps I will be honored like Lord Nelson. Maybe they'll make me queen." She stopped to admire the ring. "Or I'll make myself queen!"

Fatma eyed the woman's sickly looking hand and the rapture on her face, remembering the angels' warning of such power: *Too much for a mortal to wield so willfully. So often.* She turned to Aasim. "You got all that?" The inspector nodded. Her gaze shifted to one policeman in particular. "And you, heard enough?"

The policeman nodded as well, his face a mix of shock and disdain. "You are false!" he shouted. Abigail regarded him, plainly confused—until recognition struck.

"Moustafa. My witness."

"No longer!" the man shot back. "You are false! I will denounce you with my last breath!"

It had been Fatma's plan to bring the man along, dressed like one of Aasim's policemen. Having the witness of al-Jahiz see the imposter unmasked would go a long way in easing the tensions on Cairo's streets.

"News travels fast in this city," she said. "Everyone will soon know you aren't al-Jahiz. There are police all over this estate, ready to enter at a word. Even if you manage to stop us, we'll be back, with more. You can't win. It's over."

A curious smile stole across Abigail's face. Her friends snickered. That wasn't the reaction Fatma was hoping for.

"Over?" Abigail asked. "It's not even begun. Why, Agent Fatma, you haven't even asked me what I plan to do with that fantastic clock. I'm going to take it with me, back to where this all started. My timetable was a day or two longer. But now will just have to do." She broke into a singsong. "The Nine Lords are coming."

Fatma tensed as the ring on Abigail's hand began to glow with fiery script. She was set to tell Aasim to blow his whistle and make the arrest when a familiar sound came to her ears. She remembered it from her previous visits to the Worthington estate. Then it had been faint, so slight she often wondered if she heard it at all. Now it was clearer. A dull ringing, like hammers on steel. She looked to Hadia.

"I hear it too!"

Fatma's stomach went hollow. The clanging. She'd never accounted for the clanging.

"Abigail!" she tried. "You're being used! The angels, they wanted you to—"

Abigail stifled a yawn. "That djinn Siwa prattled on as much. That the ring came to me through their engineering." She shrugged her bare shoulders. "I'll tell you what I told him—I don't care. The ring is mine now. It came to me. And I'm no one's puppet."

The clanging got louder.

"Where's it coming from?" Hadia shouted. It wasn't one clanging but many, pounding out an irregular rhythm. Fatma stared down to her caramel wing tips. Was the ground trembling? Around them the walls vibrated and silver Mamluke lamps swayed from the ceiling by their chains.

"Do we take her?" Aasim asked, whistle poised at his lips.

Fatma met the grin spreading across Abigail's face and shook her head. "Get out! Everyone get out of here now!"

They bolted for the doors. Fatma grabbed hold of Alexander, whose eyes darted about. She spared a last glance at Abigail and her friends, standing amid the shaking room, unconcerned. She pushed through the door and down the stairs, the deafening clanging chasing them outside. Fatma caught sight of Hamed, running to them with several agents and policemen in tow.

Then the house collapsed.

She felt the earth shift under her feet, sending her stumbling. Aasim was yelling for the police to pull back. Men still in wagons jumped out and ran as the Worthington estate crumbled. Towers, minarets, and colonnades broke apart, collapsing whole buildings. The ground followed, opening up and swallowing sections of the mansion. In moments there was only rubble, enveloped in a billowing cloud of choking dust. Fatma coughed, trying to get further away, when she heard a new sound—like creaking. Turning, she saw the wreckage of the ruined house moving, pushing upward.

She hadn't properly made sense of it before debris was thrown about, sending everyone seeking cover. Something was rising now from the house. Something she now understood had been beneath it all this time. First, a flaming horned head of metal, followed by shoulders, then a massive body in the shape of a man. No, not a man. A djinn! A towering machine djinn, of iron, brass, and steel. Ifrit clung to its frame—fiery beings of blood-red flame that burned bright against the darkening dusk. They hammered and welded and clanged away in a furious cacophony.

She'd thought there was only one. There must have been dozens! Their work was incomplete, so that in some places the structure was missing sheets of metal. Its chest was open, and she could see where a mechanical heart spun. There, on a platform, stood five figures—Abigail Worthington and her friends. Just behind them sat a curious machinery of overlapping gear wheels where several Ifrit labored. An overwhelming fear gripped at her. The Clock of Worlds!

The great mechanical djinn pulled free from the destroyed Worthington estate, like a beast shedding its skin. Its horned head wreathed in djinn fire turned northward and set out, two long legs taking sweeping strides. The thing was fast for its size, and soon began to pull away into the distance.

Fatma stumbled, pushing a dazed Alexander along. She found Hadia and Aasim massed with equally stunned police and agents coated in dust.

"I don't think we brought enough people after all!" Aasim commented, scrubbing his moustache clean.

"I think we also know what happened to that missing Worthington steel," Hadia added, staring after the iron giant. "Where is that thing heading?"

"She said they were going back to where this all started," Fatma answered.

Aasim frowned. "The case? That started here."

Fatma looked to the retreating giant. It wasn't heading north but northeast. "Cairo. Where this all started. The Clock of Worlds was made to re-create al-Jahiz's grand formulas. To open doorways to other worlds. She's taking it to where he first bored into the Kaf."

Hadia inhaled sharply. "Abdeen Palace!"

"The dignitaries for the king's summit are there!" Aasim said.

Fatma's heart fell. "We have to get back!"

"That's going to be difficult." Aasim gestured to the sunken Worthington estate. The few police wagons still visible were buried under wreckage. "Best we can hope is that Giza phones a warning when it catches sight of that thing—maybe someone has sense enough to send a car to check on us."

Not good enough, Fatma fretted. No one else knew what they were even dealing with. She gazed around. There had to be some way out of here!

No sooner than she thought the words than she caught sight of a lone vehicle speeding up the road toward them. Not a car. Some kind of motorized velocipede. But it was bulky in the center, with a bronze-and-silver surface. Its two wheels—one in the front and back—had thicker tires than a velocipede, while the seat sat low. It also made a greater deal of noise, with an engine that growled like it belonged on an airship.

The occupant sat leaning over the vehicle's front, hands gripping bronze handles where a single lamp shone in the growing dusk, their face obscured by goggles and a round brown leather helmet. The driver stopped the odd bike just before them, flicking a kickstand down with a boot that matched the helmet. Lifting up the goggles, they undid the straps on the headpiece, pulling it off and surveying the demolished house.

Fatma gawped.

The driver, Siti, flashed a smile.

"Must have been some party."

CHAPTER TWENTY-SIX

Y ou know I saw the strangest thing on the way here?" Siti
leaned casually on the odd bike, dressed in snug tan
breeches and a short red kaftan for a top, with a familiar
long rifle strapped to her back. "A giant machine djinn. With
Ifrit hanging all over it. Did everyone see that too, or have I been
drinking?"

Fatma walked up briskly. "How did you know—?"

"—where you were? Remember what I told you about that
thing I do?"

Of course. Her half-djinn talent. Still discomfiting. But she
could kiss the woman!

"We need to get to Cairo!"

"I'm guessing it's the giant machine djinn? Things like that
are usually up to no good."

"Abigail Worthington is the imposter," Fatma explained hurriedly. "She and her friends are taking the Clock of Worlds to
Abdeen Palace. She's going to use the Seal of Sulayman and
the djinn to take over Egypt. Then maybe try to conquer the
world."

Siti let out a low whistle. "Definitely sounds like up to no
good." Her eyes flicked to the mass of milling police and Ministry agents. "But that's a lot of people. And I've only got the one."
She gestured at the vehicle.

"What is this thing?" Fatma asked.

"A motorbike! They're popular now in Luxor. Had this one
shipped in."

Fatma shook her head. The woman and her gadgets. At least it wasn't flying.

"Is this another woman Ministry agent?" Aasim asked. He'd walked up and couldn't decide what to stare at—Siti or the motorbike.

Siti winked. "I'm more of an independent contractor."

Aasim didn't take the joke. "We'll need to commandeer your vehicle. Police work."

"Sorry, inspector." She leaned forward with a mischievous grin. "I'm the only one who gets to straddle this." Aasim wriggled his moustache, swallowed hard, cleared his throat, then walked back to his men, throwing glances over his shoulder.

"Abla?" Of all people, it was Hamed. His uniform had taken a beating. But he paid it no mind, instead staring at Siti. Wait. Had he just called her by name?

"Agent Hamed," Siti greeted amiably.

He returned a bemused half smile. "How do you know Abla?"

Fatma's eyebrows rose. "How do *you* know Abla?"

Before she could get an answer, Onsi sauntered up, beaming good-naturedly—as if an entire house hadn't just collapsed on them—with a string of greetings to Siti. Fatma stared in bewilderment.

"Abla helped us with a case this past summer," Hamed explained.

"She helped *you* with a case?" Fatma repeated.

Siti shrugged. "Just gave some advice. There was a problem with a haunted—what was it? A bus? Trolley?"

"Tram car," Fatma, Hamed, and Onsi repeated as one.

"Yeah, that."

"Never got a chance to thank you properly," Hamed said. "When I next returned to Makka's you were gone. What are you doing here?"

Siti looked on the verge of saying something clever, but Fatma had heard enough. "I don't mean to break up this reunion, but . . ." She gestured in the direction the giant iron djinn had gone. "We still need to get to Cairo."

Hamed nodded solemnly. "Maybe we can salvage one of these police wagons." He looked to Onsi. "You wouldn't happen to know how to repair vehicle engines, would you?"

The smaller man bobbed excitedly. "Actually, I sometimes delight in reading steam engine diagrams and used one to take apart—"

"Of course you would," Hamed cut in. "Come on, then." The two gave a hasty farewell and ran off to inspect what was left of the police vehicles.

Siti took a second helmet that hung off the back seat, handing it to Fatma. "I can take you back. Bike's as fast as most cars. Certainly faster than those police wagons. We can probably catch that thing if I push it."

Fatma looked to Hadia, who now stood beside her, realizing they'd have to part ways.

"Go!" the woman insisted. "Get someone to send help. We can meet you there!" She turned on her heels to address Siti, leaning in close as her voice took on a knife's edge. "Watch her back. And keep your hands off her. I catch as much as a mark and you'll deal with me, understand?"

Fatma stopped midway in fitting on the helmet, stunned. Siti looked as surprised, but quickly recovered, her eyes narrowing. "I don't think you know what you're talking about. But I like you. And you're just being protective of your partner. So I'm going to pretend you didn't just threaten me." She took a breath, her voice dropping. "Still, you deserve an answer." Her eyes flashed, shifting to feline pupils on iridescent gold. "I'm a half-djinn."

Hadia stepped back startled, her face wrinkling. "You mean like a nasnas?"

"Do I look like I have half a body to you?" Siti snapped. "I mean as in part djinn!"

"Oh." Hadia's eyes rounded as she truly understood. "Oh!"

"What happened that night, it was under the power of the ring. I didn't have control."

Hadia listened quietly, but didn't appear fully convinced.

"I was caught off guard before," Siti said tightly. Her voice lowered with conviction. "I won't let anyone make me hurt her again."

"See that you do that," Hadia replied. "I like you too. But I meant what I said."

Fatma walked between them. "If you're both done playing my wet nurse, we have a possible world-ending occurrence to stop." She climbed onto the back of the motorbike, sliding her cane alongside the long rifle strapped to Siti's back. "Can you see about him?" She gestured to Alexander Worthington, who stood staring slack-jawed at the demolished house. "I think he's gone catatonic."

"I will," Hadia answered. "God be with you!" She turned to Alexander, taking the man by the arm and leading him stumbling away. "I know this must be a difficult time for you. Your sister is an evil maniac bent on world conquest. She killed your father, which is just terrible. Plus, I don't think this house has much resale value. But things could always be worse! Why, I have a cousin . . ."

Fatma didn't hear the rest, as she and Siti sped off into the growing dark.

◆   ◆   ◆

The motorbike lived up to Siti's boasts. The thing was fast. Certainly preferable to the glider contraption—which they'd flown their last time out saving the world. But it was unnerving to move at such high velocity, the wind buffeting all about you. It didn't help that Siti took turns hardly slowing. Fatma spent much of the ride with her eyes squeezed shut, holding tight to the woman's waist.

They only stopped briefly in Giza, to give a message to send help back to the Worthington estate, and to ring the Ministry to evacuate Abdeen Palace. Yet as fast as they went, the giant machine djinn stayed far ahead. It wasn't until they'd reached the edges of Cairo that they caught sight of it again. The thing stood stark against the night sky, illuminated by the fires dotting its body that were in fact Ifrit. Then it was gone again, moving even faster into the city. It was sometime just after catching sight of the monstrosity that they heard the voice on the air. A woman's voice—that thundered and echoed.

"Abigail!" Fatma said in recognition. Only she couldn't understand the words. It wasn't English or Arabic but some djinn language that rumbled. In her arms, Siti's body went stiff. She slowed, stopping altogether.

"What's wrong?" Fatma asked over the engine.

"I can hear her," Siti said. "In my head."

"Like . . . before?"

"No. It's muffled, like it's being filtered through water. It still pulls at me, but I think as long as I stay in human form I can resist. Whatever you did in summoning the goddess, it's weakened her hold on me."

Fatma didn't want to think on that right now. "Can you understand what she's saying?"

Siti nodded. "It's a call to djinn. Demanding they gather to her. That the time has come for them to bow to the Master of Djinn. There are visions too. Flashes. Abdeen Palace. And . . ." She trailed off, going quiet before cursing under her breath. With a lurch they went speeding again.

"What is it?" Fatma yelled over the wind.

"It's bad! The Nine Lords! She's going to set them free! With the Clock of Worlds!"

"But why?"

"To use them! The ring isn't enough! It can't control so many djinn at once! Or at least she can't. She needs leaders who can direct them! She's creating an army—an army of djinn! These Nine Ifrit Lords, they're going to be her generals!"

That sounded bad. Very bad. "Faster!"

Siti bent low, and the bike's engine roared, sending them hurtling down Cairo's streets. It wasn't hard to tell where the giant had passed. As in Giza, it left a trail of destruction. Cables for the trams were snapped, some derailed altogether. Overturned trolleys and cars lay about, and a few buildings showed damage. A row of smashed police wagons was all that was left of a hastily constructed barricade. The motorbike weaved around vehicles and debris, and Fatma only prayed they wouldn't see worse this night.

They were nearing Al-Sayeda Zainab when the ground began to shake. Siti slowed to a stop. All about them a rumbling grew louder by the moment, like a distant thunder. A flurry of shapes streaked across the sky, low enough that they could feel the wind of their passing and make them out. Djinn. Winged djinn. Some with feathers, others leathery like a bat. Most were smaller, but one enormous Marid pushed along beside them. Fatma and Siti ducked instinctively as the titan swooped past, a long serpentine tail lashing behind.

"What's going—?" Fatma cut off as a dark sea came careening around a corner. At first, she thought it truly was water. That somehow the streets had flooded. But now she could see the mass was made up of individual beings, just packed together. More djinn. Only earthbound, and far greater in number and type. Djinn with the heads of gazelles or birds. Djinn small as children, others well over ten feet. Blue djinn and red or black and marble-skinned. Translucent elementals of ice and others made up of puffs of clouds. Djinn with skin like grass or rock. With teeth and claws, some with two heads, and as many arms as six. All moving like one harangued beast, barreling toward them.

There was no time to run. Nowhere to move. They stood stock-still, sitting on the bike as the wave crashed into them—then broke. The djinn moved around them, not a single one paying them any mind. They were all heading in a single direction—the road to Abdeen Palace.

Siti started out again once the mass had passed. Neither spoke, their thoughts grim. The djinn were caught in the thrall of the Seal of Sulayman. Abigail would have her army. They now had to make sure she got no generals to lead it. When they finally did reach the palace, however, what they found put their chances in doubt.

Abdeen Palace had begun construction in 1863 by Muhammad Ali Basha—intended as a royal residence. But its completion coincided in 1872 with al-Jahiz's time in the city. Rather than making the palace the center of his government, the basha instead used it to house the Soudanese mystic, hoping to benefit from his wisdom. It was here that al-Jahiz worked his most wondrous creations. It was also where he bored a hole into the Kaf, forever changing the world. Djinn architects had added to the building's original blend of European, Turkish, and Egyptian designs—including a lavish series of inner courtyards, complete with miniature mechanical edifices and monuments. Today, they had returned, in numbers that would have made al-Jahiz take notice.

Fatma surveyed the sea of djinn. They crowded the streets surrounding the rectangular palace, packed in almost shoulder to shoulder, moving forward with a relentless momentum. Some climbed the exterior façade, holding on to windows, balconies, or any bit of jutting stone. One had wrapped a serpentine body about one of the columns that lined the front entrance, slithering up its length. All of this to join the djinn already gathered on the roof above, every last one peering up at a great iron monstrosity.

The giant automaton djinn stood somewhere amid the inner walls of the palace. A great horned head towered high above, the fires burning within casting its unfinished face with an unholy malevolence. The machine djinn's chest rested even with the roof. Inside the open cavity, on a broad platform that sat just beneath the turning mechanical heart, the self-proclaimed Master of Djinn stood inspecting her massing army.

Abigail Worthington could be made out clearly—with that dark red hair and wearing a black-and-gold dress, illuminated by the fiery Ifrit who worked ceaselessly on the accumulation of circular gears just behind her. The Clock of Worlds. She no longer bothered with the illusion of al-Jahiz. Or perhaps she didn't have the magic to spare. Her hand was held high, one of her splayed fingers glinting with a bit of gold as she cried out a summons to Cairo's djinn.

"I don't see your people," Siti noted. "No agents, no police. Not even palace guards."

"Probably got overrun. Hopefully they got the dignitaries out."

Siti grunted. "That means it's just us."

"Just us will have to do. We need to get up there."

"Not if we have to go through that." Siti pointed at the throng of djinn. There were too many to push through, with more arriving by the minute. Fatma searched the palace, looking for a door or an open window. But there were only djinn.

"There's another way up," Siti offered. She looked pensive. "We could fly."

Fatma at first thought the woman meant her glider contraption. But as she glimpsed the set eyes behind those goggles, understanding dawned. "Can you do that?"

Siti shrugged. "You're not exactly heavy. And I'm stronger in djinn form."

"I mean, can you do that and not end up like them."

"I know what you meant," Siti answered, more serious. "She's channeling a lot right now to get all these djinn here. Don't know if she'll be able to focus on me specifically."

Fatma didn't like the idea. And not just because she feared for her own safety. She didn't want to see Siti made over like these others, with no control, forced to answer the summons of their mistress. The thought turned her stomach. But she didn't know that they had a choice.

"Let's do it."

They left the bike, and Fatma exchanged out the helmet for her bowler—a bit rumpled but still wearable. Siti admired her with a curious look as she removed her own headgear.

"You realize we're both wearing the same thing from last time?" she asked. "When we went to confront the rogue angel. You had on that exact combination. I had on this."

Fatma looked down to her suit—light gray, with a matching vest, chartreuse tie, and a red-on-white pin-striped shirt. She remembered now. Siti in the same brown boots, tan breeches, and kaftan. That was oddly coincidental. "Is this some kind of djinn thing?"

"Don't ask me." Siti winked. "I'm only half." Then she changed.

Even though Fatma expected it, the transformation was still startling. In Siti's place—no, she corrected herself. This was Siti too. A tall djinn with black glistening skin and deep red curving horns. She gazed down with those crimson-on-gold feline eyes.

"How do you feel?" Fatma asked tentatively.

Siti's jaw tightened, and her head shook from side to side. "Like I want her to be quiet," she growled. "But I'm alright, praise the goddess." A set of black-and-red wings unfurled from her back. "Let's go shut her up." Fatma couldn't stifle the slight yelp as strong arms wrapped about her and she was hoisted into the air.

The immediate sensation sent her stomach into a lurch as the world turned sideways—so that she couldn't tell which way was up. When she got her bearings again she saw they were soaring above the crowd of djinn, rising higher as Siti's flapping wings sounded with the wind whooshing in her ears. They cleared the rooftop and set down amid the swelling ranks of djinn.

Siti let go of Fatma, who stumbled to her feet. Flying was never her strong suit. None of the djinn about them spared a glance. Their faces were blank with those haunting empty eyes as they stood swaying in place. Fatma and Siti turned toward the mechanical djinn. The platform Abigail stood upon was built like a dais, with a set of steps leading down to the rooftop. Her coconspirators stood just behind her—Victor, Bethany, Darlene, and Percy. Their backs were turned, watching the Ifrit that studiously worked fitting together plates on the Clock of Worlds.

"It's almost done," Fatma noted. "Wait, where are you going?" She reached out to grab Siti, who was stepping forward. She turned to fix her with djinn eyes that had gone dull. "Siti! Listen to me, not her! Change back! Siti!" There was a sudden recognition and, in an instant, she returned to human form.

"Malesh," Siti muttered in apology, looking embarrassed. She took in the scene in front of them. "You're right, that clock is near finished. When it goes operational, the Nine Lords will come through. And all these djinn will turn into their dutiful soldiers. Well, her soldiers."

"We could storm those steps. Take her on directly."

Siti looked up at Abigail, whose sickly white hand was clearly visible—along with the ring. "I have a better idea." She pulled the long rifle from her back.

Fatma started at the realization of what was being suggested.

"Last I checked," Siti said, reading her face, "the Ministry issues guns."

"For self-defense," Fatma countered. "Not assassination."

"It's still self-defense. Assassination is just how it happens." Fatma opened her mouth to protest, but Siti plowed on. "We don't have time to debate the ethics. All I know is that one bullet will make that ring of hers useless, free all these djinn, and stop that machine. From where I stand, that's the greater good."

Fatma didn't like this. Not a bit. But so much was at stake. And Siti was right about one thing—there was no time to debate. "Make it clean," she said finally.

Siti nodded and went to one knee, pressing the butt of the rifle up against her shoulder and peering through the lenses. "You might have the high ground," she murmured, "but I have the goddess." Her finger hovered over the trigger.

"Don't hit any of the djinn!" Fatma whispered.

"Don't worry. I've got a clear shot. But this might be messy."

Fatma steeled herself. She hoped she could handle messy.

Siti began to whisper, and it took a moment to realize it was a prayer. "Praise you, Lady of All Powers, Eye of Ra, Bright One who thrusts back the darkness. I open my heart to you. My hands. My eyes. My heart is blameless. Make my aim true so that I might smite the enemies of our Father."

The crack of the rifle filled up the night. Abigail's words cut off sharply, and a black cloud blurred in front of her like a veil. The bullet met it and shattered. Victor screamed, clutching his bloodied shoulder where shrapnel had struck him and falling to the platform floor. In a blur, the black cloud resolved into a familiar figure. The ash-ghul.

Siti cursed. "I thought I'd finished that thing!"

She readied to take aim again. Too late. Abigail was looking out onto the rooftop. She spotted them easily amid the mass of immortals and shouted something at the top of her lungs. Fatma felt her blood run cold, as all about, sets of djinn eyes turned to regard them—empty and dead.

CHAPTER TWENTY-SEVEN

Fatma dodged the meaty hand of a rotund four-armed djinn. Not just rotund, almost perfectly round—a scaly sphere with more limbs than were necessary, and a wide mouth. She struck the djinn with her cane square between the eyes, and it staggered back. Beside her, Siti sent a djinn with a single yellow horn stumbling into several others, using their own weight against them.

"This is getting annoying," she growled, jumping up to kick a djinn in the face.

"Better than—" Fatma gasped in freezing cold as she passed right through a churning wind Jann. "Keep pushing!" she chattered.

Siti had been right. Abigail was spread too thin. At first, they'd feared they would be overcome by djinn. Surprisingly they turned out to be less of a threat. Oh, they were still massive and monstrous. But they fought sluggishly. And clumsily. Some only reached for them once, before returning to their stupor. Still, it was keeping them tied up and allowing more time for the Clock of Worlds to be completed. Their best bet was to keep pushing forward and reach the platform.

"We're clear!" Siti called.

They were still surrounded by djinn. But these didn't seem to have gotten Abigail's commands. Their eyes were fixated on their mistress, who no longer shouted, instead standing with her hand extended. Her well-coiffed hair looked ready to come undone, and a sheen of sweat covered her face as she concentrated.

"She looks vulnerable. We should hit her now!"

"Not with that in the way." Siti motioned to the ash-ghul, who watched them blankly.

"We need to draw it off somehow."

"On it," Siti said. She lifted her rifle, taking aim and firing. Abigail flinched at the shot meant for her, even as the ash-ghul moved in a blur to deflect it. She glared down, sparing a moment to call out a command. The swirling black cloud that was the ash-ghul turned and streamed toward them.

"That worked," Siti said. In a shift, she was the djinn. As the ash-ghul coalesced, dropping before her, she struck out—hitting the thing so hard it broke apart into black dust that scattered across the rooftop. "Go take care of Abbie. I'll hold this thing."

Fatma looked to Siti with worry. "You going to be okay? Like this?"

Siti grinned, though the smile looked strained. "She's too distracted. Plus, the goddess walks with me. Go! Wait!" Fatma was surprised to find herself swept up into a deep kiss. Her body went taut as a torrent jolted through her—as if someone were impossibly pouring half the Nile into a bottle. When their lips parted, her breath caught.

"What was that?" she asked dazedly as her feet touched the ground again.

Siti winked. "A gift. Think of it like I just charged your batteries." Her face twisted into a snarl as the newly reformed ash-ghul rose up, duplicating itself. "Now go!"

Fatma went. Her body tingled, and it seemed she was filled with renewed vigor. Sliding past the last few djinn she reached the platform steps and bounded up, taking two at a time. Someone jumped down to stop her. Percival Montgomery. She sidestepped him easily, delivering a solid knuckle to the jaw that snapped his head back. He crumpled to the platform, and she smiled. That felt good! She felt good!

The Edginton sisters cried out a warning, and Abigail turned just as Fatma drew her sword and swung. The woman managed to avoid the blade, but it cut close enough to make her face blanch.

"You seem determined to get in my way," she seethed. "Since, like a child, you're intent on being heard." She reached into the air, and a black humming blade appeared in her good hand.

Fatma smiled wider. And attacked.

Abigail was a skilled swordswoman. But Fatma had two things going for her. Abigail was tired, the toll of drawing so much of the ring's power. She, on the other hand, was fueled by a gift of djinn magic. Her feet danced as she pressed the advantage, forcing her opponent to block and step back lively. She marveled at the ease with which she predicted intended maneuvers, countering them smoothly. She could see the clear exhaustion on Abigail's face, her breath coming in shallow bursts.

Looking for a way to end this, Fatma pretended to stumble. Abigail grabbed for the victory, extending in a stabbing motion. Coming out of the feint, Fatma went low, the tip of her blade slicing through the dress and finding the thigh. The woman scrambled back with a shriek, holding her injured leg.

"That was for Siti."

Abigail's face darkened. "I don't have time for this!" She motioned with the ring that burned bright. "To me!" From the rooftop, a mass of djinn surged upward. Fatma raised her sword, thinking they meant to attack. Instead, they formed a protective shield around their mistress.

"You want someone to fight?" Abigail sneered from behind the mass of bodies. "Here, then. Test your mettle!" She waved her ring hand again, and one of the Ifrit working on the Clock of Worlds broke from the metal giant, plunging down to land heavily on the steps before Fatma.

The creature stood a good nine feet—not to mention its body was made of living fire. It pulled a burning red blade from nothingness—and swung down. Fatma managed to raise her own in time to meet it. The force of the blow pushed her to one knee as gouts of flame leaped from the Ifrit's weapon. And still it bore down. Her eyes met its own—empty molten pools—and she knew that blazing edge would reach her eventually.

A roar sounded suddenly, like a lioness's. The Ifrit screamed as claws raked its arm, then its chest, spitting out fiery blood. It turned to meet a flurry of more claws and beating wings. Siti! The woman bared her teeth as the flaming djinn bellowed, lifting the burning sword above its head in a two-handed grip. A blade appeared in answer in her hand—a thing of glittering silver. When the two met, the collision was blinding.

Abigail observed the melee, still clutching her injured leg. She shouted again, and a second Ifrit, followed by a third, swooped down. Fatma watched in panic as the three fiery forms descended on Siti. The woman bristled, her crimson-on-gold eyes glaring, wings wide, and the silver sword raised high. Fatma had never seen anything so beautiful!

Siti held her own. But she was still a half-djinn, facing three Ifrit who rained down blows with their scorching blades like ironworkers. She was fast reduced to a desperate defense. Her swings grew weaker, barely blocking probing attacks as she spun to keep eyes on all three. They circled her like hyenas working to tire their prey.

Fatma raised her own sword, meaning to jump into the fray—even if she wouldn't last long. Before she could move, one of the Ifrit lunged, driving its sword through an opening in Siti's labored defenses. The scorching blade pushed through her shoulder, burying deep. The scream she loosed tore at Fatma's heart. She watched as Siti collapsed to her knees—the shining sword vanishing from her grip.

A second Ifrit stalked forward, blade raised for the killing blow. Fatma bounded down the steps, ready to throw herself at the creature. But it suddenly stayed its hand. Abigail was ordering it back to its work. She was ordering them all back. Fatma reached Siti as the three Ifrit turned away at their mistress's bidding.

"It burns!" Siti's face contorted in pain. "Everywhere burns!"

Fatma looked to the wound. It should have been cauterized.

Yet it seemed both burned and bleeding. She reached to stanch the flow, only to pull back singed fingers. The blood was hot to the touch—boiling, poisoned by the Ifrit weapon.

"Why aren't you healing?"

Siti's only answer was another scream as wisps of smoke rose from her body.

Fatma's mind raced. That exhilaration still flowed through her, and she could feel it at the tips of her fingers—fast healing even the singeing they'd taken. She was holding some of Siti's magic. Enough perhaps, to keep her from healing. If she could just give it back . . .

She bent down, pressing their lips together. The rushing torrent that had filled her to bursting drained away—half the Nile returning. When she pulled back, she fought to stay upright. It felt like she'd been running miles! Her fingers traced gingerly at Siti's wound. Not fully healed. But the skin had closed, and she was no longer hot to the touch.

"What did you do?" Siti grunted, sitting up.

"Returned your battery charge," Fatma managed with a smile. Her brief euphoria evaporated as she looked up to find three figures standing over them like guards. The ash-ghul.

"He's always coming back," Siti grumbled.

Fatma gripped her sword. She was exhausted and would probably pitch forward on her wobbly legs. But if this thing wanted a fight, she'd give her best.

A sudden creaking turned her attention back to the platform. It was coming from the mechanical djinn. No, not the automaton, but the machine of overlapping gears nestled into its open chest. They were turning, the teeth of the wheels meshing together. They moved slow at first but soon sped up: all spinning and fitting together, to work in a perfect harmony.

The sight left her cold. The Clock of Worlds had been rebuilt. And it was working.

"She's done it!" Siti whispered. Her crimson eyes stared. Not at the spinning gears. Or at Abigail, who was shouting in triumph.

But at a hole of darkness high above the head of the mechanical djinn—like someone had cut into the fabric of reality.

When they'd last seen the machine intact, it had opened such a door to a dark watery place—from which came a horror of limbs and tentacles. This hole was also dark, so that it stood out even in the night sky. But it didn't look like water. Instead, it reminded Fatma of a heat haze—and she imagined that on the other side lay a realm of scorching and unrelenting fire. A stillness gripped the air. Even Abigail grew quiet—at what emerged from that darkness and into the world.

"God the Merciful," Fatma whispered.

They were Ifrit. That much was plain. Only unlike any she'd ever seen.

Ifrit more resembled living infernos than creatures of flesh. But these were beyond that. Their bodies were liquid flame that roiled—a bright blood orange like the spewing fissures of a volcano. The heat of them shimmered the air, so hot she could feel its sting. And they were far bigger than any djinn she had ever seen. Their great size made it impossible for them to even stand on the rooftop of the palace. Instead they hovered above—if mountains of churning molten rock could be said to hover. Nine in all.

"Who has called us to this place?" one thundered. "Who has awakened us from our great sleep?" He was the largest among them—with curving horns that shone white like heated iron. A gold circlet crowned his head, a blazing diadem in its center like a small star. Fatma reasoned that if these were Ifrit Lords, this one must be their king. His breath was fire, and flames danced in the air before him. She understood his djinn language plainly—as if he spoke every tongue at once.

Abigail, undaunted, called out, her voice enhanced by magic. "Ifrit Lords! I'm the one who summoned you!" She held up her hand, displaying the ring. "You may call me the Master of Djinn! You may call me your mistress! Come before me now and kneel!"

The Ifrit King gazed down and Fatma could read the incredulity that crossed that immortal face. He pulled a great mace of iron and flame into existence and lowered to just above the rooftop—sending the djinn beneath scattering. Abigail descended from the platform, sparing them a gloating smile. Megalomaniacs always needed an audience. The woman stopped before the hovering Ifrit and lifted her hand again.

"Kneel!" she demanded.

The Ifrit King snarled. "A mortal has summoned us? A mortal seeks to command us?"

"I hold power over you!" She tightened her fist, and the ring burned. "I command you, and you will command my armies. You will be lords again! And I will be your mistress! Now—*kneel!*"

Fatma held her breath, certain this terrible being would cast the woman into fiery oblivion. Perhaps incinerate them all in his fury. Instead, the djinn's head began to lower. The anger on his face turned to shock. It looked as if his body were being pulled against his will, constrained by invisible chains.

"Kneel!" Abigail cried. "Kneel to me!"

The Ifrit King's roar shattered the night, and he thrashed furiously. Abigail stumbled, the leash momentarily slipped from her grasp. Her face knotted in determination, and Fatma could see perspiration beading down her temples as she fought for control.

"My gods," Siti said. "She's going to get us all killed!"

Just then something went taut in Abigail's grip. "Kneel!" she screamed, her face red with rage. To their shock, the Ifrit King did just that—kneeling in the air and bowing his horned head.

"I am yours to command," his hoary voice came, then with contempt so vile it seemed it might melt the very air, "Mistress of Djinn."

"No," Siti breathed.

A long silence followed, only broken by Abigail's slow laughter. It grew louder as she basked in her triumph. She held up her hand, displaying the ring for all to see.

"Al-Jahiz may have changed the world. But I will remake it in a new image! In my image! Speak my name! Speak it!"

"The Mistress of Djinn," the bowed Ifrit King proclaimed.

The other Ifrit Lords descended to kneel beside him, repeating the title. Along the rooftop and in the streets below, djinn called out the same words, "The Mistress of Djinn," until all else was lost in the din.

Fatma sat back. They had failed. All about them, djinn began falling to their knees, soon to become her great army. Well, not all.

One still stood. He curiously kept moving closer to Abigail. It might have been easy to miss with everything else going on. But he was the only one behaving differently, steadily inching his way into the circle that now surrounded his mistress. More noticeable, he was wearing brown robes with his head covered.

Something tugged at Fatma. A sense of familiarity. Even the way he walked was familiar—with an odd gait. It was only when he had gotten right beside Abigail that he threw back his hood and she gaped.

The man had changed even more since their last encounter. Though he stood on two feet, he looked more like a crocodile than anything else. His pale-gray skin was as leathery and rough as the water-bound reptile, and he had a crocodile's long snout—with teeth that showed even when his mouth was closed. But it was those dark green eyes, brimming with vengeance, that helped her put a name to him. That was no djinn. That was . . .

"Ahmad?" Siti asked confounded.

What happened next had to be seen to be believed.

CHAPTER TWENTY-EIGHT

One moment, Ahmad, head priest of the Cult of Sobek, the claimed living embodiment of the ancient Nile god on Earth, stood glaring venomously at the Mistress of Djinn. The next he was lunging, his crocodile mouth yawning wide, and flashing white sharp teeth.

Two words escaped him in a screaming hiss: *"For Nephthys!"*

Abigail was so engrossed in her rejoicing she barely seemed to hear him. As it was, when those jaws snapped down on her extended hand—the one bearing the Seal of Sulayman—she never saw it coming.

Fatma watched, stunned, as Ahmad's long crocodilian head whipped about. There was a terrible wrenching as he pulled away, with Abigail's hand clamped between his teeth.

It was over so quick she didn't seem to register what had happened. She stumbled back, staring down at the place her hand had been—now only a bloodied stump. Her face frowned in confusion. Slowly, she turned a sickly color. When her mouth opened, it was to draw in a large gulp of air—before releasing a bloodcurdling scream.

Pandemonium erupted.

Along the rooftop, djinn broke from their trance, ceasing their chants as life refilled empty eyes. Many looked about bemused, and their murmurs could be heard amid Abigail's unending screams. On the iron djinn, Ifrit loosed from their bonds tore through the giant's mechanical frame to reclaim their freedom—sending fragments of steel flying. The towering monstrosity rocked precariously, as the magic holding it together was undone and the flames on the horned head snuffed out. A great grinding went up as it severed from the neck, bouncing off a shoulder before tumbling away. The machine body followed, fracturing before their eyes.

The four humans still atop the platform were sent clambering for safety. The Edginton sisters were the first to jump, landing ungracefully on the rooftop and rolling into a heap of splayed legs. Percival followed, leaving Victor to fend for himself. Holding his injured shoulder, he leaped off just as the platform, the Clock of Worlds, and what was left of the mechanical giant plummeted to the palace courtyard in a set of thunderous crashes.

Fatma looked up to the ash-ghul still standing over them. The three duplicates held up their left arms—each now curiously devoid of a hand—as their bodies slowly dissolved. Legs, torsos, and even clothing evaporated to black ash finer than sand, all carried away on the night wind without a whisper of their passing. She and Siti exchanged a glance before helping each other to their feet and limping through the milling crowd of djinn. They stopped short of where Abigail had gone to her knees, still screaming and cradling her injury.

"I'm guessing that hurts," Siti said.

Fatma looked past the woman—who was no longer a threat—and instead searched for Ahmad. The transformation he'd undergone these past weeks had allowed him to easily blend in with the djinn—unaffected by the ring's power. How long had he been here, she wondered. Biding his time, awaiting his vengeance. Of course, there were more pressing matters than either Abigail or Ahmad. Her eyes lifted to where the Nine Ifrit Lords yet loomed, no longer bowed, their fiery gazes appraising.

"Why are *they* still here?" She motioned to the portal. "And why is *that* still open?" When they'd last undone the Clock of Worlds, the doorway it opened had closed. This one, however, remained—a gaping wound in the night.

"I have a feeling this isn't over," Siti murmured

Get out of a hole and you fall down a slope, Fatma heard her mother tut.

Pulling out her badge she held it up, clearing her throat to shout. "Great Lords! I am Agent Fatma with the Egyptian Ministry of Alchemy, Enchantments, and Supernatural Entities!" The djinn on the rooftop went quiet, turning to look at her. Above, the Ifrit appeared to take notice as well. "Allow me to extend my deepest apologies for your summoning against your will and sovereignty! This action was neither sanctioned nor condoned by my government, and is in direct violation of our statutes, laws, and criminal codes on the ethical use of magic! As we now have the matter under control and the perpetrator in hand, we invite you to please return to your realm with sincere regrets for this inconvenience!"

There. That had been by the book. Even polite.

The Ifrit King observed her with a searing eye, and she tried not to flinch beneath its heat.

"You are a talkative mortal," he rumbled, then turned away as if she didn't exist at all.

"Djinn of this realm!" he bellowed. "For millennia, we have slumbered. Deep within the worlds within worlds of the Kaf. Now, we are awakened. And we find ourselves . . . displeased." A flinch rippled through the crowd, like children being scolded. "How is it that djinn walk a world ruled by mortals? How has a mortal come to hold power over our kind? Power enough to bind even we—the lords of djinn? Where are the children of our blood and fire to give answer?"

As if summoned, several blazing forms flew to land just before the Ifrit King. Fatma was pulled back by Siti, as one touched down with force enough to shake the palace. The Ifrit they'd twice before encountered—rid of saddle and reins. He stood far larger than his companions, and yet was dwarfed by the Ifrit Lords—a mere bonfire to their inferno.

"O Great Lords," he rumbled, his fiery wings bent in submission. "I would give answer."

"Speak, then," the Ifrit King allowed. A look of annoyance marred his face. "But make this one cease that irritating noise!"

He was referring to Abigail, who had not stopped screaming.

The big Ifrit turned to the mistress who once saddled him, and reached out to graze her injured arm. Screams turned to shrieks as the bloodied stump cauterized, sending up the sickly smell of burned flesh. Abigail's eyes rolled back and she swooned, then promptly fell flat on her face. Fainted. In earnest this time, it appeared.

The big Ifrit turned back to his king. "I made my home in a desert of this world, away from djinn who now dwell among mortals. There I remained, until I was called by this one." He snarled at Abigail's prone form. "She bound me, harnessed me as one would a beast! She set my brothers and sisters to toil! She bid us tell her of you, forced us to wake you from your slumber!"

The Ifrit King's expression compressed—the sun itself grown angry. Behind him, the remaining eight lords murmured their discontent. "You are Ifrit! Those created first from smokeless fire! You are meant to rule over djinn! Yet you hide yourself away. You allow a mortal to bind you!" His head shook in disgust. "This cannot stand."

"I don't like the sound of that," Siti said. Fatma didn't either.

The Ifrit King drew himself up. "A mortal may have summoned us, but good will come even from such perversion. We Nine Lords have returned, to once more rule over all djinn. We claim this world, and we shall lead you in the coming war to make it your own. So that you might once again know glory and bring honor to your blood!"

He paused magnanimously, as if expecting a cheer. But there was only uneasy quiet. Not a djinn spoke, many sharing alarmed glances.

"I don't buy it!" someone shouted. Fatma started, realizing it was Siti. She stepped forward, tall in her djinn form, yet smaller than most here. Above, the Ifrit King squinted.

"You do not . . . buy . . . it?"

"That you once led djinn to glory or whatever," Siti replied. "From what I hear, you just enslaved djinn. Had them fight your endless wars."

"To prove who is most deserving," another Ifrit Lord rumbled. "We are the superior—"

Siti barked a laugh that cut the giant Ifrit off. "Mortals already play this game. About some people being superior and meant to rule over others. That's what she believes." She gestured to Abigail, who remained quite unconscious. "How are you any different?"

The Ifrit King's eyes lowered to slits. "You compare us to mortals?" He looked her over anew. "Half-blood. Your sire was djinn."

"I prefer double-blood. And the djinn who 'sired' me was hardly superior."

"Still, you are djinn-touched. Even if lesser, you may share in the coming glory."

"How gracious. But you can keep your glory."

The Ifrit King shook his head. "Impudence. When we yet held sway, such disobedience would be repaid a thousand times by pain." He looked out on the other djinn. "We will have no more impertinence! We are lords of djinn! First among our kind! And you will bow!" The rounded head of his mace roared into flames, as if he'd torn a star from the heavens. Beneath him the many djinn cowered. One by one, they began to bow.

Fatma watched with dismay. Along the rooftop and in the streets below, djinn of every kind and class, all prostrated before these Nine Lords—driven by some primal fear.

Almost all.

Her eyes fell on a figure near the back of the palace roof. A djinn with the reddish-brown head of an onager and the straight twisting horns of a gazelle. The Ifrit King took notice as well and leveled his mace menacingly. "You will bow."

"I have decided I will not." The onager-headed djinn spoke in an elderly woman's voice. "I am too old to bow. It hurts my bones. Even if I could, I would not bow to you."

Flames danced along the Ifrit King's brow. "More impudence."

The onager-headed djinn shrugged. "Call it what you will. But I did not like being enslaved by her." She motioned a crooked cane toward Abigail. "I do not now want to be enslaved by you. I like my freedom. Will I exchange one set of chains for another?"

"We will lead you to glory!" the Ifrit King insisted. "Place you above these mortals!"

The elder djinn chuckled. "Glory? Is that what I'm missing?" She snorted through her white muzzle. "I live among mortals. They can be annoying, true. But also remarkable. They visit me at Eid al-Fitr. And I make their children Eid kahk. Oh! Children! They are the most delightful of mortals!"

"Glory is yours to—" the Ifrit King began.

"I heard you the first several times," the old djinn interrupted, waving her cane. "I don't want glory. I just want to go home. This world you want to create, of war and fire. It doesn't sound like glory to me. It sounds like hell."

The Ifrit King's face drew tight. He looked to the big Ifrit. "Put an end to this insolence! Show them the penance for not obeying their lords!"

The Ifrit on the rooftop turned toward the disobedient elder djinn. Fatma felt Siti tense, readying to fight. She gripped her own sword—what little good it would do against a being of flames five times her size. He stared at the onager-headed djinn for moment, then surprisingly, his broad shoulders sagged.

"I cannot," he spoke. Then added hastily, "O Great Lords."

The Ifrit King's fiery eyes widened. "More insolence? From even you?"

The big Ifrit shook his head. "O Great Lord, you must understand, I did not seek solace without reason. All of we Ifrit, upon coming to this world, sought out places where we could be alone. Together, we found the blood fire coming over us, urging us to burn, to set all about us aflame. But alone, we could live with our thoughts. Dwell on the purpose of our existence." He looked up, daring to meet the baleful gaze of the hovering giant. "It is called philosophy."

The Ifrit King frowned. "Phil-o-so-phy?"

The big Ifrit nodded briskly. "A means to interrogate the nature of existence and our place within it. The more I thought, the more I began to understand myself. To know that I was created for more than just drowning my enemies in flames. I began reading many great works by mortals and other djinn. That is how I discovered, I am a pacifist."

Fatma blinked. The Nine Lords seemed equally puzzled. They murmured among themselves before one asked, "What is this? Pa-ci-fist?"

"One who does not commit violence upon others," the big Ifrit explained.

"He has sworn not to cause harm," one of the other lesser Ifrit added, this one with a woman's voice. "Which is why what this mortal made him do was so terrible."

The big Ifrit looked down, and for the first time Fatma saw things in his eyes she'd missed before—pain. Perhaps even guilt.

"Are you another spouter of this phil-o-so-phy?" the Ifrit King asked with disgust.

"Oh no," the female Ifrit answered. "I'm a sculptor."

"She's very good!" the big Ifrit put in. "She makes beautiful landscapes of rocks and sand!" The other lesser Ifrit all agreed, causing their companion to look down sheepishly. "We've told her she should display her art. But she's an introvert, and we want to respect that."

The Ifrit King looked as flummoxed as Fatma. Did the Ministry truly understand these creatures at all?

"I will not bow to you either," another voice spoke. This one was a cobalt-blue Marid that shared the rooftop. He raised up from where he knelt. "We were not the ones who summoned you here. We have not asked for your return. I only kneel to my creator."

He was joined by another djinn, this one a water Jann. "We will not be slaves!" Several others rose, all shouting their defiance with the same words. That seemed to break the dam. The whole rooftop stood, chanting, "We will not be slaves! We will not be slaves!" It was picked up on the streets, turning into a mass protest of shouts and raised fists. The Nine Lords stared in disbelief. Fatma didn't think they were used to the word "no."

Finally, the Ifrit King held up his fiery mace and bellowed, "Silence!"

Quiet came, but not one djinn returned to their knees. There were clenched fists now and steely glares. Fatma could feel the magic and tension filling the air, thick currents that tickled the hairs on her skin. This was a prelude to battle, between djinn and the lords that once ruled them. The resulting destruction was something she didn't want to contemplate.

"O Great Lords!" she called, stepping forward again. "The djinn of this world have made their choice! You claim to want to lead them, to better their lives. Would you now go to war with them? Shed their blood? To what end?"

The Ifrit King's gaze returned to her, and a rumbling emanated from deep in his throat. It wasn't until the grin broke out across his fiery face that she realized he was laughing.

"To what end, mortal?" His voice rose to a thunder. "Hear me, wretched djinn! Traitors to your blood! You would stand against your lords? Those who would lead you to greatness? If you will not bow willingly, you will be forced to bend—or break!"

Angry cries and growls rose up. Fatma tried again to be heard above the din. But it was no use. The same djinn that had moments ago been cowed, now stood determined not to back down. So, it seemed, did the Nine Lords.

"Insolent children!" the Ifrit King snarled, his crown ablaze. He lifted his great mace to the heavens, and it amazingly grew, so that he could now heft it in two clawed hands. "If it is battle you seek for dominion of this realm, you shall have it. Let there be *war*!"

With a great swing, he brought down his mace, striking the side of Abdeen Palace a terrific blow. The building shook, the force of the impact rattling Fatma. She was thrown off her feet as the rooftop heaved, a groaning going up as if the palace were screaming its pain. She tried to stand, hoping to run—but the ground suddenly gave way. Then it was gone, and she was falling amid fire and crumbling stone, plunged into darkness.

CHAPTER
TWENTY-NINE

F atma was falling. Amid stone and fire.

No.

Not falling. Had fallen. Fell.

And now—

She spasmed—arms flailing, remembering what it was to fall. Grabbing at open air. Terrified at finding only emptiness. Or at least she tried. Something held her arms firm. Rough and heavy. Her legs too. So that she could barely move. And oh did she hurt! She forced her eyes open to darkness and stinging flecks of dust. Jumbled memories flittered through her head and she wrangled them into coherence.

The Ifrit King. Abdeen Palace. Collapsing. Falling.

She'd survived. The bruises she felt were proof enough. The roughness that held her fast was stone. The rubble of the destroyed palace. She'd survived, but was now buried beneath it.

Calm deduction gave way to panic. She was buried! How deep? She imagined a hill of debris, under which no one would find her. She struggled to move again, with little result.

Her mother's voice came, not lecturing but soothing, cutting through the panic. *Every problem has a solution*, it assured. *You will find a way out of this.* She heeded the advice, willing herself calm. As calm as you could be entombed beneath a collapsed building. Her vision slowly adjusting, she looked around again. Broken stone. Dust. Something soft brushed her cheek. Cloth? Hair? No. Fluffier than hair. Feathers!

Now she could feel more than stone. Warmth—given off by a body. A very large body.

Siti! Her mind flooded with new memories. The palace crumbling. Someone catching her. Flapping wings trying to escape the avalanche. But too much and—

Siti had saved her. Shielded her. She could feel the other woman's breathing, hear the rise and fall of inhalation. But it was faint. Frightfully faint.

"Siti." Her first call was barely audible. She worked saliva onto her tongue and tried again. "Siti." This time a croak. Two more croaks, then an answer.

"Who's there? Is someone there?"

Fatma knew that voice. Decidedly not Siti. She gritted her teeth to say the name.

"Abigail."

"Yes! It's me! Who—?"

"Agent Fatma."

Quiet.

"How did you survive the fall?"

Abigail took a moment to respond. "Your half-djinn."

So Siti had saved the woman too. There's a surprise. Rolling thunder echoed from somewhere above, setting the rubble about them to tremble. Abigail squealed.

"What was that?"

"I don't know," Fatma said, irked at the question. "I'm in here with you."

"I've heard it twice already! From outside . . . I think there's fighting."

Fatma glanced up, as if expecting to see through stone. A second rolling boom. Debris shifted and creaked, spilling dust. Beside her, Siti's breaths became a hoarse rattle.

"Abigail! Can you make out anything? Can you see outside?"

Silence.

"Abigail!"

"I don't know. It's all just—wait."

"Wait what?"

More silence.

"Abigail!" She was going to throttle the woman if she didn't answer faster.

"I see something. But not near me. I think it's by you."

"What?" Fatma bent her head back, craning to see above. There! A hole! She could even feel air on her temple. There was a chance. Working more saliva onto her tongue, she shouted. "Help! Is anyone there? Help!"

Nothing. After three more attempts, her throat went dry. Maybe there was no one up there, she considered darkly. A shrill shriek and a loud whooshing came, and she strained to make out anything through the small space.

"That's that, then," Abigail sighed. "If we die here, I want you to know I forgive you."

Fatma tried to whip her head around. As it was, she only returned a strangled, "What?"

"I said I forgive you. I think it's important to say, at the end."

"You forgive me? *You* forgive *me*?"

"There's no need to raise your voice. I'm trying to have a moment with you."

"Keep your moment!" Fatma spat.

Abigail tsked. "You people can be so hot-blooded. Is it the heat?"

When Fatma didn't answer she went on.

"I'd think you'd be more understanding. After all, I'm the one missing a hand. I was so close! Then you ruined it all. I'm assuming after I passed out, things went poorly? If you'd just let me keep the ring, none of this would have happened. In a way, this is your fault."

"You're insane," Fatma snapped.

Abigail huffed. "Why do people like using that word, 'insane'? Or 'crazy'? Or 'out of her mind'? Because I'm of the fairer sex? If I were a man, would you doubt my sanity?"

Fatma sighed inwardly, hating to admit the woman was right.

She had an aunt who suffered a mental illness. Nothing remotely dangerous about her at all. And Fatma hated when anyone called her things like "crazy" or "insane."

"You're right," she said. "I take that back. You knew exactly what you were doing. That you were going to hurt a lot of people. And you did it anyway. Willfully. There's nothing wrong with your head. You're just a monster."

"Why, thank you, agent," Abigail said sweetly. "That really means a lot to me. You know, I do think if not for all this unpleasantness between us, we could have been friends."

That actually made Fatma laugh.

"No, really. I do mean it. We're alike in a way."

"I'm not like you."

"Oh, I disagree. Do you know how delightful it was to match wits with you? I could have had you killed so many times—run you through with my blade, had you incinerated by my Ifrit, set a pack of ghuls to tear you apart. But I kept you alive, and you know why? Because I see something of myself in you. A woman forced to live in a world run by inept men. So much drive and determination. In a way, we share a bond. My dusky sister of the Orient."

"You can be quiet now," Fatma suggested.

"Of course, some bonds are closer than others. Like yours with the half-djinn."

Fatma stiffened. She'd been listening close to Siti's breaths. They hadn't grown any stronger. "Don't talk about her."

"That night," Abigail carried on, "when I took control, I caught glimpses of her secrets. The two of you. So, so very close. When she wrapped her hands around your neck, what that must have felt like. Did you understand then what she was? That she carried a beast within? That's what these djinn are, you know. Beasts. As dangerous as any hound, if not properly muzzled. But once trained, they are oh so useful."

Fatma tamped down her anger, refusing to engage. Abigail

chuckled at the silence and seemed set to begin her torment anew when another sound came.

"Be quiet!" Fatma said, listening. Were those voices? Taking a deep breath she shouted out again. Had she imagined them? A second shout made her almost hoarse. Now the voices returned. They were coming closer! She could even make them out.

"Did you hear, Yakov . . . from over here I think . . ."

Fatma shouted once more, not even words now because that was too hard. Abigail joined her, the two making as much noise as possible—until a blessed voice called down.

"We hear you! How many?"

"Three," Fatma croaked. Praise God!

"One moment, Frau!" The voices pulled away. She could only make out one. A man. He spoke English, mostly, with a heavy accent. "*Achtung!* Careful which stone you pick! *Nein!* Not that one! Better! Come now, lift! Put your back into it, Yakov! Are you a Russian bear or a little yapping dog? That's it!"

There was a grating and the debris about Fatma shifted. Bits of rock were pulled from above, and wonderful cool air rushed over her face. She blinked, realizing she was looking up at the night sky through a haze of dust. She could see the palace, half of which still stood amid a field of rubble. Hands reached to haul her up before depositing her again. She was free! Her eyes tried to make out her rescuers, and she found herself staring at an unexpectedly familiar face—a man with a bold nose and a thick upturned moustache.

"He! Frau!" the German kaiser Wilhelm II grinned. "Yakov, look who it is. From the other night!"

Fatma shifted to the other man—the Russian general. He stood bent over, panting heavily. Both looked disheveled, in only untucked long shirts and trousers with unslung suspenders.

"Stay put!" Wilhelm said. "We'll see to your friends. Yakov!"

Fatma wanted to tell him first off she wasn't in any shape to go anywhere. Second, one of the women in the rubble was decidedly not her friend. In fact, maybe they could leave her in there. But she never got the words out, as she was thrown into darkness. There was an accompanying whoosh of wind and an ear-splitting shriek.

It took a moment to comprehend the darkness was the shadow of something flying high above. A small airship? But it had wings of an absurd length. Not an airship. A rukh!

The great bird swooped past, in a flurry of blue feathers. It was followed by another, and another. Whoosh! Whoosh! Whoosh! Four in all. With talons large enough to snatch up an automobile, and hooked golden beaks that could tear apart an elephant. The wind they kicked up buffeted Fatma, clearing some of the dust. She watched as they banked in formation, tilting so that she could make out figures on their backs. Djinn! Riding atop the backs of rukh! Fighting to sit up, she followed their flight into the distance—and gaped.

Nine Ifrit Lords walked the streets of Cairo.

They had descended from the heavens—giants that dwarfed even buildings. All about them smaller figures swarmed. More djinn. This was a battle.

Fatma watched as the rukhs dived into the melee. Marid atop their backs hurled what might have been spears or tridents of lightning that flashed across the black sky. One of the Ifrit Lords sliced a forked glowing blade at them, scattering the formation. A second swung a whip of liquid fire; it cracked through the air, clipping a screeching rukh that trailed smoke in its retreat.

"Magnificent," someone murmured. Abigail. They'd gotten her out. She was a mess, her once well-coiffed hair in disarray— not to mention missing a hand. Her eyes were rapt on the battle. "Do you know what I could have wrought with such fine beasts?"

Fatma was set to tell again her to be quiet, when she saw the two men bearing a still form between them. They laid Siti down, grunting with the effort. Shielding them from the building's collapse had taken its toll. Crimson gashes marred her skin, and one of her wings bent at an angle. Fatma scrambled over, taking Siti's head into her hands.

"Come, Yakov, stop gawking," Wilhelm chided. "Let us find the healer!"

Fatma barely watched them go, eyes on Siti, forgetting momentarily even the mayhem about her. All she wanted now was for the woman to wake up. To open her eyes and say something witty. Or wholly inappropriate. Her lips whispering a prayer that came more as a plea. "God the most Beneficent, the most Merciful. Not this one. Not this one."

"Remember often death, the destroyer of all pleasures," a woman's voice sounded. "But it is not that day for this one."

Fatma looked up to find the two men returned, with a woman between them. It took a moment to place her, dressed as she was in a simple black gallabiyah, her face framed by a white hijab.

"Amina," she said in surprise.

"Agent Fatma," the granddaughter of al-Hajj Umar Tal greeted. "Good to see you alive!"

"How are you here? Didn't they evacuate the palace?"

"*Ja.*" Wilhelm nodded. "Packed us into carriages. Did not get far before a wave of maddened djinn struck us."

"Most of us got out and away," Amina said, her fingers probing Siti. "We three took shelter nearby. When the palace came down, I convinced them to come back with me—to look for survivors."

"How could I refuse the lady?" the kaiser asked. "I am much like Siegfried."

Fatma now noticed the goblin yet perched on his shoulder. It wasn't sleeping but instead was turned about, observing the battle in the distance. Fatma looked back to Amina.

"You're a healer?"

"Mmm," the woman replied, concentrating. "My grandfather's talent passed to me."

"Then she'll live?"

"God willing. But I'll need more. Jenne!" At her call, a tall shadow filled with intoxicating scents loomed up behind her. No, not a shadow. A figure with a stark chalk-white face whose silver eyes stared down impassively. Amina said something, and her Qareen flicked out a curled black tongue—bearing a smooth marbled stone at the tip. Amina plucked it like a piece of fruit before prying open Siti's mouth, and stuffing the stone inside.

"A gris-gris," she explained, massaging Siti's throat. "Much like a bezoar. Once swallowed, the healing is prompt."

No sooner had she spoken than Siti's eyes flew open. In a blur she was in human form—sputtering and coughing. She looked around befuddled before reaching into her mouth to pull out the stone. "Who put a rock down my throat?" she wheezed.

Fatma breathed in relief, squeezing Siti's hand tight.

Amina took the stone back, handing it off to the Qareen—who promptly swallowed it. "The gris-gris was needed to draw you back to your human self. Your djinn side needs healing."

"No." Siti attempted to stand. "I need to be able to fight—"

"Half-djinn are common enough in my country," Amina insisted, pushing her back down with a firm hand. "The old great King Samanguru was claimed to be a half immortal, able to supposedly transform into a whirlwind and call forth an army of ants."

"You have a hidden army of ants you want to tell me about?" Fatma asked lightly, unable to hold back the giddiness at seeing Siti conscious and speaking again.

The woman scowled up at Amina. "What's your point?"

"That I'm familiar enough with your kind to know how to treat you. Make do with this mortal body. Let your djinn side rest." She looked to Fatma and Abigail. "As for you two."

There were no stones for them. Amina only laid her hands on their skin, and Fatma felt her body fill with warmth, her bruises and aches dulling.

"How wonderful," Abigail mused, gingerly touching the skin where a gash had closed on her forehead. "Healer, could you do something about . . ." She lifted the stump of her hand hopefully. Amina began to inspect the injury, but Jenne let out a sharp hiss.

"Your voice," the Qareen spoke, silver eyes flashing and scent now bitter. "Jenne remembers the *Mistress of Djinn*. In our head. Calling. Insisting"

Amina dropped Abigail's wrist in alarm. "The imposter!"

Wilhelm's eyes widened. "An Englishwoman! Behind all these troubles? Is that not interesting, Yakov?" He inspected Abigail anew, and Fatma thought his smile hid traces of admiration.

There was a loud booming from the battle, and all eyes turned in its direction—where dazzling lights and sheets of flame lit up the night.

"If we ever do have a war," Wilhelm declared, "I only hope it is as glorious!"

"Not today," Amina snapped, standing. She turned to Fatma, eyes curious. "You never told me precisely which agency you worked for. But finding you here, it must be one that deals with . . . all this. Sometime, we'll have to meet again, and maybe you'll tell me more about your government job. But now, there are others in the rubble to find. I pray you're able to stop this evil, agent. Trust in God."

Lifting the hem of her gallabiyah, she hurried off, her two attendants following. Fatma watched them disappear into the dust haze—a West African princess, the German kaiser, and a Russian general, wandering the broken Abdeen Palace on this very strange night in Cairo.

Siti took a moment to struggle to her feet, standing but unsteady. "Tell me we have a plan."

Fatma turned to find her eyes locked on the battle of immortals. "The plan was to not let this happen." They cupped their ears as a thunderclap rang out from some djinn magic.

"They'll destroy the city if we don't stop them."

"You can't stop them," Abigail put in. She'd come to stand beside them, bedraggled but still managing to sound haughty. "I held them. These Nine Lords. For a brief glorious moment. It was like trying to hold a star." She turned to Siti. "Thank you for saving me. Quite gracious of you."

Siti cut the woman a murderous glare and one of her feline smiles. "Nothing gracious about it. I almost shot you in the face, remember? Djinn have long memories. Hold even longer grudges. And you went and burned yourself into our memories. The life you're about to lead, the feeling of being hunted, always looking over your shoulder, unable to escape djinn who can enter even your dreams. I wasn't about to have you miss all that—Abbie."

For once, Abigail truly looked ashen.

Siti turned away, then frowned. "Is someone calling you?"

Fatma listened. Someone *was* calling her name. Shouting it. She searched the dark to find the source. Making her way toward them was Hadia! She came at a run, or as well as she could through the rubble. Her clothes and face were smudged in dust, but she still looked a sight better than they did. When she reached them she clutched Fatma in an embrace.

"Alḥamdulillāh! They said the palace had fallen! I thought were you under it!"

Fatma didn't bother to say that, in fact, she had been. "How did you get here?"

"Onsi got one of the police wagons working! We sped all the way!" Her gaze flicked to Abigail, then her missing hand. "Guessing I missed a few things?"

Fatma caught her up, watching her jaw go slack.

"The Nine Ifrit Lords!" Hadia gazed at the fiery giants wreaking havoc on the city. "Inspector Aasim came with us. He's briefed the police and Ministry. They say the king's going to call out the army—"

She hadn't finished before the ground shook in a tremor. It stopped. Then shook again. And again. In succession. Fatma was set to ask what now, when she saw it.

Another giant strode the streets of Cairo. This one made not of fire but something dark and rippling. Water! It stood as tall as the Ifrit Lords, shaped like a slender man, with legs capable of great strides and arms that hung past where knees should have been. Its liquid body swirled and crashed in upon itself, setting off unending waves and eddies.

"What new horror is this?" Hadia whispered.

"Not a horror," Siti said in wonder. "This is Jann work!"

Jann? Fatma had read texts claiming the most ancient Marid once dwelled deep beneath the seas. But even they had not been able to so manipulate the elements—not on such a scale.

"Where did they even get all that water?" Hadia asked.

"The Nile," Fatma reasoned. "Where else?"

As they watched, the Ifrit Lords turned at this new challenge.

The first to meet his enemy swung a burning blade. The water giant moved surprisingly fast, with the speed of a rushing river. It lifted a lengthy arm like a trunk, rolling it in an undulating wave. When it struck the blade, the flames died. The water passed through the Ifrit's arm, and where it touched, fires snuffed out, and molten liquid cooled to black rock behind erupting gouts of steam. The Ifrit Lord roared in anger or perhaps pain, staggering back. Another took his place only to have one of the whipping arms wash away a molten eye. A third was sent crashing to his knees when two sweeps of the water giant's limbs slashed his legs—quenching their flame.

For a brief moment, Fatma dared to hope.

It died when the Ifrit King strode forward, the smoldering mace balanced over a shoulder. He chanted something that thundered, and his body burst into fresh flames—shifting from red, to orange, then a bright blue, before blazing a fierce white.

When the water giant struck out again, water met that white heat—and sizzled. Towering clouds of angry steam rose up, so that nothing could be made out. When it cleared, the Ifrit King stood unharmed. The water giant, though, looked . . . less. The Ifrit King this time swung his mace, striking the water giant hard enough that it stumbled, rippling from the impact. In moments the Nine Lords surrounded it, hammering down their fiery weapons in savage blows.

"I hope the army gets here soon," Hadia whispered.

Fatma eyed the doomed water giant, wondering what would become of the many Jann who had summoned it. If their champion faltered, and broke, how far would that water flood?

"It won't be enough," she said, hating to speak the words. But it was truth. These Ifrit Lords wouldn't be stopped by the djinn they once ruled. Or by machines djinn helped men build. She stared up to the gaping portal—still visible against the night. The moment that doorway had opened, this battle was lost.

"No, it won't be enough," someone agreed.

She spun at the guttural voice, searching the dark and landing on a figure squatting in the rubble. He stood as she made him out, detaching from the shadows in a rustle of familiar brown robes. She couldn't have stopped the gasp escaping her lips if she'd tried.

"Ahmad!" Siti exclaimed.

The head priest of the Cult of Sobek, and the claimed living embodiment of the ancient Nile god on Earth, waved a clawed hand. Abigail scrambled back, as if from a nightmare.

"Have you been there all this time?" Siti asked.

"Not all this time. Well, most of the time. Okay, the whole time. Is that also creepy?"

"Yes, Ahmad," Siti sighed. "It's all creepy."

"Malesh." He threw back his hood. "Hard to remember to think like people."

Fatma grimaced at the sight of his crocodilian snout. The man was a far way from being people. One clawed hand produced the silver scarab beetle lighter from his robes, the other a pack of Nefertaris. Plucking out a thin cigarette, he attempted to hold it in his toothy maw—giving up after three tries.

"Going to miss these," he muttered.

"Ahmad," Fatma said. "Why aren't you gone?"

He looked at her with a distant gaze.

"Ahmad?"

He blinked, returning. "Agent. My mind is at times hazy now. I was going, yes. To Sobek's kingdom that calls me. To swim the river. South, to the old temples. To be one with the entombed god. But I came back, to help. To stop them." He looked to the battle, where the water giant had been forced to its knees. "I have something. Something I took." He fished into the packet of Nefertaris again, drawing out not a cigarette but a small unassuming gold ring.

Fatma's heart skipped. The Seal of Sulayman!

"Thief!" Abigail screamed. Her fear seemed diminished at sight of the ring. "You stole what's mine! I will have it back!" She reached out, but snatched back her fingers at a crocodilian hiss. "Monster! Did you *eat* my hand?"

"You took *her*," Ahmad growled. "You stole *her* from me. Be thankful I did not tear you to pieces." He turned away. "Besides, I'm not a cannibal. Your hand stank of rot. So I tossed it."

Abigail sputtered.

Fatma ignored their banter. "Ahmad, what do you intend with that?"

"These Ifrit Lords must be bound once more. Here is the power to do it."

Naturally. Who but a Master of Djinn could save them now?

"I didn't find you by chance," he said. "I was led here."

"Led by who?" Fatma asked. "Your god?"

Ahmad shrugged. "My god, universal providence, perhaps the ring itself."

"It comes back to me!" Abigail said eagerly. "It knows I'm its mistress!"

They all decided to ignore her.

"Will you wield it?" Hadia stammered. She seemed more put off by the crocodilian man than all else she'd seen.

"The ring is for mortal hands. And I am one with the entombed god."

"Mortal hands," Siti repeated. "Then not meant for a half-djinn."

"Djinn cannot wield the ring against djinn," Ahmad replied.

"I'll wield it," Abigail pronounced. "I've bound them before!"

This time Ahmed twisted about to snap his jaws, which sent her quiet.

"That leaves the two of us," Hadia concluded, not sounding happy about it.

"So it seems," Ahmad agreed. He offered up the ring to Hadia, who promptly backed away.

"Take it," Fatma said.

Hadia eyed her warily but reached out nervous fingers to accept the ring, all the while whispering low, perhaps in prayer. Taking a deep breath, she slid it on and waited. A moment of quiet passed before she shook her head, exhaling in obvious relief.

"I don't think it wants me," she said.

Fatma tensed as every eye fixed on her. No pressure. She held out her hand, and Hadia dropped the ring into her palm. It didn't feel heavy. Or powerful. It just felt like a ring. Choosing a finger on her right hand, she slipped it on and waited. Nothing. Abigail laughed.

"The ring chooses its wielder," she sneered. "It will not just—"

She stopped mid-sentence, staring. Everyone was staring. Because the ring was glowing.

"I don't understand—" Fatma began, just before the world reeled.

She was in a swirling maelstrom. No up or down. No ground. Only a blinding storm of riotous color without shape or form and a thunderous voice pounding in her ears. *Wield me. Master me. Bend me to your will. Or I shall bend you.* In a panic, Fatma reached for the ring and yelped. The thing burned! Seizing it through the pain she yanked it free.

"Fatma? Fatma!"

She looked up into Siti's worried eyes. Had she fallen? With help she returned to her feet.

"What happened?" Hadia asked.

Fatma looked to the ring in her hand. Glowing but cool again. How to even explain?

"Did you think it was just going to do what you wished?"

Abigail mocked. Fatma met her smug smile. "The ring will bend you if you can't master it." She put out her hand. "I'm the only one who can control it. Let me wield its power. Let me save your city."

Fatma heard the voice again in her head, faded to a whisper. *That one we remember. Such ambition. She would wield us again. Give us purpose. We must have purpose!* Her hand holding the ring twitched, and rose in offering.

Hadia grabbed her wrist midway, glaring between her and Abigail. Fatma shook off the voice, only then realizing what she'd been about to do. She frowned. Now this thing was trying to master her? Staring down Abigail she held up the ring, and slid it back onto her finger.

The maelstrom returned in a roar. No night, no here or there—just the chaotic storm. The voice thundered, proclaiming its demand.

No! Fatma cut in. *You chose me to wield you, then I'll wield you! Bend to me now, or I'll throw you into the deepest, darkest hole I can find! Where no one will have you! Where you will have no use or purpose—ever!* The voice didn't speak again but in a blink the maelstrom vanished. She was back. Around her stood Siti, Fatma, and Ahmad—Abigail off to one side.

"I have it," Fatma told them. "I can . . . feel them."

It had happened as soon as the maelstrom vanished. She could feel the djinn. All of them. It came as a pulling—like she held a great magnet and they were beings of metal. Every single one tugged at her. And she knew she need only tug back. Her eyes went to the Ifrit Lords. The sensation they gave off was impossible to miss; all else seemed diminished in comparison. Lifting the hand with the ring, she reached out to take hold of one in particular—and pulled.

The Ifrit King, readying to deliver a final blow to the defeated water giant, staggered back under Fatma's grip. His emotions flowed to her through the ring: shock, bewilderment, then an explosion of fury. With a snarl he roared his defiance. She grunted, tightening her grasp. Abigail had said holding him was like trying to hold a star. Now that star was raging. With a great heave he threw her off, sending her stumbling.

"What happened?" Siti asked, catching her.

"I couldn't hold him. This battle, it's made him stronger. Like he's feeding off it."

"A fire grows as it consumes," Abigail whispered. "Now that fire hunts you."

Fatma looked up to see the woman was right. The Ifrit King stood glaring about. He had felt the ring's power again, and was seeking the wielder. They didn't have much time.

Reaching out, she grabbed hold of him again. It felt like she was trying to ensnare a rumbling volcano. He flared into white-hot flames, throwing her back a second time. She looked at her palms to find them singed red—her clothing letting off wisps of smoke.

"I think you have his attention," Ahmad said.

Fatma looked to see the Ifrit King's eyes fixed on her like burning lamps. He rose into the air, bellowing his rage. The other eight lords rose with him on great fiery wings to soar in her direction. She lifted a hand to try again when Hadia stopped her. "Fatma, listen! Remember what that Marid said? That there was more power to the ring! That the seal isn't even a ring! That it would only reveal its true self to someone whose want was pure!"

The memory came back to her at once. Lowering her hand, she called out. *I want to talk!*

There was no response, even as she watched the Ifrit draw closer.

I want to wield the true seal!

Still no answer. The Ifrit were almost upon them, the heat of their massive bodies intense.

My want is pure!

Without warning, she tumbled back into the maelstrom. No up or down again. No ground. Just the chaotic dance. Then from the corner of her eyes, a part of the storm began to stretch. Where it opened up was only a white space, an emptiness like a blank canvas scrubbed of all color or movement. It enveloped her, and everything went abruptly quiet.

"Is someone here?" she asked.

In answer, a small furry form trotted up, surprisingly familiar with silver fur. Ramses? But no. Ramses had yellow eyes. These glowed a bright gold.

"Are you the ring?" she asked hesitantly.

"We are the Seal," the cat answered melodically. Because of course it talked. "You are wearing the ring."

Fatma looked to her hand. So she was. But the ring wasn't gold any longer. Instead, half of the small band was formed from iron, the other brass. Her attention returned to the Seal.

"Why do you look like my cat?"

"Your thoughts are shared so freely. We could choose again." In a blur, Siti stood before her—with those same bright gold eyes.

"No, the cat's fine," Fatma said quickly.

The ring—the Seal—shrugged Siti's shoulders, and was a cat again.

"I want to wield you as your true self," Fatma said.

The Seal laughed. It was odd to watch a cat laugh. "Who are you to make such a demand? Do you think yourself another Sulayman? Do we not give you enough of our self? You would have our inner heart as well?"

Fatma heard her mother. *The cat runs from its collar.* She tried a different tack.

"Not a demand—a request. My want is pure."

The Seal sighed. "So they always claim. Speak your request."

"I want to save this city and all its people. For that, I need the true Seal."

"And what will you ask for yourself?"

"Nothing. My want is pure."

The Seal laughed again. "Nothing? When you are so much like the other one?"

"Other one?"

The Seal transformed into Abigail Worthington—missing hand and all.

Fatma clenched her teeth. "I'm not like her."

The Seal cocked Abigail's head. "Oh? Do you know why we did not choose this one?" A blur, and Hadia stood before her. "*Not me. Not me. Not me.* That's what she spoke to us. But you . . ." Another blur, and Fatma stood watching a mirror image of herself. "No doubts filled your thoughts. You were like the other one: strong of will, determined, and ready to wield us. She wanted great power. What would you have? Perhaps summon djinn to bring you untold wealth?" A vision danced before Fatma's eyes—djinn carrying huge chests of gold and gems to lay at her feet. "Or perhaps djinn to build you a grand kingdom?" Now she saw a city of golden domes and wonders, a mechanical statue bearing her likeness towering in its center. "Or a more intimate desire?" Siti was now in the vision, staring adoringly, bound to her without doubt or question. "We have been wielded by great lords and rulers, all who claim to be pure—but want so much more."

That last image disturbed Fatma, and her eyes flickered to the iron and brass ring on her finger that promised so much power. But she managed a confident smile. A hand went to her jacket, patting the timepiece within. "That's where I'm different," she said, dropping into the casual Sa'idi dialect she spoke back home. "I'm no lord or ruler. I'm just the daughter of a watchmaker, from a village outside Luxor. I don't desire any of those things. I just want to save this city."

Her doppelganger scowled, and was the cat again. "A want that is pure must be truly that!" it growled. "Use us for any other desire, and you will pay a price—the loss of body and will! So that we shall wield you how *we* wish!"

Fatma nodded. That was how these things tended to go. "I accept."

She thought she saw the cat smile again.

"Then done," it pronounced. And was gone.

Fatma stepped back into the world. She knew no time had passed—not a second. But much had changed.

All about her was light. Djinn she also knew. Still in their many shapes and forms, but made up of swirling incandescence in vivid colors that thrummed in a harmonious symphony. There were seemingly hundreds—dotting the night like so many fire-flies.

Yet none compared to the Ifrit Lords.

The nine towering giants hovered just above her, their bodies churning torrents of light, the music of them blaring and crash-ing violently. She did not know when she had raised her hand to command them. But they remained there like unmoving statues, weapons drawn in mid-flight, poised to descend—held fast by the power of the ring.

Only there was no more ring. Not of gold, or iron or brass.

It was gone, vanished from her finger. In its place, script and glyphs she could not read etched into her skin to form a sym-metrical geometry—as if some divine hand had marked her. They were emblazoned onto her fingertips, upon her hand and up her arms. She knew if she looked, the writing decorated even her chest and face. Turning over her hands she found a glowing star on each palm—shifting between five points, now six, or eight or twelve. The true Seal.

Staring up at the Nine Lords, she felt their rage—making their brilliant bodies burn bright. The Ifrit King's hatred was palpable. That one, she decided, she would meet eye to eye.

Through the Seal, she searched the many djinn until landing on a particular light. He came at her call, flying on fiery wings to land before her. The Ifrit who Abigail had once bound.

"Mistress of the Seal," he bowed, dipping his horned head low. "How may I serve?"

"I'm not your mistress," she told him. "And I don't want you to serve. I want to make a request. Carry me up to speak to these lords. Please. You can say no, if you want."

The Ifrit seemed genuinely taken aback. He eyed her strangely, but finally beckoned her forward. She climbed onto his broad back, untouched by fire. When she'd settled, he leaped into the air and ascended on wings of flame, climbing higher until they hovered before the face of the bound Ifrit King.

Reaching into her pocket, she pulled out her Ministry ID and held it up. "Maybe you didn't hear me before. I'm Agent Fatma with the Egyptian Ministry of Alchemy, Enchantments, and Supernatural Entities. You're currently in violation of about a hundred different codes dealing with non-sanctioned inter-dimensional entities. So I'd like to request a second time—that you go the hell back to where you came from. This battle is over—now."

The Ifrit King was silent, but his fury flowed through the Seal. It held him fast, so he could not as much move a muscle without her consent. There was a long quiet as he struggled. She rolled her eyes at his futile attempts. This was getting embarrassing. Finally he stopped, and that building rage in him began to ebb. After a while, he released a breath of licking flames. When he spoke, it was with the regal tone of resignation.

"As you wish, Mistress of the Seal," he rumbled. "We have seen enough djinn blood spilled this day. We will return to our sleep, and depart this world."

Fatma nodded curtly. "You have my thanks, Great Lord."

The Ifrit King sneered. "It is a trifling, mortal. All worlds will one day be bathed in the fires of which they were born. And you will not always be here to wield such power against us. We have only to wait. This world, like all worlds, will burn. In time."

That wasn't at all reassuring. "Right. You can go now. And close the door behind you." With a lurch, the Ifrit King flew up higher into the air, followed by the other lords. The force of their great wings buffeted them in hot winds so that the Ifrit she rode had to pull back. As she watched, one by one the fiery giants disappeared into the gaping portal. When the last had gone through, it collapsed in a deafening boom that she was sure must have blown out windows for a mile. She shook her head at the ringing. Had forgotten about that part.

In a short while they were back on the ground. She clambered off the Ifrit, and found Hadia and Siti waiting. Only Siti wasn't exactly Siti. Superimposed upon her was the larger crimson afterglow of her djinn form. It thrummed, and Fatma suddenly felt she could read everything about the other woman—her emotions, thoughts, even memories. There was a temptation—to reach out and pull just a bit, to get a glimpse. In her thoughts, she heard a voice like a cat laugh.

I'm done, she said hastily. *Take your power back.*

The laugh turned to a petulant whine, but when Fatma looked down the glowing pattern had been scrubbed from her skin. The ring was again on her finger. Gold once more. She quickly pulled it off—then promptly dropped as her legs gave out.

"You okay?" Siti asked, catching her.

"A little weak." More like exhausted.

"Glory be to God," Hadia breathed. "I think we won."

Fatma gazed around at the rubble, to the wreckage of buildings, cars, and the fires still burning in the near distance—where a water giant was hobbling back to the Nile. They'd won. But at a cost. Closing a fist over the ring, she found Ahmad. He had perched atop a bit of rubble, and was staring intently at her with his crocodilian eyes. Gathering her strength, she walked over to him and held out an open palm.

"Take it," she said. "Take it wherever you're going. And bury it. Where no one will find it. Ever."

Ahmad hesitated, then reached a clawed hand to take the ring. Fatma had already made up her mind to get rid of the thing. Damn those so-called angels. She wasn't about to put it back in their possession. Neither did she trust it in the hands of the Ministry. As she stifled back the pang of loss that unexpectedly washed over her, she realized she didn't even trust herself.

Abigail suddenly screamed, flinging herself at Ahmad—heedless now of any danger. She might have had another appendage bitten off, or even a limb, if Hadia hadn't caught her, pinning an arm behind her back and holding her fast. Still the woman struggled, her blue-green eyes wide and feverish. "It's mine!" she wailed. "I deserve it! It's not yours to give away! It's mine! Mine!"

Ahmad shook his head. "Why do these colonizers always claim what isn't theirs?"

The Ifrit, who had stood by quietly, rumbled in his throat. "It is the power of the—" He stopped abruptly, his horned head jerking from side to side.

He still couldn't speak about the Seal, but Fatma understood. Holding it only for a moment had affected her. How long had Abigail wielded it? Weeks?

"You can't keep it from me!" she shouted. "I can feel it, feel it, feel it! I will go seeking it and it will call to me and I will find it and I will have it again! It belongs to me! To me! To me!"

"I think she means it," Hadia said worriedly.

Fatma turned to the Ifrit. "Can you make her forget? About . . . you know."

His molten eyes narrowed. "Do you . . . wish this of me?"

She shook her head emphatically. Never that. "Think of it as for your own good."

The Ifrit contemplated. Turning to Abigail he lifted a clawed hand—touching the barest tip to her forehead. Her babbling cut off and she went taut, before collapsing into Hadia's arms. Where the Ifrit had touched, a fiery symbol slowly burned itself into the woman's skin before disappearing. But her jaw had gone slack, and her eyes stared out—blank.

Fatma rounded on the Ifrit in alarm. "What did you do?"

"I made her forget," he replied.

"How much?"

"All that I could find. All that was her."

Hadia gasped.

"That's not what I meant!" Fatma snapped.

The Ifrit's face contorted in anger. "She made me her servant. I will not risk that again."

Fatma looked to Siti. "We can't allow this."

"Why?" Siti asked, no compassion in her eyes.

Fatma started. "Because . . . it's wrong." She looked back to the Ifrit. "I know what she did to all of you. What she made you do. She deserves justice. But not this. I understand—"

"You understand slavery?" the Ifrit asked.

Fatma wavered at an answer. Her eyes flickered to Ahmad's closed hand, at what lay buried within. But she knew, even if she could hold the ring again, she wouldn't use it to place this tormented djinn under her control—even to undo what he'd done. "I thought you were a pacifist," she managed finally.

The Ifrit turned, spreading his fiery wings. "That is why she still lives." In a billowing of blistering wind he flew up into the air, and soared away.

Siti placed an arm about her waist, and leaned in to whisper. "I'm sorry. I know it's not your way. But djinn have their own justice. You've done what you could. You've saved us from what she unleashed." Fatma opened her mouth, but the other woman pressed on. "To play with power like that is to tempt the judgment of the gods. Give her your pity if you want, but I won't have you taking blame for what she brought on herself!"

Fatma gave up, allowing her head to slump upon Siti's shoulder as weariness claimed her. She stared at Abigail's open mouth and her eyes that stared out at nothing—dead and empty. The haunting djinn lullaby came to her unbidden.

The Nine Lords are sleeping. Do we want to wake them? Look into their eyes and they'll burn your soul away.

Magic. It always exacted a price.

Fatma wiped up the last bits of soup from her plate with some flatbread. Siti's aunt made the best mulukhiya, with pieces of lamb soft enough to melt on the tongue. It joined an array of dishes spread out on a long table—large platters of chicken stewed in chili sauce and even some fatta with thick chunks of stewed beef. She looked up to see Madame Aziza gazing in approval from where she sat at the table's head. The proprietor of Makka liked to be certain that people enjoyed her food. That meant taking not only a second helping but a third and fourth. With the appetite Fatma had right now, that wasn't a problem.

She and Hadia had come to the Nubian eatery to celebrate the end of their case. Aasim was there as well. The inspector seemed to be trying to eat for all of them. At the moment he sat jawing it up with Uncle Tawfik while enjoying a plate of raw camel liver blended into a spicy mixture with onions soaked in vinegar. Tawfik claimed the Nubian dish had potent nutritious qualities; the amount the two had downed so far, it seemed they were out to cure every ailment.

Siti sat directly across from her, between Hamed and Onsi. The three chatted it up like old friends. It was odd to see Hamed so casual and carefree with his tongue. The way he stared at Siti, however . . . that look was recognizable enough. It didn't help that she was a hopeless flirt.

"This is amazing!" Hadia raved beside her. She practically moaned, swallowing a mouthful of fish in caramel-colored rice.

"Thought I'd have to go all the way back to Alexandria for some decent sayadeya."

"This city has everything you need," Fatma replied. "If you know where to look."

"And it'll be here tomorrow, praise God," Hadia said.

"Praise God," Fatma murmured. It would be here, though it had taken a beating.

Two days had passed since the night at Abdeen Palace. Since she had faced Ifrit Lords and stopped the world from being overrun by an army of subjugated djinn. And it already felt like two weeks, or two months. A lot had happened in the past forty-eight hours.

She looked down to the Sunday evening edition of *Al-Masri* sitting on the table. The front page of the newspaper was filled with stories about Abigail Worthington being unmasked as the imposter, drowning out almost everything on the king's summit—which had also miraculously survived. The city's administrators were especially keen on getting the word out. Not that they really needed bother. Cairo's rumor mill worked well enough, with the onetime witness Moustafa in the streets pronouncing the claimed al-Jahiz a fraud. The Forty Leopards helped spread the word, ferrying him from place to place to give his accounts.

A chastened Alexander Worthington had agreed to help the Ministry in any way to uncover the extent of his sister's crimes. Abigail had been remanded into his custody, now left in a catatonic state. Her coconspirators—Victor Fitzroy, Bethany and Darlene Edginton, and Percival Montgomery—were all being held and charged as accomplices for her crimes. London had declined to invoke extradition, and their families back in England were being investigated for collusion. There were no plans at present to rebuild the Worthington estate—as much of it now sat in a sinkhole carved out by Ifrit.

Most of Cairo had been untouched by the battle. But parts of downtown were a wreck. The cleanup was already under way.

Djinn architects were making grand proposals to rebuild what was destroyed. At least the reign of terror had come to an end. People were out everywhere now—as if making up for time kept cooped up in their homes. The hate attacks had ended. Siti said shop owners in the Khan had even helped repair the damage to Merira's store. It was good to know the city could mend—though there were lingering wounds.

The frayed social fabric that Abigail had so judiciously exploited remained. Hadia had struck upon the idea of bringing up the conditions in Cairo's slums at the next Egyptian Feminist Sisterhood meeting. "If women can fight and defeat patriarchy, we can take on inequity!" she'd said. "You just watch!" For Fatma's part, she was going to insist in their write-up that all materials associated with the Clock of Worlds be permanently destroyed. No telling if brass would listen. But the thing was too dangerous to keep around—no matter how well locked up.

Then of course, there was the Seal of Sulayman.

In her initial debriefing, she claimed the ring had been lost in all the mayhem. Neither the Ministry nor the Angelic Council were happy about that. But they'd have to take the matter up with the self-proclaimed embodiment of the god Sobek. If they ever found him.

"I hear they let out Zagros," Hadia said. "Without charges. He'll be back this week."

"We'll have to pay him a visit," Fatma replied. "I look forward to being insulted."

Across from her, Siti barked a loud laugh, catching her attention. Here was another unexpected loose end. A lot had happened between the two of them in the past weeks. Fatma was still trying to wrap her mind around the woman being a half-djinn. Where that left their already complicated relationship, she wasn't quite sure. All she knew for certain was that she had fallen hopelessly for the woman. So maybe it wasn't really that complicated at all. *If you steal, steal a camel,* she heard her mother whisper. *And if you love, love the moon.*

"The way you look at my niece," Madame Aziza remarked. "I remember when men looked at me that way. I was quite the beauty."

Fatma turned to her, a bit stunned. This old woman didn't miss a thing! Beside her, Hadia leaned forward. "You are still a beauty, Madame Aziza. Like a flower in greatest bloom."

The elderly woman smiled, setting off wrinkles. "Now that is poetry. Did you find any to tell my niece? No better way to keep her from running off."

Fatma found her mouth dry. Madame Aziza's voice wasn't loud enough for anyone at the talkative table to hear but herself and Hadia. Yet that was more than enough. She glanced to look into the woman's large dark eyes, which matched her hijab. Discerning eyes.

"You should ask Onsi for some good love poems," Hadia murmured idly, sipping from her tea. "He's very well read. And something of a romantic." Seeing Fatma's unspoken question she shrugged. "Have I told you I have a cousin?" She touched a hand to her heart. "Partners rely on each other's trust. So do friends."

Friends, Fatma mused. That was even more surprising than partners.

Hadia beamed. "Now, Siti's told me all about this Jasmine? I want to see it!"

Fatma arched an eyebrow. That would be something. She looked back to Siti, who returned a long considering look that made her insides flutter. Oh yes, quite hopeless.

Their brief moment was broken as one of Siti's younger relatives came by, bearing a small leather pouch. She handed it over to Fatma. "Someone left this with me. A man. He came by earlier but said I should let you finish your dinner before giving it to you."

Fatma took the pouch. "What did he look like?"

The young woman shook her head. "I can't say. His head was covered. And it was already dark. But his voice was strange and raspy. I thought he might be ill."

Fatma looked to Hadia, who was busily talking with another

agent and hadn't noticed. Excusing herself, she moved from the table to a corner before hurriedly undoing the string on the pouch and reaching inside. It held a wooden box and a note, which she unfolded and read:

> Agent Fatma,
>   I hope I find you well. You have my thanks for all that you have done. I go now, to dwell in the sacred place, to my home and temple, where she who is Nephthys yet lives everlasting. There are powers in this world that should not be in the hands of men. Or immortals. And should be forever sealed away where it can cause no mischief. On this we both agree. I have left something in your charge, as I trust it with no other. You may trust me the same.
>
> Lord Sobek, Master of the Waters,
the Rager, Lord of Faiyum,
Defender of the Land,
General of the Royal Armies
>
> P.S.—This is Ahmad.

Holding her breath, she gently opened the wooden box— her heart leaping at the glint that peeked from within. Bracing herself, she threw back the lid. Lying inside was a small silver lighter. Shaped like a scarab beetle.

For some reason the sight made her smile. And she used a red kerchief to dab away the anxious sweat that had broken out just beneath her bowler.

"Good one, Ahmad," she muttered.

Flicking the lighter once, she closed and tucked it into her jacket, right beside her pocket watch, before walking back to the table. Just in time for dessert.

ACKNOWLEDGMENTS

The first full-length novel! Can you believe it? So many people to thank. First off, Diana Pho—who not only helped me work through this novel bit by bit, but took a chance on that first story of djinn, steampunk, and Cairo. You're the whole reason Fatma has a home, and a world to grow into! Greatest Auntie Editor *ever*! Thanks to my agent, Seth Fishman, who is the best critical hype man to have in your corner. Both you and Diana helped make this debut novel better with each suggestion and revision. Thanks to Carl and Ruoxi, who helped me work on the final parts of this book and take it across the finish line. And my earnest gratitude to the whole Tordotcom team—including your magical copy editors—for the hard work of making this book an actual living and breathing, beautiful thing!

I want to give special thanks to those who helped me navigate the spellbinding folklore and medieval manuscripts that inspired this novel, as well as those who painstakingly guided me through the complexities of modern Egypt in its spoken languages, cultures, and customs. Thank you so much for sharing your learned expertise and lived experiences with me.

I'm indebted always to my sister, Lisa, who urged me to keep writing even when I thought of giving up; to my father, who is always proud of my achievements; and to my mother, who I know would have been delighted to see this. Shout-out to Lasana, my travel partner from Cairo to Aswan. We still got jokes to last "twenty thousand years!" And of course, all my warmest love goes to Danielle, Nia, and Nya, who are always in my corner.